JERICHO'S DAUGHTERS

By PAUL I. WELLMAN

History

DEATH ON THE PRAIRIE

DEATH ON THE DESERT
  (Republished together as
    THE INDIAN WARS OF THE WEST)

THE TRAMPLING HERD

GLORY, GOD AND GOLD

Novels

BRONCHO APACHE

JUBAL TROOP

ANGEL WITH SPURS

THE BOWL OF BRASS

THE WALLS OF JERICHO

THE CHAIN

THE IRON MISTRESS

THE COMANCHEROS

THE FEMALE

JERICHO'S DAUGHTERS

JERICHO'S DAUGHTERS

A NOVEL BY PAUL I. WELLMAN

DOUBLEDAY & COMPANY, INC., GARDEN CITY, N.Y., 1956

All of the characters in this book are fictitious, and any resemblance to actual persons, living or dead, is purely coincidental and not intended by the author.

Library of Congress Catalog Card Number 56–10775

To that wee, winsome sprite

WENDY

who, on arriving in this vale of woe and worry five short winters ago, brought a new wealth of gaiety, charms, and graces into it, and (as a very unimportant side incident) conferred upon me, for the first time, the honorable and happy (though I fear somewhat ancient) title: Grandfather.

JERICHO'S DAUGHTERS

One

When Mrs. Mary Agnes Wedge entered the flower-bowered lobby of the Beverly Hills Hotel, she created quite a little stir, even in that place which is accustomed to and somewhat blasé about the visitations of rajahs from India, oil millionaires from Texas, and world-publicized nymphomaniacs from Hollywood. This was perhaps natural, since she was a rather important and regular guest, who expected, received, and paid for the very best the house afforded in accommodations and services.

The desk clerk, a polished young man with a well-groomed thin mustache, advertised his recognition of her with a smile and almost a flourish.

"Good morning, Mrs. Wedge," he said in his best brisk-cordial manner. "Delighted that you're to be with us again. Pleasant flight across, I trust?"

"Dull," she replied wearily, signing the registration card.

The clerk clucked sympathetically. "Monotonous, of course—all that water. You'll be wishing to rest, no doubt. The luggage you shipped ahead arrived in due time and we took the liberty of depositing your things in the suite we set aside for you. I hope you'll find everything in order. Is there anything special you desire?"

"You might send up a gin-and-tonic. And a breakfast menu."

"Thank you. At once, ma'am." The clerk was unsurprised. It was not yet nine o'clock in the morning, but this guest was just off a transpacific plane from Hawaii, and perhaps a gin-and-tonic before breakfast was indicated in her case.

A girl at the switchboard behind the desk spoke to him.

"Oh, yes, Mrs. Wedge," said the clerk as Mary Agnes turned away from the desk. "Long-distance has been trying to reach you."

"From where?" she asked.

"Your home, I believe, ma'am. Jericho, Kansas."

"Oh." Flat, uninterested voice.

"They've been calling the past hour," volunteered the clerk.

"I suppose so. The plane was late."

"Will you take it in your suite?"

"Yes. I'm going up now."

"Thank you. The operator will get your connection."

Preceded by the bellboy, she passed toward the elevator, slender in an angularly graceful way, her dark traveling suit, the mink stole on her arm, her jewelry, hose, and slippers all advertising expensive good taste. Nobody could call Mary Agnes Wedge beautiful, yet she caught every eye in the flower-filled lobby in that brief parade.

The suite into which she was ushered overlooked the hotel's gardens, which are famous. She glanced from an open window, inspected the closets to see that her dresses and coats had been hung in them carefully, directed the bellboy where to place the two bags she had brought on the plane, tipped him and dismissed him. Then, with a woman's immediate instinct, she went to a full-length mirror and gave herself a quick survey, with a particularly searching scrutiny of her face.

The face was not without its charm, although it was too thin, almost emaciated from continual dieting. Cheekbones and chin were prominent, the greenish eyes deep set with a light etching of lines disguised with make-up at the corners, the nose delicately aquiline, and the mouth firm and straight—too firm and thin, perhaps, so that she found it necessary to soften it by widening and curving the lips with the red smear of her lipstick. Her crisp hair, cut in a fashionably short mode, was brown, almost black, with a stylized streak of gray, and her skin was darkly tanned—she was fortunate in always taking a good color under the sun, and she had devoted some weeks of idleness to this end in Honolulu.

All in all, she saw in the mirror a rather haughty face, a face faintly hinting discontent, a face men sometimes found attractive, but women, with healthy feminine hatred, often described as "hard as nails."

"I'm looking a little scrawny around the neck," Mary Agnes said to herself, half aloud.

She had passed her fortieth birthday; and she was becoming increasingly conscious of fading youth, and dreading the appearance of what women call a "crepe throat." Indeed, she had begun to arrive unconsciously at an age when she dressed not so much to attract men as to annoy other women.

Leaving the mirror, she sat down beside a table on which a telephone rested. This morning she felt tired and debilitated. Habitually she traveled by air, because habitually she was in a hurry to get places. Yet, though she always assured herself that air travel is the safest mode of transportation and quoted to herself those figures about millions of passenger miles per accident, she was never quite at ease during a flight; and the one from the Islands had been a long one. She had taken Dramamine to counteract her tendency to air sickness, and it was supposed to make one sleepy. But while it numbed her senses, the drug did not induce slumber, and she spent the hours in a sort of dulled wakefulness, unable to dismiss from her mind the inevitable little gnawing worry that always was with her when she was flying over all those interminable miles of menacing gray ocean. Now she confessed to an inner sag of weariness, and it made her impatient with herself, and with life in general.

The telephone on the table suddenly jingled. She lifted the receiver.

"Mrs. Wedge?" inquired an operator's tinny voice.

"Yes. This is she."

"Ready with your call from Jericho."

"All right."

"Go ahead, Jer-r-r-richo," the voice trilled.

Over the wire came a tentative questioning. "Hello? Hello?" She knew the voice. It was her husband.

"Hello," she said. "Hello, Wistart."

"Mary Agnes? Is that you, honey?"

"Yes."

"I've been trying to reach you——"

"Yes, I know. The plane was late. Head winds."

"Bet you're tired, poor girl."

"I'm fine. I can never sleep on a flight, but otherwise fine."

"How's good old Honolulu?"

"Oh, all right. About as usual. Nothing out of the ordinary."

"Anyone interesting at the Royal Hawaiian?"

"Some movie people. Making a picture in the Islands. I met a few of the cast—John Wayne, Lana Turner, John Qualen. Danced with admirals and sugar millionaires and all that sort of thing. Oh, just about what you'd expect at that hotel."

"Get a good suntan?" he next said.

"Yes. I simply lived on the beach."

This senseless preliminary of banalities annoyed her. Why was Wistart calling her so soon and so insistently and then spending all this time talking about minor, unimportant things?

"Listen, Wistart," she said impatiently, "this call is costing money, isn't it? What did you want to say to me?"

A moment's hesitation at the other end of the wire. Then, "When will you be coming home?"

"I don't know. A month or so. You know I plan to go down to Balboa with the Kerstings. And there are a lot of other things I want to get done—shopping and so on——" She grew vague.

"Well——" He hesitated again. She could hear him breathing over the phone. At last he said, "I wish you could arrange somehow to come on now, honey."

It grated on her to have him call her "honey." The word was commonplace, and besides neither of them, really, felt in the least that way about each other.

"In heaven's name, why?" she demanded sharply.

"Oh—just wish you could."

"Is something wrong?"

"No—not exactly."

"Wistart, is it the *Clarion* again?"

She could almost see the sullen, defensive look come into his face at her tone. He said, "It's a pretty long story over the phone."

"There's no reason to be mysterious!"

Now he grew dogged. "You know I hate discussing matters over the long-distance."

She knew that stubbornness of his, which was his substitute for strength, and it exasperated her.

"Listen, Wistart," she said icily, "if it isn't important enough to discuss over the phone, it certainly isn't important enough to bring me back to Kansas in January weather."

He seemed to consider that, but for some obscure reason he evidently had made up his mind. "Well, then, when will you be coming?" he asked.

"I've already told you I'm not sure yet. I can't stand Jericho in mid-winter!"

"Well—if that's the way it is—I suppose that's that——"

"Is this all you wanted to say?"

"Yes, I guess it's all."

"I think we'd better hang up then."

"If you change your plans will you wire me?"

"Yes. Of course."

"Then good-by. Give my regards to the Kerstings and—and any-one else you see out there that I know. And take care of yourself, honey." His voice seemed to drag.

"Good-by, Wistart."

The receiver clicked.

2

Almost at once there was a knock on the door: it was the waiter with the gin-and-tonic. Mary Agnes took a sip of the bittersweet drink while she glanced over the menu and ordered a slender breakfast. Then, after the waiter departed, she sipped again at the gin-and-tonic, found that she did not want it, left it on the table, and went over to the open window.

This was midwinter, and she reflected that it probably was bitter-cold and snowy at home. Yet in the gardens below her window the trees were in full rich leaf and the flower beds rioting with bloom. Linnets warbled their twittering songs in the vines and the soft California air touched her cheek like fairy fingers.

Such a contrast should have given her pleasure. Yet, gazing out at the semi-tropical luxuriance, she knew a feeling of discontent akin to bit-terness.

When a woman has not seen her husband for more than three months, a conversation with him should have some meaning to it, even when conducted over the long-distance telephone. But the conversa-tion she had just concluded with Wistart was empty, or irritating, or both. She and he simply meant nothing to each other—less than noth-ing. It was one of the things wrong with her life. Wistart constituted a failure in it; an annoying, apparently irremediable failure.

She pictured to herself her husband's broad fair face, his pale-lashed blue eyes, his plump large frame, and all these things seemed, to her mood, traits singularly unlovely. Wistart Wedge, she thought, was one of the most ineffectual men she had ever known; and she believed that she knew men measurably well. After all, she had been through the valley of matrimonial humiliation known as divorce thrice before she was thirty: a childish high school elopement, annulled; a college girl campus romance, quickly ended in a somewhat juvenile disagreement; a crush on a visiting actor in Jericho's "little theater," who had a profile and almost nothing else, concluded almost as soon as begun.

Mary Agnes was the spoiled and headstrong only daughter of the oldest propertied family in Jericho, the Timothy Coxes. From her parents, both now dead, she inherited a very considerable fortune, chiefly in the ownership of the great and prosperous department store known as Cox's, Incorporated. Money provides excuses for erratic conduct in the minds of many people; nevertheless, three divorces before she was thirty constituted something of a record in Jericho, and the spiteful tongues made the most of it.

But then she married Wistart Wedge, whose mother owned the only newspaper in the city and whose late father had been a United States senator. To be sure, they took each other on the rebound: he had been infatuated with Gilda Westcott of the packing house family, and she, secretly, with Dr. Murray Clifton, a society physician—and she had never forgiven that couple for marrying each other. Nevertheless, for ten years now she had been Mrs. Wistart Wedge; and the criticism over her three divorces had stilled.

Curious, she sometimes thought, how the simple fact of living in conventional wedlock invested a woman with standing and respectability she could hardly otherwise attain. She might be lazy, incompetent, stupid, shrewish, but her status was secure if she was *Mrs.* Somebody. It was like standing still to win a race.

Mary Agnes was habitually cynical concerning the conventions: she considered them stereotyped and dull. Yet she subscribed to them, at least publicly. And though her ten years of marriage with Wistart had been ten years of boredom, she endured them for the reason that it was necessary to do so if one were a woman, and a somewhat prominent woman, and lived in a community like Jericho, Kansas.

She revenged herself on the conventions by sometimes shocking her Jericho friends with derision.

"You can't do this, you can't do that!" she once snapped at Bess

Attwater, whose husband, Sidney, was cashier of Jericho's largest bank. "Why can't you? Who made all those rules that keep women from doing almost anything that's any fun? I'll tell you. *Women* made them —and women maintain them, like self-established concentration camps of custom, because women prefer the imprisonment with its indolence and protection to freedom with its risks and dangers!"

Since Mary Agnes was known to be sarcastic by habit, feline by temperament, and sophisticated in a brittle-glass manner, Bess Attwater did not dare take issue with her—nor did any of the other women present, for that matter. They were all afraid of her, of her edged tongue, of her superb manner, which carried off even wild acts of rudeness or unreason, of her assumption of superior experience and knowledge of the world, of the sometimes deadly penetration with which her intuitions sought out and laid bare their most deeply hidden secret thoughts.

Her husband was afraid of her also. She thought of Wistart with a little twist of scorn on her lips. She was older than he by three years, although she did not like to remind herself of the fact, and that may have been one reason why she held an ascendancy of will over him from the very day of their marriage. In no respect was she dependent on him: she was wealthier in her own right than was he, and she did not permit him to forget it. And she considered herself in every way his intellectual superior.

It was characteristic of Wistart that, though he was fully aware of how she felt toward him, he accepted her attitude without much resentment or even thought. She had made it very plain to him in the first months of their marriage that she could not abide him, even to be fondled by him, much less the physical crudity of sex. Thereafter, in all the years since, they occupied separate rooms in their home, the intercommunicating doors of which remained closed. In all those years they had gone their separate ways, with different associates, different interests, different tastes, journeying in divergent directions when they left Jericho for business or pleasure.

Mary Agnes, to be sure, was gone from home far more often than was Wistart, since she was dedicated to a life of idleness, and could leave the operation of her store to her capable manager, and had the money and taste for travel, and was almost constantly weary of Jericho. She did not permit him to inquire into her comings and goings, and she was too contemptuous to care about his.

Yet a contradictory emotion entered here. Wistart's very subservience, his oxlike acquiescence to her every wish, his acceptance of her scorn, comprised part of her discontent with life, of her resentment toward her husband. A man should not, after all, be an ox . . .

In the recent telephone conversation, she remembered now, he had sounded somewhat agitated about something. She shrugged a thin shoulder: Wistart's agitation made little impression on her compared to her irritation at his childish secretiveness. He was forever being agitated in a rather feeble sort of way, and his agitation invariably bored her.

She asked herself: I wonder what it's about this time?

And she answered her own question: It must be that damned *Clarion* again.

Wearying. It seemed to Mary Agnes that every time she went to Honolulu something happened to Wistart's newspaper. Seven years ago, for example, when she was in the Islands, Wistart's mother, Mrs. Algeria Wedge, died suddenly of something called a coronary thrombosis.

Mary Agnes and Algeria Wedge never got along well together, since both had strong wills and were not averse to saying the cutting thing when it seemed called for. But with Algeria seven years in her grave, Mary Agnes could concede to herself that Wistart's mother was an enormously capable woman, a person who did difficult things so well that she made them appear easy. She combined an adroit mind, the ability to get people to do things she wanted of them, and a feminine lack of scruples so well that she put her husband in the Senate: although his own political blunders soon lost him his seat in that august assemblage. After the senator's death Algeria took over the publication of his newspaper, the Jericho *Daily Clarion*, with such ability that she brought it to a high state of success.

Algeria was competent enough, there was no doubt of that, but after she was gone the responsibility for the family newspaper fell on Wistart's not very competent, or even willing, shoulders. Under his management, or perhaps lack of management, the *Clarion* actually succeeded in losing ground, both in circulation and revenue, in spite of the fact that it seemed to be in an impregnable position, alone in its field in Jericho.

Then, three years ago, when Mary Agnes again happened to be in

Honolulu, a rival newspaper, the *Morning Sentinel,* suddenly burgeoned into publication in Jericho. Wistart, she recalled with half-amused scorn, was at the time dreadfully upset, in a panic almost.

His alarm was occasioned by his fear of his own inability to meet opposition that might be very tough: a fear that was hardly without good grounds. The new *Sentinel* brought to Jericho as its publishers two brothers, Eddie and Tony Ender, strong-arm artists, trained under a high-binding big-city newspaper in dirty back-alley fighting and guttersnipe tactics. They sneered at ethics, believed in blackmail, disdained dignity, and from the first created enough noisy, blatant, vulgar confusion to make life a misery for Wistart Wedge and the poor old *Clarion.*

And now, once more during one of her trips to Hawaii, something evidently had happened again. She wondered what was the matter with that damned newspaper this time; and she was sure Wistart wanted something from her. He hesitated to ask it offhand, over the telephone, so it must be something rather important that he hoped he could make her see in his light, perhaps by a rather long and involved argument and presentation of facts and viewpoints. The mere thought of a session like that with him was so distasteful that she made a little grimace of petulance.

Whatever it was, she said to herself, it could damn well wait. She certainly had no intention of returning to Jericho just at present.

She decided that when she had her breakfast she would take a bath and a nap. After that she would consider plans.

3

Toward two o'clock in the afternoon the telephone awoke her from a sound sleep.

"Hello," said a voice through the receiver with brittle cheerfulness. "Mary Agnes?"

"Yes."

"How are you, darling? This is Mims Newman."

"Mims? Oh, yes, Mims! How wonderful to hear from you!" The rather overdone cordiality of women over the telephone.

"I just this minute learned you were in town," Mims said.

"How on earth did you find out?" asked Mary Agnes.

The question was purely rhetorical. She knew Mims Newman as a confirmed celebrity hunter, with an expensive home up one of the Beverly Hills canyons, which she seemed to feel a need for justifying by rounding up in it more or less "brilliant" assemblages as frequently as possible. To this end she maintained a regular source of information at each of the fashionable hotels in Los Angeles and Beverly Hills—a desk clerk or a telephone operator—who for a fee kept her informed as to the comings and goings of "interesting" people. Mary Agnes had met Mims only two or three times, in the homes of other persons in the city, and at this moment she could hardly remember what the woman looked like save that her hair was dyed a raw orange hue, and she was short and dumpy and wore expensive clothes that did not suit her.

"Oh, a little bird told me," giggled Mims gaily. "I thought—if you happen to be free this evening, darling, we're having a few people in for cocktails—about five o'clock——"

"Why, thank you, but——"

"Oh, do come, darling!" chirped the voice. "Informal, and you'll have fun, I promise! I'll have someone bring you out—it's murder trying to get around in this town without a car, as you well know. Let's see— you were with Erskine de Lacey that evening at the Carvels', weren't you? Of course he's gone—lovely boy, and so talented—we all miss him. But there are plenty of other eligible males"—Mims was quite arch— "who'll jump at the chance to come for the very attractive Mrs. Wedge!"

Mary Agnes ignored the archness. "Erskine de Lacey?" she said. "What's become of him?"

"You mean you don't know? Why, I thought you, of all people——"

"Why me, in particular?"

"You live in Jericho, Kansas, don't you, dear? He's gone *there*—to live."

"He has?" Genuine astonishment. "For what reason?"

"I understand he's to be head of some art museum."

"That's quite interesting." Mary Agnes gave a little laugh. "I hadn't heard. Actually. Of course, I've been away more than three months, and I have to confess I'm not much of a correspondent——"

"Well, really, it only just happened, you might say," said Mims eagerly. "A Mrs. Butford was out here a few weeks ago—Mrs. Simon Bolivar Butford. Of course you know her—darling old thing, isn't she?"

"Yes, I know her," said Mary Agnes. She did not add that the adjec-

tive "darling" hardly had occurred to her in connection with Mrs. Butford.

"She took quite a fancy to Erskine," Mims prattled on. "You know
how he is—makes himself agreeable to everyone. He really did a job on
the old lady. She practically fell in love with him—called him 'Dear
Boy' until it was almost ridiculous—and since she seems to have a lot
to say about the museum, whatever it is——"

"It's an art gallery. Just being started."

"Yes, I suppose that's it. Anyway, she insisted that he go back with
her. Between you and me, I don't think she had to talk very hard. He
was probably glad to get that kind of a job. He's very talented, of
course, but he isn't the kind of an artist that sells many paintings—
he's hardly sold anything at all, actually. Except a little real estate his
mother left him. And that's gone now."

"I'm sure Erskine will be an acquisition for Jericho," said Mary
Agnes. "But—about the cocktail party—I'm afraid it just isn't possible,
Mims, and I'm so sorry. I have some plans I can't very well change—
you understand, dear, don't you?"

"Of course. And I realize it's short notice." But Mims obviously was
disappointed. "Well, then, some other time, won't you? Toodle-oo,
darling."

4

Mary Agnes lay on her back and stared up at the ceiling. Mims Newman, she reflected, had been remarkably prompt with her invitation:
and in its way this was quite a high compliment, proof that Mrs.
Wistart Wedge was sought after, even here on the Coast. But why not?
She had been coming to California for years; and she had friends who
were rather important socially in Beverly Hills, Westwood, Bel-Air,
Hollywood, and other places in this crazily far-flung sprawl of population known collectively as Los Angeles. She dressed as well as the best,
could be charming when she wished, and knew how to lift a conversation from banalities to a bright, even a daring plane. And she had
money, which counted nowhere more heavily than in this money-
hungry film capital.

But another thought gave her less satisfaction: the news about Erskine
de Lacey.

Mims had suggested having one of Mary Agnes' masculine acquaintances pick her up and bring her to the cocktail party. It was a usual procedure, and Mary Agnes accepted escorts on occasion if they were entertaining and well groomed and unattached and behaved themselves at least moderately well. In Jericho, of course, she would not have dreamed of it, because Jericho would have been aghast.

But she enjoyed society; and she disliked going unaccompanied to places, especially here in Los Angeles. It offended her aesthetic taste. A woman by herself was somehow incomplete, a half creature socially, like a statue which is beautiful from one angle only. She is, furthermore, the object of a faint shadow of something combined of pity and contempt from her own sex, a thin feeling more an instinct than a thought, as if she were unable to interest any man, and therefore were a failure in her femininity. This was not true, of course; but Mary Agnes acknowledged the implication, and here, more than fifteen hundred miles from home, she saw no harm in accepting, without any false hesitation, invitations of various kinds, with the companionship of men as a corollary, to parties and night clubs and even, on one occasion, a weekend yachting cruise over to Catalina Island.

Masculine attention was easy to attract if one was a wealthy, well-dressed, and amusing woman, very much the mistress of her own actions, and with a husband half a continent away. Mary Agnes was nothing of the prude, and found it amusing to play the game of coquetry with her companion of the evening—if she was in the mood —being quite secure in her ability at the end to keep the situation under control.

The woman is, after all, the final arbiter in such matters: and perhaps it was fastidiousness, and perhaps it was a definitely arrived at policy against becoming involved in any personal entanglements, and perhaps it was simply a coolness of temperament that never permitted Mary Agnes to warm, even when her companion was most attractive and showed an inclination to warmth.

This coolness she possessed in an abundant degree. In dealing with men she found it rather an asset: she could sometimes excite their emotional interest merely by being indifferent to them. She gained a certain pleasure out of arousing and thus subduing a man without any intention of rewarding him, but only for the sense of power over him that it gave her. She herself felt no emotion, she only played at emotion as a game, a technique.

All of this, curiously, gave Mary Agnes a pleasant sort of character in Hollywood and Beverly Hills circles: a woman young enough to be interesting, yet old enough to be wise; amusing, gay, and playful, even a bit daring to a certain point without being stupid about it. And furthermore, unattainable—which in itself made her a challenge to some men, particularly in Hollywood, where wolf reputations are highly prized.

The same sort of behavior at home in Jericho, of course, would have given her quite another kind of character: and the realization that Erskine de Lacey, with whom she had gone out perhaps more frequently than with any other man in Los Angeles, had been carried off to Jericho by that egregious old frump and almost pathological prude, Mrs. Simon Bolivar Butford, was slightly disquieting.

This was for a reason beyond the mere fact that Erskine had been her squire frequently and at many places. She supposed he had the good taste to keep that to himself, and even if he spoke about it she could shrug the matter off.

Something else concerned her more deeply. In all her visits to Los Angeles she had conducted herself with such excellent judgment and coolness, even when she drank rather more than was good for her, that she could think of only one indiscretion she had committed.

One indiscretion. One wild prank—it was really no more than that —carried out on a night when the treacherous fumes of rum drinks, concocted to delight and betray, wreathed through her brain, filling her with laughter and recklessness, a momentary discounting of consequences in the impulse to do something unconventional, something that seemed daring and fun at the time. Nothing very terrible; yet a little embarrassing to look back on. An act of rebellion against all the metes and bounds of custom, carried perhaps a step too far.

Erskine de Lacey . . . that strange soul, Erskine de Lacey. She could not yet quite understand herself or the thing that had happened between them.

Two

1

The previous September, when Mary Agnes stopped at the Beverly
Hills Hotel—as she usually did between planes on her way to Honolulu—Los Angeles was having one of its heat waves. Through her
open window in the hotel she listened to the roar of traffic on Sunset
Boulevard, and she knew that wide avenue, like every other roadway
leading toward the sea, was jammed with cars filled with people rushing to the beaches and the cool ocean airs and waters.

Along the seashore, from Malibu to Laguna, the hot sands of the
beaches stirred yeastily with a mass of scantily clad humanity, a froth
of it wading out or even swimming into the blue-green waves, life-
guards watching from towers, young men bronzed and shouting and
bounding and splashing, girls molded in skintight swimsuits screaming
and laughing and running and being splashed, children dabbling at the
wet surf's edge or making sand castles, older people, some almost hideous with the deformation of age, but still conforming to the convention
of the revealing beach garment, lolling on the sands or under umbrellas.

In the city's expensive residential areas a thousand blue-tinted swimming pools surrounded by green grass and languorous flowers were
gathering places for beautiful young people, also in the inevitable swimsuits, who poised and plunged from diving boards, rose and splashed,
laughed and shouted, or stretched out on mats and towels on the concrete aprons to augment their fashionable tans.

Everywhere, on the clipped lawns and amidst the pruned shrubbery
of those costly homes with the swimming pools, tens of thousands of
sprinklers sprayed water, brought at infinite expense and labor through
great concrete conduits across mountain ranges and deserts from sources
hundreds of miles away; and the trucks of Japanese gardeners, laden
with hoses, garden implements, and bags of trash, stood along the curbs
as those patient urban peasants toiled to keep the beauty of grass and
flower serene and unblasted by the heat.

Along Sunset Boulevard elderly women with sunglasses and battered wide straw hats flapped maps at passing cars, advertising "Home Addresses of 100 Movie Stars." In Hollywood, now long degenerated from a city of glamour into a seamy town of second-class shops, tourists gazed reverently at cement footprints before Grauman's Chinese Theater, or hung about the intersection of Hollywood and Vine in hope of catching sight of some celebrity, or crowded in sweltering lines at the entrances of television and radio studios.

Down in the poorer sections of Los Angeles husbands and wives yelled at each other over bottles of beer and dirty-faced kids swirled in and out. On Skid Row, where the eyes smarted with the smog and buildings wore a dirty coat of grime and soot, old forgotten men queued up in front of gospel missions, where they could get soup with their psalms. The old forgotten men made no pilgrimage to the ocean. Their one concession to the heat was to strip down to their gray, grimy undershirts.

This was Los Angeles on a heat-smitten, smog-ridden day; and Mary Agnes was glad that her plane left for Honolulu the following morning. Meantime she was waiting for Erskine de Lacey to come for her. They were going out for cocktails and she was willing to be amused.

At six he telephoned from the lobby, and she made him wait only fifteen minutes before she came down from her room in a wide-flaring cocktail dress of aquamarine and black that made her waist seem small, with a filmy scarf about her bare shoulders.

Erskine came over to her quickly. He was of medium height, slender and small-boned, with a preserved boyish look, his crew cut brown hair slightly graying; about her own age, she judged. She thought his face rather good-looking: tanned like all these sun worshipers, with wrinkles on his neck and jaw muscles strong as if he had been grinding his teeth for years. He wore a simple blue suit with a string tie, and his shoes were black, pointed, and narrow—a shade too narrow for a man, perhaps—and very well polished and elegant.

"Did I keep you waiting long?" was her stock feminine greeting.

"Oh, not at all!" was his stock masculine reply. "Shall we have a cocktail in the lounge before we go?"

"I suppose we're a little late already——"

"It really doesn't matter—those things go on forever. Still, my car's at the porte-cochere. Mind a little wind?"

"No, I have my scarf."

Erskine had escorted her before: they were, indeed, quite good friends. He always treated her with unvarying and almost exaggerated politeness, and this was one reason she sometimes preferred him as an evening companion.

She was not especially offended with a man if he grew ardent perhaps under the influence of a few drinks. She was not even above permitting a few kisses, if she felt like it: everybody kissed everyone these days. But there was a line she drew, and if her escort attempted to go beyond that she extricated herself, and in such a manner that she usually left him, if somewhat frustrated, at least accepting defeat with good humor and even with hope of better luck at some later time; for she managed usually to leave things with a half promise hanging in the air, as some women almost invariably do.

All this, however, required effort, and the summoning of tact and firmness and perhaps humor, for laughter is a great quencher of fire. It was much more restful to know that your man was not going to stop his car suddenly under the pepper trees and begin reaching for you. In the case of Erskine this not only was restful but a little puzzling to her. She wondered why he seemed to like her so well, yet only at a distance.

Erskine's car was a small MG convertible, a fire-engine red. She never had liked the little foreign sports cars, preferring comfort; and she wondered if the MG was evidence of something or other in Erskine, perhaps juvenilism of mind. But she seated herself in it, wound the scarf about her head, and he swung out from the hotel drive into the rushing traffic of the boulevard.

"How long do you want to stay at this brawl?" he asked her.

"No particular length of time. Why?"

"You've never seen my studio." He made a swoop with the diminutive car along the curb inside a truck, so that she held her breath when it seemed there was not room to pass without a collision. But the MG slipped through the narrow space, roared past the truck, and raced on.

She breathed normally again. "No, I haven't," she said.

Though she knew he was an artist she had never seen any of his work. In Hollywood he was considered an "advanced" painter, which probably meant that he was excessively modernistic.

"Isn't it about time you did?" he asked. "Suppose we have dinner

—after we pay our respects out here—and then perhaps take a peek at my workshop?"

She considered. Studios . . . rather well-known devices of gentlemen with something on their minds besides art, or music, or whatever it is. But Erskine was different from most men she knew in this city, and besides, she had that complete confidence in herself.

"Let's see how the cocktail party is," she temporized.

2

The cocktail party turned out to be a typical Hollywood herd movement: a playroom larger than the rest of the house, overdecorated with indiscriminate modernistic prints and modernistic furniture, and overfilled with people standing, sitting, talking, drinking while servants in white mess jackets flitted about with trays of hors d'oeuvres and cocktails.

Mary Agnes knew some of the guests, minor denizens of the film colony chiefly, bit-part actors and actresses, assistant directors, script writers, song writers, and others whom she had difficulty in cataloguing. It was characteristic of this kind of an assemblage that when you were introduced to someone you received an odd, searching look, as if that person were trying to decide what might be your particular claim to distinction. Thereafter, if you were an outlander, or nobody in particular from a Hollywood standpoint, the person might try to ignore you.

But one did not ignore Mary Agnes successfully. She was sufficiently striking in appearance and manner so that she made a rather passé actress, still living on her success of a dozen years before, seem somewhat inferior by comparison. And though the rather passé actress was rude enough to address all her remarks to her male companion of the moment, she was no match for the keen feminine intellect which had just joined them, and she soon found that the male companion was engrossed in conversation with the invader; to the point that when she somewhat resentfully detached herself and went elsewhere, her departure was hardly noticed by the gentleman.

With this kind of minor triumph Mary Agnes was familiar, and she passed from group to group. Snatches of the kind of talk one forever heard at gatherings of this type came to her:

". . . makes you almost weep for her. She's had a nervous breakdown—her last husband committed suicide, you know, while she was in Las Vegas with that Argentine boy friend of hers, and she blames herself . . ."

". . . and the idiot gave all that up for the blonde, when everyone knows she's nothing but a Pacific Palisades pushover . . ."

". . . married again, is she? To that human cartoon? This is her fifth or sixth, which? The old boy must have plenty . . ."

". . . rotten luck. A role in this TV series and one in the new MGM picture came up at the same time. Couldn't take both . . ."

". . . says she has to sleep with every leading man she works with, because that's the only way she can get the emotional feeling for him that makes her performance valid . . ."

The Hollywood jungle, a restless stirring of frustrations and fears, prowlings and preyings, backbitings and bitterness. A few years ago glimpses like this into the shadowy inner world of the film colony had interested, even excited Mary Agnes. But now they wearied her, and when she found Erskine beside her, suggesting that they leave, she assented.

3

They drove back to Hollywood, and to the Beachcomber's: all bamboo and raffia, dimly lit through Japanese colored-glass net floats, with soft Hawaiian music whimpering in the air, exotic Asiatic food, and treacherously delicious rum drinks. Erskine was amusing and she was grateful to him for taking her from the boredom of the cocktail party. And after the two martinis she had there, and a pair of rum drinks with curious names—a Donga, one was called, and a Sumatra Kula—which she allowed herself here, she found herself more than usually relaxed and inclined to laugh very easily at things which really were not so very funny.

But enjoying herself seemed to be the main object at the time, and so when they finished their dinner of strange Chinese and Hawaiian dishes, she took a third rum drink at his smiling urging—a Don's Pearl this time, with a little seed pearl at the bottom. You had to drink it to the bottom to get the pearl, and she laughingly was determined to do so, and did.

By then she felt slightly dizzy and a little reckless, and when he suggested again his studio, she agreed without any particular hesitation. The night was very warm, as the day had been, and perhaps that had something to do with the way the drinks affected her, but she remembered only foggily that they drove up one of the steep narrow roads in the Hollywood Hills and stopped before an old pseudo-Spanish house overlooking the neon signs of the city.

"This is it," said Erskine. And when he ushered her into the house and switched on a light, "It's rather a mess, but you may be interested in some of my things."

She sat down, feeling a little unsteady on her feet, and gazed around. The room was quite large and evidently designed for a living room, with false beams and a sloping Spanish fireplace; but it was Erskine's studio and it was wildly disarrayed. An easel covered with a paint-daubed cloth stood near a window, and canvases, finished or unfinished, were stacked along the walls. The furniture was old and shabby and upholstered in red. The walls, too, were a dull brick red. To her the colors seemed to swirl and pulse.

He pointed to a large sideboard, painted red like everything else— a rather dreadful magenta red in this case. "I did that myself. Color is everything. That's not a *cozy* red—it's not a strong *virile* red—but it's rather a treasure—don't you think?"

She nodded.

"When I work I like harsh colors about me," he went on. "They stimulate me, stir me. Don't you feel it, too?"

His voice seemed insistent, almost quivering, as if this were a very important tenet with him. The rum drinks sang in her ears, and she felt airy, her head and heart light, careless of thought or ordinary matters. She nodded again, acknowledging that the fierce blare of colors acted on her as Erskine said, beating at her emotions and senses like bludgeons of light.

On the wall opposite hung a painting—a nude, evidently, of a strange deep fuchsia pink, with montane breasts and legs thick and heavy, the face a blob as if a child had daubed it.

"Lush, isn't she?" asked Erskine, following her glance.

"You painted it?"

"Yes. Empirical—*trés* empirical. Sensual. The way I felt at the time. Emotional."

So this was the kind of work he did. She found the thing repellently ugly, yet in her mood oddly, almost mesmerically fascinating to her gaze.

"What does it say to you?" he asked.

She hesitated. "I'm not . . . sure."

"Oh! You don't like it!" It was an accusation.

She said, "I didn't say I didn't like it——"

"The trouble is you won't *let* yourself like it!"

She felt defensive and groped for her thoughts. "Perhaps I—just don't understand it."

"You needn't understand it!" he exclaimed. "In art that's the least essentiality. No two souls feel alike—ever. But if you just *let* it enter you, touch you, take possession of you, it will mean something to you —something immense and creative, like the sensation the artist felt, and the model felt with him, when they were doing it together!"

She wanted to ask if he actually used a model for that, but felt it would be impertinent since obviously he had.

"Feel—you must feel!" he insisted. "To feel nothing, or even to feel little, is like death. Only when we begin to feel acutely do we begin to grow!"

She stared at the painting and the colors seemed to run together in tones and designs almost harmonic. She wished to feel, she wanted to understand, the great creative thrust Erskine had experienced when he painted that—it must be godlike, an otherworldly exhilaration.

The rum drinks were more potent than she realized. She shifted her gaze to him, sitting opposite her, swinging a leg rather jauntily over a chair arm, slender, with a cigarette in his fingers, and he seemed to her compelling and powerful in the thoughts he was expressing to her. Her mind, with the pleasing, irresponsible glow of the alcohol, was willing to be dominated, whereas when it was sober it was unwilling for such domination.

I wonder if he knows I'm a little drunk, she thought. And an inner voice said, Knowledge that a woman is a little drunk is an advantage men frequently seek to improve upon.

As if fearing to have the conversation stop she spoke almost faintly.

"I think I see now what you're achieving, Erskine."

Words, meaningless words, an excuse to gain time and summon order in the maze of her thoughts.

4

He remained sitting where he was, swinging that narrow pointed foot and looking at her. She felt his gaze go over her features, over her figure with strange intimate candor. And she found that she did not resent his intimate gaze. It seemed to caress her; she yielded to it almost dreamily.

"Mary Agnes," he said in a low voice. "Mary Agnes, I want something."

"What is it?" she asked, alarm faintly stirring.

"I've wanted it a long time, darling—ever since I first knew you." In his voice was an odd, entreating earnestness.

Now it is coming, she said to herself. He wants something . . . and by his voice I know what it is.

Instinctively she tried to sit more erectly, to marshal her thoughts.

How shall I deal with him? Be insulted, or angry, or just laugh? Or shall I . . . wait and see what happens, putting off decision until the time?

He spoke again. "I want to paint you."

To *paint* her! Not the crude masculine intention she had expected, after all. She leaned back in her chair with a sensation of relief and of surprise at herself, at her own confused emotions. It seemed suddenly so simple, her necessity for decision allayed.

She gave a little laugh.

"Why are you laughing?" he asked.

"Because . . . I couldn't imagine why you'd want to paint *me*." It was not why she laughed, but it was all she could think of to say.

"Why?" he said. "I've always wanted to paint you. You have superb bodily architecture—and you have a soul. I feel it. I feel I could do something wonderful with you. Will you pose for me?"

Her mind was still foggy, but she was no longer alarmed. It seemed a small thing he asked of her.

"If you really want me to—I don't see why I should object," she said after a moment. "When would you wish to do it?"

"Here—now!" He was eager. "I have in mind already the mood I want to create—soft light—mystery, almost indefinable mystery—subdued, shadowy, elusive—holding like a perfect jewel in a rich case the white purity of the female figure——"

"*Nude?*" The word almost jumped from her.

He stared.

"Nude, of course. How else? The nude is the great classical expression of art." He gazed at her closely. "You're not prudish, are you? Some of the greatest women of history have taken pride in being painted in the nude. All generations of artists have done their supreme work in it. You needn't fear it. The nude, to an artist, is an abstraction —the beauty of line, the modeling, the tones of color alone matter. At the same time it's the supreme compliment that art gives to the most beautiful thing in the world—the feminine form. Artist and model combine, the one with his brush, the other with her loveliness, in the great act of creating!"

He had not moved, or so much as gestured. After her momentary apprehension she felt inclined to him strongly out of the reaction of relief. And she felt that she owed him something for some reason which she did not very well define to herself. After all, other women, countless women, as he said, had not blushed at posing for artists in the nude. It was an experience, one might almost say a feminine function; and it was something, certainly, that not every woman could say she had done.

She noticed again the picture on the wall opposite. If *that* was the way he painted . . . after all, what harm could come of it? Nobody, in a thousand centuries, would ever recognize the original in Erskine's picture . . .

"Why not?" she heard herself saying to him.

She pushed herself up from the chair and stood rather unsteadily, conquering an impulse to giggle as the room seemed slowly to revolve around her.

"My models use that room to dress," he said in the same calm voice. "You'll find a robe and slippers in there. I'll be mixing my paints. Please go and get ready. The sitting won't take long."

Walking carefully, she moved toward the door he indicated. It seemed very silly, the thing she was doing, but for a reason she could not explain the whole idea was attractive. Even exciting. She desired to be painted. To be painted as she was, a woman in pure naked femininity, unfettered and unconcealed. To be viewed as an artist views beauty. To be unashamed in giving the beauty of her body to the canvas.

5

Still in the strange state of mind where volition seemed to be absent, she came out of the dressing room. Only a vague question was in her thoughts, hinging on what he might think of her when he saw her. The gray flannel robe she had found and wrapped about her body was the only garment she wore.

Erskine stood beside his easel, on which he had placed a fresh canvas. He had donned a smeared smock and was mixing paints with a palette knife. Laying down his palette, he came toward her, his face now strangely pale, strangely remote and introspective.

"I've decided just how I want to place you," he said. "Here, stand on this rug, with the red sofa behind. This lamp with the red silk shade will be beside you to illuminate the figure on that side with a delicate rosy tint, contrasting with the opalescent white of the opposite side. There. Now let me take the robe."

For just an instant she clutched the robe closely about her. To surrender every protection for her body in the presence of a man not even her lover was a novel and suddenly shocking experience. But his quiet air of doing the accustomed, natural thing and his hands held out expectantly for her garment overcame her reluctance. After a moment she opened the robe, drew it off, and handed it to him.

A sudden shrinking came over her. She stood before him half huddled, one arm drawn across her body at the confluence of her thighs, the other as if seeking to conceal her small breasts, the attitude of a woman confused and shamed.

Erskine clapped his hands softly.

"Perfect!" he cried. "Perfect! Don't move—hold that!"

He brought a scarlet scarf with fringed edges. "Here—I want you to hold this in your lower hand—trail it thus, down along your hip and thigh across the floor at your feet. So. It counterpoints the red lamp and provides a touch of drama—as if the woman is surprised in the intimacy of her bath. Remember that pose; fix it in your mind! I'll paint fast—I promise that I'll paint very fast——"

Holding the scarf gave her something to do and she gained confidence. She kept the pose and somewhat hazily reflected that nudity, after all, is not so unnatural to a woman . . . she is at her most effective in that state, and she knows it.

He returned to his easel and for a moment looked at her intensely, as if he would fix her image in his mind forever.

"I shall call it *Odalisque!*" he exclaimed, and began rapidly to sketch on his canvas.

Very quickly he took up his palette and began to paint. He seemed imbued by a kind of fury that surprised her. The room was warm, and she saw the sweat beading out on his forehead. Even in her nudity she felt a dampness beneath her arms and under her breasts from the warmth, but she steadfastly withheld from movement.

After a time the pose became tiring, but he spoke to her continually, praising her figure, her patience, her intelligence when she obeyed his wishes and showed her understanding by slight shifts of feet, body, or head. She knew he was flattering her, but she found it pleasing to have him gaze upon her and speak of her form as if it were a vision from heaven.

Gone was her alarm and confusion. She was only interested, now that her instinctive shrinking had passed, in being a good model, in giving him what he desired for the painting. She tried to feel his joy, to share companionship with him in the creation they were bringing into being together, and to a degree she did succeed in this, though her arms began to ache, and her back also, from her long-held position.

She wondered what kind of an abstraction he was making of her simple white female body, and now as she grew fatigued she did not greatly care. Perhaps she would not even understand it, but she could say to herself at least that she had posed for an artist who was mad about her form. A little fillip to life. She tried to continue in this reckless light mood, but it grew less light, then faded under the soggy weariness of her flesh.

For the first time now she observed the expression of his face. She was struck by it. He seemed transformed, his expression resembling that of a man in profound suffering. His mouth was half open, the lines from the corners of the nostrils deepened in a strange, almost sinister manner, in his eyeballs was a glare like that of a madman . . . or something else.

It almost frightened her.

"Erskine, Erskine!" she cried out. "I can't! I'm too tired to do any more."

In the act of putting on a brush stroke he paused, gazed at her as if uncomprehending, the wild glare still in his eyes. Then he completed the stroke, and the expression smoothed itself from his face.

"Of course, darling," he said. "I've overworked you. Forgive me——"

He put down the palette and brush and drew the smock over his head.

She straightened, rubbing her aching arms and bending her back. The gray robe was thrown over a chair and she took it up. Strange how quickly the habits of the model take possession. She seemed to have lost all self-consciousness toward him, no more than drawing the robe over her shoulders and loosely about her.

"Can I see the painting now?" she asked.

"Yes," he said in a voice strangely heavy. "It's not finished by any means—we'll have to complete it later."

She went over and gazed at the canvas, and gave a startled gasp.

"Why—it *looks* like me!" she cried.

She beheld a swirling of subtle and subdued hues of red, a cloudlike nimbus of color, and in the midst of it, as if shrinking from the gaze yet by the same act inviting it, a white female body—*herself*. It was her body, idealized only a little, the slim hips and thighs, the sloping shoulders, the softness of the small breasts with their delicate nipples, every sign and symbol of her sex made manifest and evident. And it was *her face* . . . recognizably her face, the greenish eyes, the hollowed cheeks, the arrogant nose, the dark hair with its widow's peak, even its little streak of gray.

"It *is* you," he said. "It's beautiful."

"But—I thought you painted only abstractions——"

"Some subjects merit being painted exactly as I see them."

She felt stunned, somehow apprehensive and helpless.

"I—I didn't know you were going to do *that* kind of a painting . . ."

"It's a triumph, isn't it?" he asked.

Half mechanically she gave a little nod.

"Thank you for it," he said in a low voice.

She recognized the voice . . . *that* kind of a voice. As if mesmerized, she felt herself drawn into his arms. The gray robe slid from her shoulders to the floor and a hand cupped her naked buttocks, drawing her thin body hard against him, the fabric of his shirt front almost bruising her tender breasts.

She felt him tremble violently, and her gasp was smothered by his lips on hers. A long kiss. A hard, burning, searching, lingering kiss. The rum, or the warmth, or some other thing created a vast thudding of drumbeats in her ears. Trouble faded in the chaos of her mind. An enormous lushness crept over her, draining her of every thought save a blind urgency of instinct. She was ready, naked in his arms, expecting, the mysterious starchiness gone suddenly out of her, as if already she had fallen willingly from some stupid estate. In frantic capitulation she responded to his kiss, pressing her body to him, closer, harder.

All at once he released her and stepped back.

"There . . ." he said, in a voice half muffled, as if something were finished.

Dazed, not understanding, she stood looking at him, naked and alone, her arms still half open as when he stepped from them.

He gazed back at her, all the passion, the look of suffering washed clean from his face.

"Go dress now, dear," he said. "I'll take you to your hotel."

She could not believe it. Her eyes still fixed on him with an almost fearful question in them, she bent her knees, groping on the floor for the robe. Trailing it behind her, dizzy, her heart still pounding, she stumbled to the dressing room.

6

Her awakening next morning was attended with anguish. Her head thumped with a twisting ache, its red torque at first depriving her of thinking.

"Oh, God," she said aloud. "What a fool. I never was so tight before."

Then she sat up, the movement sending a spasm of pain like a blow through her skull, but the ache was secondary to another pain, the pain of a half-vague recollection.

Aspirin. Three aspirin tablets. A cold wet towel for the forehead. After a time the ache was better.

But the recollection was not. It grew clearer, almost quite clear to her now.

I did *that?* she said to herself. How could I have done that? Drunk, naked, and making a holy show of myself!

But I was posing . . . I was a model.

I suppose women have done it before, drunk and naked.

Another thought brought her bolt upright again, with another searing anguish in her head.

The *painting!*

She remembered the painting a little vaguely, but she was sure it was none of Erskine's hideous daubs. Something almost beautiful, and shameless, and recognizable . . .

She had seen *herself* in that graceful white figure, rose- and opaltinted, surrounded by the red swirl of color, and she had been, she remembered, pleased with it, complimented by it in a swirling unsteady way that seemed to chime with the swirl of colors.

Yet also she was vaguely troubled; and even in the condition of mind in which she was the evening before the trouble would have grown to a warning, and from that to a decision. She would have demanded the picture, or insisted that he destroy it at once.

But what followed drove the picture itself and her half-formed protest clear out of her thinking.

She remembered again Erskine's face, working in that strange manner, and his sudden embrace of her. She felt once more his long searching kiss from which she did not withdraw, clinging to him rather in an almost wild willingness to surrender, unprecedented in her life before.

Then the strange denouement. His release of her. His stepping back as if in withdrawal, all his excitement of the moment before faded, and his one word, *There* . . .

As if something were finished. *What* was finished?

He had rejected her when she offered herself to him. In this was shame and a betrayal. When a woman has been brought to the point where she drowns every consideration in surrender, the humiliation of such a rejection lies as much in her shame over having thrown down all defenses as in the fact that the man did not see fit to accept her.

With the humiliation anger came to Mary Agnes: savagely wounded pride.

She reached for the telephone beside her bed and dialed Erskine's studio. She would get that painting. He would sell it, she was quite sure of that. A hundred—even a thousand dollars. He needed money, and the picture was of no value to him, at least in the sense it was to her. She would get it, whatever it cost, and personally see it destroyed.

But there was no answer on the telephone. After a long wait she dialed again. Still no reply. Erskine had gone out, probably for the day.

Her plane was leaving in two hours, and she must get ready. After all, the painting was unfinished. He probably would expect to complete it on her return from Honolulu. She decided to let the matter rest for the time and get in touch with him as soon as she got back from the Islands.

Yet all the way to Honolulu on the plane the question kept returning to her. Why? *Why?*

She was sure he had been as pent and mindless with desire as she. What had happened? Had she done something wrong, made some mistake?

She did not regret the outcome: on the other hand, she was intensely thankful it had turned out as it did. But the instinctive searching inherent in her sex for reasons of behavior in a matter so intimately personal vexed her: with herself, with the man who could have had his will of her that night and did not.

7

Still, it might in time have faded out of her mind completely, or at most remained only as a dim infrequent speculation, had it not been for two rather strange women she encountered who came to the Royal Hawaiian as guests, having landed from the liner *Lurline* a few days after her own arrival.

The older of the two attracted attention at first merely by so obviously not belonging in the gay, cosmopolitan, cocktail-drinking crowd that disported itself in the bars, along the exclusive beaches, and on the ball-room floors of the hotel. She was not young and far from smart, in fact quite dowdy in appearance, given to plain, dark-colored, rather loose and shapeless dresses that hung from her shoulders to her feet, her gray hair combed in some nondescript old-fashioned manner, always wearing glasses, and usually with a book in her long-fingered hands.

Her companion was younger, perhaps about thirty, with a thin unformed figure and a quaint little snub-nosed face, who attended the older woman with such assiduity that Mary Agnes put her down as a secretary-companion. When she had the opportunity, however, she occupied herself with acquiring a tan on the beach like so many of the other guests, female and male. Both seemed aloof and reserved toward strangers.

At first Mary Agnes paid little attention to either of them beyond wondering why they came to this expensive and ultrafashionable hotel instead of taking some light-housekeeping rooms where they could potter about and knit or get their own little meals, or do whatever else they did to keep themselves busy. But she revised her opinion quite drastically concerning them one afternoon.

She had gone down to the beach to lie in the sun, spreading her rug on the sand and seating herself on it in her swimsuit to put oil on her arms and legs and shoulders, when she saw the younger of the two women lying on a mat not far from her.

"Hello," said the young woman with an odd tentative little smile.

"Hello," responded Mary Agnes, busy with her suntan oil.

After a moment the other said rather hesitantly, "I'm Miss Isham—Julie Isham."

Mary Agnes nodded and smiled rather distantly. "I am Mrs. Wedge."

She was willing to let things drop there, but Miss Isham, for some reason, seemed determined to persist with the conversation.

"It's beautiful here, isn't it?" she said, gazing out at the ocean, dark blue beyond the dazzling white surf and growing indigo blue toward the horizon, with Diamond Head crouching against the skyline.

"Yes, I've always thought so," said Mary Agnes.

"This is the first time I've been in Hawaii," the other ventured. "Dr. Lewin needed a rest, and she decided it would be nice here."

"Oh?" said Mary Agnes, glancing at her with slightly increased interest. "Your friend is a doctor?"

"Yes! Oh yes! One of the very greatest in her field. Dr. Flora Elizabeth Lewin, of New York." Miss Isham pronounced the name quite impressively, but Mary Agnes was unimpressed; she had never heard it before.

"What's her specialty?" she inquired.

Miss Isham's expression said she could hardly believe this benightedness. "Why—psychology, of course. She's one of the world's foremost authorities—her books are read everywhere——"

"You mean she's an analyst?"

Miss Isham sat up. "She's a student of human problems," she said solemnly, as if reciting a lesson. "She tries to help people find values and stability in their inner world to stand over against the sufferings and fears and frustrations which are the diseases of our time. She has degrees from Johns Hopkins and Edinburgh, and she took intensive work in Zurich, under Jung himself!"

"Really? She sounds interesting."

"She's a very great woman, Mrs. Wedge. I'm a patient of hers myself —xenophobic tendencies with anxiety neuroses. She brought me here with her and I'm coming out of it. You see—I spoke to *you* just now without your even saying anything to me."

Mary Agnes looked at her. Back in Jericho, as everywhere else, it was thought smart to talk glibly, although not necessarily intelligently, on the vaguely fascinating subject of psychiatry. To this end Mary Agnes, in common with most of her feminine friends, had done a little haphazard reading, more to acquire a smattering of the curious jargon of the psychiatrists than for any real knowledge or understanding. She remembered now that the term xenophobia referred to fear of—or was it resentment of?—strangers, and she felt that this young woman probably had done much self-examination and study, as was usual with those who became preoccupied with psychiatry from an amateur standpoint.

Miss Isham was like a new convert, zealous to proselyte others. "Do you ever suffer anxiety neurosis, Mrs. Wedge?" she asked. "Everyone does. Dr. Lewin would be glad to talk to you."

Mary Agnes laughed. "I don't care to be analyzed, exactly. But I'd like to meet your friend because she seems unusual."

"Very well. You shall. I'll see to it." Miss Isham gave her a smile. "I think I've had about enough of this sun now. I don't want to blister —I've been here quite a while, you know. Shall I see you this evening?"

She took up her mat and robe and bottles of unguent and went off to the hotel, her brown legs twinkling.

Mary Agnes completed the oiling of her body, stretched herself on her back, and adjusted her sunglasses. There was something more than a casual motive in her expressing a willingness to meet Dr. Lewin. It had occurred to her that someone who was truly conversant with the shadowy world of the inner mind, as Miss Isham said Dr. Lewin was, might give her an insight into a question—*that* question—that again had arisen in her thoughts.

She approached her objective in her usual oblique way. That evening Miss Isham, showing off her patron with a childish sort of pride, introduced her to Dr. Lewin in the lanai. The "student of human problems" was quite plain, with a long, horsy face and deep lines in her forehead above her glasses; yet her expression was not unpleasant, and she proved to have a dry sense of humor, and they wound up having dinner together.

Not at first did Mary Agnes bring up the subject that interested her; not that evening at all. She met the two casually, here and there about the hotel, or in the shopping districts of the city, and was always cordial and friendly, rather seeking to get on an easy footing with them, although her own activities, quite social since she knew a good many people on the Island, forbade spending much time with them even had she wanted to do so.

But the opportunity she had been looking for came one day about a week later when she happened to find Dr. Lewin alone, reading on the terrace.

She sat down near, and the older woman looked up with a smile.

"Where's Miss Isham?" said Mary Agnes.

"She's sunning herself."

"I was noticing your book, *Two Essays on Analytical Psychology*— it's by Jung, isn't it?"

"Yes. Are you interested in psychology?"

"I'm interested, but I don't know much about it."

"Nobody knows much about it. The subject is too vast."

"Miss Isham says she's a patient of yours."

Dr. Lewin smiled again. "Not very much of a patient. More of a friend. She was a little confused, and perhaps uneasy, but she is adjusting herself well. I'm not concerned about her future."

"Perhaps," said Mary Agnes, "since you deal in matters of the mind, you can explain something that's rather mystified me since I heard it."

She tried to speak casually, but she felt that Dr. Lewin glanced at her rather keenly through her glasses.

"I can at least try to give some sort of a suggestion," she said.

"I have a friend," Mary Agnes began, "a professional model. She told me of a peculiar incident during a sitting for a certain artist."

Dr. Lewin nodded.

As tersely as possible, always relating it as if it had been told her by her fictitious "friend," Mary Agnes described the occurrence in Erskine de Lacey's studio.

At the end Dr. Lewin said, "Did you find the experience shocking, Mrs. Wedge?"

"I?" cried Mary Agnes. "Why do you assume it happened to *me?*"

"There are certain signs. Your preoccupation with the matter. Over-emphasis of this friend you describe, showing that you are anxious to have me accept such an identity. Minuteness of detail in one or two respects almost necessitating firsthand observance. It's really nothing to be concerned over, you know. Obviously you're no professional model. You agreed to pose for an artist you knew, didn't you? An artist you perhaps did not know as well as you thought you did?"

Mary Agnes hesitated, and then, a little shamefaced, gave up and nodded.

"What you've just described," Dr. Lewin went on in a voice quite matter of fact, "is known among sexologists as a 'deviation of object,' perhaps related to fetishism. The term sometimes applied to it is Pygmalion-eroticism. The subject obtains release, sometimes only psychic, sometimes both psychic and physical, out of the act of painting or modeling in clay a human form, usually of the opposite sex. In rare cases it becomes obsessive."

When Mary Agnes returned to her room, her face was blank with thought.

So he was *that* kind.

Pygmalion-erotic—they gave names to everything, the psychiatrists, based usually on some Greco-Roman myth. Thus, Oedipus complex, a child's fixation on a parent; thus, narcissism, the worship of one's own body.

Pygmalionism drew its name from the fabled king and sculptor who fell in love with a statue of a woman which he himself had carved.

Mary Agnes saw it now, she was sure of it: Erskine de Lacey painting so furiously, his intense lascivious gaze, his hands on her naked body, his single heated kiss—*they comprised a sexual act.* His face, like a man suffering, was the face of one in the paroxysm.

A curious tangent thought came: so he had not rejected her after all! From the first Erskine had wooed her, a strange wooing, a seduction leading to an unnatural consummation.

Her shoulders twisted in repugnance and she felt degraded.

Gradually, however, she thought more clearly. She did not fancy the role she had played, yet, offensive as it was, no harm had been done to her, except perhaps to her pride. It came over her that Erskine probably could do no real harm to any woman . . . in a normal way. He was perhaps to be pitied more than hated.

Then she remembered that he had asked her to return, to pose for him again when she was back from the Islands. Decidedly not! The mere suggestion was revolting.

But what about the picture? Not finished but *recognizable:* Mary Agnes Wedge, very much in the nude.

She could imagine what people would whisper in Jericho if someone who knew her ever saw that painting:

". . . you could *recognize* her just as plain as anything . . . not a *stitch on,* mind you . . . what can she have been *thinking* about? . . . a woman who would do *that* would do *anything* . . ."

With that she became more anxious than before to get possession of that picture as soon as she returned to California.

8

Well, she was back now, in Beverly Hills, and she had just learned from Mims Newman that Erskine de Lacey had gone, of all places, to Jericho!

Jericho . . . and Mrs. Simon Bolivar Butford. Mary Agnes knew Mrs. Butford quite well—aged and rich, the town's chief dowager, to whom everyone kowtowed because it was hoped she would someday leave her money to one or another of Jericho's civic institutions. She knew Mrs. Butford's selfishness, and shallowness, and smugness, and greed for flattery and praise. And also she knew how impregnable Mrs. Butford was in her huge old house with her huge old fortune to maintain it and her.

Erskine would know very well how to handle her. He had a way with old women. For years he had taken care of his mother as if he were a nursemaid prior to her death. Madame de Lacey was a widow, suffering from palsy, with one side of her mouth drooped down, talking in a low sepulchral voice. She handled the purse strings, and he handled her.

He was foot-loose. He had never married, and Mary Agnes knew now why he would shrink from marrying a normal woman.

But he knew every trick of dealing with an old woman, and he no doubt turned this to advantage with Mrs. Butford, dancing attendance on her, playing unceasingly to her enormous vanity, never venturing to disagree with her on any subject, coddling her, performing services for her, making himself indispensable to her.

And now he had gone to Jericho with her.

That was what caused Mary Agnes abruptly to change her plans in the middle of her conversation with Mims Newman. She had half intended to accept the invitation to cocktails, and fully intended to go to Balboa with the Kerstings, until Mims dropped that word about Erskine.

Instead she canceled all her engagements, sent a wire to Wistart, and that evening boarded a plane for Jericho.

ANNALS OF THE *DAILY CLARION*

The High and Noble Works of Journalism in Jericho

Jericho, Kansas, possessed two newspapers. Or perhaps it would be more exact to say that Jericho was possessed by two newspapers, in somewhat the manner that the celebrated devils possessed the Gadarene swine of Holy Writ, and with almost an equally confusing effect.

Neither paper ever came close to winning any Pulitzer prize for outstanding journalism, being alike shoddy, acrimonious, and carrying the freedom of the press to the point of license, particularly when discussing politics, scandal, or one another.

Of the two, the *Daily Clarion* was the less objectionable. It once had been a journal of some dignity, being the Wedge family newspaper, established by Senator Tucker Wedge and edited and published by him until his death. The senator was a man of intense self-assertion and considerable glibness that in some quarters went for wit, in others brilliance, and in others for superficiality or malice. He loved a phrase so well that he would out with it if it stabbed his dearest friend. As a result he accumulated so large a complement of enemies, at home and throughout the state, that eventually the sovereign voters kicked him out of his seat in the United States Senate.

Nevertheless, Senator Wedge did possess a curious streak of integrity, which propelled him from time to time into big, popularity-sapping fights. For example, he was for prohibition at a time when the issue was highly unpopular in honestly wet Jericho. At another time he fought the Ku Klux Klan in a day when that sheeted order could muster a parade of three thousand devotees in regalia, equipped with all the prejudices, intolerances, and sadistic inclinations fostered by the kleagles and the klaxons; and including not only the stupid and illiterate, but also ornaments of the city administration, the bar association, and the ministerial brotherhood, who belonged to it for reasons of expedience, political, legal, or divine.

None of these battles were waged for money. In fact, Senator Wedge lost advertising and friends in all of them. Nevertheless, the *Daily Clarion* out of them gained a sort of reputation for honesty of conviction that continued throughout his lifetime.

When the senator passed on to his reward—because of a heart attack due to too much golf at the Jericho Country Club after overeating at lunch—his widow, Mrs. Algeria Wedge, carried on in much the same manner, even ordering a delegation from the Rotary Club out of her office when they waited upon her to protest the *Clarion's* attacks on a brother Rotarian, who also happened to be a very venal city manager.

The delegation consisted of twenty important advertisers, and they hinted they would withdraw their advertising if Mrs. Wedge did not see fit to comply with their ultimatum. For answer she called for someone to rummage cuts of all the businessmen present and dared them to do their worst—she would have a story printed that day proving that the popular city manager had his hand in the public till, and was prepared to write a front-page article herself about the members of the delegation, showing forth the manner in which the free press was being intimidated. The ultimatum bearers quit like twenty chastised dogs.

All this somewhat top-lofty journalistic attitude changed after Mrs. Wedge's death, and particularly after the *Morning Sentinel* began publication.

The *Morning Sentinel* was established, with outside money, by the brothers Eddie and Tony Ender. Not news, but revenue, was their chief and only concern, their editorial department only a vassal to the advertising department. Any kind of advertising was accepted, providing there was cash to be paid for it. The pages of the *Sentinel* sprouted a poisonous fungoid growth of patent medicines, quack practictioners, potency pills, occultism, and fake investment opportunities. Every advertisement could, and did, command a news story in the paper's columns. It was Tom Pollock, the elderly barrister, who one day paraphrased:

> "Count that day lost whose low descending sun
> Finds not some blurb upon the front page run."

But the *Sentinel* had another source of income; achieved by suppressing stories as well as publishing them. Private detectives on regular retainers made periodic reports from Kansas City, Wichita, and Denver —the most popular joy spots for errant Jericho lotharios. Among the fish caught in this net at various stages of history were some of the city's most prominent businessmen—and even a matron or two of high social standing—who were engaged in extracurricular dalliances of one kind or another.

The *Sentinel* was always most tender and discreet about such matters, as witness its regard for the sensibilities of Mr. Julius Simpson, the popular undertaker, owner of the Simpson Family Mortuary ("Dignity and Service Conveniently within Your Means") and the Tower Memorial Lawns cemetery.

Mr. Simpson, rubicund, benignly solemn, in his fifties, a grandfather, and rich from a busy and fruitful lifetime of planting at outrageous prices the city's defunct, was superintendent of the Sunday school of one of Jericho's most important churches. His grandfatherly interest in children was highly esteemed; but people did not know that he carried his grandfatherly interest so far as to transport one of the children under his wardship to an out-of-state city for her education and his refreshment.

The pupil in question was Charlene Peckham, fourteen years old but precociously rounded and pert, whose father, a local truck driver, believed her to be visiting a girl friend in Denver, whereas she was occupying a hotel room with that portly old frog, Mr. Simpson. This liaison was duly reported by a detective to the brothers Ender.

But observe the tact and the gentle ruth of the Enders. Instead of cruelly exposing this affair to the public, they merely called its regrettable circumstances—with affidavits sworn by a reliable investigation service—to the attention of the elderly lothario himself on his return to the city.

Mr. Simpson, when he was confronted with this information, lost his customary rubicund hue and resembled rather strikingly one of the cadavers which had been lying about nine days on a slab in the rear of his own embalming rooms.

But he survived, and it might have been noted that thereafter the pages of the *Sentinel* were heavy with advertising from the Simpson Family Mortuary, to the amount of ten thousand dollars above the

regular budget. Since, however, this maintained the press in its freedom, and since no whisper concerning Mr. Simpson and his idyll with
the precocious young nymph Charlene ever got out, and since Mr.
Simpson thereafter lived a rigidly exemplary life, being almost afraid
to look over his shoulder for fear a gumshoe was following him, the
results might be considered in some degree worthy.

It should be added that the truck-driving father of Charlene never
knew; it would have been cruel to wound his feelings with knowledge
of his daughter's betrayal, and he did not have the money to purchase
any advertisements in the *Sentinel* anyway.

Three

To the stranger within its gates Jericho offered a convenient introduction to itself in the form of a handsome booklet, issued by the Chamber of Commerce, printed in four colors, and entitled *Richest in Peace, Safest in War*. It contained a map showing the situation of the young city almost in the center of the continent, far from the perilous seacoasts and borders of the nation, from which enemies, identified by Jericho people as "the Rooshians," might attack.

The booklet contained also a summary of the city's advantages as a place to live, including a rather hasty reference to the weather: "An outstanding feature of Jericho's weather is its variability. As everybody knows, the people of the world who amount to anything live in regions of swift and sudden changes in temperature and weather, with scurrying winds."

The "swift and sudden changes in temperature" was a neat touch of understatement. Occasionally Jericho enjoyed beautiful, calm, balmy days; but more often the conditions were either sweltering or freezing, so that if, indeed, the erratic behavior of the thermometer is an index to what is required to "amount to anything," the people of Jericho should have been blessed above all mortals.

The "scurrying winds" was good, too. Sometimes they scurried at ninety miles an hour, and they had been known to scurry with gale force for days and even weeks at a time, in summer with a searing edge of heat, in winter with ice fangs of cold.

On that particular early January morning Debs Dorn hardly considered himself blessed by the sub-zero wind which rasped like a file on his cheek. He tucked his head deeper into the upturned collar of his overcoat, pulled his hat low on his forehead, rammed his fists into his pockets and half ran, half skated down the snowy sidewalk toward Jolly Herron's Drugstore.

It was before sunrise and the streets were dark. Save for a solitary bus grinding along up the block and a few furtive automobiles appearing to be frozen at the slippery curbs, no sign of life was visible. But the windows of the drugstore were alight, although the frost which frescoed them prevented one from seeing who might be giving patronage at this early hour of a winter's morning.

Herron's Drugstore was ancient, foul, dilapidated, and frowsy, with a row of sticky booths for patrons of the soda fountain, spindle-legged stools at the counter, a faded mirror at the back, a display of much-thumbed magazines and comic books, a cigar counter, and the usual shelves of proprietary medicines. Nevertheless, it remained open twenty-four hours a day, and for an excellent reason. Uninviting as it appeared, Jolly Herron's place possessed a certain significance, for it stood about halfway between the newspaper offices of the *Daily Clarion* and the *Morning Sentinel,* and hence provided a curious neutral ground where members of the staffs of those two eternally feuding journals could meet with taunts and gibes, and unprintable stories, and occasional exchanges of information, more or less friendly.

Debs opened the door, stepped from raw cold into fetid warmth, carefully closed the door, brushed a few flecks of snow from his sleeves, and turned down his coat collar. He was thus revealed as a compact, dark young man, bony-faced, with an oddly sensitive mouth and eyes oddly alert and oddly secret. Habitually he wore a look of weary cynicism—a pose with him, perhaps, for he was no more than thirty—and he was a person of some consequence, being the city editor of the Jericho *Daily Clarion.*

Debs Dorn's name was part of his background. His father, a bookish visionary who operated a small, eternally dusty and eternally littered secondhand bookshop, was too busy upholding his militant theories as a philosophical atheist, a vegetarian, a prohibitionist, and a socialist ever to make much of a living. There were days when the table in the Dorn household had scarcely enough even of the cheapest vegetables to satisfy hunger. The elder Dorn was dead now, being predeceased by his wife, but he had named his only son for his chief hero of socialism, Eugene V. Debs. This name the son bore with a sort of ironic truculence. But except for his name Debs Dorn espoused none of his father's lost causes. He liked beefsteak and bourbon for dinner, when he could afford them; never took the slightest interest in any kind of religious discussion; and though his leanings were liberal, he did not permit his own political views to influence in any manner his handling of the news strictly according to the rock-bound Republican policies of the *Clarion,* which paid him his salary.

"Hi, Smoky," he said to a cadaverous youth with pimples, who stood behind the counter waiting for the drugstore's day shift to arrive.

"Hi, Debs," said the youth.

The drugstore was empty, but Debs jerked his head toward the rear.

"Brummitt and Yates," said Smoky. "And Jeff."

Debs walked to a rear door, opened it, and entered a room even dirtier and less appealing than the drugstore itself. There was a long table, seared and scarred with cigarette burns, standing on an uncarpeted floor littered with half-smoked stubs, burnt matches, and dried mud. Two unshaded electric bulbs hanging from the ceiling gave a bilious light, and scattered about were half a dozen battered chairs.

Jutting out in one corner was a jerry-built box of cheap siding, concealing a filthy lavatory and stool. An old-fashioned steam radiator bore rather rakishly a rusted tin coffee can containing water to "humidify" the air: and some treatment of this or another kind was indicated, for though the day was hardly beginning the room was stale and blue with tobacco smoke. The walls were of rough plaster, painted a faded gray and decorated with three or four torn theatrical posters, a "mural" of pornographic nature drawn by a drunken newspaper artist with a copyreader's grease pencil, and sundry stains where tobacco chewers had spat.

Women were never admitted to this back room, which was facetiously referred to as the Press Club, and was the reason for the popularity of Jolly Herron's place. It was for newspapermen only, a haven where they could drink or gamble or gossip or even sleep, unobserved by the lay public.

A balding, young-old man in a baggy suit, Ed Brummitt, of the *Sentinel,* was shaking dice with Harry Yates, a fellow staff member, for nickels on the scarred table. Another man sat behind a newspaper, his chair tilted back against the wall, both hat and overcoat on.

"Hi, gents," said Debs nodding.

"Mr. Dorn, of the evening bladder, I believe," said Brummitt.

Yates, plumpish and smelling of whiskey, did not look up. Brummitt returned to the game and the small cubes rattled.

"My point," said Yates. "That's forty-five cents I'm into you."

"I gotta quit and go home," said Brummitt. "Payday tomorrow."

Yates nodded. It was a peculiarity of the Jericho newspapers that though printers and advertising solicitors were paid by the week, members of the editorial staffs were paid semi-monthly. It also was a peculiarity of the two papers that their reporters were paid so little that at the end of each half month they rarely had enough money to satisfy even a forty-five-cent crap-shooting debt.

Brummitt and Yates put on their overcoats and prepared to depart. They had just finished their night's work on the morning paper and would sleep through the day. As they left, Brummitt halted beside Debs.

"Hear Madame Wedge is back from Honolulu," he said.

Debs nodded.

"Hear the Big Deal is on again," Brummitt added.

Again Debs nodded. He, too, had heard the rumor.

Curious how information, no matter how secret, managed to seep through both newspaper offices. The "Big Deal" to which Brummitt referred was a hardy perennial—a rumor often revived, but always denied, of a merger of the two newspapers. It was dreaded by both staffs, for a consolidation meant that some reporters would find themselves in the surplus category, and therefore without jobs.

Brummitt and the other *Sentinel* man went on out.

Throughout this exchange, to which he paid not the slightest attention, the young man beside the wall remained tilted back in his chair, reading the final edition of the *Morning Sentinel*. He was Jeff Linderman, assistant city editor of the *Daily Clarion*, lanky and serious-faced, perhaps five years Debs' junior. Hat pushed back on his head and overcoat unbuttoned, he read carefully, with deep concentration, the opposition newspaper, page by page, column by column, until he had digested every item in it.

Debs said nothing until he finished and looked up. He himself had read the rival paper with equal thoroughness before he left home that morning.

"About time to get over there, Jeff," he now said.

Jeff straightened his long thin legs, rose, buttoned his overcoat, pulled his hat down on his forehead, folded the paper, thrust it into his pocket, and belched.

"Reckon so," he said.

"Find anything startling in the opposition?"

"Nope. Blurbs. Routine. That yarn about the vice ring is a phony. The old Draggett story dug up again and worked over. Any truth to the scuttlebutt about the Big Deal?"

"Don't know. May only be talk, because Mary Agnes came home."

Debs should perhaps have been more respectful of the wife of the publisher of the *Clarion,* but newspapermen speak thus irreverently of their betters.

Jeff belched again. "I dread the day."

"Seas rough last night?" asked Debs without solicitude.

"It's the hooch they sell in this damned state. Didn't drink so much, but it turns my guts upside down."

This was a rather usual complaint of Jeff's, who had no stomach for liquor and really did not drink heavily, but had an innocent vanity in being considered an abandoned sot. He was intelligent, a loyal lieutenant, and one of the two men with some writing ability on the *Clarion,* the other being Debs Dorn himself. These two, who might have added a little brightness to the paper's drab columns, were assigned to "desk jobs," leaving the writing to the less able. It is a disease that affects most newspapers.

Together they left the drugstore and stepped into the bitter wind which whirled scattered snowflakes down the bleak dark street.

2

The ground floor of the Daily Clarion building was reserved for the advertising and circulation departments in order that customers in those cash-paying divisions might be spared the labor of mounting stairs. A private elevator provided easy ascent to the publisher's office on the second floor. But nobody thought of sparing the legs of a newsman, so the city room, which also was on the second floor, was reached only by a rather steep flight of stairs from a street entrance.

It was not yet seven o'clock when Debs and Jeff arrived in the city room, and the place was as yet untenanted, looking shabby and disordered as usual. Two teletype machines beside one wall clicked a soulless staccato in queer unison, though their messages were different since they each reported a different press service's budget of news. They had been turned on an hour before when the first printers arrived, and already long curling trails of yellow paper with neat lines of type, all in capitals, festooned the floor about them.

Rows of battered desks, typewriters even more battered, yawning wastebaskets, calendars and maps on the walls, and a PBX box at the head of the stairs constituted other furnishings. The PBX box would be presided over presently by a gum-chewing telephone girl, but now its wires all dangled, save for two, one connected with the city desk, the other with the circulation department below.

Debs switched on the lights above the large central desk and began going over a heap of galley proofs left from the previous day, marking *Kill* on some and *Hold* on others, while Jeff glanced at the trailing teletype reports. After a moment he tore the long strips from the machines, and seating himself opposite Debs, began with a brass rule neatly to cut the items one from the other by tearing, sorting them, piling complete stories to one side, and pasting up others which came in separate "takes"; for in addition to being assistant city editor, Jeff also was in charge of the telegraph report.

"Anything big on the wire?" Debs asked.

"No," said Jeff. "Steel strike looks like a sure thing."

Debs grunted.

On the wall at the end of the room an electric clock gave a sharp *ping.* Seven o'clock.

As if at a signal the stairs became noisy with feet and voices. The staff was arriving for work. Debs hardly glanced up as the men passed him and went to their various desks, where some looked over the *Sentinel,* others began pecking at some unfinished story, and others simply smoked or gossiped.

It was not a staff of which a newspaper could be particularly proud. The *Clarion* and the *Sentinel* hated each other to a degree seldom seen even in the journalistic world, which is long on newspaper hatreds. But however furiously they disagreed on every other matter, they agreed perfectly on one thing: they employed the cheapest help they could and kept it as low-salaried as possible. As a natural result both editorial staffs—hardest hit by this dollar-pinching policy—were composed in far more than ordinary measure of incompetents, misfits, and drunks, most of whom could work nowhere else and therefore took jobs in Jericho "for peanuts."

A big, jovial-seeming man in a rakish hat and loud yellow topcoat stopped at the desk. "What you got for me?" he asked Jeff.

He was Larry Cameron, the sports editor and also the staff's lustiest lecher. Big, round, and ribald, he was filthy of mouth and mind to a degree bordering upon the supreme, but engaging for all of that. Reputedly he knew every woman in town who was sexually available— within his purlieu of women, that is, which included only primroses somewhat soiled.

Withal, he was a tremendous sentimentalist. Upon the shabby females with whom he lay in the back seats of automobiles or on chigger-swarming grass clumps in cemeteries and on golf courses, he lavished the same sort of soupy admiration found usually in pimply adolescents at their first awkward great loves. Similarly he had high enthusiasms for pork-and-bean prize fighters, bush-league home-run hitters, and star halfbacks on minor college elevens that never won games. A ragged little kid singing for pennies on a street corner moistened his eyes. He was devoted to his friends and would demonstrate his affection by tenderly attributing to them cuckoldry or venereal diseases. Those he disliked he invariably maintained were homosexual.

He liked both Debs and Jeff, and sometimes asked the latter to keep an eye on the sports report in case something broke big enough to warrant making over his page while he drove off into some lovers' lane with whatever drab excited him at the moment. Always he followed the same routine—building up to asking the favor by ingratiatingly accusing Jeff of contracting syphilis or the like.

Then, "Watch sports for me, will you?" A leer. "I'm going *duck* hunting."

An hour or two later, when he came back, Jeff would glance up from his work. "How many ducks did you get, Larry?" he would ask.

"Oh, just the one," would come the airy reply.

Larry now picked up the heap of telegraph stories Jeff had indicated and gave Jeff a scrutinizing squint.

"You look like you've got the crud," he said genially.

"I *am* a little tired this morning," said Jeff.

"You ain't tired, you're stale," said Larry. "I can cure that. Come out with me tonight. You'd be surprised—this town's full of beds and the beds are just full of women."

Jeff grinned and shook his head. It was a perennial offer which he perennially refused. Larry took his sheaf of copy and swaggered back to the sports desk in the corner by the wall.

Presently Debs called out, "Canfield!"

Joe Canfield, the police reporter, rose slowly and came to the desk. He was slim, fox-faced, with sandy hair and shifty eyes, in his thirties. Debs often wondered what a psychoanalyst would have made of him. He was not to be trusted, a liar who would have been notable even in a more populous and mendacious center than Jericho. Yet, though his handling of the English language was no more than adequate, he could telephone in a fair story. Moreover, as police reporter he got news from others than the minions of the law—he was a consorter with unsavory characters and had his own scattering of stool pigeons among the petty thieves, prostitutes, and confidence men of the city.

"How about the vice ring story?" Debs asked.

"Nothing to it," said Canfield. "No ring. Just Earl Draggett and his tavern, the Chesterfield Club, again. Sheriff's office caught someone smuggling redeye to the tables, contrary to the statutes, so Draggett's under bail, to be tried next term of the district court. That's all there is to it. He's got one strip-tease act. But no pimping. I know the gal."

"Sure she's not doing a little hustling on the side?"

"Say, listen, I went back one night and talked to that dame. Bonnie Bonner. She'd just finished her act, naked as a jaybird except for a G-string, and was in her dressing room. When I walked in on her, she was wearing a wrapper, sitting at her make-up table, reading the Bible."

"Go on!" said Debs incredulously.

"So help me. She belongs to some little off-brand religious sect. Dumb as they come. It says nothing in the Bible, according to her reading, about being a sin to strip naked in public, and she gets two hundred bucks a week for doing it. So she does it. Otherwise she'd be hashing for what she could pick up in tips. She's married. Husband's a carpenter. Queer on religion, too. He works in the day and she works at night. They sell religious tracts and do considerable praying and Bible reading together."

"There's a story in that."

"Yeah, maybe," said Canfield.

"Sunday feature—*Bible Reading Burlesque Queen*. Can it be handled without libel?"

"I reckon."

"Give me an outline on it. And check the libel business. Okay."

Canfield lit a cigarette, tilted his hat on the side of his head, and went down the stairs to his beat. On consideration Debs decided against having him write the story about Bonnie Bonner. In the first place Canfield could not write well enough. In the second place it might be safer to have the facts checked by someone more reliable before they were published in the newspaper.

Other men began coming to the desk for assignments. Telephones jangled as the switchboard operator took her place. Reporters hurried in and out, the teletypes maintained their ceaseless clicking, voices were raised in shouts for the copy boy, for someone to hurry up that goddamn story, for somebody to get that phone: a welter of noise and confusion, the normal heartbeat of a newspaper, the inherent excitement that keeps newspapermen at an otherwise somewhat thankless task.

Debs felt a lift, almost happiness, the sense of power and accomplishment he always knew when the *Clarion* was in full operation, with himself sitting at the throttle, the key figure in its complicated machinery.

3

The society editors would not come down until nine o'clock, because it was presumed in Jericho journalistic circles that no lady of social importance ever rose before that hour. When they did arrive they would have an item of unusual significance for their columns. Mrs. Wistart Wedge was home from Honolulu. The *Sentinel* had ignored this news as a matter of policy, and much would be made of it by the *Clarion*.

It was, as a matter of fact, real news such as the society page rarely carried, for the story of Mrs. Wedge's return would be read not only by those who usually perused the so-called Snob Sheet—mistresses of fine homes who were acquaintances as well as rivals of Mrs. Wedge, and women of humbler homes and vocations who lived vicarious social existences through following the activities of those in loftier stations—but also by certain persons interested in cold matters of business and finance, to whom this return would have important meaning; and above all by everyone connected, however remotely, with the newspaper business in Jericho. For the whisper of the Big Deal had reached every journalistic level in the city, down to the scabbiest newsboy.

At eight o'clock Samson J. Hudson, the managing editor, came up the stairs from the street. He paused at the city desk.

"Anything doing, Debs?" he asked almost paternally.

Hudson was a graying, burly man, nearing sixty, with horn-rimmed glasses, a loose upper plate, and bowlegs. He was bitter with disappointment because he knew he was on a toboggan ride downward in his profession. Once he had for a time held a position as managing editor of a much larger paper in a much larger city, but he drank himself out of that job. Then, after clinging to various minor posts, he met Wistart Wedge, of the *Clarion,* two years before at a political convention and convinced him he would be of value in "modernizing" the paper.

It was a job, such as it was, but to Hudson it was a long step down. He despised both the *Clarion* and Jericho, and he hated Debs because Debs was rising and he was going down, and because he knew secretly that Debs was a far better newspaperman than he, and was afraid that someone else would discover it and put Debs in his place. He still drank, but he did it secretly now, and made great show of frowning on the use of liquor by members of his staff.

Sometimes Hudson assumed the kindly, paternal manner. But from that, at any pretext, he might go to the opposite extreme, flinging his frustration in frenzies at his staff, behaving in the manner that non-newspaper folk imagine is typical of managing editors—skating around in his chair, wearing out two or three trousers seats to every coat, yelling, abusing, a bullying tyrant to those under him, but always a sycophant to those above. Behind his back the staff called him Shrieking Sam and cordially detested him.

Debs Dorn bore him patiently, as one of the burdens of life, knowing his hypocrisy and vindictiveness as further obstacles to be taken into consideration in the already rough road of getting out the *Clarion* daily.

He answered Hudson's question in the negative.

"How're you handling the story on Mrs. Wedge?" asked the managing editor.

"Thought I'd just let the society desk use it. It's their department——"

Hudson exploded.

"Hell's fire, man! You consider this a routine society item? Good

God! Why, this woman's been to Honolulu! World travel! The best known woman in town, bar none! Everyone wants to know what she did, what she saw, what she thinks! Get a reporter on it right away —have a cameraman out there—put it on page one! Double-column feature head! God Almighty, how can I be expected to get out a paper when nobody—but *nobody*—knows what's news when he sees it staring him right in the face!"

The last sentence, addressed to the ceiling in a despairing appeal to whatever gods there be in the Olympus of journalism, was uttered so loudly that everyone in the city room heard it, and everyone knew that Shrieking Sam was working himself up to one of his frenzies.

"Okay," said Debs, seething inwardly. "I'll send——"

But Hudson had a new idea. "Forget it—just forget it! I'll handle it myself! Goddamn it all, if anything's done decently around this place, I have to do it! Well, I'll take care of it! But don't you make any mistake about this—hold a place for that story on page one! Understand?"

Debs nodded without speaking. He knew the direction this was leading. Hudson had seen a really magnificent opportunity to curry favor. The call to the Wedge home would be personal, a honeyed flattery over the telephone; Mrs. Wedge would be informed by Mr. Hudson that he, the managing editor, was devoting his own personal time and attention to seeing to it that she received proper recognition—recognition befitting her station and the wide public interest in everything she did. The story, when it appeared, carefully filled with panegyrics calculated to please her, would be earmarked in Mrs. Wedge's mind as the work of the alert, the capable, and the faithful Samson J. Hudson, who truly appreciated her importance and worth. And this, when and if certain decisions concerning the *Clarion* and its staff were made, might very conceivably redound to the credit of Samson J. Hudson.

The staff took due notice. Evidently the Big Deal was very much on Shrieking Sam's mind also.

Four

I

Wistart Wedge came downtown that cold January morning somewhat earlier than usual. He had been surprised when his wife wired
him the day before that she had changed her mind about staying in
Los Angeles and would return at once to Jericho; and he had hoped
from this that she was interested in his problems and was coming home
to discuss them with him. But she was wearied from two successive
nights on planes and she was so chillingly sharp when he met her at
the airport shortly after midnight that he did not then dare broach the
subject that most deeply concerned him.

This morning Mary Agnes was sleeping late. Even under ordinary
circumstances she made it her practice, taking breakfast and sometimes
doing some telephoning to her friends before arising, so that often she
did not appear downstairs until almost noon.

Wistart, barred by long custom from his wife's room, found himself
awake early and could not return to slumber. He rose, had breakfast,
read the *Morning Sentinel,* estimated with a sickly bitterness how
much greater its advertising linage was than that of his own *Clarion*
of the evening before, and at last told Suey, his Negro butler-chauffeur,
to bring the small car around to the front. He would drive downtown
alone. He felt he could not contain himself if he waited until noon for
Mary Agnes. Too much depended on her mood; and the long wait,
spent in wondering what frame of mind she would be in this morning,
was too much like a convicted prisoner's long wait for his sentence to
be declared.

As he drove down from Tower Hill, his gaze was vague, his mind
deeply preoccupied with its own inner problem. He parked his car in
the newspaper's small parking lot and took the private, self-operating
elevator up to his office.

"Good morning, Mr. Wedge," said Miss Finch, his secretary, as he
entered the reception room.

She was a waspish, thin-faced, elderly woman with thick-lensed glasses whom he had inherited from his mother, the late Mrs. Algeria Wedge; and she had greeted him in exactly that same voice, without the slightest change of inflection, every day in all the years she had worked for him.

He merely nodded and went into his inner office, where he seated himself at the large carved desk with its dull glow of polished rosewood, its various table ornaments, and its pile of letters, already slit open and neatly arranged for his perusal by the efficient Miss Finch. Going through the mail usually was his first business, but today he did not touch the correspondence. Instead, he took from a humidor of hand-tooled leather a fine cigar, lit it, and for a few minutes puffed on it silently.

Opposite him, on the paneled wall, hung a portrait: his father, the late Senator Tucker Wedge. Painted nearly thirty years before, when the senator was enjoying his first and only term in the upper house of Congress, it pictured a bald, paunchy man with a strong jaw and a harsh black eye.

Force was inherent in the attitude and expression of the man portrayed; but the force that was in the father was not discernible in the son who sat at the carved desk. Wistart Wedge was thirty-seven years old, although he hardly looked it with his round boyish face and fair complexion. His expression was kind, almost gentle, rather than aggressive; his eyes were light blue with pale lashes, and his hair, blond and silky, was becoming rather thin on top. Plump without being actually corpulent, he appeared to be easygoing, even somewhat placid ordinarily; but his look this morning was withdrawn and worried without being determined.

For a time he puffed the excellent cigar, debating whether he should call in Miss Finch for the morning's dictation. But he felt an aversion to the task; and he found that the cigar did not taste as well to him as usual, so presently he discarded it and rose from his chair.

Should he telephone his home and find if Mary Agnes had risen yet? He glanced at his wrist watch. It was only a little after ten o'clock. No, on second thought he decided it would be unwise to awaken her if she was still sleeping—today of all days, in particular.

So he took a turn or two across the room, his eyes hardly seeing the rich leather-covered furniture, or the shelves of books, or the framed photographs on the walls picturing occasions more or less important in which he had been a participant, or his father's portrait, or the beautiful velvet rug which covered the floor. The office had been designed by a skillful decorator for peace, contemplation, and tempered decisions. But the man who paced restlessly back and forth in it was far from peaceful, and unable to arrive at a decision, tempered or otherwise. He was wrestling with a problem that vexed him nearly beyond himself.

2

Almost exactly three years ago, Wistart remembered, the problem first became manifest to him, when he sat in this same office with John Giddings, the *Clarion's* business manager. Giddings was gray and dry, with huge, almost elephantine ears, and old-fashioned pince-nez glasses perched on his large nose. He was a senior employee who had begun his service in the *Clarion's* earliest days as a printer's devil, progressing upward with earthworm slowness until by the very inertia of accumulating years he became business manager.

An efficiency expert would not have approved of Mr. Giddings. Indolent and not very alert, his management of the advertising and circulation departments, nominally under his direction, was loose and far from effective. On that morning, three years before, he had news for Wistart.

"The Audit Bureau of Circulation people have given me their preliminary report," he said.

"Ah, yes," said Wistart. "This is our present circulation?"

"Not complete. An estimate really—the official report comes later——"

"But this is pretty close?"

"Well—in the neighborhood."

"You mean we've lost all that circulation in the past year?"

"Only about ten per cent," said Giddings a little uneasily. "We can make it up by a vigorous circulation campaign."

"What about the drop in advertising?"

"There's been a slight retail recession——"

"But the national space is off as well as the local."

"I'll have a talk with the advertising department," Giddings said. "We need to spur things up a bit, I admit. Especially now."

Wistart glanced up from the report. "Why especially *now?*"

"You mean you haven't heard?"

"I don't know what you're talking about."

John Giddings squirmed uncomfortably and pulled at one of his flapping earlobes. "I thought you'd been informed—the report came in this morning——"

"Mrs. Wedge is flying to Hawaii," explained Wistart. "I was seeing her off at the airport and only just came to the office. What is this report?"

"Well—according to my understanding—there's going to be an attempt to start another newspaper in Jericho."

Another newspaper! Wistart stared, feeling the blood rush from his face to his heart.

"Has anyone tried to verify this?" he managed to ask at last.

"Yes. I made inquiries. I'm afraid—that maybe it's so. Oh, nothing to worry about, I think. Some syndicate's bought a building over in Jugtown, near the courthouse. I understand presses and linotype machines are ordered and contracts signed with newsprint companies. The usual preliminaries. But it's been tried before, you know. Jericho won't support two newspapers—it's been proved. Nothing to worry about, as I said."

Nothing to worry about! And with the *Clarion* already losing ground, though it was alone in its field? Wistart was not a great newspaperman, but he had enough experience to know how difficult it is to get a newspaper under way again once it has slipped back. Inertia is a terrible weight to overcome in the journalistic world. A newspaper is dependent not on the habits of one, or a few, but of all the thousands of its readers; it must change all those habits to regain ground it has lost.

Although the winter day was cold outside and the office no more than comfortably warm, Wistart took a handkerchief from his pocket and wiped his suddenly dampened forehead.

"John," he said, "this is serious. Who's going to run—the new paper?"

"All I know is that they're brothers named Ender—Eddie and Tony."

"Never heard of them. Where are they from?"

"Chicago, originally."

"Get some wires out and check on them."

"All right, Wistart."

"And report back—the first minute you hear!"

Giddings was somewhat startled by the vehemence of the command.

If the boss was so jumpy, there might be something to worry about after all . . .

The report came back quickly. A national advertising agency which represented the *Clarion* telegraphed:

Eddie and Tony Ender formerly here in Chicago. Grew up in big circulation—advertising rat race during period of hottest newspaper fight between Hearst, News, and Trib. Reported sharpshooters. Tony circulation specialist, Eddie advertising shark. Hear they have cornered available comic, feature releases in Jericho. Any truth?

Wistart glanced up from the message. "What about the features?"

Giddings laughed comfortably. "Haven't touched us. We've got everything we've always had. They may have taken what we didn't want."

"Are you sure we've got the best?"

"All I can say is they're the ones we've used for years—Dr. Hazlett, the Lonely Hearts, Quilt Patterns, Crossword Puzzle, and all the others. And the comics have been adequate in the past——"

"The *past?*" Somehow the word struck fear in Wistart. "What about the present?"

"I never read comics myself," said Giddings easily, "but I haven't heard any complaints about ours."

"What complaints would there be when we're the only paper? Check and see if they *have* cornered the features."

A day passed, and again Giddings was in Wistart's office with word from the big feature syndicates. The word sounded ominous. Yes, the Sentinel Publishing Company had contracted for what seemed an endless number of syndicated features, including all the comics of the newer vintage, various special departments, and every available column of opinion.

"What'll they do with them all?" Giddings asked. "They won't have the space to publish them."

"I'll tell you what they'll do," said Wistart with sudden prescience. "They'll pay for them and use only what they want—and keep us from using the rest."

"That costs money——"

"And they've got money. They want to kill us, and they'll run at a loss for years if they can choke us out. Know who's behind them? One of the biggest newspaper chains. And who they're tied up with locally? Tom Pollock's their attorney."

Giddings gave a scornful sniff. Tom Pollock—Judge Thomas Jefferson Pollock—was a Democratic politician reputed to control the vote in the city's poorer districts, commonly called Jugtown. The *Clarion* often had peeled him rather unmercifully, and he was reputed to be the newspaper's bitterest enemy.

"If that's the kind of disreputable element they want," Giddings said, "they'll not last long in Jericho."

Wistart stared at him. So steeped in his own inertia was old John Giddings that his mind could not grasp this new peril. Clearly there was no help here. Wistart let him go back to his desk. All at once he knew that he himself, and he alone, must grapple with this problem, without any aid, counsel, or encouragement from anyone.

He was beginning now to see the full picture: he, and Giddings, and the entire *Clarion* force, had been caught asleep, drowsing when they should have been alert, in a smug belief of security, so that they were perhaps already overwhelmed without even knowing it.

The very next day, on every billboard that could be rented in the city and around it, a blatant, shrieking announcement appeared:

Dedicated to the Greatness of Jericho
THE MORNING SENTINEL
New—alert—progressive—friendly.
A stride forward in progress.
Watch for it!
First in news, first in features, first
in sports, first in comics, first in
ideas, first in service to the community.
Three Wire Services.

Jericho people discussed the announcement eagerly, and there seemed to be a general feeling that a second paper would be good for the city. There even appeared to be a little current of rejoicing over a setback to the *Clarion,* which long had dominated opinion, politically and otherwise, to the resentment of some dissenters.

To Wistart it was like defeat already sustained. He cabled Mary Agnes in Honolulu, but she had only just arrived there, and he received an indifferent reply that she would not be back for at least

two months. It was obvious that she was utterly unconcerned over
his dilemma.

There was nobody with whom he could even share his great worry,
and he was bewildered and terrified. In desperation he flew to Chicago
to discuss matters with his advertising representatives there, only to
receive from them the coldest of discouraging information.

Yet there, in the very midst of his black slough of despond, something happened to him that changed his life . . . the only good thing
that ever had happened to him, he sometimes thought . . . something
that enabled him somehow to keep up a fight he thought was lost for
three long years—until now, when he was facing the gravest crisis
of all, the crisis that caused him to telephone Mary Agnes in Los
Angeles.

Mary Agnes . . . he fell to wondering what, after all, had induced
his wife to change her plans and come home immediately when she
told him she would not. Certainly she seemed far from interested either
in him or his problems when he met her plane the night before.

"I'm too tired to talk," she said to him in the car, throwing back
her head against the seat with closed eyes. "Please, Wistart, I can't
stand being bored just at this minute."

That was the end of their conversation. They rode home in silence,
and parted in silence to go to their respective rooms. She seemed aloof,
not at all inquisitive, and quite uncompassionate.

3

Presently Wistart ceased his pacing and went out into the reception
room. Miss Finch glanced up to see if he wished her to come with her
pad and pencil, but he did not speak or even look at her, so she returned to her typewriting. Without any particular plan or reason he
passed out and down the hall toward the city room of his newspaper.

At his appearance in that busy place Hudson, the managing editor,
came to his feet with surprising celerity, an expression of anxiety in
his eyes. The boss did not make a practice of visiting his subordinates:
he sent for them. Hudson reasoned that it must be something serious
that brought Mr. Wedge in person to the city room. Moreover, he
thought with a thrill of fear that he knew what it was.

Only a few minutes before he had finished a telephonic conversation
with Mrs. Wedge at her home, and he was still tingling from it. Mrs.

Wedge could be extremely prickly when she was annoyed; and obviously she was annoyed by his call. He wondered why.

His proposal to her, that he send a special reporter and photographer to interview her and make a truly memorable story of her recent travels, with an assurance that he would give it his personal oversight to make sure they handled it as she would like to have it written— which in his mind meant with all possible superlatives and encomiums —should have been flattering to her. In his entire newspaper experience Samson J. Hudson had hardly known anyone who was not flattered by being mentioned prominently and admiringly in a newspaper, and who did not feel correspondingly friendly and grateful toward the man who made such mention possible.

But Mrs. Wedge had said no, that she did not think much should be made of it. And when he rather insisted, on the surmise that she was playing coy and wanted to be wheedled, she became at first stiff, and then cold, and finally biting. She left him with a flea in his ear that still was burrowing painfully in that tender organ, and he was very fearful that he had made a serious mistake in going so strongly into the matter.

Moreover, he was angry. At whom? Debs Dorn, perhaps. Yes, Debs should have warned him. What was the fellow there for if not to help a worried managing editor in such matters? Undoubtedly Debs was smirking to himself secretly now, since he had allowed his superior to blunder into so unhappy an impasse. It was treachery, really! Mr. Debs Dorn would have occasion to regret it . . .

But at this moment Wistart Wedge walked into the room. Instantly all rage, all thought of Debs Dorn, fled from Samson J. Hudson's mind. Inwardly he shook. Without doubt Mrs. Wedge, angered by his well-intentioned but evidently ill-timed efforts to convince her that she should be photographed and featured on page one, had telephoned her husband expressing her displeasure. Now her husband had come to take Hudson to task. The managing editor gulped at the thought of his own evil fortune and groped in his mind for some excuse with which to appease his employer's wrath.

At first Wistart did not speak. Wordlessly Hudson stood gazing at him, trying to read his expression. Then Wistart made a scraping sound in his throat, shifted his feet, his lips almost twitched, and with a sudden sensation of acute embarrassment his eyes fell.

Mary Agnes had not, as Hudson feared, telephoned him. As a matter of fact, now that he had wandered into the city room, Wistart did not know what to say to this man, his subordinate, to explain why he was here.

After a tense moment Hudson relaxed slightly. He was accustomed to interpreting the looks of others, particularly those above him in station. And he knew certain symptoms, or thought he did. Sometimes after drinking a little too much—discreetly, of course, and secretly— he felt the inevitable aftereffect next morning. He believed now that he recognized an unsteadiness of hand, a dullness of eye in his employer.

Relief swept over him. Far from feeling alarm now, he almost had to repress a chuckle. The boss himself? Well, why not? After what had just happened over the telephone, Hudson could imagine that things did not run exactly smoothly in the Wedge home. That woman —she had a nasty temper and a nasty tongue. Who was to blame her husband if he overindulged a little? It was only human.

Hudson liked to think that other people were "human," because to him the word signified that they were weak, and he felt he knew better how to deal with the weak than with the strong. All at once he saw a chance to repair the damage of his unfortunate conversation with Mrs. Wedge. He could at least win her husband's gratitude.

His manner underwent a change. "Excuse me, boss," he said in a tone of respectful understanding. "You don't look as if you feel quite like yourself this morning."

"I didn't sleep well, to tell the truth," Wistart mumbled, glad to cover his slight embarrassment.

"Just as a suggestion," said Hudson confidentially, "you'd feel better if you took a little nip." Rather furtively he glanced around. "It just happens I have a bottle of pretty good scotch in my desk. Don't have any use for it myself, of course, but somebody gave it to me yesterday, and it's still there, unopened. If you like, I'll slip over to your office with it after a while. Quietly."

Wistart nodded vaguely. Perhaps a drink would be of some help. He turned and went out.

Five minutes later, with the air of a conspirator, Hudson entered his office and from the side pocket of his coat took a square bottle. The conspiratorial manner was hardly necessary, for the purchase of liquor, after decades of state prohibition, had become legal in Kansas, but Hudson wished his employer to see and appreciate his discretion in making sure nobody suspected he was having a drink in his office. To Wistart the man's manner was rather annoying. Nevertheless, he permitted Hudson to pour him a stiffish drink, adding water from the carafe on the desk.

"Have one yourself, Hudson?" he asked.

"Oh, no indeed, sir," the other said virtuously. "I hardly ever drink —never on duty."

"Well, then, thank you," said Wistart. He drank. Curious how the alcohol, to which he was unaccustomed so early in the day, warmed him and took some of the edge from his trouble.

"Anything else I can do for you, sir?" asked Hudson.

"No, thanks."

"I'll just leave this bottle——"

"No, take it along with you."

"But you might——"

"Thank you, but no!" Wistart spoke rather more firmly than he intended.

Quickly Hudson pocketed the bottle and left. When he returned to the city room, the staff took note of his face. Its look said, as plainly as if the words were spoken aloud: Big Deal.

Five

I

Richest in Peace, Safest in War, the chapbook of Jericho, quite ecstatically described in many illustrated pages its sources of wealth, such as wheat, hogs, and oil; its industries, including the airplane factories, the flour mills, the evil-smelling oil refineries, and the still worse-smelling packing houses; and the larger commercial and financial enterprises, prominent among which were such principalities of power as the First National Bank, and Cox's, Incorporated.

The latter, Jericho's biggest department store, was an institution which dated from the days when the city was no more than a land shark's townsite boom on the vacant prairie. It had survived drouths, blizzards, a county seat war, a major tornado, and several business depressions, local or national, to become an ornament and bulwark of the new progress and prosperity. But though old in history—it dated from 1889, and sixty-six years was *very* ancient for Jericho—there was nothing antiquated about Cox's present establishment. Only four years before the big, modernistic structure that housed it was built, covering half of a city block, of steel and concrete faced with cut stone and mosaic tile, speaking of "levels" rather than "floors," its *décor* and appointments elaborately tasteful.

You could buy almost anything at Cox's; it was the first store in town to install escalators in addition to elevators; and its tearoom on the upper level was the smartest in Jericho, offering, in addition to its menu, living models who displayed the latest creations from Cox's various apparel departments in stately parades about among the tables.

It was not to be expected, of course, that *Richest in Peace, Safest in War* should describe or even list minor businesses, such as the struggling little shops which huddled about Cox's, as if hoping rather pathetically for a few crumbs of trade from the overflowing commercial table of that giant mecca of money-spending women shoppers.

When, shortly before noon, Wistart Wedge left the Clarion Building, he hesitated before going for his car. Almost nobody was on the street because of the cold. For the moment he decided against the car and instead walked a block to the intersection where the First National's austere brick and Cox's chaste tile-and-dressed-stone confronted each other across Main Street. Near the corner, diagonally across from the bank and directly facing the department store, was a small shop which—of all things in this weather—had a display of beachwear in its windows.

Wistart considered this display for a moment: two wax models on a simulated seashore with driftwood and sand, the one in a sun costume of shorts and jacket of bright print, the other in a most frankly revealing swimsuit and wide hat of palm straw. Inasmuch as most women's apparel shops in Jericho were still displaying fur coats, it seemed to the male eye an incongruity. But there was no lack of planning in it. This shop catered not to the ordinary Jericho housewife, but to those fortunate creatures who could afford to go to Palm

Beach, or Bermuda, or Laguna for the winter and required garments suitable for such hegiras.

Above the door, in slender gilt type, ran a legend:

GREY RUTLEDGE, SPORTSWEAR

As if arriving at a decision, Wistart entered. The little shop was smartly appointed, as any woman would instantly have seen: although a man might not be expected fully to appreciate the kind of taste displayed in it. Wistart had only a rather vague impression of showcases filled with various feminine articles of wear, racks with coats and sports dresses, and a counter covered with purses, jewelry, scarfs, and the fantastic belts women affect. In the place were no customers because of the weather, but at the rear of the store, talking together, two women stood.

One of these Wistart dismissed with barely a glance. She was Mrs. Hettie Hedcomb, a saleswoman, middle-aged, bosomy, with glasses secured from falling off her sharp nose by a cord running from the ends of the bows around the nape of her lean neck, and thin ankles which had the appearance of forming capital L's with her long, flat-heeled shoes.

The other, however, was far more worthy of appraisal. She was not old, yet not quite young—in her late twenties, you would venture—with something about her suggesting the tempering of experience which deepens girlhood into womanhood. Severely simple and hardly ornamented, save for white collar and cuffs, her black wool dress gave an effect almost nunlike: except that no nun ever donned a garment which so clung to the lines of her body, fitting and flattering curves so symmetrical; nor did any nun ever reveal legs so graceful or feet so small and prettily arched in high-heeled slippers. The black dress dramatized the blondeness of her head, and you knew it was a natural blonde, and also that the way she carried her head was in itself something to admire.

She was Grey Rutledge, the proprietress of this shop.

Over her eyes, quickly masked, passed a fleeting shadow of surprise or some other emotion when she saw Wistart enter. Everyone, of course, knew the publisher of the *Clarion,* if only by sight, and she had known him more than well for a number of years; but this was almost the first time he had ever entered her place. After just the slightest hesitation she spoke to Mrs. Hedcomb and herself went forward to greet him.

"Good morning, Mr. Wedge," she said, formally cordial. "What a surprise, having you come in on a cold day like this!"

In her eyes was a question. And he was conscious, as he always was, of her eyes, her magnificent eyes. He remembered the first time he saw her, years before, when she was working in Jed Rutledge's real estate office. He thought her very young and lovely then, and asked her name.

"Grey," she said simply.

"But I mean your first name."

She smiled. "Grey *is* my first name."

Odd name for a girl—family name, he learned later. But some women have the power of making the most unlikely names triumphantly and gracefully their own just by being the kind of persons who enhance everything that touches them. Grey, for example—how perfectly it suited her. It would be hard to imagine her with any other name. Grey Norcross it was then—Grey Rutledge now. No matter what her last name, there were those eyes of hers—wide, clean, beautifully gray, with wonderful curved black lashes. They glorified her face and invariably disturbed his tranquillity.

"Can I help you?" she was asking him.

It brought him out of his abstraction, and at the question he gave her a sudden, unexpected look, as if she had surprised something in him. For a moment there seemed to be in his face a cold shadow, suggesting dreariness and an eloquent silent appeal. Then his eyes fell, and the expression fled as swiftly as a hallucination.

But she had seen it and felt there was a great trouble in him, exactly what she did not know. A rush of pity went over her, and an indefinable kindness, and a wish to help him, for this man was secretly dear to her.

She gave him a smile. Her face was clear and good to look at, with a trim little nose, arching brows, and lips delicately modeled. Sometimes in repose the face appeared a little tired. But with the smile the tired expression fled, and her face was bright, the magnificent gray eyes giving it a touch of real beauty.

He realized she was waiting for his answer. "I'm looking for something—I hardly know what—Mrs. Wedge came home last night. I want a little gift for her." He looked up, half abashed. "I didn't want to go to Cox's. Her own store, you know."

"Of course," she said. "I understand what you mean. Buying something for her which she already owns, you might say. Did you think of something to wear, or perhaps jewelry?"

Jewelry. The word drew his eyes to her again. Her hair, gleaming honey gold, was thick and wavy, and she wore it swept back, her ears fully revealed. Only a woman with beautiful ears would dare wear her hair that way, and Grey Rutledge's ears were small and perfect, and set off by earrings with large pearls.

People took it for granted that the pearls were artificial, because real pearls that size cost a small fortune. But people did not know. The pearls *were* real and they *had* cost a small fortune. They were a gift, with a special meaning, and Grey wore them often because she loved them, and because she knew nobody suspected their real value, and because it gave her a little sensation of amused daring to flaunt them, as it were, before the eyes of the gossips—such as her own saleslady, Hettie Hedcomb, for example—who would have made the most of scandalous speculation out of them had they known.

"What can you show me?" Wistart said, answering her question.

He spent a little time selecting his purchase, almost as if he were unwilling to leave. Once Grey asked, "How is Mrs. Wedge?"

"Fine. A little tired from her trip."

"Isn't she home earlier than you expected?"

Once more she caught that momentary fleeting look of dreariness in his face. He glanced toward the rear of the store. Mrs. Hedcomb was arranging some dresses on a rack.

"Grey," he said in a desperate low voice, "if you only—just once——"

"You promised," she said.

"I know—but things are so bad—I hoped——"

He broke off. Mrs. Hedcomb was coming slowly toward the front of the store.

For a barely perceptible instant Grey bit her lip, her eyes shadowed by some inward thought. Then her face cleared.

As if to cover the slight pause in their conversation, she said, "If you'd come in a little later in the month, Mr. Wedge, we'd have a much better selection for you. Our stock's low just now because of the Christmas trade. But I'm going to Chicago on a buying trip and I hope when I return we'll have a much better offering."

He looked at her. "Oh? When?"

"Why—tonight, I think. As a matter of fact, I was just going to wire the Sherman Hotel for a reservation."

For a moment he seemed to consider that unimportant bit of information. Then he purchased an expensive little handbag on her suggestion that no woman can ever have too many nice bags, and waited for it to be gift-wrapped.

When he paid for it, he said, "Thank you," as if Grey had done him a very great favor.

She watched him go out. A woman customer entered the store and Grey left her to Hettie Hedcomb while she walked back to her small office and seated herself at the desk.

For a time she sat quite still, thinking. When Wistart first came into the shop, she had felt something very like a thrill of apprehension. It was not like him. They were lovers, it was true . . . a strange, unwilling fidelity in which she had lived for three years now . . . but it was not wise for him to come to her here. He had never done so before and she wondered what extraordinary thing moved him to do so now. Certainly he could have purchased the handbag in any of a dozen places.

But she knew him so well, and in that look of misery she sensed some cruel trouble in him. Three months before they had agreed solemnly that they would never meet again. She told him she could no longer go on with it, because of the fear, and the guilt, and her little daughter. And he agreed with her that she was perfectly right, it was selfish of him, and he loved her too much even to wish her to continue if it made her unhappy. They understood each other and the need for breaking off very well then, and they parted rather sadly, although it was with a sensation of relief, truly, on her part; and Wistart's kindness, which she knew so well, had never seemed finer to her than it did then.

Yet with that decision firmly made, she had in the moment that she bit her lip reversed everything. She felt that he was suffering, and something . . . duty, perhaps, or a pitying love . . . made her change all her plans. For this one time. Just once, and this the last.

Already now she regretted that she had given him that information of her buying trip, which meant far more than that. She wished she could recall him and tell him it was a mistake, she had not meant that at all. And then she remembered his voice when he thanked her: for something infinitely greater than the gift wrapping of the package she placed in his hands. She could not be so cruel. Hate it, hate it, hate it, she would go through with it this one more time, for his sake.

2

Driving his car up Tower Hill, Wistart was still thinking of Grey. She was the finest thing his life had ever known, the only love he ever had experienced, the only understanding, the only entirely unselfish friendship, and he had told her so many times. Losing her, when she told him it was over, had been to lose the only true happiness in his life. It was the more wonderful, therefore, that she had relented to him. He wanted her, her kindness, her sympathy, her sweet self, and he was almost happy when he thought of her.

But the warmth left him when he turned his car into the circular drive before his white-pillared colonial home: it was replaced by cold like a stone.

Cold . . . the thought focused itself in dull resentment, directed at no one in particular, but rather at the bitter day. Why did Jericho have to present itself in an aspect so hostile just when Mary Agnes came home? The weather had been deceptively pleasant, for a Kansas winter, then turned treacherously frigid overnight, and today, though it was noon, the thermometer was still down near zero, with a cutting wind and a flurry of snow. He knew Mary Agnes would hold him responsible, not actually for the weather itself, but for bringing her back from California just at this time.

Unfortunate, most unfortunate. She was difficult enough ordinarily, and he had hoped after three months' vacation she would be in a humor comparatively good. He looked for no love or even friendship from Mary Agnes. But he had a business problem to discuss with her, a problem of gravest importance, and she held the key to it.

He left the car in the driveway and went up the steps of the veranda. Beside the front door hung a thermometer, which he consulted before entering. Suey, the butler, came into the hall to help him out of his coat and take his hat. Suey was tall and thin, with a kindly wrinkled black face and the courtly manners of a veteran of the Pullman service.

"Is—ah—is Mrs. Wedge down yet?" asked Wistart.

"No, suh," said Suey. "But I understan' she has arisen. She ordered her lunch served in the library."

In Wistart's hands was the package from Grey Rutledge's, but he hesitated a moment. "Cold today, Suey."

"Yes, suh." Ordinarily Suey would have grinned and made some sally about the weather. But today he did not relax. From this Wistart argued that matters were not progressing smoothly in the household. Perhaps Mary Agnes was in one of her tempers.

He cleared his throat. "Six above zero by the thermometer outside." "Yes, suh."

No point in pursuing this. Wistart went from the hall into the living room, rich with its subdued beauty of costly furniture, hangings, and objects of art. He did not pause there. Instead, he crossed the thickly carpeted floor toward the far end, where the library opened. Before him, rather in the manner of a votive offering being borne to appease an angry goddess, he held his package with its smart gold and brown wrappings and fluffy gold ribbons.

A fire was burning in the grate of the library, and the room looked cozy and pleasant with its ceiling-high bookshelves.

His wife, however, was not there.

Wistart glanced about in a manner somewhat indecisive and laid his package on a coffee table. Then he went and stood before the fire, holding out his hands to the warmth of the crackling blaze.

3

In her bedroom Mary Agnes was just preparing to go downstairs for luncheon. Although it was noon, she actually had risen earlier this day than she intended, because of a stupid telephone call from that man at the *Clarion*. For that reason, and others, her temper was not at its sunniest, and she had yelled at the maid and had difficulty with her hair when she combed it.

After those two successive long nights on planes she was sleeping in utter weariness when, shortly before ten o'clock, her bedroom telephone tinkled and awoke her. It was someone from the *Clarion*— Hudson, or Judson, or some such name—and it appeared that he wanted some sort of an elaborate article about her Honolulu trip, with a picture of her taken by a news cameraman.

She did not like news photographers. Invariably, she thought, they made her look hatchet-faced. Furthermore, she did not consider a routine pleasure trip worth being blazoned in the paper as if she had discovered a new continent. After all, she had been to Honolulu several times previously, and she felt it would make her appear slightly ridiculous since everyone knew her husband owned the *Clarion*—as if she had insisted, out of vanity, that the story be printed in this overstressed form.

Mary Agnes had her vanities, and it was one of them that she considered herself above petty vanities of this kind.

So she did not take kindly to the suggestion. "A short paragraph in the society columns will be sufficient," she told the man.

But he persisted. Mary Agnes was inclined to be impatient with insistence. Before she could get rid of Judson—or was it Hudson?—she had been forced to speak quite plainly and sharply to him. Nobody knew better than she how to be cutting when it was warranted. Probably she had wounded the feelings of the man Hudson—if that was his damned name—when at last she lost patience with him. He apologized hastily and got off the phone. Then, a while later, some young woman named Miss Sayre called back rather diffidently, and received from Mrs. Wedge the barest kind of an announcement, with instructions to place it inconspicuously on the society page.

The episode ruffled Mary Agnes, not only because it shortened her sleep, but because it offended her sense of good taste. Some women in Jericho might think it an achievement to have their names and doings in the *Clarion,* but she hardly considered herself in their category. After all, she spent more time away from Jericho than in it, and when one has been mentioned in the columns of great journals in New York, Los Angeles, London, even Paris, and has had her picture more than once in magazines like *Vogue* and *Life,* to be mentioned in a small hinterland newspaper is rather trivial.

By the time she settled the question of the article in the *Clarion* she was so thoroughly awake that she buzzed for the maid, ordered breakfast, scolded when the pillows were not fixed to suit her while she ate in bed, and called for the mail to be brought up.

The maid brought the letters and informed her that Mr. Wedge had gone to the office. There were no communications of importance, she saw as she shuffled the envelopes. Nothing personal, at least. How could there be? She was not expected home for at least another month.

It was after eleven when she rose, had her bath, and dressed. And all the time her mind was vexed by her paramount concern. She decided she would get hold of Mrs. Butford as soon as possible and find out just what was the status of Erskine de Lacey. Later she would have a talk with Erskine himself. She wanted to know the whereabouts of that painting, although she really did not anticipate too much trouble over it. Erskine still needed money, she was sure. A short private interview, an offer of a good check, and she supposed he would not find it difficult to part with the picture, especially since it was admittedly unfinished.

Six

I

It was at this moment, when the lady's spirits were at a stage of unhappy depression, that she descended the stairs and found her husband in the library, his backside to the grate, his expression as he glanced up at her half questioning, half defensive.

"Hello," he said.

"Back already?" She was indifferent.

"I came home early."

"Have you had your lunch?"

"No, I thought I'd take a bite with you." He gave a feeble grin.

Without speaking or changing her expression Mary Agnes reached for a pull cord by the wall. Then she seated herself near the oriel window, her elbows on the arms of her chair, her chin leaning on both hands, gazing out at the bleak day with a look of loveless displeasure. In the room silence reigned, broken only by an occasional crackle from the fireplace.

After a time Wistart said, "Honey—I brought you something."

He offered the votive gift in its brown and gold wrappings.

The goddess accepted it without any enthusiasm and laid it once more on the coffee table without opening it or giving it more than a glance.

A colored girl in white apron and cap appeared at the doorway.

"You rang, ma'am?" she asked.

"Yes, Clara," said Mary Agnes. "You may serve luncheon here for both Mr. Wedge and myself."

"Yes'm," said Clara.

She disappeared rather like a rabbit bolting into its hole. The servants, when their mistress was in one of her moods, spent as little time as possible in her presence.

Wistart gazed at his wife somewhat aghast. "Aren't you going to open your package?" he asked.

Mary Agnes viewed the brown and gold parcel as if with disfavor. Then she said, "From Grey Rutledge's?"

He nodded. "I thought buying for you at Cox's was a little like carrying coals to Newcastle."

The poor fellow was full of such clichés, but it was not worth Mary Agnes' effort just at this moment to wither him.

"I thought I recognized the wrapping," she said.

She spent some time opening the package, working at the ribbons as women do, pulling them around the corners rathers than breaking them, as if the ribbons were perhaps more precious than the contents they held. At last the wrappings were off, and the smart little handbag revealed in its nest of soft white tissue, to be lifted and inspected.

"Grey Rutledge always has good taste," Mary Agnes said listlessly.

Wistart took this as a form of thanks; and was grateful.

Clara, the maid, entered with a silver tray, on which were sandwiches, fruit, and a silver coffeepot with cups, which she set on the low table. Mary Agnes poured coffee, and for a time she and Wistart sat silent, consuming their sandwiches and sipping the hot liquid.

Presently she put down her coffee cup and returned her gaze drearily to the out-of-doors.

Feeling that her expression of bored disfavor was an arraignment of him, Wistart did not break her silence. He heard the grandfather clock in the living room chime. Half after twelve. For lack of anything better to do, he consulted his wrist watch. He had set it by the electric clock at the office, and he found that the grandfather clock was exactly on time. Good old clock. Dependable. One of the few things he could depend on these days.

Still Mary Agnes said nothing. Whatever small appetite he had departed. He put what was left of his sandwich on the small plate and sipped his coffee. Then he stopped even sipping his coffee.

2

Again silence lengthened and grew. The library was cheerful and warm, with the books and the fire, but to Wistart the atmosphere seemed chilling. This once had been his mother's study, in the days when she ruled the destinies of the *Clarion;* and all of Jericho, for that matter. After her death, when he and his wife took over the house, Mary Agnes had changed this one room very little. The mellow shelves of books from floor to ceiling, the furniture, even the table which his mother had used as a work desk, were full of memories to him, like shadows of former days.

His entire remembrance of his mother was that of a being superior to all others in her wisdom and justness. It was a picture perhaps slightly warped, since there can be no question that Mrs. Algeria Wedge, in her lifetime, had her human failings and weaknesses. Nevertheless, to her son, brought up under her dominion, which was fond but nonetheless complete, she represented Infallibility. Though at times it was irksome, he gave up rebellion quite early in life and accepted Infallibility as an unconscious source of security.

Not until it was gone did Wistart know how much he depended on his mother's strength. With a habit of self-deprecation which somehow had become a part of his nature, he compared himself to his mother, and the comparison was discouraging. To a man with pride it might have been humiliating, but Wistart did not have pride so much as resignation.

The realization did come when suddenly one day she was dead and he found himself with the protecting Infallibility shorn away from him. At that time he and Mary Agnes had been married three years, and from almost the very first day they had known how little suited they were for each other.

Mary Agnes was clever, polished, sophisticated, and lean. She made no secret of her derision at his plumpness and slow awkwardness, and he came to accept her scornful little cruelties as a matter of course; even when their acquaintances sometimes noticed and were amused by them. It was generally supposed by people that Wistart was too obtuse to understand, really, his wife's continual malice. But he did understand well enough; he could feel pain and resentment too, although he took refuge in his reputation for stolidity and showed nothing of it in his face or manner.

He was sure his wife hated him. Sometimes he hated Mary Agnes, hated her bitter tongue, her eyes which seemed to probe his most secret thoughts, her leanness and hardness, her arrogance; and there were times when he dreamed secretly of freedom from her and wished she would walk out on him, leave him alone. But thus far, though they had been married ten years, neither of them had made a move toward separation, at least legally and openly, because they both had need to subscribe to the mores of Jericho in order to make up for their own shortcomings and previous violations of Jericho social codes.

In the final analysis, Wistart's feeling toward Mary Agnes was more fear than hatred. At this present moment he was in an agony, combined of terror and practical certainty of failure in what he hoped for from her. He had to ask a favor of Mary Agnes: something so important that his whole life seemed to hang on it. And he could not remember ever having asked of her anything, however trivial, which she had granted easily, if at all. He wondered how, this morning, he could possibly bring the matter up, particularly since, very obviously, her humor was bad.

3

It was Mary Agnes who broke the unhappy silence. In spite of her detachment, irritation with him was not her sole preoccupation. She had other problems more pressing to her. Nevertheless, he was there, and he had managed to arouse in her a slight curiosity, although perhaps not a sympathetic curiosity. Her way of opening the discussion was characteristic.

"Well, Wistart, let's have it," she said suddenly.

He almost started. "Have—what?" he said somewhat stupidly, for now that the issue was to be brought in the open he felt a sudden intensification of his fears.

"You had some reason, I suppose, for calling me back in this atrocious weather—or didn't you?" She spoke acidly, ignoring the fact that she had her own reasons for coming.

"Well—yes. Yes, I did, honey——"

"I've told you I hate being called 'honey'!"

He drew a deep breath. "I'm sorry. I'll try not to do it any more. But about—wanting to see you—I did—I do have a reason."

"No, really?" she drawled with sarcasm.

He seemed to gather himself. "I'll give it to you straight. I'm going to have to sell the *Clarion*."

She sat up at that. "Sell it? Why?"

"The *Sentinel* people have made me an offer——"

"The Ender brothers? Those horrible little vulgarians? Why, this is insolent!"

"Not as insolent as you think," he said unhappily.

"Wistart, stop talking in riddles!"

"Well—to tell the truth—the sale is being forced on me."

By now all her lassitude was gone. Her gaze on him was concentrated, a little frown line between her eyes. More by reputation than otherwise she knew Eddie and Tony Ender. She had met them a few times—at the sort of civic affairs, Chamber of Commerce dinners and the like, with which she was occasionally bored.

Round-bellied little men, she thought of them. Eddie, the elder, was dark, a few hairs plastered tight across his bald spot, continually smiling a detestable loose-lipped grin, and with a handshake limp as a dead fish. Tony was red, with fox-colored hair and foxlike cunning, which he masked, however, behind a bulbous nose and an expression of unspeakable stupidity. Horrible little vulgarians she had called them, and it seemed to fit them better than well.

She gave a shudder of distaste—the Enders were the essence of what her nature abhorred, bold in an oily smirking manner, badly gotten up in clothes too flashy, perspiring slightly and smelling too strongly of cologne, none too sure of their grammar or syntax even in the few brief words she exchanged with them out of politeness. The very idea of calling them newspapermen was funny in a disagreeable way— they were gangsters, perhaps, but certainly without any single quality of the intellect, the grasp of affairs, and the ability to present those affairs to the reading public. They represented the new trend in journalism gone to its farthest extreme, prostitution of everything that gives it dignity and respect, for grimy, greasy dollars.

Mary Agnes had snubbed the Ender brothers properly, and she did not think they had much love for her. The mere thought that they might presume to meddle in affairs connected however remotely with herself was an affront of a personal nature.

"How can they *force* a sale on you?" she demanded.

He undertook to explain. "The *Clarion* was only about breaking even three years ago when the *Sentinel* was established——"

"It was a gold mine when your mother had it."

"I know it. But—well, I'm not my mother. Anyway, we've been losing ground ever since the other paper started. When a newspaper begins to lose money, it loses it faster than any other kind of business."

His voice had taken on a pleading, self-defensive sound. She glanced at him with contempt. What a bungler!

"I don't believe those Enders have the kind of money to buy the *Clarion*," she said.

"Maybe not. But they can get it. And—well, the paper's in a vulnerable position just now——"

"For what reason?" she pursued mercilessly.

His eyes fell. "We've had to borrow—to correct antiquated methods and equipment—and—well—just to keep going. I think we've done it —the corrections, I mean. New presses and linotype machines, and some better talent in both the editorial and business departments. But it's cost money—a lot of money. And we aren't making money. I've kept hoping we'd pull out of it, but the truth is we've only fallen behind. It's hard—very hard—to get a newspaper started up the hill again once it sags. And—well, to cut it short, the *Clarion* as of today is practically in the hands of the bankers."

Now it was her turn to draw a deep breath—a gasp, rather. She had not imagined such straits. Often in the past she had tossed off satirically the phrase "married to a newspaper" as a joke. And she had never taken Wistart seriously, always speaking of him and his paper in the half-humoring way that a busy elder uses in referring to a child and its footling little toy. But all the time she had taken for granted the *Clarion's* permanence. It was, she suddenly realized, one of the solid bulwarks of her existence, of which, until now, she had hardly been conscious. With this thought, she was for the first time alarmed.

"The worst of it," went on Wistart tonelessly, "is that we're badly
in arrears to the paper mills——"

"How much?"

"About a hundred thousand dollars."

"And other debts?"

"To the banks and other creditors, about four hundred thousand."

She was startled. "Half a million! But the *Clarion* is worth more
than a million, isn't it?"

"I—well—yes, I suppose you could say so—counting intangibles like
good will and its subscription lists and the fact that it's a going concern, and so on. But the actual physical assets are nowhere near that."

"The paper mills are pressing you?"

He nodded ruefully. "The banks refuse any more credit. And now
we've been notified that unless we do something about the paper debts
the mills will cut off our newsprint. That means suspending publication."

"The *Sentinel* knows about this?"

"Yes, that sort of thing gets around in the publishing world. And
some smart people are working with the Enders. Tom Pollock, their
attorney, for one, is no fool——"

"I should say not! And he's got plenty of reason to hate you, hasn't
he? The kind of things the *Clarion* has said about him."

"You can't run a newspaper without making enemies," Wistart said.
"You simply can't avoid stepping on somebody's toes sooner or later.
Pollock's always been in the wrong political camp——"

"So you've cast your bread upon the waters—of the wrong kind.
And now it comes back to you?" For a moment she mused. "Tom
Pollock can get even for those years the *Clarion* has maligned him—
he can stick in the knife and turn it in the wound——" She seemed to
derive a gloating zest out of the contemplation of this fascinating
cruelty behind the dull, routine façade of business.

He nodded. "I guess that about says it. If our newsprint is cut off,
the *Clarion* must take bankruptcy or accept the offer——"

"What's the offer?"

"Not very much. Not near what the *Clarion's* worth. They've got us
over the barrel, and they're not interested in paying for good will or
other intangibles. They'll get us from the receiver in bankruptcy if
they don't get us outright. What they're offering is to take over the

debts, and pay us a little more—fifty or sixty thousand, maybe. I don't know exactly how much until the audit is made."

"And that's *all?*"

"Either that, or lose everything."

"The end of the Wedge dynasty. Rather sad, isn't it?" Her voice was half dreamy, as if she were watching, without participating in it, the acting out of a stage tragedy.

He nodded with a gulp.

"And you'll be—a nobody."

"I suppose you could say that," he agreed drearily.

"And rather indigent besides, won't you, by the time you've settled your personal liabilities besides those of the paper?"

It did not occur to him to suggest that his wife was wealthy and that she might share her wealth with him.

"Broke," was all he said.

"A nonentity where you've always been such a big shot. And the *Clarion* will be in the hands of those awful bastards, the Enders, and Tom Pollock."

Whether or not Tom Pollock would twist the knife in the wound, given opportunity, Mary Agnes knew how to do it with exquisite torture, and her husband winced.

4

But she was thinking. It had not escaped her that Wistart was by no means the only one affected if the *Sentinel* crowd got control of the *Clarion*. In her mind, which was acute enough, this realization suddenly deranged all perspectives, altered the proportions of all things.

The fat, oily, cologne-scented Ender brothers! Once they owned both newspapers they would be unassailably the lords of Jericho. She pictured Cox's, Incorporated, independent, serene, dominant—and her own—suddenly finding itself without that serenity and independence, forced to pay a different kind of tribute and show a new kind of loyalty if it wished to prosper. And another consideration, purely feminine, entered. The Enders had wives—overdressed, overjeweled, and overfurred. In bad taste as they were, it was not too much to imagine that they would have social pretensions. Even Mrs. Wistart Wedge might find herself forced to accept the pushing, ill-bred creatures. The thought was an affront to everything in her fastidious nature.

Being "married to a newspaper," in spite of her derision, suddenly meant something. Prestige, for one thing. And power. And protection . . . from certain contingencies, like a painting for which she had posed on an irresponsible night and which seemed to haunt her.

Mrs. Wistart Wedge, with the *Clarion* at her beck, carried heavy guns, very heavy guns, socially and otherwise. What armament would Mrs. Wistart Wedge have without the poor old *Clarion?*

The thought stung her into rising.

"What do you intend to do?" she asked.

"What can I do?" he said. "They've got me in the wringer——"

"Surely you can do something! Not just sit there like a lump on a log and let them run over you without lifting a finger!"

Her metaphors were somewhat mixed but her meaning was clear and so was her indignation.

"Everything's been done," he said meekly. "I've tried every line—except——"

"Except what?"

"Except—you. You're the only hope I've got left, Mary Agnes. Honey—oh, excuse me! I mean—if you could just arrange to lend me the hundred thousand dollars for the paper companies——"

"*I* lend you a hundred thousand? To throw it away like the rest?" She almost screeched it, and she began walking around, her silks swishing, her face blanching with anger. "You fool! You weak, blundering fool!"

All at once her pacing ceased, and she shot him a glance containing a new expression. Her anger faded, was replaced by something else, perhaps the dawning of an idea; and then an expression almost like elation grew in her face. She half chuckled with some thought of her own.

"Oh no, I'll not lend you the money, Wistart!" she said. "By no means will I!"

Now she did laugh, a little sharp, almost gay, tinkling laugh. The *Clarion* assuredly was not going to the Ender brothers. Instead, she saw suddenly how the *Clarion* was going to enter a new existence.

For a moment the shadow of the dead Algeria Wedge seemed to stand in the room and Mary Agnes almost mocked at her. Algeria had been great in her world through the *Clarion*. Now another woman was going to stand in her stead. Hitherto Mary Agnes had kept her fingers out of the newspaper's affairs. From this time forward she intended to have her fingers in those affairs very much indeed. An entire vista of new interests, new enterprises, new motives of life seemed to open before her, challenging and exciting.

"I'll not *lend* you the money," she said. "But I'll furnish the one hundred thousand dollars to keep off the paper mill wolves——"

He gazed at her, almost incredulous, hope dawning.

"And for that I'm *buying control* of the *Clarion!*" she went on, her voice ringing. "You'll make over exactly fifty-one per cent of the ownership to me!"

Hope suddenly fled from him. He felt trapped. This was not what he wanted. A loan, yes. But to have her invade, poison, dominate this last free corner of his life—no, not that!

He wanted to protest, to run from the room, to reject her and her pitiless proposal. He could not.

Seven

1

A little before noon that morning Debs Dorn's telephone on the *Clarion* city desk rang. It was Joe Canfield.

"A murder," said Canfield. "Woman killed."

"Where?"

"That Draggett roadhouse. Sometime after midnight. Just found the body."

"Who was she?"

"Remember the dame I was telling you about—Bonnie Bonner?"

"The Bible-reading strip-tease girl?"

"Yep. It's her. Happened after closing hours. Found her this morning when they opened up the office. In her dressing room. Head bashed in. Blunt instrument."

"Photo?" Debs asked.

"Theatrical cheesecake used by the management."

"Bring it in. Any suspects?"

"Not yet. The cops are grilling Draggett and his people, but I don't think they know anything about it. No robbery. Purse here with a few bucks in it. Maybe rape, but they don't know any boy friends she had."

Debs made rapid notes on a pad of paper.

"All right," he said. "Get all the dope you can and come in and write the story for the home edition."

He hung up the receiver and found Hudson leaning over him.

"Murder?" exclaimed the managing editor. "Woman? Jeez—get out an extra!"

Debs nodded. Murders, even of roadhouse entertainers, were considered extra-edition material in Jericho journalistic circles.

"*Jericho Beauty Found Slain!*" gloated Hudson, quoting an imagined headline. "Who's writing it?"

"I am. I talked to Canfield."

"Make it quick! Make it good! The opposition's going to come out with this! Copy boy! Tell the composing room to get ready for an extra! Phone circulation, somebody!"

Debs pulled to him a typewriter on a rolling stand and swiftly, accurately, wrote a clear account of the tragedy in about two paragraphs.

As he wrote, Hudson peered over his shoulder.

"Goddamn it, Debs!" he exploded. "You call that a story? Gimme some adjectives! Ghastly murder! Had her head bashed in, didn't she? Put blood in—we can correct it in the next edition if there wasn't any. Beautiful! She was, wasn't she? Had to be if she was a strip tease. Shapely siren! Divorcee, probably—that always adds interest. No? Well, skip that. Love nest! Roadhouse seraglio! Give 'em something to read! Sex orgy! Slain after sex orgy! Put that in. Quote the police as speculating it. They'll stand for it. Imagination! What you need, Debs, is imagination!"

Debs shoved back the typewriter. "Listen, Sam, I know about this girl. There wasn't any sex orgy. If there was any sex, it was rape. She was only nineteen years old, and she was religious—in spite of the strip teasing. Married. We'd get in one hell of a libel suit if we used that sex orgy angle!"

"The hell you say! Well, leave the sex orgy out—this edition at least. Haven't much time anyway. Gimme the story and make it fast. We're holding the forms. Jeez-us! Nobody around here knows a thing! Got to do everything myself! Jeez-us! Goddamn!"

Debs wrote and handed the sheet of copy paper to Hudson.

"That's all they'll have time to set," he said.

Already Jeff, across the desk, had sent out the headlines. Hudson glanced at the copy, added another adjective or two of a lurid order, handed it to the copy boy with orders to rush it out, and turned on Debs. He was still rankling from the rebuff he had received that morning from Mrs. Wedge, and this was his chance to vent his anger on somebody.

"You gotta do better than this, Debs!" he said, his spectacles glittering dangerously. "I can't have a city editor who doesn't know how to play the news. This whole staff needs shaking up. There'll be changes around here—some great big changes—if I don't see everyone more up on their toes!"

Tingling with anger at the loud criticism which he felt was unmerited, Debs went out to the composing room to supervise the quick change of make-up of the front page and send the form to the stereotypers on its way to the presses and the shouting of the newsboys in the streets.

When he returned to the city room, Canfield was back and Hudson was examining a handful of theatrical photographs of a scantily clad dark-haired young woman, voluptuously curved, and—perhaps with some assistance from the retoucher—rather handsome in a somewhat vacant-faced way.

"Look—I said she was beautiful!" exclaimed Hudson triumphantly. "Use that—two columns, page one. Full length. Readers like legs, bare legs. Get a four-column layout for inside—Draggett, her husband, that sort of thing."

A layout artist took the photos off and began to work on them.

"Any suspects yet?" asked Debs of Canfield.

"Nobody. The Draggett people are clean. Ironclad alibis, all of 'em. Besides, no motive."

"Who's on the case from the police department?"

"Nibs Galloway and Walt Benson."

"Galloway's a good detective."

"Dumb," said Canfield. "Walt Benson's the best man they got." Debs remembered that Canfield did not care much for cops, but seemed to be on friendly terms with Benson.

"Write a new lead for the home edition," he said. "Feature a police dragnet or something like that. I'm going to lunch."

2

As with all newspapers, luncheon periods on the *Clarion* were strictly regulated according to edition deadlines. Leaving Jeff sitting at the city desk, Debs put on his overcoat and hat and went down the stairs to the street.

On nice days he customarily walked over to Jolly Herron's for a sandwich, because he was pretty sure of meeting other newspapermen there. But this day was cold, so he raised his overcoat collar about his ears and crossed the slippery street to a small cafeteria. He disliked cafeterias, but they had the virtue of saving time, and the distance to this one was short, and the food cheap.

Within, he hung up his hat and coat, took a tray, slid it around the aluminum track by the steam tables, placed on it such dishes as he desired, and having paid the gaunt woman at the cash register, looked around for a table. A girl was sitting alone near the wall. He had not noticed her when she came in, but her eyes were on him, and when he looked at her she smiled. She was quite young and quite pretty, and he knew her—Sally Sayre, helping with society on the *Clarion*. So he went over with his tray.

"What's big in your department, Sally?" he asked, seating himself.

"Not much. A couple of engagements. Mrs. Wedge returns home."

"What are you doing with that?"

"One paragraph. *Very* definite orders from Mrs. Wedge." The words were respectful, but there was an irreverent note in her voice and a crinkle at the corners of her hazel eyes.

Sally was twenty. She graduated from the state university the previous spring with a major in journalism and a sorority pin, and since her family moved in the somewhat outer circles of Jericho society, she was thought qualified to assist at the society desk. Sally, however, considered herself a newspaperwoman, something quite different from a society reporter, and wanted a news job. She had imbibed the idea that women are discriminated against in a man-made world, and she considered herself a feminist and a career woman; but the way she wore her slim-waisted suits in winter and her fluffy dresses in summer, and the way she used her eyes and her smile, rather indicated a very normal and healthy interest in men and romance. Upon Debs she looked with a species of awe, which did not, however, entirely quench her young pertness.

"What was Shrieking Sam blowing his top over this morning?" she asked.

"First about how to play the yarn on Mrs. Wedge. Then about some details on the murder story."

She said, "It flips me when he yells at you like that."

She was wide-eyed and serious. He noticed she had a cute nose and soft lips.

"Don't let it bother you," he said. "Managing editors are like that."

"*You* wouldn't be."

"How do you know? I'd probably shriek and swing from chandelier to chandelier just like Sam."

"No, you wouldn't. You wouldn't have to underline your own importance. That's why he does it. Sometimes, quite cheerfully and without compassion, I could poison that man!"

He grinned, and decided he had better change the subject.

"How do you like newspapering, Sally?"

"I don't know. I haven't tried it."

"After six months on the *Clarion?*"

"Sitting and calling up Tower Hill snobs? Gushing over table decorations, describing every stitch some dumb little doll wears up to the altar, salaaming before Mrs. Rich-bitches and listening to the nonentities they're having in for canasta? That's hardly what I call newspapering, thank you."

She had a point there, certainly, Debs thought. He found her attractive in her young way, and felt almost paternal toward her.

"Sure newspapering's what you really want?" he asked.

"Yes."

"I'm not."

"Why?"

"I don't think it's a good lifetime game for women. Want to look forward to becoming a tough old bag of a she-scribe with a wilted cigarette hanging out of the corner of your mouth, the smoke getting in your eyes, while you pound out some routine story for the Sunday bulldog?"

The point was not lost on Sally. It was a pretty pat description of

Kay Roberts, who wrote Sunday features and handled exchanges for the *Clarion*. Kay really was not so old, being no more than forty-five, but to Sally she appeared ancient. She wore ill-fitting mannish clothes, smeared her make-up, was careless to the point of being untidy with her dyed red hair, laughed too loudly at obscene jokes, and sometimes, when she was off guard, looked woefully dejected. Kay Roberts was not even her real name. She was born Gussie Zeller, and married and divorced a Polish oil field worker named Joe Yampolski. Obviously Gussie Yampolski was no name to sign to an article, so she took Kay Roberts as a nom de plume, and eventually adopted it as her real name, even signing it to her checks.

But Sally shook her head. "You don't have to be that way. Look at Dorothy Kilgallen. And Margaret Bourke-White. And Clare Boothe Luce. They're all newspaperwomen."

"Exceptions to the rule: They had something more than ability— luck. Connections, and so on. They went in through the front door of journalism. You'd have to go in through the back. Do you know what happens to most career girls, even the ones with ability?"

"What does?" she asked defiantly.

"Second string. Always second string. And getting leaner, and more frustrated, and bitterer every year. You think normal women's lives aren't important? Believe me, they are. Want to know who the first team women are? The ones who have weddings, and husbands, and homes, and babies, and canasta parties, and table decorations, and all those things that seem individually trivial to you, but which taken together become mighty important—life."

She was looking down soberly, not answering him, and he realized he was being somewhat pontifical.

So he grinned. "Disagree?"

She raised her eyes. "Sure, I disagree. And it makes me mad to have a man talk that way."

"You're mad at me, Sally?"

Suddenly and surprisingly she smiled at him. "No, I'm not mad at you. I think you're swell!"

It was so direct and femininely innocent, somehow, that it took him back.

But she was gazing past him.

"Speaking about what we're speaking about," she said, "there's somebody who proves everything I've said about women in careers. And she's everything I'd like to be."

He turned his head. Looking slim and elegant in a thick loose gray coat and a small black hat that made her blonde hair seem brighter by contrast, a young woman was sliding her tray by the steam tables.

"Grey Rutledge," said Sally. "I've known her for years. She's smart, attractive——"

"Granted," he said.

"Successful——"

"Yes."

"Independent."

"Maybe."

"Of course she is! What makes you say that? Do you know her?"

"Sure I know her."

"How well?"

"Very well. She lives in a house right next to the one where I room. Betty Jean—that's her little girl—plays jacks in the summer on the sidewalk in front of our steps. Sometimes they have me over to dinner—Grey's mother, Mrs. Norcross, is a wonderful cook. There's a sort of little neighborhood club, too, that plays penny ante poker a couple of times a month. Sometimes Grey comes to that."

"With you?"

"Once in a while."

"Oh . . ." An odd little flat note in Sally's voice.

Debs laughed. "Grey Rutledge doesn't have time for a guy on a newspaper salary. Doesn't have time for *any* man—that anyone knows about, anyway."

"Wonder why? She seems so attractive."

"Widow. Maybe she's disillusioned about men."

"Women don't get *that* disillusioned," said Sally.

Grey saw them, and Sally smiled invitation, so she came over.

"Hello, Sally. Hello, Debs," she said. When she smiled she had a trick of half closing the lower lids of her eyes, making bright dancing gray half-moons of them. "May I join you? But you're almost finished——"

"I've got to go in a few minutes," said Debs, rising. "But I know Sally's in no particular hurry to get out in that cold. Have a seat."

He helped her with her tray, and she sat across from him, beside

Sally. He compared them: Sally, twenty, very young and untried and eager; Grey, twenty-eight, not so much older, but poised and with a light armor of sophistication. Both femininely desirable and provocative, yet somehow both with an air of strained alertness, as if their bodies were full of trembling wires.

Career girls, he thought. The new combination of sex and efficiency, bringing not only their particular feminine abilities and skills, but also their particular feminine problems, their emotions and instincts and disturbances, to business and the professions. He liked them both, rather more than liked them; but at the moment he half resented them, too.

They were chattering together, the inevitable small talk of women, and he pushed his chair back. At once they stopped talking to each other and turned their attention to him.

"You're not going already?" asked Grey. In her voice was a little note of disappointment, of question: the feminine instinctive wish to hold a man near, the feminine instinctive concern that she has not devoted enough attention to him. In its way this was more flattering than the full original attention would have been, and yet Debs, who felt it, was sure that he was only a man to her, on a plane with many other men; that he meant nothing more than a casual friend to her, although she could have meant far more to him had he permitted himself to think of it.

He nodded. "Got to get back. Will you be playing poker with us at the Barnestables' tomorrow night?"

"No, Debs. I'm leaving for Chicago tonight. Buying. I'm going to be sorry to miss it."

His face changed slightly. "I'm sorry, too. Well, got to get back."

Both young women followed him with their eyes as he left the cafeteria.

3

Across the street, as he reached the door to the stairs that led up to the *Clarion* city room, Debs halted. Coming along the sidewalk, his head lowered against the wind, was a rugged, bull-necked young man with powerful shoulders and torso which seemed oddly to belie his boyish, pug-nosed face. He wore a black pseudo-alpaca overcoat and a black felt hat pulled low on his forehead. Debs knew him: Nibs

Galloway. They had been friends, in the curious way newspapermen and policemen sometimes are friends, ever since Debs was a police reporter and Galloway a rookie motorcycle patrolman.

"Hi, Nibs," said Debs.

"Hi." Galloway halted, turned his back to the wind, and held his hat down on his head. His red face wrinkled as a few sleety flakes of snow skidded past his cheek.

"Hear you're on the Bonner case," Debs said.

"Yeah."

"Anything new?"

Galloway shook his head.

"Any theories?" Debs asked.

"Wasn't sex—I don't think. From everything we can find out the gal was respectable even if she did shake a naked fanny—some kind of screwball religion. Of course, some sex maniac might of gone crazy for her an' got in her dressing room after the show. But it don't look like it. The city doc examined the body an' says she wasn't criminally assaulted. Besides, there wasn't no struggle. There must of been people still in the building when it happened, because she always left right away when her last act was finished. Whoever it was hit her on the head, probably from behind. Likely she didn't even see him, because she didn't scream. He must of been hiding in there when she come in. Nobody knew it happened—supposed she'd gone home. It was after her last act, like I said, an' the roadhouse closed up for the night pretty shortly. First time anybody knew about it was when the janitor force come to clean up this morning."

"Anybody have it in for her?"

"Nobody we know of. That kind of thing, with a woman, is generally a jealous lover, or a man she done wrong. She had no truck with any man except her husband. We talked to him. Poor guy's dazed, an' pretty dumb anyway. Name of Dewey Bonner. Hipped on religion to where he wears a beard like one of them prophets. In his spare time from work he goes around tryin' to sell religious tracts an' books. He told us they give everything him an' her earned to their sect. Haven't hardly nothing for theirselves—live in a little shack out beyond the packing house. Housekeeping rooms, nothing more. He got worried when she didn't come home last night—they have an old broken-down jalopy she always drove, an' it was still out at the Ches-

terfield Club this mornin'. But he didn't know what to do about it.
He jest shook his head an' kind of mumbled. No, she didn't have no
enemies we been able to spot."

"Then what do you think?"

"Well—could be that somebody shut her up. She was a hallelujah
lassie, you know. If she got the goods on somebody—a crime, say—
she'd go to the sheriff's office, or the police, first chance she got."

"Something on Draggett, maybe?"

"Don't think so. The county attorney issued a padlock order on his
place this morning after this happened, but he seems to be clean as
far as the murder's concerned."

"Somebody that frequented the Chesterfield Club, then? A guest,
maybe?"

"Could be—but we ain't got no leads along that line."

Glancing across the street, Debs saw Sally emerge from the cafeteria
with Grey. Sally waved at the other girl, and then came over toward
them.

"Miss Sayre," said Debs, "this is Detective Galloway."

Sally always gave a man her full treatment of eyes and smiles.
Galloway said, "Pleased-tuh-meetcha-miss," and seemed abashed.

"Come on, Sally," said Debs. "See you, Nibs."

He took her arm, finding it slender and firm in the loose sleeve of
her coat. Together they went up the stairs to the city room.

As they reached the top, Hudson glanced up at them, his face dark
and serious. Debs hung up his coat and hat while Sally went to her
desk. When he turned, the managing editor was coming toward him.

"I may have a new lead on the Bonner murder," said Debs.

Hudson seemed hardly to hear him.

"Read this," he said, his face heavy with portent.

Debs took the small square of blue paper and read:

Memo from the Office of the Publisher:
As of this date, the names of Wistart Wedge and Mary Agnes Wedge
will be carried jointly on the masthead as co-publishers of the *Daily
Clarion*. Employees in all departments will accept and carry out implicitly
any orders or directions given by Mrs. Wedge, who has fullest authority.

"What do you make of that?" asked Hudson.

He was thinking of his own blundering insistence over the telephone when he talked to Mrs. Wedge that morning, and how curt and cutting she had been. And he was wondering, quite fearfully, how much of a grudge she might hold against him, and how this change would affect his status.

"I don't know," Debs said, "but I'd better get those new lines set for the masthead."

He walked out toward the composing room. He did have plenty of notions about the change. It meant that something big had happened at the summit level of the newspaper. Perhaps the Big Deal was off—if it ever had been on. Certainly new problems were provided.

Debs wondered when Mrs. Wedge would come down to look over her new principality and begin giving orders. From what he knew of her, she had more than her share of temperament, and probably liked to throw her weight around. She would have screwball ideas, undoubtedly, and it would be his task to carry them out—*implicitly,* the memorandum said—or in some manner convince her that they were impractical, or unwise, or wrong. And, if possible, do it without offending what probably was a pretty touchy female, used to having her own way and out looking, very likely, for opposition and determined to break it down at any cost just to show who was boss.

At the moment Debs felt weary. He detested his job, and the *Clarion,* and the whole damned profession of journalism.

ANNALS OF THE *DAILY CLARION*

The Broad-mindedness of Ramseur Jackson

To understand Jericho, one must understand its eccentricities, among which is the fact that it has not one, but two separate civic centers. The focus of business and prosperity is along Main Street, where stand such pillars of finance as the First National Bank, Cox's, Incorporated, and the *Daily Clarion,* with, to the north, the better residential areas, including Tower Hill. Eight blocks south, along Commonwealth Avenue, is the center of political activity, represented by the old courthouse, the new post office building, and the *Morning Sentinel,* with the poorer homes straggling beyond until the poorest of them become shacktowns near the city dump.

These two disparate divisions of the city are called, locally, Jerrytown and Jugtown, and this goes far back in history, to the county seat fight of the eighties between Jericho and Bedestown, an embryo hamlet then existing a few miles away across the prairie. Men went out with weapons in those days and bushwhacked one another over which town should have the county seat with its tax-supported offices. When Jericho finally won, Bedestown gave up the ghost and dragged its dried-up shacks over the intervening miles of buffalo grass sod to move in with its victorious rival. So the two settlements existed together, and continuing down to the present day there has been a difference between them.

Jerrytown, so called because it was the old Jericho center, has always been proper, prosperous, and a little superior. Jugtown, named thus because the old Bedestown crowd had a hankering for the whiskey demijohn, has always been inclined to be poverty-stricken, sinful, and irreverent.

A personal feud, which is still a Jericho legend, once underlined this divergence. It happened around 1910, an election year in which the race for county attorney received the biggest attention because of the personalities of the rival candidates.

One of these was the incumbent, Jasper Peddigrew. He had been at the public trough ten years, and there was nothing brilliant about him as a lawyer, but he was a party wheel horse and had the support of the Republican organization, including the G.A.R., which still wielded influence.

His opponent was Ramseur Jackson, better known as the Ramrod. He had an imposing manner, compounded of a glaring blue eye, a gray mustache and goatee, and a "presence," which is to say, a potbelly. He was devoted to the Democratic party, unhandicapped by any sense of humor, gifted with a single-minded and undeviating admiration of himself, and filled with antiquated notions of honor, being a professional Southerner with, as he put it, "Alabama antecedents and Virginia upbringing."

Nobody gave Ramseur Jackson much of a chance. Not only was the county strongly Republican, but people figured that even if he had a party to support him, his high-flown language would intimidate the natives thereabouts. Nevertheless, the Ramrod believed in himself, if no one else did.

He had a wife, Essie, a good deal younger than he: a dark little creature with straying eyes, rather pretty, about whom occasional whispers floated, for she was known to be susceptible to masculine admiration. Jackson was uneasily aware of her flirtations, but seemed unable to stop them.

Only two weeks remained before Election Day, and the campaign approached its height. In the midst of this the whispers concerning Mrs. Jackson increased suddenly to open scandalous talk. Neighbors had seen a man coming from the Jackson home late one night; a night when Mrs. Jackson's husband was known to be away campaigning in a distant township. Gossip went farther and even named the man— one Jehu Norkle, immigration agent for the railroad.

It has always been supposed that Mrs. Jackson became fascinated with Norkle because his pride and boast was the finest pair of mustachios in Jericho. People remembered Madame de Staël's saying that "Kissing a man without a mustache is like eating an egg without salt," and to a lady with an eye for that kind of decoration, Jehu Norkle must have been well nigh irresistible. His mustachios had the proportions and general appearance of the prize spread of a Texas longhorn steer.

When Ramseur Jackson returned home from the hustings he was ignorant of what was being said around, being in the proverbial position of a husband who is the last to hear of the indiscretions of his wife. But a story so universally savored could not forever be kept from him. And one day, just a week before election, Jericho was treated to a roaring, snorting pageant of indignation. Having at last learned what all the town was talking about, the Ramrod got himself drunk, and like a gray-haired nemesis in a black campaign hat and frock coat, stalked the streets with a long-barreled Colt revolver seeking his rival, who, however, kept himself warily out of sight.

Young Tom Pollock, then a fledgling lawyer but later to be a federal judge, with some others, reasoned with the rampant Southerner. It happened that Pollock deprived him of his weapon, and for that the Ramrod gave him a cursing that was classic for its all-embracing blasphemous description. Though Pollock understood he had made a mortal enemy, he helped sober Jackson up enough so that he recovered from his immediate thirst for Norkle's gore, and except for the indiscretion of Jehu himself, the affair might have ended there. The railroad man, however, as soon as he was sure Jackson was disarmed, rushed to the courthouse and swore out a peace warrant against the fiery barrister before old Judge Hutto, who, though he was crippled with arthritis and feeble with age, occupied the district bench.

To Ramseur Jackson's mind this was the ultimate injury, since he esteemed an invasion of his professional purlieu an affront even graver than an invasion of his home. Shortly thereafter Jericho learned he was in jail; facing charges of assault, threat with a deadly weapon, malicious destruction of property, tampering with the records of the district court, forcible illegal entry, vandalism, refusal to submit to a peace warrant, and contempt of court.

The charges were all-embracing, but not surprising in view of the facts of the case. The Ramrod, it appears, got himself drunk again and went to the courthouse, breathing fire, with the intention of throwing old Judge Hutto out of his own office for issuing that peace warrant. The judge, though stiff with age and all bent up with arthritis, straightened out like a quarter horse and came sailing into the hall when the Southerner burst into his chambers. Thereupon, cheated of his quarry, the Ramrod took out his ire by throwing most of the judge's furniture out of the window, and the four winds of Kansas scattered the papers of the court. It required the united efforts of the sheriff and four deputies to subdue him and put him behind the bars.

Tom Pollock visited the prisoner in durance and after talking with him bailed him out. Jackson pumped his hand, breathing hard through his nose.

"Let me assuah yo', seh, of my deep sens'bility of obligation," he said. "Yo' air, I understand, from the South yo'self?"

Pollock said he happened originally to hail from Missouri.

"In soul and manner Missouri is part of the South," said the Ramrod magnanimously. "And yo' tharfore will understand that a gentleman—especially, seh, a Southern gentleman—must be allowed some leeway fo' his emotions."

After that he departed with a snort of such furious indignation that it rattled the windows of the sheriff's office.

Within an hour Ramseur Jackson had been shot.

It seems he hunted up his wife to upbraid her. The lady dug a pistol out of her reticule and wounded him in the left leg.

After a doctor bound up the injury, the Ramrod had himself carried to the Apex Hotel, where he lay in bed raising hell and shouting for vengeance.

The better element of Jericho's citizenry was critical of him, holding that he was an old fool who got what was coming to him. Young Tom Pollock, however, felt like overlooking most of his vagaries, since nobody had been hurt but himself, and he was, after all, a gentleman under considerable harassment. And he thought later that Jackson would be even more harassed when the *Clarion* appeared on the street with its version of the affair, including an editorial in the best and most trenchant journalese, in which it referred to Ramseur as disreputable, drunken, and a disgrace to the city.

Pollock considered it a little hard on the Ramrod, and remembered he was a proud man and inclined to direct action. When, half an hour later, he received a personal summons to the injured barrister's bedchamber, he went with some misgivings, since it was he who had disarmed Jackson. His misgivings appeared justified, for he had an unpleasant surprise when he entered the Ramrod's room. The South-erner got instantly out of bed, limped across the floor, and locked the door. Having not foreseen that the man would be able to move about, Pollock was somewhat chilled by the action.

He was chilled even more when Jackson stood up in his nightshirt, with his red face and potbelly, snorted like a buffalo, pulled from the bureau drawer his huge six-shooter, and laid it on the table. To young Pollock's distempered imagination it looked all of three feet long. Yearningly he glanced out of the window. It was thirty feet down to the sidewalk below, yet he said afterward that he believed he would have leaped it head first if the Ramrod had so much as said "Boo!"

It quickly developed, however, that the Alabaman had no wish to shoot him; nor was he really incensed over the *Clarion* editorial, being rather inclined to be flattered by this public attention. What he desired was that Pollock witness him in an oath.

"This is a Bible—observe I place my right hand on it," said he. "Now listen to me, seh: I hereby do solemnly swear upon my honah as a gentleman and an Alabaman that I will make that unspeakable sonofabitch, Jehu Norkle, get down on his knees and apologize to me on the principal intersection of Jericho. So help me, God!"

He kissed the book devoutly. With his rumpled gray head, his belly-distended nightshirt, and his earnestness in his ridiculous oath, he made an almost irresistibly funny picture, but if Tom Pollock had any desire to laugh, he mastered it. That piece of Colt artillery lay in too easy reach. He therefore complimented the Ramrod most politely and departed, not even forgetting his hat.

As for that oath, ridiculous though it might have been considered, Ramseur not only carried it out, but he carried it out double.

It happened in this wise: the whole town soon knew he had sworn to make Norkle apologize on the principal intersection, and an imme-diate heated debate took place over which was the principal intersec-tion. Jerrytown had no intention of permitting anything to lessen its claim to the chief intersection; nor would Jugtown bow to Jerrytown's pretensions. At last a committee was formed to wait on Ramseur Jackson at his hotel and demand what he intended to do and which intersection he proposed to elevate.

The Ramrod was magnificent. He heard the committee out, then said that, by thunder, he was too important a man to become involved in any piddling sectional issue of this kind, and he proposed to dignify it by no personal endorsement of either location. The committee departed, and the question of what he was going to do became the chief topic of conversation, with considerable speculative betting, on both sides of town.

But Jericho was not left to wonder long. After all, the Ramrod's injury was only a slight flesh wound. The following morning he rose from his couch of pain, attired himself in his best Prince Albert coat, his best campaign hat, his best pair of varnished boots, lit a twisted stogie, and limped over to the railroad offices. There he stuck his pistol into the midriff of Jehu Norkle.

The nose of the freight agent, ordinarily the color of a ripe plum, turned a peaceful pearl gray as, without a demur, he marched out before the muzzle of the gun. A good many people were witnesses when Jehu Norkle knelt at the First National Bank corner on Main, still with that pensive pallor on his face as Jackson flourished his weapon, and in a trembling voice apologized for the peace warrant and also for calling on Jackson's wife.

Nobody interfered, partly because of the ancient aphorism of the West, *Let every man kill his own snakes;* and partly because of overwhelming public curiosity as to what else would take place.

Ramseur Jackson prodded Norkle into arising with the pistol barrel, and followed by a crowd which grew in size every minute, marched his victim, who was trembling and perspiring so freely that his magnificent mustachios had quite wilted down, eight blocks south to the courthouse corner on Commonwealth. There the railroad man knelt again, and in a shaking voice repeated his apology.

It was a sweeping gesture. People later made many admiring comments on Ramseur Jackson's broad-minded and careful conduct of his affairs so as to wound no faction.

As a sequel, Jehu Norkle departed rapidly and permanently for climes more salubrious. Mrs. Jackson obtained an uncontested divorce from her husband, and having become interested in a drugstore clerk with a tenor voice, dropped out of the public eye.

And in the meantime the sovereign voters elected Ramseur Jackson, by a most handsome majority, to the high office of county attorney.

Eight

In the night the street lamps made a pallid glimmering on the thin snow, the wind wailed beneath the wintry stars, and the city seemed to be lighted by a little dazzling frost cloud that lingered over the moon. The tire chains of the taxicab in which Grey Rutledge rode kept up a monotonous whirring that seemed to chime with her mood of depression as the vehicle turned down Forest Boulevard toward the railroad station.

She was looking forward to her Pullman compartment on the train as a place to think. Alone, surrounded by the four narrow steel walls of the little cubicle, with nobody to intrude, no telephone, no immediate responsibilities, it is possible to ponder deeply and long. Grey had need to think. She was on her way to Chicago. To keep an appointment. It was an appointment she had not planned, which she did not in her soul really want to keep, but which she must keep for reasons too deep for any logic.

To the left she saw the Butford house loom up suddenly in the night, a huge black silhouette of four-story brick walls, steep slate roofs, and ornamental chimneys, with only one or two windows alight. It was unique in Jericho: the only mansion remaining in this central part of the city, all other homes of wealth long ago having gone to more fashionable districts. Remote and aloof it stood in its wide grounds among its leafless trees.

As if the sight of the grim, dark house brought an involuntary shiver, Grey drew her coat up about her throat. She knew that imposing old pile as one knows a drab and ancient weariness. She knew also the implacable old woman who dwelt in it: Mrs. Simon Bolivar Butford, widowed almost thirty years, who had inherited her dead husband's house and his fortune, his selfishness and cruelty, his vanity and love of ostentation, but not his brains or his strength, which were the only redeeming things about him.

It was night, and midwinter, but in the backward arch of her mind Grey saw a midsummer day, and a slim girl in a black dress going hesitantly up the walk toward the old Butford house. The girl was herself: Grey Rutledge. And she was that day going to begin a special kind of slavery which she did not even then imagine; a dreadful period of her life, sad even in the remembering, and the beginning, it seemed to her now, of all the fatefulness that since had enmeshed her, predetermining this act or that, almost as if she had no will or way of her own.

As the tire chains whirred on, biting the light icy snow, the Butford house was left in the night behind and Grey's face cleared. But her thoughts continued to race back; and it seemed to her they could not be stopped, or that there was any solution to what confronted her now and in the future.

2

Save for the dim lights in the passage, the Pullman car was dark. Grey followed the redcap to her compartment and waited while he stowed her luggage away. When he came out, she tipped him and thanked him with a smile. Her smile was one of the things you liked about her, and people had a habit of responding to it. The redcap did so now, with a surprised grin of his own, a touch of fingers to his cap, and a "Thank you, miss," spoken with more than usual sincerity.

Grey went into her compartment and locked the door. One of the conveniences of modern travel which she intimately appreciated was this being able to enter her sleeping car before train time, settle herself for the night, and even go to sleep before the train came along much later, the car was coupled to it, and she was started on her journey.

A Pullman compartment is not a large place to move about in, but then neither was Grey large. At once she began undressing, hanging up her suit neatly, cleansing her face at the little mirror, slipping out of her underthings and into nylon pajamas, and creeping between the crisp sheets of the berth. She had a feminine love for nightgowns, lovely, sheer, full-length nightgowns that mistily reveal the form within like a dream of beauty; but when she traveled she wore pajamas for their practicality.

In her berth she lay awake with the light on. Not that she had any intention of reading. She simply lay flat on her back, her eyes wide open. After a time she lit a cigarette.

Close beside her, right on the next track from the sound of it, a freight train passed, steam heaving and snorting at first, a vibration of her berth at the pounding of heavy drive wheels, and then what seemed to be an interminable rattle and clank as the long string of cars moved slowly by for some unguessed far destination.

Nobody had said good-by to her at the station; but then nobody ever did. She was on a business trip . . . officially, at least. And she was a businesswoman: the attendance and gallantries surrounding women who have men and are precious to them were not to be expected by her.

Grey was the buyer for her little store and a buyer must always be months ahead of the seasons. She had been buying four years now and her guesses on the unpredictable trends of women's styles had never been too bad. Better than good, in fact. She had a flair, an instinct, based on her own preferences and tastes. Women shoppers in Jericho sometimes found at Grey Rutledge, Sportswear, things indicating almost a prescience of things to come. Perhaps they might seem a little bizarre or extreme, if the customer had the daring to wear them—until the fashion magazines came along three or four months later and showed exactly the same styles. And then everybody was wearing them, and the original pioneer of the mode in Jericho could feel smug over cleverly anticipating and leading fashion—although in her own most secret mind she might perhaps give a little credit to Grey Rutledge, also.

Nobody questions a buyer's judgment of the time to go to merchandise showings, and Grey had things fairly well organized. At the store Mrs. Hedcomb and the fitting woman would carry on for a few days. At home Betty Jean and Grandma would continue their routine as usual.

Betty Jean . . . dear little thing, just starting school and already asleep when Grey left home, her eyelids like flower petals closed over her eyes, her childish face peaceful and untroubled. She knew her mother was going and on this occasion, for the first time, begged to go along.

Of course she could not. There was school. Betty Jean was bringing home good marks, and looking forward to belonging to the Brownies, and sometimes had her small friends over for the night. She was well adjusted and happy, Grey was sure. And it was important that she miss no school . . . or was it?

No, really. Grey confessed to herself that an absence of a week or so would do no damage to her daughter's education. And it would be fun to have her. Betty Jean was six now, and company: with funny childish thoughts and winsome childish ways, so pretty and spritelike that any mother would be proud to have her just to show her off.

Yet Grey could not even consider taking her.

She lay in her berth waiting for the train to come from the west, pick up her car, and begin rushing her across the continent on an errand behind an errand, having to do only secondarily with buying women's trivia or estimating the unimportant variations in style by which women set such store. She was going to Chicago, all the way to Chicago, to meet a lover. She did not want to go. Yet nobody was forcing her to do it: she was acting on her own volition, really on her own thought and suggestion.

Lover. She said the word to herself. When a woman has an affair with a man, he is called her lover. An equivocal word, with an equivocal meaning. A lover can be honorable and admirable. Or a lover can be something furtive, a paramour . . . she disliked the word and shrank from it. She preferred to say lover, though there was nothing in it about which she could take any pride from her own connection with it.

The word for a woman in a love intrigue is less equivocal. Mistress. At first she had shunned it, but now she could say it because it was true.

Mistress . . . when she was sixteen she first began reading about mistresses, and she thought the word glamorous and exciting and sophisticated. But she never thought she would use it for herself.

A mistress, traveling hundreds of miles to a forbidden tryst. Always traveling great distances for a few brief hours. Ridiculous? No, the only way it could be for safety. Chicago, with its millions, was a human jungle where nobody ever could be found. New York was another. Also Los Angeles. Even Miami—once. All those thousands of miles, stolen meetings at distant places, for what?

The shuddering ecstasy of sex? No, beyond that, something quite different. Something going back to the years before. The years that began the story of Grey Rutledge.

It was a slow beginning. Sometimes it seemed to Grey that she was on a tide of fate, being carried whether she would or no to some sure doom. Was this something in her mind? A helpless determinism? She did not believe so: it was not characteristic of her temperament or her thinking. Yet there was the record.

Her mother, now at home taking care of Betty Jean, was born Marianna Grey, of a family with somewhat decayed Southern pretensions, long on charm and tradition and short on worldly possessions. Marianna married Barnaby Norcross, a lawyer, not particularly brilliant but strong on dignity and decorum, who practiced in Sedalia, Missouri. There they lived, and there Grey was born and named after her mother's family—rather a Southern custom, but a name which seemed to suit her with those eyes of hers.

Sedalia, with its elm-shaded streets and its old red brick houses and its railroad shops: the Norcross girl grew up there, thin and frail at first, and then slender and graceful, and people said she was pretty. Grey remembered her mother's constant iteration of the word *background*. Her mother had background, which meant the right kind of associations and training that she considered necessary for the life of a nice girl.

So Grey had music lessons and French and dancing in addition to her high school studies; and her mother saw to it that she did not become too much interested in any of the ordinary town boys. After high school she wanted to go to Missouri University, but her parents decided on a private college, because her mother felt it carried more éclat. And since Barnaby Norcross never was overly successful as a lawyer and they simply could not afford a school like Vassar or Bryn Mawr, Grey went to a small women's college in Tennessee, which her mother had attended before her, and which could be relied upon to teach a girl nothing but the more useless accomplishments considered suitable for a "lady."

It was in the middle of World War II, and the war was like a cloud in the air, with far-off excitements that she hardly understood. It affected her little, except that in the years when she might have fallen in love, young men came and went too rapidly for any permanent attachments, even though she had romantic thoughts about one or two and kept up a rather erratic correspondence with several. The war ended when she was nineteen, and she got her diploma, and that summer her father died.

It was a shock, for the family was affectionate and close-knit. It was a shock in another way, too, for Barnaby Norcross, who was a lawyer and should have known better, left his estate tangled and muddled, and by the time the other lawyers got through with it there was not much left of it. Grey's mother had the old house and barely enough to live on. It was evident that Grey must begin earning her own living.

Considering what she had to offer, she discovered that she had nothing except good looks and good breeding and a few accomplishments that added up to no practical values: unless one had a home and could use them for the kind of life a home should have. She loved clothes, and when she had thought previously of working, or a career—which wasn't often—she had vague notions about perhaps fashion modeling at first, and then maybe becoming a buyer and going to New York several times a year, or even to Paris now and then. But there were no particular openings for buyers without experience in Sedalia, or even for fashion models, and the whole future looked pretty dark.

Then Jed Rutledge came home from the war: a major in the Army Air Force, with a lot of combat missions to his credit and a lot of ribbons on his chest. She had known him before he went away because the families saw something of each other, but Jed graduated from Missouri University the year before she graduated from high school, and he looked upon her then as a fledgling to be twitted in a rather superior way.

Now, however, things were somewhat changed. She was nineteen and he was twenty-five, and the difference between their ages mysteriously meant nothing any more, for all his war experience. He was interested in her and they had a date or two; and she thought him good-looking, and besides, there was an aura of heroism about him.

She might even have become romantic about him if he had stayed a little longer, but he was home only a few days, and left for Kansas somewhere.

Later, around Christmas, he came back, no longer in uniform, and took her to a dance one night. That evening he offered her a job. He had gone into real estate, he told her, in Jericho, Kansas, which had airplane factories, and a packing plant, and flour mills, and a couple of oil refineries, and was making large strides in expansion. And why didn't she come out and sell real estate for him?

She took the idea to her mother, and to her surprise Mrs. Norcross agreed. Selling real estate did not require special technical training, and Jed said many women were taking it up—it was rather natural, when you thought about it, since women are interested in houses and homes, for them to engage in selling them. For some obscure reason it seemed to Grey's mother a rather genteel position, a little above ordinary office work in the social scale, and this was to her the clinching argument.

So Grey went out to Jericho, a sprawling city growing too fast for its own good, but full of optimisms and beliefs in its future. She did some studying, of course, to pass the real estate board's examination. And after that, with her license paid for, she went out and showed cottages and tract homes for the Rutledge Realty Company.

3

The Rutledge Realty Company was not a large concern. It was comprised, in fact, only of Jed himself, his pretty salesgirl, and a middle-aged, part-time stenographer, who answered the telephone and did not like Grey because she was young and cute.

Jed was a smiling extrovert, dark, curly-headed, and athletic. He was a confirmed joiner and belonged to all the clubs he could get into, including the Jericho Country Club, where he was a four-handicap golfer. He drank well and moderately and was so personable and likable that he sold quite a lot of real estate.

But Grey discovered she was not very good at it. There were so many angles to be figured, and so much information you had to carry in your head, and there was that final pressure to be put on at just the right psychological moment—she almost always missed somewhere along the line. She made a few sales, but not many, and Jed watched her with some amusement.

Occasionally he took her out to dinner, although he made no sort of a specialty of her, circulating quite freely in his bachelor role among the unattached girls of good family in Jericho.

One evening when they were dining at the Country Club and Grey was in her best dress, and looked rather charming even to her own critical eyes, he said to her, "The trouble with you women in real estate is that you're more concerned with getting the lowest price for your prospect than the highest price for your client. You spend your time trying to talk your client down rather than talking your prospect up."

She dropped her eyes, because she knew what he was talking about.

"I just couldn't bear seeing that young couple disappointed today," she said. "They wanted the little Hersberg house so badly."

"It goes deeper than that," he said. "The bargain instinct. Because you're a woman, you're on the buyer's side by nature. You talked to the Hersbergs and tried to get them to accept a thousand dollars less?"

"Yes."

"And when they wouldn't, you offered to pare your own commission to give the couple some kind of a reduction?"

"Y-e-es . . . a little, maybe."

"And even then you couldn't make a sale?"

"They couldn't afford even that—and I was so sorry for them——"

Jed laughed. Then he grew serious. "Grey, selling real estate is just not your dish. Do you know that?"

She had been expecting it, because she knew she had not been doing well enough. "I'm sorry—so sorry—I tried—really tried—but—but I guess you're right."

He went on talking. "Well—I wouldn't worry about it if I were you. Any old bag can sell real estate."

Her head was bowed, her voice subdued. "You're going to—get someone else?"

"Yes. I have to. An experienced salesman who knows property values and the tricks of the game."

"I see." Very crushed, she gazed down at her plate. "Then I suppose —that means——"

"It means you don't belong in any office," he said.

And then the most surprising thing happened. Suddenly he leaned forward earnestly.

"It means, too, that I can't get along without you," he said. "Grey —darling—you're the cutest thing I ever saw, and I'm in love with you. Let's get married, Grey. Will you—would you—consider being Mrs. Jed Rutledge?"

It took her breath away. In sheer astonishment she raised her eyes.

"You mean——" she began. "You mean you're going to—to fire me —because you want to—marry me?"

"Yes," he said with a half-smile, "I guess that's about what it amounts to."

Suddenly they both were laughing—laughing almost hysterically, so that people at other tables glanced over at them, wondering what the joke was.

Later Grey thought it was the strangest proposal she ever heard of, and one of the nicest, in a way. A complete surprise, too. She had speculated about him, of course . . . every girl always runs every eligible man through her mind. But Jed was older, and he was her boss, and so busy with all his activities, and dating other girls far more frequently than her, and he had never been serious or intimate before. So it really was unexpected, in spite of the fact that a woman is supposed to be able to read a man's intentions before he puts them into outright words.

She might have gone through the customary clichés of hesitations and ponderings, and this-is-so-sudden-I-must-have-time-to-think. But she didn't. After all, she had always liked Jed, and if she was not quite sure she was in love with him, she was sure she could be, once she became accustomed to the idea. And all at once it seemed to her that it was the answer to every one of her problems, and she was grateful and happy and breathless, and she said yes and meant it.

He didn't even kiss her—not there, among all those tables, with everyone looking on. But since neither of them cared about dancing any more that night, he took her home at once. They sat for a long time in his car in front of the house where she roomed, and they made some plans, and she was all rumpled and rosy when he let her out to go to her room, and that night she was too excited to sleep much.

4

They were married in the little Presbyterian church which Grey attended now and then; and Mrs. Norcross came up from Sedalia and wept when the promises were being made, perhaps with relief at getting her daughter properly and safely wed.

After that they went to the Colorado Rockies for their honeymoon— which is par for the course in Jericho.

There were adjustments: she was not yet twenty, and she had never

really been in love, and the thought of the awesome physical intimacy
with a man was a little fearful in prospect. The first night, when he
slid under the sheets with her and his hard male body pressed against
her tender form, her heart thumped so that she thought it would stop
her breathing. But she had resolved to be courageous, and Jed really
was gentle and he soothed her and told her she would never be sorry
about it.

It was not so frightening once it began . . . far from frightening . . . not bad . . . it was good . . . very good . . . very, *very*
good . . .

And so sex became a part of her life, and she felt she had taken a
vast step in experience and knowledge, and justified herself and him
and their marriage, and she was dreamily happy in her bridehood.

By the time they returned to Jericho they were used to each other,
and they already had their little bywords and jokes and teasings. And
their first quarrel, too, about nothing, really—just the kind of a small
spat that is sometimes needful to clear a nerve-charged atmosphere.
They rented a house and Grey began housekeeping on the lower slope
of Tower Hill.

5

Tower Hill was the name of the only eminence in Jericho, and even
it was not very much of an eminence as hills go. Originally, in the
city's youth, it had been occupied by a water tower, and bore the name
of Water Tower Hill. But as the town grew, someone with a pro-
moter's imagination laid out an exclusive residential district on it; and
the standpipe was removed, giving way to a more modern and less
conspicuous city water supply system. Shortly thereafter the acclivity
dropped the utilitarian part of its name and became known simply as
Tower Hill, which had an aristocratic sound in keeping with the
large houses of wealthy people erected upon it.

From the front porch of her new home Grey could look up the
avenue and see at the top of the hill the mansions of the Jericho peer-
age, a collection of handsome and expensive residences, with shaved
lawns, spreading trees, blooming flower beds, and all the appurtenances
of wealth, including large cars, magnificent furniture, butlers, chauf-
feurs, maids, and gardeners. Overlooking the city's lesser dwellings
and business places, these prairie palaces stood around a circle made

by the avenue on top of Tower Hill, like haughty sentinels guarding against the encroachment of the plebeian or the upstart, in this Valhalla of the Jericho mighty.

Among the Tower Hill homes was a handsome white colonial structure with gleaming pillars, the residence of Mrs. Algeria Wedge, owner of the *Daily Clarion*. Once in a long while the fine-featured, white-haired old lady visited the Country Club, usually with her son Wistart and his wife. Since Jed liked golf and believed that playing the game was a help to his business, and since Grey liked to dance, he took her to the Country Club frequently; and so she saw Mrs. Wedge several times, rather from a distance.

Then chance, one evening at a pre-Christmas ball, placed the Rutledges at the same table with Mrs. Algeria Wedge; and Grey was so impressed by her, and so happy to be noticed by her, that she excused herself from two dances to sit with Mrs. Wedge, who no longer danced.

This did not escape Mrs. Wedge's attention. It was one of the interesting traits of that remarkable woman that she liked having young people about her. And since the youthful Mrs. Rutledge was neither gushy nor dull, nor yet wholly preoccupied with dress and household affairs; and especially since there was no mistaking the awed admiration in her eyes—rather handsome eyes they were, Mrs. Wedge conceded—nor her willingness to listen to an older, far wiser woman, it followed that they had a pleasant conversation.

"You're rather new to Jericho, aren't you, my dear?" Mrs. Wedge said to Grey.

"Yes, I just came here a few months ago. I was working for Jed—trying to sell real estate. I guess he felt sorry for me, I was so bad at it, so he married me."

Mrs. Wedge smiled. "I can imagine other reasons why a young man would want to marry a girl like you. So you gave up a career for a home?"

"It wasn't much of a career."

"I used the phrase in the light sense. We hear so much about careers and women these days. Even a stenographic job, or a stint as hostess in a tearoom, is erected into a 'career.' Members of our sex seem somehow impelled to give high-sounding names to prosaic things. But tell me, do you regret leaving the world of business, with whatever challenges it offers?"

"Not especially. Being a wife is quite a job in itself, I think."

The older woman's smile grew almost benignant. She was past seventy but she was handsome with her snow-white hair and serene face.

"It *is* quite a job," she said, "and not an easy one. I'm really glad to hear someone your age believe in it."

"I thought you might think otherwise, Mrs. Wedge—with your own wonderful career—which really *is* a career."

"My career, as you call it, was rather imposed on me. I was ambitious to be sure, but until my husband died, my ambitions all were for him."

"Oh . . . ?" Grey murmured.

"The world has changed, perhaps because of the cataclysm of two world wars, and with the change women have a new status. Sometimes I wonder if it is a healthy status. By that I mean, I wonder whether most women who work are really happy with the necessity of working. They think they are, but are they?"

"If they aren't, why do they do it?"

"Economics have much to do with it—living standards which we've grown to think are necessary, but may not be as necessary as we think. Even married girls today feel they have to work to eke out the family budget and pay for that new house or that new car, or perhaps just some new clothes. But there's another factor, also. It's become smart —the fashion—to be 'independent.' When a girl gets a job where she can earn a living, she thinks she is a self-determining unit—which she never really is."

"Why not, Mrs. Wedge?"

"Because she's a woman, and no woman is entirely complete by herself. We've heard a great deal in my lifetime about the emancipation of women. Well, women are pretty well emancipated today from almost everything except the most important thing of all."

Grey was intensely interested. "The most important thing?" she echoed.

"Their sex," said Mrs. Wedge. "A girl is a girl and a man is a man. Putting them in an office or behind a counter doesn't alter that inescapable fact. It's an overpowering and healthy feminine instinct to attract men, and a woman working among men can hardly help it that they are attracted to her. The working girl is exposed to her own desire for love, and since she associates freely with men, in a way which would have been deemed unconventional a generation or two ago, the opportunities offered by propinquity, the arch entangler, are increased."

"So they get married—like I did."

Now Mrs. Wedge's smile was gently pensive. "Some do. But too often it happens that the man to whom the girl turns cannot be hers conventionally. So we have the unconventional relationship; and regardless of all the pride she may have in being 'emancipated,' an unconventional love, not safeguarded by all the ancient laws and customs, is an unhappy love for her. I've known many cases, and I never knew one where it did not mean tragedy of some kind, for the girl at least."

"Then they ought to be wiser!"

"What's wisdom when the heart's involved? One can't blame them, the career girls and the men. Perhaps they're working together on a task of mutual interest, giving it their mutual effort and attention, becoming a team in their dealing with the public, or with correspondence, or with statistics, or with machinery, or with test tubes—or whatever it is. It's asking too much of nature that they remain entirely insensible of each other."

Grey drew a deep breath. "You think girls shouldn't work, Mrs. Wedge?"

"Oh, but they must! Women are in business to stay: somehow they must work out their problems, somehow society must help them. It's a transition period, I think, from the long centuries of the cloistered, protected sex, to this new freedom, to which none of us are entirely adjusted yet."

Mrs. Wedge paused and smiled at Grey's wide eyes.

"No, girls must work, and will work. I was only stating their problem—a problem more important to the girls than to the men, because in the relationship of the sexes it's so much more fateful to be a woman. And in stating it, I was trying to say to you that you're a very lucky girl yourself to win a husband and a home, and do it without a heartbreak."

Nine

The Pullman car moved slightly, a mere nudge which translated itself into a steady acceleration. Then the berth swayed and Grey heard the rattle of rail frogs squeezed beneath heavy wheels. From some far-off western place the train had come, picked up her car, and she was under way, lying warm in her lighted steel compartment while a locomotive up ahead hunted with its headlight through the winter night toward her distant destination.

Train movement, once it was steady and smooth on the level road-bed, often made her sleepy. But this night she found it difficult to summon slumber.

Names ran through her mind.

Wedge. Algeria Wedge. Wistart Wedge. Mary Agnes Wedge.

Odd, the way people tend to become like their names. Algeria had an exotic foreign sound, a feeling of mystery like a coiled serpent, fascinating but somehow perilous.

Wistart. Strange name. A family name no doubt, but not a masculine, aggressive name. It reminded Grey only of wisteria vines, clinging to some latticed support and trailing long sprays of lavender bloom.

Mary Agnes, however, sounded hard and canny as chrome.

Then there was Wedge, the family name. Solid, cleaving, intractable, driving.

Wedge—and the *Clarion*—and Cox's, Incorporated—and Tower Hill —and Jericho . . . names twisted like a strange pattern in the fabric of her life.

Grey did not forget that night at the Country Club, and her talk with Mrs. Algeria Wedge, and what followed. Not long after New Year's the Rutledges were invited to dinner at the top of Tower Hill.

It was a large surprise to Jed, who was more elated over it than was Grey. He was making headway in his business, was active in the Country Club, program director of Kiwanis, and a member of the Chamber of Commerce and the real estate board. All these were pegs in the

Jericho ladder, but an invitation to dine at the home of Mrs. Algeria Wedge was the summit of that ladder, and correspondingly gratifying to him.

Grey dressed in her blue taffeta, which made her hair look like soft gold and her gray eyes almost violet in the lamplight, and went with some misgivings to breathe the rarefied social atmosphere. But she need not have worried. After all, the "background" instilled in her by her mother was a splendid asset, and she found that she knew how to behave, and talk, and look among these people, as anywhere else. Afterward she remembered that dinner party—the gleaming napery, the silver and crystal, the dinner dresses, the attention she received particularly from the gentlemen, and the graciousness of the hostess —as a misty dream, a glimpse into a heaven of wealth and luxury and assured position, impossible, of course, ever to be equaled again.

But strangely enough it was equaled again, or at least approached. Among Mrs. Wedge's guests that night were her son Wistart and his wife, Mary Agnes. Grey had met Wistart Wedge once, before she was married, when he visited the Rutledge office on some kind of business while she was working there. She remembered him as diffident, or abstracted, and also that he seemed surprised when he asked her name and she answered "Grey"—surprised, that is, when he found it was her given name.

She did not suppose he would remember the occasion, but when he did remember it, and spoke of it, she was surprised and pleased.

She met other couples that evening, like Dr. and Mrs. Murray Clifton, and Mr. and Mrs. Charles Sinclair, Jr. With some awe she learned that Mary Agnes Wedge had been born Mary Agnes Cox, and owned Cox's, Incorporated, the big department store; and that Mrs. Clifton was the former Gilda Westcott, daughter of the great meat packer; and that the Charles Sinclairs were of a family who owned some of the most important business and residential property in the city— including, as it happened, the very house which the Rutledges then were renting.

Young Mrs. Rutledge was pretty and charming, and Jed Rutledge was acceptable, and Mrs. Algeria Wedge in a manner sponsored them. Hardly realizing what was happening, Grey found that they had been "taken up," and were often included in social affairs on Tower Hill.

Not all of them, of course. One did not expect that. And when one returned hospitality, since one's home was slightly less than palatial, it was at the Country Club. This had the disadvantage of being expensive, but one had to keep up appearances. Appearances, in fact, became a constant problem and requirement. The Rutledges felt impelled to acquire two cars, although they could have managed with one. Jed wanted Grey to dress well, and she did her best to comply, although the clothing bills sometimes ran high.

She had a gift for dress—a natural instinct and taste, almost of elegant witchery at times. She had the gift also of becoming her clothes as much as they became her: to the point that on one occasion she even wrung a compliment from Mary Agnes Wedge, who was notoriously chary of compliments to other women.

"How do you do it, pet?" said Mary Agnes with her critical little smile. "You look like an angel with a touch of sophistication—really, it's quite immoral, you know, for you to look that way!"

It was the highest sort of compliment Mary Agnes could give. Being "immoral"—theoretically, of course—was to her something to be arch about rather than to be condemned; although she herself lived a life of sufficient actual propriety, at least as far as Jericho knew.

Mary Agnes had a sharp edge to her tongue, a waspish quality which was especially evident in the way she treated her husband. By her, Grey noticed, and in fact by most of her crowd, Wistart Wedge was regarded as rather stupid, something of an oaf, a buffoon who had not the perception to see when he was snubbed or derided in public, or the fire to resent it if he did see it.

All the cool, superior assurance that poor Wistart lacked, Mary Agnes possessed, and she knew how to wither him when he very occasionally offered some futile opinion or half-burgeoned idea of his own.

"Oh, Wistart, don't be such an ass!" she would exclaim bitingly.

Or, in a tone of wearily amused indulgence, *"Please,* Wistart, you're not writing editorials now in your little newspaper."

Of course, Wistart did not write editorials for the *Clarion.* He had no writing ability, and this was well known to everyone, so it added a further subtle sting to his wife's sneer.

When Mary Agnes turned on him thus, Wistart invariably wilted. Sometimes Grey saw a weak look of self-defense come into his eyes; sometimes a mere appeal for quarter, but usually he simply retired as quickly as possible into the background without any particular show of feeling, like a big, awkward dog that has been kicked and told to lie down and cease making a nuisance of himself.

Most of the crowd accepted Mary Agnes' appraisal of her husband and treated him with a sort of humoring disregard. But Grey was not so sure about him, and she found that she did not like Mary Agnes very well.

2

She liked Mary Agnes still less as time went on.

One evening while they were at the Country Club, the crowd had stopped dancing to watch a championship prize fight on the television in the lounge.

Grey noticed Wistart sitting alone at a table with a highball glass, looking expressionlessly at nothing in particular. She was not much interested in pugilism, and just to be companionable she went and sat down at the table with him.

"Don't you want to see the fight?" she asked him.

"No. I guess not. The champ will win."

"I don't care about it either."

For a time they sat silent, then he said, "Can I get you a drink?"

"No, thank you." She was not, at the time, drinking much.

Another silence.

All at once she smiled at him. "Do you know the Rutledges are expecting an addition?"

Thinking back on it afterward, she really could not explain to herself why she imparted to him this piece of intimate news. It had not yet been announced to anyone; as a matter of fact, she had only just become sure of it herself. But somehow it was as if she wished to hold forth the little personal matter to him as an evidence of her interest and friendship.

"A baby?" he said. "When?"

"In June."

"That's wonderful." He pondered a moment. "Mother will be delighted, she thinks a great deal of you. Mary Agnes will be happy for you too——"

"Oh, you mustn't tell anyone!"

"Why not?"

"We're not ready to make the announcement yet——"

"You mean—nobody knows?"

"Just Jed and I—and now you."

"I'm the *first?*"

"Yes," she nodded. "Yes, you are."

She was surprised at how his face lit up. "Why," he said, "that's a compliment—a real high compliment! Thank you. I—I'd just like to tell you that—that I feel honored to be the first to know, and—well—thank you!"

It was almost touching. She thought that if a simple small thing like that had so much meaning to him he must be very starved for friendship and sympathy. His phlegmatic appearance was certainly misleading, she decided—he had feelings and emotions for which nobody credited him.

The crowd remained around the television, where the fight continued for the full fifteen rounds, and it gave Grey and Wistart time for quite a long talk: an odd, exploratory talk on her part. She discovered that he was shy, self-deprecating, and too humbly grateful to her for simply being nice to him; and it seemed too bad that he should be so.

By the time the televisioned fight was over, and the champion had won, and the crowd came back to get its glasses refilled and resume its dancing, Grey had formed some rather definite opinions about Wistart.

He was not witty or very amusing in the usual meaning of the words. But this, at least in part, was due to his painful lack of ease. She discovered in him a natural kindliness and eagerness for friendship, if he knew how to gain that friendship. And he had a continual habit, almost an obsession, of excusing in others what he would not excuse in himself; taking the blame for things, referring apologetically to his own awkwardness and lack of force, to which he attributed his failures and unhappiness.

Grey did not like to see that in a man. Any man. But she could begin to understand why it was so with Wistart. The reasons were twofold: the two women in his life.

His mother, Mrs. Algeria Wedge, was a woman of such brilliant gifts and strong determination that she could not help dominating everything with which she came in contact, though she did it with deceptive grace and charm. She had dedicated her life to the success

of the *Clarion* and rearing her fatherless son to take over its publication one day. Her mistake was inherent in her: so all-envelopingly did
she wrap her heart about him that she almost crushed the manhood
out of him. In her anxiety that he make no mistakes, she made every
decision for him. She was not cruel to him, at least consciously so: she
was just so unassailably right in everything concerning him that it was
hardly to be wondered that he came to feel his own inadequacy very
early. That feeling increased after he married Mary Agnes. Where his
mother was dominating in a kindly way, his wife domineered him in
a cruel way. Between the two of them, the wife and mother almost
deprived him of strength of character or the ability to make decisions.

In the weeks following, with this new understanding of him, Grey
came to feel profound pity for Wistart as she saw him beaten with
sarcasm and scorn, time after time, like a poor old horse beaten about
the head with a stick of firewood. He seemed to hold no resentment
against his wife for this, any more than the horse would resent the
one who was beating him; but staggered this way and that, almost
blindly, with a patient, pathetic sort of endurance and resignation.
When he was left alone at last, he was not even angry, but retreated
into himself, made himself as inconspicuous as possible, and somehow
lived on in an existence that must have been joyless and rather hopeless.

3

But if Wistart did not resent his treatment, Grey resented it; so
much so that the day came when she could not help taking up arms
for him.

"Oh, Mary Agnes!" she burst out after a particularly cruel gibe.
"Leave poor Wistart alone! Why are you so hard on him? *I* understand what he means——"

Mary Agnes turned on her a face like a white mask except for the
quizzical arch of her brows.

"My dear——" Her voice was cool, trickly. "*You* understand him
. . . ?"

She gave a little icy laugh, and it was joined by the others.

Grey felt humiliated, and she could see Jed across the room, and
knew Jed was blaming her for what he considered an impertinence—
what all these people, obviously, considered an impertinence. After all,

she told herself, Mary Agnes and her crowd were very important to the Jed Rutledges, and she supposed she should be grateful to Mary Agnes and refrain from intervening in something that assuredly was nothing of her affair. She remembered that Mary Agnes had put up her name in the Jericho Art Association, not *quite* as select as the Junior League, but good; and she tried to feel that she was in the wrong.

She even managed a smile, hoping that it looked like a smile beseeching forgiveness. But beneath the smile she was hating Mary Agnes. And she never forgot the episode; or forgave it.

Sometimes, even now, years later, she wondered if Mary Agnes remembered the episode also, and sometimes she was almost sure she did. Mary Agnes was sphinxlike. There was no telling what she was thinking.

Once in a long time Mary Agnes came into Grey Rutledge, Sportswear. She did not buy often: her things usually came from New York or Paris, or, in the case of ordinary staples of apparel, from her own store. But she was not above shopping now and then to pass the time, or perhaps out of curiosity . . . very sleek and confident, her eyes calm and arrogant, her long, sharp-tipped fingers touching everything with intimate disregard.

She had a way of entering the store as if she owned it and was rather contemptuous of it; a way of speaking to Grey with an aloof little smile, as if she only half remembered who she was but was making an effort to be gracious about it.

But Mary Agnes assumed that manner for her own reasons, and she was very much aware of Grey. Once Grey was conscious of a cold, very intent stare from her; her greenish eyes shining with the cruel expressiveness of a falcon's. It was startling: then instantly the look flicked away, and Mary Agnes left the store almost at once.

But the chilling stare had been there and Grey's mind was uneasy over it for days, wondering what inspired it. After a time she put it aside as something she must have taken for more than it was: growing out of a guilt she felt . . . guilt toward that very woman, not guilt of remorse, but guilt of fear.

Ten

Her berth tilted slightly as the train went around a smooth banked curve, and outside Grey heard the bell of a road-crossing signal: a clanging growing steadily louder as she approached it, then receding as she was past it until the sound was lost.

A bell. And a road. She thought of another bell and another road, which had marked fateful moments for her.

The other bell was a funeral bell, tolling.

In the June after the party at the Country Club, where she came to know and somewhat understand Wistart Wedge, two events of mighty importance in Grey's life occurred almost simultaneously.

Grey's baby was born in St. Matthew's Hospital. And the same night Mrs. Algeria Wedge died in her sleep at home.

Mrs. Wedge's death was quite unexpected. She had seemed in good health, and people commented on how strange it was that both she and the late senator had passed of heart attacks, though of a slightly different nature. And the same people also commented, quite philosophically, that a death like that was, after all, the best. It is a favorite pastime of people to discuss the best ways to die; when they are not discussing their own deaths.

The funeral at St. Albans Episcopal Church was one of the most notable in Jericho's history, the bishop coming all the way from Topeka to officiate. The front-page columns of the *Daily Clarion* were ruled in mourning black, and the story of the demise of Jericho's most notable woman occupied two of those columns on the first page and three columns more on the second, being a full account of her life and times, her achievements, benefactions, activities, interests, and personality. There also was a three-column portrait of Mrs. Wedge on the first page, and a full column of tributes, headed by a brief telegram from the White House itself, and including expressions of esteem and grief from the governor of the state, two senators, and many other personages notable in politics and business. All Jericho took a melancholy sort of pride in such post mortem notice of one of its own citizens.

Mrs. Wistart Wedge, who was in Honolulu at the time of her mother-in-law's death, flew half around the world to be present at the obsequies.

Grey did not attend the funeral, though she read everything about it. At the time she was in the hospital with her new baby—a little girl, tiny, helpless, beautiful. Betty Jean was the name Grey chose for her, an old-fashioned double name, charmingly simple and sweet, she thought. Jed rather fancied Shirley, or Lisa, or Dorothea, but he surrendered to his wife's wish, being far more interested in having her through her ordeal safely than he was either in the infant or the infant's name.

The nurse had left the baby with her, and Grey was alone with it, adoring its little red, wrinkled, sleeping face as it lay beside her in the hospital bed, when she heard the tolling of the distant bell in the tower of St. Albans. The sound gave her solemn thoughts. An old life ended and a new life begun almost at the same hour. A famous woman had concluded a brilliant career and a tiny girl, for whom the future was a dim secret, was entering on the long struggle which life is.

The thought of Algeria Wedge's death brought Grey even closer in spirit to her baby, because it underlined the miracle of life giving and made more precious the little spark of humanity in the curve of her arm, filling her with new hopes and wonders and fears for it.

Listening to the far, tolling bell that day, she felt for some reason almost a premonition of some terrible, unreasonable disaster.

That summer the heat set in early, and by the time she and Betty Jean were home from the hospital most of the people of the Tower Hill mansions had gone to cooler places—California, Bermuda, Colorado. So Grey saw few of her friends, which did not much matter to her since she was occupied with her baby; undergoing those three months of anxiety and confinement of first infancy; keeping feeding hours, bathing and changing and oiling the little body, taking the tiny thing to the doctor; suffering with the heat because she feared it was bad for the child rather than because of any discomfort to herself.

She really had little time even for Jed: and Jed was restless that summer. He was feeling the reaction, the disquiet, that comes to many a war veteran. There were days when he was deeply discouraged, when he wondered whether he had been wise to leave the peacetime military service, in which he could have kept his commission and perhaps won rapid promotion in the new Air Force. He had maintained his reserve flying commission and sometimes was gone for days on training flights, even trying out the new jet planes. This terrified Grey, because it seemed a needless risk of his life in machines which as yet hardly had been perfected enough to be trustworthy.

Then, one day, Jed came home with a new, great, grandiose plan. In a gesture of mighty optimism he took an option on a tract of farm land north of the city. Excitedly he told Grey that he was going to subdivide it himself. It would have to be done on a shoestring, but no matter. He would succeed: he was sure of it and his future.

What he proposed was a veterans' housing project, and his mood swung from discontent and depression to almost exaggerated enthusiasm. It concerned Grey that he already had begun counting his profits, because it meant he was trying to justify the depth to which he was plunging with his scheme. He was gone from home much as he put forth every effort to consummate his project, pulling wires, borrowing every cent he could raise, committing his entire future because, as he told Grey with eyes gleaming almost feverishly, once the lots began to sell and the small homes to go up the whole thing would carry itself and climb dizzily in value.

They would be rich . . . *rich* . . .

2

When the report came that day in August, she was so stunned that at first she did not accept it. But gradually she knew.

It was not a jet flight, which she had feared. Not even an airplane. It was a road . . . that other road.

A "jack rabbit driver," so they said—a reckless young fool with his girl in his car, showing off to her, who got out of his lane on the highway in his hurry to pass someone ahead with a flashy burst of speed.

Jed was alone in his automobile. The crash was head on and nobody survived. It occurred five miles out of Jericho, near the nascent housing project on which such hopes and plans had been built by him.

In its essence that was the grim story.

Grey bowed under the stunning blow of her grief and bewilderment. Hardly did she understand and hardly remember the days following

Jed's death. Her mother arrived from Missouri to help her through her time of great sorrow and take the care of the baby off her hands. There was the funeral, and there were the inevitable visitors. And there was the long period while lawyers sorted out the disheveled details of Jed Rutledge's business.

Grey had never known much about her husband's affairs. She knew they were not wealthy, but they lived well. Sometimes she worried about his borrowing so heavily for the real estate development. But the actual dread facts of her situation left her aghast.

Not only had Jed obligated himself disastrously for his land venture, but she discovered that for a considerable time they had been living far, far above their means. Keeping up with the Tower Hill crowd had cost money, but Jed thought it worth while since he believed it was good business, and she had never questioned him. After his death it was made evident that everything they possessed, to the very furniture of their rented home, was mortgaged to the utmost limit of possibility. He had borrowed until he could get no further loans from any source, and even allowed his small insurance to lapse for its cash value. Furthermore, bills were coming in, unpaid bills, some of them months old, from grocers, clothing stores, automobile financing companies, everywhere . . .

Grey was made to understand there was nothing left: she and her baby were paupers.

Worn, silent, inarticulate, helpless to assuage her daughter's pain and fear, Mrs. Norcross patiently did little odd jobs around the house, working in the background, caring for Betty Jean, seeking silently to extend comfort and sympathy. But she could not help Grey in her most terrible problem.

A Mr. Cronin, representing the Sinclairs as a rental agent, called. He inquired if Grey expected to keep the house, and when she told him she could not afford its rental, he said, very kindly she thought, not to be in any hurry. It would not be necessary to give possession of the house for a month, he added, and she could take her time moving her things.

Moving her things! *Where?*

She could not return to Sedalia with her baby. Her mother had barely enough to subsist on; she worried, saved, and scrimped as it was to make ends meet. But where else?

In those days there were times when Grey thought that tiny Betty Jean, now growing round and rosy, with great, wide questioning eyes, sensed the dreadful trouble in the air. The child slept fitfully and sometimes wailed at night as if with nightmares. So tightly would she be locked in the terror of her sleep that it often was difficult to waken her; and when she did wake she clung desperately to her mother for a long time, seeming to fear to let slumber steal up on her again. That her baby should suffer this terror, not understood but felt, was a further source of anguish to Grey.

In utter despair and exhaustion one day she lay on the bed beside Betty Jean, and the tears welled up unbidden and trickled from under her closed eyelids. While she was thus silently weeping, a tiny hand touched her cheek like the fluttering wing of some miniature bird, and opening her eyes, she saw her child regarding her almost as if she understood.

She reached out her arms and held her baby to her breast, feeling for her a despairing love akin to madness, beyond a mother's normal passion, growing out of her hopelessness and fear; something fierce and almost dangerous, like that of a tigress for her cub.

"Oh, baby . . . darling," she sobbed. "I'd do anything—*anything*—for you . . . if only I knew *what* . . ."

3

Gilda Clifton was Dr. Murray Clifton's wife, and they belonged to the Tower Hill set. But Gilda was different from Mary Agnes and others of that chrome-plated crowd. She was dark-eyed and dark-haired, with two children of her own, and to Grey she seemed beautiful and refined and deepened, as if some tragedy in her life had left her with kindness and sadness, thoughtful and sweet.

Always Gilda had been sincerely friendly toward Grey, and one day she called up on the telephone.

"I thought I'd tell you of something, dear," she said, then hesitated as if not sure whether she should go on. "You know Mrs. Butford? She's lost her secretary." And then apologetically, "I'm not suggesting . . . unless you think you'd be interested."

"Oh, but I *am* interested," said Grey, quite eagerly.

"Well, then—Mrs. Sloane, her former secretary, was with her about ten years," Gilda went on. "She resigned this week. I understand it's because she has a brother in Omaha who's a widower and ill and she feels she must go and care for him. Mrs. Butford is quite at a loss without her and anxious to find someone suitable to take her place."

Grey had seen the former secretary, Mrs. Sloane . . . a pale background adumbration, attending her mistress with a rather fluttering concern, bringing a knitted stole for the old shoulders, or a stool for the old feet, or directing the servants with the tea things. What her first name was, Grey never learned. She dismissed her as one of those colorless personalities who would always be lost in any kind of gathering.

"I've met Mrs. Butford, of course," she told Gilda. "When the Art Association had tea at her house that time——"

Gilda Clifton gave a little laugh. "She appears to be quite formidable, but I think it's only her manner. She's old, and perhaps a little set in her ways, but it ought not be too difficult to take that into account. I don't imagine the work is too demanding, and you might find it interesting to handle affairs for a woman like Mrs. Butford, who has many activities in spite of her age."

"Yes, I think so, too," said Grey. "If she'd want me," she added.

"Anyway, you might see her. Why not make an appointment with her?"

"I will! And—thank you, Gilda—I can't tell you——"

"Don't thank me, dear. I just happened to hear about it and thought —it might at least be a stopgap for you."

It was like Gilda Clifton. Grey could have gone on her knees to her in gratitude. If she could get that position with Mrs. Butford! At the moment it seemed to her a solution of her most terrifying difficulties, temporarily at least.

Somehow she must earn money; and her only business experience was selling real estate, in which she had rather failed. But being private secretary to a wealthy woman was an occupation in which she might use the very kind of training she had received . . . the politenesses, and the niceties, and the graces of the girl's college and her mother's insistence on "background."

So she dispatched a note to Mrs. Butford, and having received a formal summons to come for an interview, left the baby with her mother and took a bus to the Butford house.

4

As she told Gilda Clifton, she had been in the Butford mansion once and knew something of its history. It was built by Simon Bolivar Butford, a portly and piratical business buccaneer, with a bloodsucking instinct for money-making, who was deceased these many years, but not especially regretted. By profiteering in World War I, and pyramiding those profits during the Florida land boom by selling mangrove swamps as choice building sites to innocent human sheep from the hinterlands—dealing always unethically and sometimes skating very close to the edge of the law—he became Jericho's first millionaire.

In 1927, a year after the Miami hurricane which wrecked finally the Florida land boom, Simon Bolivar Butford, who had defrauded hundreds out of their life's savings in that flimsy semi-tropical bubble, built his Jericho house on grounds occupying a full city block. Those grounds he surrounded by a cast-iron fence, reinforced with hedges to keep interlopers at a distance; and he beautified the premises with flower beds and lawns and trees and drives, and a fountain with a grossly fat stone cupid imported from Italy. In the midst of this rose his mansion, four stories of red tapestry brick, white stone facings, and slate roofs, with a brick garage combined with servants' quarters in the rear. The fact that he died less than twelve months after his house was completed did not prevent it from being a monument to him and to his money; and also to his tastes, which were ostentatious, old-fashioned, and ornate.

That warm day when Grey paid her visit to the house, Simon Bolivar Butford had been in his grave more than twenty years, and in the intense heat of late summer the grounds looked dusty, the grass withered in spite of the sprinklers that were playing, the fountain with the stone cupid out of repair and dry.

Nevertheless, the huge old house itself still was imposing, and as she stood before the bronze and glass doors which everyone knew had come from the Tiffany studios, Grey smoothed down the simple black dress of her new widowhood, and felt her heart beating a little wildly when she pressed the bell.

The door swung open and a squat, elderly woman in a black uniform and white cap and apron regarded her with small blue eyes set in a red face.

"Yah?" said the woman with a broad German accent.

"I'm Mrs. Rutledge," said Grey. "I have an appointment with Mrs. Butford."

"Oh, yah. Coom in."

Grey entered a vestibule entirely of white marble, with wide marble stairs leading up to an archway and two sets of narrower marble steps, one on either side, leading down to a lower floor. All that marble was somehow chilling and she felt depressed.

Up the central stairs waddled the German woman, and Grey followed her through the arch and into a large hall paneled with mahogany. She had been there before. This second floor, she knew, was used only for social affairs. To her left two doors opened, one to the music room and the other to the drawing room. At the right was the entrance to the grand dining room. A somewhat jarring note in this archaic grandeur was the iron cage of a self-operating elevator at the far end of the hall. Mrs. Butford was old and found it difficult to climb stairs, and the lift had been installed for her convenience.

The German maid led the way to the open door of the drawing room.

"Missis R-r-rutledge, moddom," she said.

5

Almost timidly Grey went in alone.

The room was ornate, as was everything in this house: walls of mulberry tapestry with woodwork and high ceiling painted an old-ivory hue, and hangings at the windows of mulberry shade. There were huge chandeliers with glass prisms, a fireplace of glass mosaic, and mahogany furniture, old-fashioned and heavily late Victorian.

In a wide armchair, as if on a throne, sat Mrs. Simon Bolivar Butford, stroking a wheezing Pekingese dog which lay in her ample lap.

She was old. Grey had seen her before, but now she was struck more forcibly by the impression of age in her—unbending, determined age. The silk dress of dark purple, with heavy lace on bosom and sleeves, too elaborate for this hour, seemed funereal; and the feeling was enhanced by her dead-white face, without expression, and her hair, arranged rigidly in set waves, which should have been dead white also, but had been given a bluish tint by the hairdresser. The face once had been plump, but the plumpness had fallen away with age and now lay in ugly folds and wrinkles about her jowls. She was a heavy woman, especially in the lower part of her body, and when she walked she used a gold-headed ivory cane, which was always beside her chair. Her feet rested on a mulberry-upholstered footstool. On her plump fingers rings sparked and glittered, and bracelets clinked on her wrists as she stroked the lap dog. About her sagging throat hung a heavy necklace of amethysts and gold links.

"Good afternoon, Mrs. Butford," said Grey, attempting a smile.

For what seemed a very long time the old woman continued to stroke the lap dog, surveying her coldly without replying. Grey's smile faded.

"You're Mrs. Rutledge?" she said at last. Her voice had a curious rustling quality as if it came from behind a heavy curtain.

"Yes," said Grey.

"We have met before, I am given to understand?"

"I was here—with the Art Association," said Grey hesitantly.

The blue-white head inclined slightly. "I cannot be expected to remember them all. I do not see as well as I once did." Mrs. Butford screwed up her mouth, sucking at her dentures, a habit with her.

"No," Grey said. "Of course not."

She stood before the old woman holding her handbag tensely in both hands. She was not invited to sit down, and remained standing nervously throughout the interview.

For a time Mrs. Butford continued to peer at her with eyes that were tufted above with white hairs and surrounded by an interlacing network of wrinkles, a look almost reptilian; while without cessation the jeweled flabby hand stroked the lap dog, a continuous motion, hypnotic in its effect.

"You are a candidate for a position as my secretary?" said the old rustling voice at last.

"I—well—it was suggested——"

"Are you, or aren't you?" rasped Mrs. Butford so sharply that Grey almost gasped.

"Yes. Yes, I am," she gulped.

The blue-white head bent toward her. "What is your age, Mrs. Rutledge?"

"Twenty-three."

"You are somewhat young. I do not like unnecessary frivolity. My secretary must at all times behave with proper decorum." The old woman scraped her throat harshly. "But since you were a member of the Jericho Art Association, I will assume that you are a lady."

Grey noticed the peculiar use of the past tense, as if she were no longer a member of the Art Association, although her dues were paid up to the end of the year.

"I try to be a lady," she said diffidently.

Mrs. Butford's myopic eyes peered grimly. "Very well. I shall acquaint you with the duties of the position we are discussing. I do not require arduous labors, but I do require what the name of the service implies—careful attention to detail, attendance to correspondence, making arrangements under my direction for such matters as social affairs and travel, personal presence when I desire it, the efficient performance of such other tasks as I shall give you to do, willingness and good humor."

"Is—shorthand or typing a requirement?" Grey asked.

"No. I do not consider the typewriter an implement of polite correspondence. You will write my letters by pen. The example of chirography in your note asking me for this appointment indicates that you write a clear and neat, if undistinguished, hand, sufficiently good for secretarial purposes."

She paused, and Grey waited.

"I travel at certain seasons. For the winter season, to Washington. In the spring I frequently go to Bar Harbor. Sometimes in the summer I spend a few weeks in Beverly Hills. You will, of course, accompany me."

Grey said nothing. The thought that her baby would be a problem to be considered during these travelings away from home aroused new perplexities. But she could think about that when it came time.

"You will receive a salary in addition to your living," Mrs. Butford continued. "I paid Mrs. Sloane, my recent secretary, one hundred dollars a month. She was able to save almost all of it, so that when she left me after ten years she had quite a little nest egg besides enjoying throughout all that time a genteel existence."

Grey nodded. The salary was not much, but as Mrs. Butford pointed out, it was practically all clear.

"Do you wish to undertake the task under these conditions?" asked the old woman.

"Yes. I would like to do so——"

"Very well. We will make the experiment. Now, young woman, when can you come?"

"Why—when you need me, I suppose."

"I shall need you at once." The blue-white head nodded sternly. "You will live in this house. Your sleeping room will be next to mine, in case I should require your services at any time, and especially because I like to be read to after I retire to bed——"

"Live *here?*" gasped Grey. "But—what about my baby, Mrs. Butford? If our quarters were so near to yours, I'm afraid she might disturb you——"

The old woman threw herself angrily back in her chair. Her hand, which had never ceased stroking the lap dog, became rigid. Presently the animal lifted its supercilious nose and nudged at her jeweled fingers. The hand resumed its stroking, the dog relapsed into wheezing content, but the white bristles of Mrs. Butford's brows remained bent in a scowl.

"A child?" she said. "Nobody informed me of this child! There can be no child in this house, Mrs. Rutledge. I cannot abide children. Young children, untrained children, especially. I fear this makes the matter impossible."

Grey was stunned. This was something she had not even considered. All her hopes, her hardly formulated little plans for the future, were suddenly ruined. She clutched her handbag more tightly. A timid idea suggested itself to her.

"Perhaps," she said tentatively, "I can find someone to care for my baby during the daytime, while I'm at work, and see her at night in my off hours——"

"There are no hours, Mrs. Rutledge! We do not watch clocks around here. As I told you, this would be your home—your life. Do you understand?"

Not to see Betty Jean even at night? Grey could hardly conceive of it.

"I would like—could you give me—a little time to think it over——?" she began.

"I will remind you," said Mrs. Butford coldly, "that there are numerous well-qualified persons available for this position. If you cannot make up your mind——"

"Oh, but I don't mean that! Of course——" Grey seemed caught in a whirlpool of desperation. The present was her great emergency, and this seemed the only thing available to her.

"I'd like to take the position, Mrs. Butford," she said humbly. "But I must have three or four days' time."

"For what purpose?"

"My mother is with me at present. I'm going to ask her to take my little girl for me, and I'd like to go with them to Sedalia, where my mother lives, to make arrangements——"

The wrinkled white face grew rigid. "That is out of the question! Three or four days is utterly out of the question, Mrs. Rutledge. I have an important social event—a musicale—scheduled for Thursday next. I can give you two days, no more!"

"But how can I pack, and go to Missouri, and return——?"

"I suggest, Mrs. Rutledge, that your mother may be perfectly capable of taking the child back alone. It would save time."

For a moment Grey struggled within herself. She wanted to cry out at the threatening old woman, to tell her to take her job and fly to the nethermost regions of hell with it. But she fought back the impulse.

"Well, Mrs. Rutledge?" the cold voice asked.

No way out of it. Grey swallowed. "I'll do it the way you suggest, Mrs. Butford."

"Very well." The old woman seemed triumphant. "Report to me before dinner on the day after tomorrow. At six o'clock."

Helpless and numb, with a sense of being treated cruelly and unjustly, and able to do nothing about it, Grey nodded.

The blue-white head inclined once more. "Then I will excuse you now. Bear this in mind: I do not brook lateness in appointments."

6

It was the beginning of what seemed, to Grey, an eon of misery, of serfdom, of humiliation. She discovered at once that Mrs. Butford was an inflexible tyrant in her household, that she was vain to the point of mania, and stupid and unread, yet with a streak of cunning.

Routine was rigid. Breakfast was exactly at eight each morning, and

Mrs. Butford invariably had fruit, a bran mush with cream and sugar which she thought important for her bowels, Postum because she considered coffee too stimulating, and heavily buttered toast with orange marmalade. Grey breakfasted with her in the sitting room on the third floor, which was connected with the sleeping suite, where all meals were served except when guests were present.

"Mrs. Rutledge," said the old woman the first morning, "you're not eating your bran mush."

"I don't really care for it," said Grey. She had seen Betty Jean and her mother off on the train the afternoon before, and she was worried about them. Mrs. Norcross seemed so tired already, with the new burden which she assumed patiently, and the baby somehow looked pathetic and deserted. Grey had little appetite this morning.

"Eat it," said Mrs. Butford. "It will regulate you. Everyone needs regulation."

Grey recognized it as an order—a very definite command. She must force herself to swallow the unappetizing stuff or risk her employer's displeasure. She obeyed, hating her own abjectness but unable to see how she could do otherwise . . . so much depended on keeping Mrs. Butford in good humor.

The bran mush episode was a piece with a gross pattern of domination which seemed an obsession, almost a passion with Mrs. Butford. Sometimes it seemed to Grey that the old woman had a planned purpose to break down, and keep broken down, every will in the household.

With Grey not even the most personal matters were allowed to pass uncommented upon, sometimes outrageously.

"Mrs. Rutledge, go take some of that lipstick off your mouth," Mrs. Butford said the very first day. "I have no objection to a slight and discreet tinting of the lips, but this trend of women nowadays to smear their mouths so heavily is disgusting. I want none of it around me."

So Grey went to her room and took off her lipstick, and then, gazing at her face, thought it looked too pale after her ordinary make-up and applied a "discreet" touch of the color again, hoping with tears in her eyes that it would pass inspection.

When she returned, Mrs. Butford glowered disapprovingly, but evidently decided to accept the compromise without comment at this time.

Other matters, however, did come in for comment. She criticized Grey's wardrobe, and Grey found herself confined to wearing only the drabbest of her dresses and almost no jewelry at all. Cigarettes were absolutely forbidden, even in her own room, and Mrs. Butford had a hound's nose for a smell of tobacco smoke.

These invasions of her private rights seemed intolerable, but there was something worse.

In Mrs. Butford's mind the world was divided into classes: the privileged, who were worthy of meeting socially Mrs. Simon Bolivar Butford; and the rest of humanity, beneath notice, or to be noticed only because they served the Mrs. Simon Bolivar Butfords of this world. The touchstone by which everyone was judged was money; or if not money, official position of the higher ranks; or, occasionally, family connection, particularly a claim to aristocratic European blood.

The old woman had "assumed" in their first interview that Grey was a "lady," and from this Grey supposed that her status was that of a companion and perhaps even a friend, if one could be one's employer's friend. At least she was quite ready to be Mrs. Butford's loyal companion and take a more than required interest in her welfare.

But the second morning Grey heard Mrs. Butford snap her fingers. A moment later the old woman exclaimed, "Mrs. Rutledge! I snapped my fingers!"

"Yes, I heard you," said Grey in surprise. "I thought you were calling your little dog."

"I never call Carlo by snapping my fingers!" Mrs. Butford glowered. "When I snap my fingers, I want your attention—at once!"

To have fingers arrogantly snapped at her—when it was not even done to that pampered, wheezing, supercilious, revolting little lap dog!

Tears of anger and humiliation started in Grey's eyes.

Then she remembered herself and fought back the tears. Very definitely she had been made to understand that she was in the servant class in this house, along with the old German maid, the cook, the houseman and housekeeper, and the chauffeur and yardman. Her pride was painfully lacerated and rebellion swelled in her, but she could do nothing. Betty Jean and her mother depended on the money she must send to them; and she could think of no other employment, at least at present.

She made a painful but necessary decision. However unpalatable, however humiliating it was to a girl with pride, she had entered into this servitude and she must make the best of it as long as it lasted.

She found that her servant status meant something else upon which she had not counted: she was not to attempt to maintain any of her friendships with persons she knew, who were now "above her." Not even with someone as kind and affectionate as Gilda Clifton. She had a "place," a subservient position which she must keep. Mrs. Butford would not think of allowing any of her servants to be on familiar terms with anyone whom she recognized socially: in some obscure manner she appeared to think it diminished her own standing. Yet part of this also was a natural cruelty.

7

This streak of cruelty, sometimes apparently motiveless and the uglier for that reason, was illustrated by an episode one day.

After breakfast each morning Mrs. Butford required the reading of the newspapers, not only the *Clarion,* but papers from New York and Washington. Headlines first.

"Not that," she would say if the item did not interest her, and most items did not. But she had an uncanny instinct for pouncing on obscure little articles on back pages.

"Read that," she ordered when Grey casually read a small one-line headline over a one-paragraph story in the *Clarion.*

The Bemis Music Company, said the item, was announcing a closing out sale of pianos, television sets, radios, records, and musical instruments at greatly reduced prices. To Grey the item seemed too unimportant to merit notice, a blurb inserted by the newspaper in connection with one of its advertisements.

But to Mrs. Butford it possessed immediate significance.

"Bankruptcy!" she gloated. "I knew it! Willard Bemis never had a head for business." She seemed to derive intense satisfaction out of the news of a failure. Then her thoughts took a different turn.

"And to think that I've had them here, in this house, as my guests!" she said.

Her face grew harsh, as if the unfortunate Bemis couple had committed a treachery by allowing her to invite them.

"That wife of his," she went on with growing rancor, "putting on airs and making a career—an absolute career, mind you—out of the piddling fact that she sang on a radio program one winter ten years ago! Insufferable, the way she brought that up constantly in conversation. I never liked the woman. An instinct told me something was wrong with them. False fronts, both of them. Fourflushers, as Mr. Butford used to say. He had no use for pretenders, and neither do I. Well, they've found their true place—nowhere!"

This last she uttered with malicious triumph. For a moment she paused, her lips screwed up as she sucked her dentures, then another thought came.

"Why," she exclaimed, "that woman has a book of *mine* this very minute! One of my leather-bound classics, which she borrowed two weeks ago from my library! Mrs. Rutledge, write a letter!"

Grey went to the escritoire, took a sheet of stationery with Mrs. Butford's name engraved at the top, dipped her pen in the inkwell, and prepared to write. Her mistress dictated:

"Mrs. Bemis: Kindly return the copy of Thackeray you borrowed. It belongs to our set, which you do not. Mrs. Simon Bolivar Butford."

Grey wrote, and she could hardly believe it. Surely the old woman did not seriously intend to send this causeless insult to someone already bitterly beset by misfortune.

But Mrs. Butford cackled with glee. "Clever, isn't it? The play on words. Oh, *she'll* writhe, I promise you! That will show her where she stands in no uncertain language! Send it at once."

This stabbing a person whose only offense was that her husband had been unfortunate in business was rather typical of her employer, Grey was discovering—a curious unwholesome streak of venom, the wish to wound others, perhaps growing out of some hidden resentment in her own subconscious mind.

Very soon after Mrs. Butford's note was sent, the book she demanded was returned with a very abject little letter of apology from Mrs. Bemis. To this Mrs. Butford did not deign to reply. As far as she was concerned, the incident was closed and Mrs. Bemis sentenced to oblivion.

Eleven

I

Mrs. Butford was a creature of mysterious, almost eerie qualities at times; a composition of moods and instincts perverse, often hateful. Yet Grey, who by nature tried to understand and sympathize with others, sometimes thought her, unpleasant as she was, almost pathetic.

She had a curious preference for purples in her garb; almost everything she wore was purple, or had strong purplish decorative touches. Some people said unkindly that this was an indication of her snobbish arrogance, pointing out that purple was the imperial color of the ancients. Others held that she affected purple because she believed, though erroneously, that it became her odd bloodless complexion.

Grey came to have another theory: purple was the color of mourning.

Mourning for what? Something she had lost, or never possessed? Youth? Love?

During her husband's life, Grey had been told, Mrs. Butford was submerged, almost ignored by the dominating and self-assertive Simon Bolivar Butford. At times she was brutally humiliated by him, and may have hated him often. But when he died she seemed to think that all that was most significant in her existence died with him; she had been so completely contingent on him, his thoughts, his wishes.

All that Simon Bolivar Butford ever really had been interested in was his wealth, and when he left it to her she came to feel about it as he had. She discovered the power of money and the relishing sense of importance it gave her. And in her widowhood she had set out without really thinking it through, but rather as a blind reaching instinct, to be all her husband was, remembering his ways, his selfishness, his lack of consideration, and his greed, and imitating them.

In this, a stupid woman's evolution out of resentments and yet abject admiration toward the man who ruled her like a slave, was something with which Grey almost could sympathize; except that Mrs. Butford grafted on her imitations of her husband certain added traits of her own with which sympathy was impossible. The unnecessary cruelty to Mrs. Bemis was only one instance of many cruelties in which the old woman seemed to find a psychic satisfaction. Her vanity also was her own quality; and an insistence that she be attended constantly, waited on, and ceaselessly flattered was a poisonous outgrowth of this trait.

Grey was expected to praise her jewelry, which she wore constantly and in bad taste, her house, her dress, her blue-white hair in which she took pride, even her disgusting and overfat little lap dog. Sometimes Grey could hardly force the words, but she made herself give this slavish flattery because it was her chief protection against periods of sulking and fits of spiteful anger on Mrs. Butford's part.

Indolent herself, the old woman could not bear to see anyone around her idle; and she devoted much of her attention to inventing tasks, often useless, to keep her servants busy. The silver, of which there was much, must all be polished twice a week. The cars were washed daily. Every room must be kept free from a fleck of dust and the kitchen spotless. Each day, accompanied by Grey, Mrs. Butford made a slow, cane-tapping, angry inspection of the house, going from floor to floor by the elevator, and woe to the employee who was found delinquent in even the smallest duty.

All the servants in the house feared her, and Grey sometimes wondered why they did not leave her. They seemed to be held in her employment by a mysterious bond which Grey found difficulty in understanding. In her own case, it was sheer economics. She desperately needed the work and its small salary; and Mrs. Butford saw to it that she was kept too busy from morning to night ever to seek a position outside, keeping watch on her almost like a predatory animal with a cornered prey.

Toward one creature only she was the opposite of cruel: Carlo, the wheezing, fat lap dog. Constantly she fondled and pampered the little beast, fed it choice bits from her table, even allowed it to sleep on her bed with her. Though she complained about every other expense and berated her staff continually for wastefulness, she never questioned any bill from the veterinary, the dog manicurist, the hair thinner, or anyone else performing a service for Carlo. Grey sometimes wondered if here was an indication of something else in the old woman: desire, perhaps, to be loved, which she would not permit in any human being out of distrust; or even desire, very latent and subconscious, for a motherhood she had never known, an instinct transferred to the dog as if it were a child.

But though Grey understood or felt some of these things, they did not make her life any easier. Days all were alike. Everything moved by schedule. They rose at half after seven, and from that moment Grey was kept occupied all the livelong day. She ate her meals with her mistress, read to her, brought her things, wrote her letters, gave her directions to the other servants, arranged flowers, listened to her constant bragging, helped her change her costume two or three times a day, and did a hundred other tasks, all to the maddening clack of a carping tongue.

But even all this was not enough. Mrs. Butford was a hypochondriac, taking pills and medicines, and forever complaining of ailments, some of which, due to her age, were undoubtedly genuine.

"My back aches—I must have arthritis," she moaned one day.

She looked over at Grey. "Mrs. Sloane used to massage me when I suffered so."

The implication was obvious. "If you want, I'd be glad to try," Grey said.

"Very well, Mrs. Rutledge. Wait. Let me get my dress off, and my corset. Here—help me with this." Mrs. Butford began eagerly to remove her outer garments to enjoy the full pleasure of the massage.

Grey shrank from it, finding it distasteful, but Mrs. Butford, looking like a fat old reptile, stretched herself face down on her bed, and the girl bent over her to rub and knead the loose folds of her aged body. It was as unpleasant as she feared. A stale, fetid odor came up from the torpid figure. The rolls of fat were flabby and rubbery. The skin was a grayish unpleasant color, mottled in places with brownish spots. But Grey performed her task as well as she could.

Long before Mrs. Butford felt she had been sufficiently relieved, the girl's arms and hands ached with weariness. At times the old woman gave little moans and grunts of sensuous pleasure, and at other times she lifted her head to give directions that a new area of her vast expanse of hide be rubbed.

Thus began a new routine. Each day thereafter there must be a massage, sometimes two or three times a day; not always the back, but the hips, the arms, the vast flabby thighs and calves, even the feet and the nape of the neck. Grey grew to dread Mrs. Butford's smirk and her "Well, it's time now for my little rubdown."

She found the old-age smell which became evident when the body was unclothed almost sickening at times, and the old-age look of flabby, wrinkled, and folded flesh disgusting. It was, furthermore, no part of the usual duties of a personal secretary to perform bodily services of this nature, particularly when they were not really necessary, but only an indulgence.

She became sure in her mind, at last, that Mrs. Butford's reason for demanding the massages was that they were a new form of abasement for Grey, besides being one more task to keep her eternally occupied.

2

Mrs. Butford had a grand house in the late-Victorian style and she gave in it occasional grand entertainments, also somewhat Victorian in mood. One of Grey's first tasks was to manage the details of the musicale which her employer had mentioned in their opening interview.

The design of the house was such that elaborate functions apparently were its ordained reason for being. On the night of the musicale the guests—black tie specified—were met at the door by the German maid and directed down the marble steps to the "lower" floor. They found themselves in a great room in English oak, with walls festooned with large framed photographs of notables whom either Mrs. Butford or her late husband had known. Two presidents—Harding and the second Roosevelt—eight governors, five senators, and other assorted dignitaries were in this gallery.

Two billiard tables, covered and never used since Simon Bolivar Butford's death, occupied the center of the floor. From this central hall opened dressing rooms where guests left their coats and wraps. There also was a smoking room, in English oak and red leather, with a large fireplace, a Korean money chest, Hindu and Japanese medieval arms, three or four ugly Tibetan devil masks, and other Oriental curios, the fruit of a Butford tour in Asia. The gentlemen idled in the smoking room while their ladies powdered their noses before going upstairs, but there was no smoking, since it was understood that Mrs. Butford, who did not use tobacco, disapproved of its use by others.

This arrangement of rooms occupied one half of the lower floor.

The other half, walled off from it, was occupied by the kitchen, pantries, and the furnace room, from the last of which a door, kept locked, opened into the smoking room.

When they went upstairs the guests were ushered into the music room on the second floor, which was ostentatious like the rest of the house, in ivory tints, with a grand piano of cassian walnut highlighted with gold tints, and a forty-thousand-dollar pipe organ with an echo effect from the top floor. The music room was thrown together with the drawing room by opening the wide connecting doors. Near the piano, on an easel, was a life-sized oil painting of the late Simon Bolivar Butford, the *embonpoint* and choleric complexion symptomatic of his death—which was from apoplexy—being evident. It was customary for guests to speak of this portrait to Mrs. Butford so that Mrs. Butford could tell them it had cost eight thousand dollars.

During the serving of the "collation" and the musical program that followed, Grey stood near her mistress. This was necessary, because the old woman had bad eyes and her vanity forbade her wearing glasses; and an equally bad memory, so that her secretary constantly prompted her in a whisper as to the names of people who approached to speak to her. If any guests spoke to Grey herself, however, she tried to appear not to notice them, and if she was forced to do so, acknowledged their greeting only with a smile. For the "suitability" of "keeping her place" had been strongly enjoined upon her.

It was noticeable that the women guests seemed quite to understand and readily accept this arrangement, especially Mary Agnes Wedge, who spoke to Grey exactly as if she were a maid when she asked for her wrap at the end of the evening.

At least one of the men, however, did not understand it.

Somehow, as the guests were leaving, Wistart Wedge cornered Grey.

"What's the matter, Grey?" he demanded. "Aren't you speaking to your old friends any more?"

"Mrs. Butford does not desire members of her staff to be recognized socially by her guests," said Grey primly.

She left him staring after her.

All in all, it was a difficult evening, and a wearying one, as well as a rather dull one, Grey thought. Yet the following day the *Clarion* devoted a gushing article to the affair, which occupied the chief space on the society page. Some of the more inspired paragraphs of this journalistic effort, which Grey read aloud to her mistress, will give a general idea of the whole:

"Mrs. Simon Bolivar Butford, in an exquisite gown of purple lace and wearing the diamond necklace given her by her husband, the late industrialist and empire builder, was as usual the most charming and gracious of hostesses to the exclusive assemblage of guests at her palatial mansion on Forest Boulevard.

"For a time there was the hum of pleasant conversation as the guests spent a delightful half hour eating delicious hot dishes in the rooms which were filled with light from pink candles in crystal and silver holders, and with the perfume of American Beauty and La France roses in silver vases. The serving table was covered with a cloth of rare old filet lace and Italian cutwork.

"After the collation Mme. Josefina Cateri-Callopini, soprano, and Oscar Emil Streugen, at the organ and piano, both brought from Chicago by Mrs. Butford especially for this occasion, rendered a magnificent program.

"At the end of the evening, which seemed all too short, the guests took leave of Mrs. Butford, thanking her for her gracious hospitality and receiving the smile of the hostess, so well known to all, as a happy memory of her charming personality, which impresses everyone who has ever met her."

There was a good deal more in this line, and the program of music and the full list of guests were given. As Grey finished reading the article, Mrs. Butford gave her smile "so well known to all," which, it must be confessed, was a rather crocodilian grin of gratified vanity, and nodded in approval.

But Grey was left wondering. Remembering the stiff, dull affair which nobody seemed really to enjoy, she found it hard to understand how a newspaper could be so extravagantly, almost servilely laudatory about it.

3

Though she was busied with these matters from waking to sleeping, Grey had one continuous thought: she missed her baby.

As the weeks passed, the girl's longing, instead of abating, only seemed to grow, until it was a constant pain which she felt sometimes with wonder as to how much sorer it could become. Motherhood was mysteriously greater than she had imagined: an emotion belonging to deeper and more subjective significances than any other relationship . . . having to do with the spirit and the soul. Her child was like another self, or perhaps even more truly a bit of her own being, which she loved more than she loved herself. She and her tiny daughter had been a natural unit, unbreakable except at the cost of pain and unhappiness to both. To be deprived of her baby had caused her bitter suffering already, and she feared her little girl might be suffering more than even she was.

At times she tried to picture in her mind what Betty Jean must look like now, and she found she could not do it, because the child would have changed so greatly already. An almost irresistible yearning to see her baby grew daily like a hunger of the body, and at the same time fear began to oppress her: suppose her baby, her own baby, would forget her . . . had forgotten her already! Such a little thing, how could she be expected to remember?

Daily she tried to find time to write a little note to her mother, and Mrs. Norcross dutifully kept her informed once a week in her old-fashioned letters, telling her that Betty Jean was getting along well, and seemed to like her new home, and was gaining weight, and learning new tricks and ways: she could hold her own cup of milk now.

But this was not enough, not nearly enough to appease the longing in Grey, and by October it had become so desperate that she screwed up her courage to ask a weekend leave from her duties.

At once she saw that Mrs. Butford was not pleased. "A weekend off? For what reason?"

"I want to see my little girl."

"The child is ill?"

"No—at least I hope not—not that I've heard. But she's lonesome for me——"

"A childish whim! We must be adult, Mrs. Rutledge. It's impossible for me to spare you now. My fall reception is coming up——"

"But I'm lonesome for my baby!" Grey almost wailed.

The girl's pleading cry would have melted most persons, but Mrs. Butford only grew the more grim.

"Impossible," she repeated. "My reception requires elaborate preparations. You must begin on the invitations at once."

"I haven't seen my daughter in three months!" Grey flared.

Mrs. Butford knew perfectly well how to quell an outburst of this kind. For a full minute she sat silent, staring coldly.

"Never let me hear you raise your voice to me like that again," she said at last, her white tufted brows drawn down. "I wonder if you realize, Mrs. Rutledge, how lucky you are? A pauper. A complete pauper. And I've given you shelter and an occupation which any woman in your circumstances should envy. And for this I've asked very little. Only courtesy and willingness to do the simple and small tasks assigned, and perhaps a little appreciation of my many kindnesses." Then her voice raised raspingly. "But do not think, Mrs. Rutledge, that you are essential here! If you are not satisfied, speak. Speak out any time! There are plenty who would be only too glad to fill your place. Do you know that?"

Grey stood mute, head hanging, knowing how impossible it was to answer, situated as she was.

"Now go!" commanded Mrs. Butford. "Go to your room, young woman, and think of all I've done for you! And try, if it is in you, to be a little grateful. And a little humble. When you've thought it out, you may come back to me."

Dismissed like a naughty and unreasonable child, almost unbearably humiliated, Grey ran to her room, threw herself on her bed, and allowed the tears to flow wildly. Her thoughts were wild also.

She could not go on like this. Anything was better . . . she would get another job . . . in a laundry, or a restaurant, anywhere. If she only had time to hunt for work. If . . . if she only had the *time*.

Gradually hopelessness took the place of anger. She felt as if she were choked by a creeping, entwining tangle of inescapable circumstances. Not even her own child could she call her own: this was how a slave must have felt in the terrible days of human chattelism.

In this new spirit of blank despair she rose after a time. Her weeping had ceased. She composed herself, bathed her eyes, and sat staring out of the window, numb with misery.

Some time later Minna Horst, the German maid, knocked at the door with word that Mrs. Butford wished to see her. Grey found her mistress sitting and fondling her lap dog as usual.

"I've just had the cutest idea!" she exclaimed to Grey, chuckling with self-approval. "You'll love it, Mrs. Rutledge."

It was evident that she had forgotten or dismissed as trivial the scene of a short time before. Grey stood waiting to hear what magnificent conception she had to announce.

"I was listening to the radio," Mrs. Butford smirked, "and I heard one of the commentators—he's a favorite of mine, he's so sound in his political doctrines—talking about his dog. His *dog*—imagine! A wonderful talk, over the air! I was so touched by his love for his dog that it made me think of my own little Carlo." The wrinkled old face grinned coyly down at the small beast in her lap. "Then I had my inspiration! I'm going to write a letter from *my* dog to *his!* Did you ever hear anything so clever and unusual? Get your pen and let me think what to say. When we finish the letter, dear little Carlo is going to sign it his own precious self. Can you guess how?"

Grey shook her head.

"That's the best part of it! My Carlo will sign it with his own cute little paddy-waddy, of course! We'll press his foot on an ink pad and then on the paper, à la fingerprint!" The old woman quaked with mirth at her own consummate cleverness. "Isn't that wonderful, Mrs. Rutledge?"

Grey said yes, that it was. But she wondered bitterly about a mind that could go into such sentimental fatuity over an animal yet contained no sympathy for real human unhappiness.

"Oh, it just came over me—the *Clarion* must know about this!" exclaimed Mrs. Butford, her idea gaining sweep. "Get Wistart Wedge on the phone for me."

Now fully carried away by the brilliance of her own conception, Mrs. Butford took the telephone after Grey had the connection for her.

"Wistart, dear boy?" she said with a gay chortle. "This is Mrs. Simon Bolivar Butford. I've had the most *wonderful* inspiration! I *had* to let you know!"

Gushingly she went over the details of the dog-to-dog epistle.

At the end she said, "I thought you'd like to print a story about it, something like this: 'Mrs. Simon Bolivar Butford, one of Jericho's and Washington's wealthiest and most sought-after society leaders, was so impressed when a radio commentator talked over the air about his dog that she sat right down and wrote a letter from her dog to his.' You know—something like that. You can finish it yourself. Isn't it the cleverest idea? I thought you'd think so. What's that? A copy of the letter itself? An excellent idea. As soon as I get it written. Who? Mrs. Rutledge? Yes, I'll send her down to deliver it to you personally, and then you can give her the address of the radio man so I can mail the letter to him. Hee-hee! So cute, isn't it?"

4

The elms were becoming bare of leaves, and in many front yards little heaps of the dried leaves were burning, the smoke adding to the blue haze of the Indian summer day. In the black Butford town car Grey was driven down to the Clarion Building by Larsen, the silent thin chauffeur, and found her way to the reception room of the publisher's office.

A thin-faced elderly secretary, wearing large, thick-lensed glasses, took her name and disappeared within. A moment later she was back.

"Mr. Wedge will see you at once," she said.

Entering the office, Grey saw Wistart standing behind his big rosewood desk.

"Hello," he said, smiling. "It's good to see you, Grey. Honest, it is. Won't you please sit down and tell me about yourself?"

Genuine warmth was in his voice.

She perched in one of the large leather chairs and he seated himself once more behind his desk.

"I brought this from Mrs. Butford," she said, extending the envelope. "And I'm to get the address——"

"Yes, I know. The commentator. I've had it looked up. Here it is." He gave her a slip of paper, which she put in her handbag, and began to read the dog-to-dog epistle she had given him.

"Mrs. Butford was the author of this?" he asked, looking up.

"Yes. She dictated it."

"I knew *you'd* never be guilty of such twaddle. It's almost enough to make one gag."

"Then you're not going to publish it?"

"Oh, but I certainly am! Every word. Exactly as it's written."

"But if it's so bad—why?"

"For one thing, Mrs. Butford wants it published, and the *Clarion's* policy is to keep her happy. Ever wonder why everybody, including this newspaper, makes so much over her?"

"I'll confess I've been puzzled at times—but I suppose it's because she's so rich and socially prominent——"

"It's because she's so rich—and has no close relatives." Wistart grinned. "We hope that when she dies she'll leave her money to Jericho, so we try to keep her happy with Jericho."

"I see." Grey nodded; it explained some things to her.

"But there's another reason why I'm going to print this," Wistart went on. "I'll have to tell you I had a little plot. I specifically asked Mrs. Butford to send you to me with it, and I must justify that request."

"I can't imagine why you asked to have me bring it—especially——"

"Just because I wanted to talk with you, Grey. It's a long time since we talked together. I miss it. I hope you don't think it's ridiculous of me—but I prize your friendship, very much indeed."

The simple statement, made half apologetically yet sincerely, so struck her that she could not think of any reply.

For a moment there was silence while he wrote a note on a blue memorandum pad and summoned his secretary with a buzzer.

"Miss Finch," he said, "take this note and copy to the city desk. Tell them to run the letter verbatim with a suitable lead on page one."

Silently Grey sat gazing at him. Here in his office Wistart presented a different aspect to her; his diffidence and social awkwardness were not evident in this place of business. She thought to herself that if some of his acquaintances, even his wife, could see him thus, they might feel a somewhat higher respect for him.

When Miss Finch was gone, she said, "What did you want to talk about?"

He did not answer directly. For a moment he looked at her, unsmiling. Then he said, "It's a pretty heavy strain, isn't it?"

"I'm not sure I know what you mean, Mr. Wedge——"

"Let's get one thing straightened out," he interrupted. "You said something to me at the musicale, and there's been a lot of talk—women, of course, gossip about such things—and I understand that it's one of the rather odd requirements of your present job that you can have no contacts or associations with your old friends. Now it happens to burn me up. Can you explain what it's all about?"

"I—suppose it's just Mrs. Butford's way—her notion of how things should be done properly——"

"*Properly?* It's a damnable and shocking piece of snobbery! Listen to me, Grey—your friends are still your friends—and I hope you consider me one of them. Please don't carry that old tyrant's orders right into my own office, will you? Here at least can't we just call each other by our first names, as we've always done?"

She looked down at her hands folded in her lap, confused and yet warmed by a feeling of gratitude.

"I know you're unhappy," he went on.

She still fenced. "I hoped I didn't look too—different. Maybe it's because Mrs. Butford doesn't approve of very much make-up——"

"It's not that. You look brave and nice, like you always have. But you're too subdued—something makes me feel you're in trouble. I'm sure it's Mrs. Butford."

She had not expected so much discernment in him, and she felt a little like tears, so that she did not trust herself to speak.

"I hoped you *did* still consider me your friend," he said quietly after a moment.

"Oh, I do!" she cried. "Wistart, of course I do—I—I know it! And I'm . . . grateful for it."

His face did not change. "Then I'm going back to my first question. It *is* a strain working for Mrs. Butford, isn't it?"

"Not too bad," she said tonelessly.

"Tell me about it, Grey."

At that moment she felt that she liked Wistart more than she had ever liked him before. She found suddenly that she wanted to confide in him.

"Perhaps it's my own fault," she began. "But sometimes—I just feel I can't go on with it much longer. She—she seems so demanding—and—well—hard to please at times——"

He nodded.

She felt a pang of conscience. "Really, Wistart, I feel sorry for her. It isn't her fault—not all of it. She's so dependent on others. She has to be doing something, has to be occupied. She can't sit still, you know, because she really has nothing substantial in her personal life to keep her busy when she's alone. She doesn't read, she doesn't sew, she just can't be alone. She wants attention, she must be waited on all the time. I don't think she's intentionally cruel or selfish—perhaps she's just childish——"

"She allows you no life of your own?"

"Well—nobody has much who works for Mrs. Butford."

"But *you*—I'm interested in you."

"All right, me. It's true, I guess, that I'm at her beck and call all the time . . . sometimes even in the night she calls me out of my sleep if she's wakeful. I'm another pair of feet, you see, another pair of hands, another pair of eyes for her—I have to be with her every minute."

"What on earth does she keep you busy at all the time?"

"Well—a hundred things. And if I have any leisure, I read to her. I spend hours every day reading to her."

"What kind of things does she have you read?"

"Well, the newspapers, of course. She keeps scrapbooks—or rather I do—whole volumes of leather-bound scrapbooks, with every item that has ever been printed about her. Aside from the newspapers, anything that isn't heavy—I get magazines like *Reader's Digest* and *Coronet* and read from them."

"It must be terribly boring for you."

"No, not really. I like to read."

"But you *don't* like to complain, do you? Well, there's some deeper reason for your unhappiness than even this constant and exhausting attendance on Mrs. Butford."

She hesitated. "It's personal. It can't be helped."

"Tell me about it."

Her gray eyes suddenly were wide and beautiful with pain.

"Wistart . . . I want to see my baby."

"Why can't you have your baby with you?" He frowned. "It's a big house."

"Oh, Mrs. Butford wouldn't stand for that!"

"She dislikes children?"

"I wouldn't want to say such a thing about her——"

"But she can't stand them around her."

"Oh, Wistart, I don't know——"

"But I do!" His scowl deepened. "She doesn't want anything to take attention away from her. I know her—selfish, self-centered, demanding everything and giving as little as she can—that's our Mrs. Simon Bolivar Butford! How can you stand her?"

"She's my employer," Grey said simply.

"Where's your baby now?"

"With my mother—in Missouri. I send money to take care of her. I haven't seen her for three months . . . and she's so little——" Her voice caught. "I'm sorry, Wistart. I don't know why I should be burdening you . . . but you asked."

She mustered a smile for him and it touched his heart. For a few minutes he was silent, then he said, "Have you noticed that Mrs. Butford never attends church?"

"Yes," said Grey, "and it's surprising, too, she seems so pious."

"I'll tell you a story about that, because it may explain some things to you," Wistart said. "The late Simon Bolivar Butford belonged to a generation of robber barons whose methods of getting rich would land them in the penitentiary today. They were gay old dogs, most of them, and the ones who were at the top rather considered that a man wasn't a success in life until he had a mistress and could afford to maintain her in luxury in her own establishment. Old Butford had his mistress—Gertrude Carling, her name was. I understand she was quite beautiful in a Lillian Russell sort of way. She was a grass widow in the days when it wasn't exactly respectable to be a grass widow. He built her a house over toward Tower Hill. Among her various other talents, Mrs. Carling had a soprano voice, and she liked to sing in a church choir. So Simon Bolivar Butford built her a church. It's still standing—the Community Church on Bratton Avenue."

"I've been there," she said. "It's a beautiful little church."

"He built it, or most of it, out of his own pocket, partly to show he could do something big in the line of public benefactions, but chiefly, so the story goes, in order that his mistress wouldn't have to walk more than half a block on Sundays to sing in the choir."

Grey looked at him incredulously. "Are you joking?"

"Not at all. It was one of the open secrets of the day."

"What happened to—Mrs. Carling?"

"Sold her house and left Jericho after old Butford's death. Went to Florida, I understand. He left her well fixed financially."

"Do you suppose Mrs. Butford ever found out?"

"Yes, she knew all right—all the time it was going on."

"What did she do?"

"Nothing. Old Simon Bolivar Butford was a pretty hell-for-leather guy. He dominated everything and everybody, especially her. She never, by word or sign, gave anyone the notion that she had an inkling of it. But she never entered the portals of that church, or any other church, before or since her husband's death. It was her rebellion."

Grey drew a deep breath. "Poor old thing! I'm sorrier for her than ever."

"She had compensations," said Wistart. "Wealth and respectability. And, after all, it wasn't so uncommon in those days for rich men to have their lights o' love. Mistress-ship is an ancient and not entirely dishonored institution in the past history of this world, you know."

"I still feel sorry for her."

"I don't." His seriousness deepened. "Whatever crosses Mrs. Butford may have borne have been considerably lightened by the fact that she's always had more money than she knew what to do with—to buy clothes and furs and jewels, and travel and give costly parties, and live in luxury and indolence, and have someone like you, whose little finger is worth more than her whole fat carcass, to wait on her, baby her, be bullied by her, and build up her vanities—just as if she'd done something worth while instead of being a stupid parasite throughout her whole worthless existence!"

Grey was surprised by Wistart's heat. And she could not help knowing it was occasioned by personal feeling which, in some curious unformed way, was involved with herself. She felt almost abashed.

He leaned back, the blaze fading from his light eyes.

"Why don't you leave her, Grey?" he asked.

She spread her hands helplessly. "How can I? I've nothing else I can do."

"Do you know why her other employees stay with her?"

"No."

"Minna Horst, the maid, has worked for her ever since the days of old Simon Bolivar Butford. She wouldn't know where else to go. The houseman and housekeeper—what's their name——?"

"Hajek—Jan and Carla Hajek. They're married."

"I know. They're D.P.'s from Czechoslovakia. Came over after the war, and they're obligated to stay with her, or think they are, since she took them in and guaranteed them a job. Larsen, the chauffeur, is a parolee from prison—convicted of embezzling a few thousand dollars from a bank where he worked, although I heard that someone else, higher up, actually got the money——"

"I didn't know this," she gasped.

"Those people *have* to stay with her. She likes it that way, because she holds a whip hand over them. But you—*you* don't have to stay."

"I haven't time to hunt a job, and besides, I don't know how to do anything——"

"You know one thing. Better than almost anyone I know."

"What's that?"

"How to wear clothes—and buy them. I couldn't help notice it, as I've noticed it many times, when you came into the office just now. May I ask what that outfit you have on cost you?"

"This suit? It's old—why—thirty-nine ninety-five—at a sale a year ago." Again she felt embarrassed. She had worn the suit the previous fall . . . before she was a widow.

"On you," he said, "it looks as if you'd bought it from some exclusive New York shop for a couple of hundred just because of your taste and the way you wear it."

"Thank you," she murmured, dropping her eyes.

"Did you ever think of turning your instinct for clothes into something profitable?"

"You mean working in a dress shop?"

"Not clerking. I mean going into business for yourself."

She stared. "That takes money, doesn't it? Look, Wistart, this is *me* —Grey Rutledge—the girl that doesn't have a dime."

"We're friends, aren't we?"

"Y-e-e-es."

"Grey, you've done things for me that I couldn't begin to express— maybe you didn't even realize it."

"You were always nice to me, too," she said in a low voice.

"Friends ought to help friends, if there's a way to do it."

She sat silent, her eyes lowered.

"I have a little idea," he said. "There's a business building, a small one—the Boyd Building, across the street from Cox's. I happen to own it. The offices upstairs are occupied by a dentist and a law firm— reliable and stable. There are two spaces on the street level. Soule's Drug is next the intersection. It's an old established company, too, and reliable. But the other's the Model Dress Shop—that cheap-john little place."

"I've been in the Model."

"They're closing out. Cheap goods, phony 'bargains,' and all that stuff, with the big department store across the street looking right down their throats. Bound to fail."

She nodded, wondering where this was leading.

"Do you happen to know a good tenant for that building?" he asked.

"No."

"I do. I'd like *you* to open a shop there——"

"*I?*" She was utterly astounded. "Why, Wistart—I haven't the finances—it's impossible——" She almost gulped at the thought of it.

"Finances could be arranged."

"Or the experience."

"You have something better—instinct and taste."

"Why would I succeed when the people there now are failing?"

"Because you'd do just the opposite—be a little exclusive, offer people what they wouldn't get anywhere else."

Grey closed her eyes and gave her a head a little shake. When she opened them again, she said, "Wistart, I think this is about the sweetest thing anybody ever said to me—but I can't do it."

"Why?"

"Because, for one reason, I wouldn't dare risk somebody else's money——"

"I'm not trying to do you any favor, Grey. It's all selfish on my part —I'm thinking of my property, and getting a good tenant for it would increase its value. You could do it, I believe in you."

She rose. "Thank you. I can't thank you enough. But no. It's impossible."

"Think it over, anyway, won't you?"

She went out and he stood up at his desk, looking after her.

On the way back to Mrs. Butford's she felt almost tearfully tender toward him, because she thought all at once how alike they were— beaten by life, though in different ways. A kinship between them . . . and he had held a hand out to her. She could not take the hand he offered, but she would always be grateful to him for it.

Twelve

She said it was impossible, and she meant it. But she could not keep herself from thinking about it.

In spite of her, it kept coming back and back to her in the weeks that followed. She thought of it while she slaved on the details of Mrs. Butford's ostentatious fall dinner-reception, while she wrote Mrs. Butford's long and inane letters, while she sent "articles" about Mrs. Butford to the society editor of the *Clarion,* while she pasted clippings concerning Mrs. Butford's doings in the leather-bound scrapbooks, while she read interminable hours the drivel Mrs. Butford preferred to hear, while she did a hundred other things, some of them distasteful, like kneading Mrs. Butford's flabby body in the massages which her mistress demanded, and especially when she lay in her own bed of nights, sleepless . . . wishing, wishing . . .

In November, Mrs. Butford prepared to make her annual trip to Washington. It was a regular part of her schedule. She reserved a suite of rooms in one of the large hotels of the capital and held receptions for stuffy diplomats and politicians. She had been doing it for years, blandly shifting her social allegiances with the shifts in political complexion of Congress and the White House, and this, she informed Grey, was because she was "above petty politics."

That morning the house was bustling and Grey had been packing the trunks under Mrs. Butford's eye, listening to unnecessary directions on everything, even to the folding of each individual garment, when the mail was brought up by the German maid.

Mrs. Butford took the letters and went through them, peering at each closely, as if to decipher its contents through its envelope. Household bills, which she recognized by the open-faced envelopes, she placed on a small table at her side. Personal mail went into her wide lap. One letter she glanced at several times, looking over at Grey as if unwilling to have her stop working.

Finally she said, "Here's one for you, Mrs. Rutledge."

Grey took it, recognizing her mother's handwriting. There had been nothing in Mrs. Norcross' previous letters to cause her concern, but when she looked at this one she felt a sudden premonition. So much so that she did not read it at once, but placed it on the escritoire and went on silently with her packing.

After a time she found courage to open it. Her mother wrote:

Dear Daughter: I would have written you sooner, but have been much occupied with Betty Jean. The child has been ill & pining. I had in Dr. Wright for her & it cost me $5.00, which we can ill afford. He said she was suffering from a virus going around & did not think it was anything much to be worried about in itself, but said the baby seemed run down & not doing well & inquired if she was perhaps lonely for her mother. I told him of the circumstances & he said of course that could not be helped, but sometimes a little child, even if unable to express itself, feels a sense of loss & he thought if you might be able to visit her even for a day or two it might help her condition. Of course, this may not be possible & Betty Jean is eating a little better now, although not as well as I would like to see. I know the railroad fare is expensive also, but I merely suggest it in case it is feasible, since the Dr. mentioned it, for I know our dear little girl would love to see her mother . . .

There was more, but this was the important part. It left Grey silent and sick, so that at lunch she had no appetite.

"What's the matter with you?" Mrs. Butford asked.

"My little girl's ill," said Grey.

"Seriously?"

"I don't know. I hope not dangerously. But she's pining for me, my mother writes. Mrs. Butford—could you let me have a few days——?"

Instantly the old woman was on the alert to scotch such a suggestion. "What are you asking? You know very well, Mrs. Rutledge, how ridiculous such an idea is when we're on the point of leaving for Washington for the season! Ridiculous? It's ungrateful and thoughtless of you even to ask!" Mrs. Butford glared, the white hairs above her eyes bristling. "We have little enough time as it is. Certainly I can't let you go. You know that as well as I do. I'm surprised at you—especially when, even by your own saying, there is no emergency!"

Grey said nothing. To debate the matter would be worse than useless. She folded her napkin and looked silently out of the window.

"For pity's sake, don't sulk, Mrs. Rutledge!" Mrs. Butford said peevishly. "Come, straighten your face. We have work to do. There's still the large brown wardrobe trunk." She paused a moment, sucking her dentures and thinking. "That reminds me, I've not yet made a public announcement of this. There should be something in the *Clarion* about my annual winter junket to the capital. I shall prepare a little article about it."

Thereupon, she dictated to Grey the following:

"CLEAR THE SOCIAL DECKS.

"Mrs. Simon Bolivar Butford, one of the most notable social figures in Jericho and Washington, will leave next week for the nation's capital, where she has an elaborate suite in the ultra-fashionable Mayflower Hotel.

"Mrs. Butford is a popular and much sought-after figure in Washington society, and many will be the gay and notable affairs at which she will be an honored guest. She will, in turn as usual, be hostess at many brilliant and memorable receptions and dinners, among which are her annual banquet for the diplomatic heads of the various foreign governments represented at Washington and her series of morning concerts and luncheons, which are justly celebrated and at which the elite of Washington society will be present."

Grey copied it carefully, not forgetting any of the self-adulatory adjectives.

She gave a glance over at her mistress. "Mrs. Butford——"

"What is it?"

"Don't you think it might be well for me to take this down for you personally? I mean, it's so important, it ought to be delivered to Mr. Wedge himself so there can be no slip-up——"

The old woman considered for a moment. Then, to Grey's relief, she nodded. "Yes, this is, as you say, most important. Take it down—but be sure to hurry back. We have much to do."

2

This time Wistart had not requested that she bring the article to him. He did not even know she was bringing it. Perhaps he did not want to see her again. But she at the moment wanted very much to see him.

When she entered his office, he seemed surprised. But he took the envelope, on which she had written *Mr. Wistart Wedge, the Jericho Daily Clarion,* opened it, and read the article in it through.

"So you're leaving for Washington," he said.

"Yes."

He glanced up. "You don't sound very enthusiastic about it."

She remained silent and did not look at him.

"Grey," he said, "something's wrong, isn't it?"

She looked at him then almost desperately. He was her friend, she was sure of it. More important, he was a man. A woman should have some man in whom she could place reliance. She was tired of carrying the burdens of her troubles alone. At the moment she thought his broad, somewhat pink face with its pale blue eyes and thinning blond hair was good to look at and comforting, if only because it was male, and she had grown up all her life believing that what was male was strong and re-sourceful and dependable.

"Oh, Wistart!" she cried. "Something *is* wrong, and if you want—if you *really* want to know—I'll tell you!"

It came out then, all in a rush, the things she had not told him before: how unbearable was her concern and longing for her baby, how be-wildered she was with what life had done to her.

Tears came, too.

Wistart said nothing, but he rose and closed his office door. He had that terror of feminine emotion that affects most men, and he came back and sat silently but rather anxiously, hoping she would regain her composure. At last she dabbed her eyes with a handkerchief and faced him again, rigid and shaken.

"I'm s-sorry," she told him with a pathetic attempt at a smile.

Looking at her, he thought that her eyes, gray with their tear-damp-ened lashes, were more beautiful than any he had ever seen. But his face did not change.

"I'm glad you told me all this," he said. "Do you know what I'm going to advise you? Go see your little girl—right away—regardless."

"I wish I could—how I wish it," she said dully. "But Mrs. But-ford——"

"To hell with Mrs. Butford!"

He rose from his desk, walked over to a window, and stared out scowling. Then he came back and stood before her, looking down at her bent head.

"You've got to leave her, Grey," he said. "I can't stand it, seeing you so unhappy all the time. No, don't interrupt me—you've got to make a decision. And I'm going to help you whether you want it or not."

She looked up at him, waiting, and he regarded her very gravely.

"I'd do it for an ordinary friend," he went on. "And you're not ordinary—to me you're special. You've got to notify Mrs. Butford that you're through. Right away. Without any notice, even, because the old bitch doesn't deserve it, the way she's treated you, and your baby needs you—right now, not a week or two weeks from now. Will you do it?"

She was somewhat dazed, almost appalled. "I—I don't know—I can't——"

"If you don't want to do it, I'll do it for you."

"No. Oh no—if I did that, I'd have to tell her myself. I'd want to do it —kindly. But——"

"Now listen to me. Remember our talk about the store? I'm serious about it. Are you game, Grey, to go into business—with me as a sort of partner—at least until you get well on your feet? Would you object to that?"

"Having you as a partner, Wistart? Of course I'd not object to it. And I'd be game—but——"

He thought she misunderstood him. "You ought to know me by now, Grey. This is on the up-and-up. For friendship, just friendship. Nothing, absolutely nothing, more than that——"

"I know it," she said faintly. "That wasn't what I meant. But what if I shouldn't make a go of a store like that—you'd lose——"

"You won't fail. And if you did, I'd take an income tax loss that might even come in handy. From your standpoint there's nothing you *could* lose, is there? Starting from nothing—you can't take anything from nothing. And you've got everything to win—you'd be your own boss again, have your own home, your baby back with you——"

It was too tempting, it sounded like a dream, she could hardly grasp it, but she wanted it so badly . . .

She nodded, gulping.

"It's settled then," he said. "You take the train tonight for Sedalia. No, better—fly. I'll get the plane reservation for you. Is it a deal?"

Her moment of great decision. She rose and stood before him, her face rigid, almost white.

"It's . . . a deal," she said.

"Then I think you'd better go now—and tell Mrs. Butford. I believe your plane leaves about nine o'clock tonight."

"Yes. I will." She felt frightened, shaken, as she began to realize fully the revolutionary thing that was happening in her life.

"Don't let Mrs. Butford back you down," he told her. "Don't tell her—or anyone else—about my part in this. Don't tell her *anything!* She'll try to find out about your plans, but let her guess. It'll do her good. After you get back from Sedalia, we'll sit down and go over things. Above all, don't worry—don't worry about anything."

She gazed up at him almost tearfully. She believed in him, his assurance, the help he would give her. All at once her fears left her. And with this the thought of his kindness and unselfish friendship, all hidden under his self-assumed stolidity, swept over her in a wave of feeling.

"Oh, Wistart, darling!" she said in a small fluttering voice no louder than a whisper. "You're so wonderful to me. So good—so kind and good —I'll never, *never* be able to pay you back for what you've done for me——"

All at once he felt her arms about his neck in a little flurried hug, her head for a moment against his shoulder, and then for a breathless instant a kiss, the warm living softness of her lips against his.

Stupidly he stood still, his arms at his sides, not even offering to return the quick embrace she had given him, and she went out, almost as if she were fleeing.

3

Grey was hardly mindful of what she had just done. Her quick little embrace, her kiss, her words of endearment were no more than an impulsive expression of pure gratitude and affection, feminine currency really innocent as tokens of a feeling wholehearted and sincere. Already she had almost forgotten it as she passed Miss Finch in the reception room and hurried out into the hall—with some shrinking of heart as she considered the probably unhappy scene when she made her announcement to Mrs. Butford.

But Wistart, alone in his office, had gone white. For a long minute he stood just where she left him as if unable to move; or as if he were trying to believe what had just happened, yet really not believing it.

After a time he seemed to rouse himself. He went into his office washroom and looked into the mirror. On his lips was a little smear of red. Lipstick. Yes, her lips had been there. He hesitated, then with a dampened towel removed the small mark so exquisitely personal and feminine. He would carry the lipstick mark in his heart, but it was not for the eyes of such as Miss Finch.

Still in a daze he returned to his desk and mechanically picked up one of the letters on it. The sheet of paper trembled in his hand and he could not read it, did not wish to read it. He replaced it on the desk and sank into his chair, staring for some time unseeingly into space.

"God," he said at last. *"God . . ."*

He was profoundly shaken, too shaken to do any more work. Presently he left the office without saying where he was going and took a long, lonely ride in his car, far out along the concrete ribbons that spanned the Kansas plains beyond the city. The day was calm, a beautiful late-autumn day, for once windless and with soft haze on the horizons. In the cornfields the fodder, brown and sere, stood in conical shocks like Indian tepees. A white farmhouse, pretty in its nest of leafless trees, sent up a straight thread of smoke from its chimney toward the fleckless blue above. But Wistart did not notice the day, or the fields, or the house, or the sky. He saw a face, and a pair of gray eyes wonderfully moving with their tear-dampened lashes, and knew still that moment of surprise, of wonder, when he felt the soft sweetness of her lips.

Just before dinner he returned to his home. Mary Agnes was gone—for the winter—to California this year. He was glad she was not home, because he did not think this evening he could have borne her caustic tongue. At dinner he hardly spoke to Suey, who waited on the table. Very early that night he went to bed, but it was long before he found sleep.

Next morning there was a letter in his office mail marked *Personal:*

Dear Wistart: I'm here at the airport, and it's 9 o'clock at night, and I'm waiting for my plane which is due to take off in half an hour, so I'm going to put this in the mailbox and hope you get it tomorrow.

Oh, Wistart, how can I tell you what you've done for me? I feel like a new person, altogether, entirely different, happier than I've been for so long I've forgotten when.

Mrs. Butford took my resignation rather hard. It seemed to surprise her that I would leave her, since she knows my financial condition. At first she wouldn't accept it and tried to get me to reconsider by using endearing words and telling me how much I meant to her, even offering me a better salary. But I promised you, so I just told her I meant it and I was going. Then she tried to find out what I was going to do, asking me all sorts of questions, but I gave her no satisfaction. So at last she became upset and said some rather unpleasant things.

It was really very distressing, for she had counted on me to go to Washington with her, but I really don't feel badly about it, because I have gotten her all ready for her trip and she can easily get somebody to replace me—after all, there are plenty who would like to go to Washington who would probably be better for her than I.

I kept my temper and didn't tell her my baby was more important to me than her social season, and took my things and left. Now I've burned my bridges behind me and look forward only to the future. As soon as I return to Jericho I'll get in touch with you, and I hope I have the ability to do for you what you expect of me.

Oh, Wistart, I could never say what I'd like in a letter, but only this, I never had a friend like you in all my life, and thank you, thank you, thank you!

Devotedly, Grey.

He read the letter over twice. It had the effect of clearing his head for it seemed to phrase exactly something he had been in danger of forgetting—he was Grey's *friend*, nothing more. Anything beyond that was unthinkable. Even if Grey felt toward him as he did toward her—which he was certain she did not—she would never permit such an emotion to grow in her toward a man who was married. She was too decent, too high-minded and clean.

So, rather patiently, as he had condemned himself to other unhappinesses before, he now condemned himself to bury his feelings, seek to forget them if possible, and be that good friend to her that she believed him to be.

By the time Grey returned from Sedalia, he was able to converse with her quite naturally. The opening of the little store, with the name plate *Grey Rutledge, Sportswear,* occasioned some comment but not much, for after all, there were many small shops of about the same caliber in the city. Since she had just been home, it was presumed some family money had been placed in the enterprise. She took a small house in a modest neighborhood and presently brought her mother and Betty Jean to live with her in Jericho.

Launching a business was exciting and there was very much to learn in a very short time about such matters as short-term bank loans, and taking merchandise discounts, and markups, and credit, and advertising, and budgets, and government tax requirements, and buying. But she worked furiously, spending every possible minute of every day on it.

By early in December she had redecorated and had a small stock of rather good merchandise on display, and though the shop started slowly it did well toward Christmas, particularly in accessories and gift items. People came in out of curiosity, and commented favorably on Grey's taste in decorations and fixtures, which were modern and attractive, and her sportswear, which was new and fetchingly displayed. Her prices were not cheap, and she began with a small place and kept it small. But customers kept coming, and it appeared that the store and she herself were successful in a small way as soon as Jericho knew what they stood for.

That Christmas a card went out to all the store's customers, with a quite clever *New Yorker* type of drawing on it, and a printed message:

To you and yours, our warmest Christmas greetings and sincerest thanks for your patronage and encouragement. Grey Rutledge, Sportswear.

On the particular card of this mailing that came to Wistart Wedge's desk in his office there was a small handwritten addendum: *All this and a thousand times more to you, dear friend. G.R.*

Grey did not know how childishly happy it made him, or that it went into a private filing case which he kept locked, the key to it on the chain which was with him always. In the private file were some other items: a note for five thousand dollars signed by Grey Rutledge; a canceled check for the same amount made out to her by Wistart Wedge, with which she had opened her bank account; and the one letter she had written him from the airport that night when she broke with Mrs. Butford.

4

All that happened late in 1951, and here it was January of 1955. More than three years had passed, and three years can teach one many things.

As she lay in her berth in the darkness, feeling the movement of the speeding train beneath her, Grey considered that one of the things that must be learned in that length of time is the impossibility ever of keeping matters on a basis of impersonal business between a man and a woman, especially when there are debts and obligations of kindness and sympathy and regard on each side.

In the darkness she thought of an evening long before, and of Mrs. Algeria Wedge, white-haired and stately, talking to her at the Country Club. Some sentences of that wise woman came back to her:

Women are pretty well emancipated today from almost everything except the most important thing of all . . .

And also, *A girl is a girl and a man is a man. Putting them in an office or behind a counter doesn't alter that inescapable fact . . .*

Working girl . . . the career girl, Grey thought. Is there no just compromise whereby she can guide her life as a woman, or must it be always a wild and confusing conflict? Unhappily, how unhappily true it is that no one can bring about a compromise by herself alone; it can only be brought about, in this respect, in relation to the other sex.

Grey wondered if the time would ever come when a woman could find means to reconcile loyalties and love with the moral code. She herself could not throw off her responsibilities and say, "I could not help it, life was too difficult for me." The obligations were too fundamental.

She had striven to be loyal to the best within her, but she knew that from the standpoint of society and conventional morality she was a sinful woman.

And, she thought almost despairingly, though she had tried to safeguard the others dear to her, who were involved with her . . . her little girl, her mother, even her lover . . . they could not be protected completely, and at any time something might occur which would mean hideous disaster to them through her. And that was more important and more tragic, she felt, than what possibly might happen to herself.

Why, oh why is it, she asked herself, that the most important problems of life must be fundamentally insoluble . . . ?

Thirteen

I

When Grey awoke next morning and looked out of the window by her berth, the weather outside was gloomy and snowy. She dressed and went to the dining car, and sat at a spotless damask-covered table, sipping coffee and looking out as the train pulled into the ramshackle ugliness of Chicago's outskirts: the sprawling settling tanks of the sewage disposal system, the scattered industrial plants, the mud flats, the rows on rows of soot-stained flats, all turning their dreary posteriors to the railroad.

January, in Chicago, is not a month to be recommended except to those hardy souls with the instincts of polar explorers, and Grey could tell that across the frozen mud flats and tiered homes of poverty a bitter wind was sweeping from ice-locked Lake Michigan, adding to the discomfort and misery.

At the thought of going out into that bleak chill, she felt a little shiver, and it carried her mind back to another day in January, when the elements and chance and need and sympathy had combined to alter her life perhaps for all time to come.

That was the January a year after her store opened. She was in Chicago for some spring style openings, her first visit to the city for that purpose, and she was alone, of course. For once Chicago was enjoying a few days of pleasant weather in midwinter. The air was crisp enough to be invigorating, but not cold enough completely to numb; in the Loop the traffic roared almost cheerfully; and on the sidewalks the noontime crowds streamed at the peculiar half trot which is characteristic of Chicagoans, paying scant attention to the absurd bird-twitter of the traffic cop's whistles.

That morning Grey had attended two style showings, and she was walking back to her hotel, trying to clarify in her mind what she had seen, and staying near the shop windows, partly because she wanted to look at the merchandise displays, partly to allow the rush of the crowd to pass as she took a more leisurely pace.

Fur coats were much in evidence: at the showings most of the women buyers wore furs, usually mink; and on the street almost every woman in view was in fur of some sort, from dyed rabbit to sables.

Grey did not possess a fur coat. Nevertheless, in her wool coat with its stand-up collar and her little velvet hat, gray like her eyes, she was pretty enough to attract second glances even in hurrying Chicago. Of this she was not unmindful, though she was indifferent to it. She was accustomed to glances: critical, appraising women's glances; men's glances, also appraising, but with a different interest. Eyes upon her made her in no wise uncomfortable, and she appeared not to know the eyes were taking her in, adding her up, estimating her, approving, envying, disliking, or coveting her.

A voice said, "Grey!"

She turned. "Wistart!" she cried in surprise. "Golly, I'm glad to see you!"

They both laughed.

"Imagine running into you like this—among all these people!" he said. "About one chance in three million, isn't it?"

"If that's the population of Chicago, you're about right," she laughed. "What in the world are you doing here?"

His animation faded suddenly. "Business," he said.

"Oh?" She felt that he did not wish her to question him.

After a moment he said, "Where are you headed?"

"For my hotel. The Sherman."

"May I—walk that far with you?"

"Of course, if it's on your way."

They fell in step. It was only two blocks, but they found hardly anything to say to each other. Not since that day in his office and her sudden little act of emotion had they conversed except on business. They saw each other occasionally: at the bank, perhaps, or casually passing on the sidewalk. And when they did happen to encounter, they greeted each other almost formally and briefly, and went on without glancing back, because that was their compact with each other.

But as they walked along silently together now, Grey knew that he was thinking of her all the time, as she was thinking of him. She felt some outstretching of thought, almost as if he were trying to tell her something; and she almost feared to have him tell her, as if she knew already it was some trouble in which she could not help him, however much she wished to do so.

When they halted at the hotel entrance, he said, as if he were summoning up a sudden boldness, "You're busy for lunch, I suppose?"

"Not exactly," she said, "but I haven't very much time. I have another showing at one-thirty."

He nodded with the peculiar acceptance of disappointment which was characteristic of him and said good-by.

But as he turned away, a sudden impulse seized her.

"Wistart!" she called.

He halted and looked at her with a question on his face.

"I have two showings this afternoon," she said, "but the second—will be over by five o'clock."

He took up the suggestion eagerly. "Then what are you doing this evening?"

"There's a dinner and theater party for some of the buyers. But I wouldn't have to go——"

"Would you—could you—have dinner with me instead? Oh, but you probably want to go—the theater and all——"

She laughed. "Do you want to take me to dinner, Mr. Wedge? Or are you trying to talk me out of it?"

His eagerness returned. "You will?"

"Of course I will. Most of the buyers are women—and the rest might as well be."

"Then—then—what time?"

"Seven?"

"That's fine. I'll come for you then." He thanked her almost humbly.

All that afternoon as she sat through the showings, she kept thinking of him, wondering about him; what so profoundly depressed him; his eagerness—so ready to accept disappointment—to be with her and talk with her.

In this was something deeper than mere curiosity. There was a mystery in him; the curious sensation of loneliness she had felt in him at times was underlined again in the brief walk with him to the hotel. He seemed somehow lost: lost in an icy labyrinth of perplexities and worries, terribly unhappy, and perhaps terribly afraid.

On the way back to the hotel after the exhibitions, she thought idly that the weather seemed to be changing, with clouds sweeping in a leaden overhang from the northwest and the temperature much colder. But she forgot about this when she was in her room, and she set about preparing herself, as a woman does when she wishes especially to please a man.

She undressed and showered, soaping herself thoroughly and painstakingly, feeling the smooth elasticity of her flesh under the spray, until, soapless and sweet, she stepped out of the cabinet. Standing on the bath mat, she thoroughly dried herself with a towel and delicately powdered her slender, femininely contoured, youthful body.

After that she put on her prettiest fresh underthings, and with a terrycloth robe about her, spent some time arranging her hair: a work of art, really, its gleaming masses brushed up above her forehead with dips at the temples to make the head seem narrow and elegant, and a soft cascade of rich honey-hued curls at the back, leaving the ears uncovered and delicate, lying close to the sides of her head. Then she made up her face, added just the right subtle touches of perfume, put on her best earrings and necklace, and donned a cocktail suit which she had purchased as a sheer extravagance: a gray silk twill, slender and tenderly curved, and glowing with a softness like moonlight.

She was ready; indeed, she was waiting and looking out of her window at the snowflakes which were beginning to float rather thickly across the street when the telephone rang and Wistart was downstairs in the lobby.

2

When he saw her, the look on Wistart's face could not fail to please the woman in her. She knew that to him at that moment she appeared beautiful. Perhaps, she thought, she really did not look too badly; and perhaps it was just the mood he was in. But in any case she liked him very much and felt in a holiday mood, glad to be with him, glad they were going out together to some gay place. Tonight she was resolved to enjoy herself; and more importantly, to help Wistart enjoy himself.

Not in more than two years, since Jed's death, had she really had a "date" with a man—widowhood, and Mrs. Butford, and her preoccupation with the store had combined to keep her from much activity socially. She had been asked by men, but for some obscure reason which she could not clearly define did not go with them even if she could afford to take the evening off from her after-hours work, which was not often. Perhaps not the right men had asked her. But whatever it was, she welcomed this evening the more happily now, as if she were breaking a long deprivation.

"I've got a dinner reservation," Wistart told her. "It's up north, not too far from the Edgewater Beach—pretty near to Evanston, in fact. A little place, and quiet, but good food. Mind a rather long cab ride?"

"Not if the cab has a heater," she said gaily, tucking her little gloved hand into the crook of his arm.

The cab did have a heater, and the driver was not averse to a fare that took him a long way north, which was, as it happened, in the direction of his regular station. Already his windshield wipers were working to clear away the snow that was plastering stickily and threatening to block his vision whenever they stopped twirling.

"It wasn't doing this when I phoned the tavern early this afternoon," Wistart said, peering out at the whitening sidewalks and the swirling flakes. "Maybe I ought not have planned going so far. At least we won't run into much traffic—people won't be out."

She gave a little laugh.

"Did I say something funny?" he asked.

"Oh no." She glanced at him from the corners of her smiling eyes. "It was just that I caught myself thinking a ridiculous thing."

"Tell me." He was smiling also.

"It's too silly."

"Please."

"Well, I'll tell you, because it *is* silly. I caught myself, when you said there wouldn't be many people out tonight, thinking how lucky it was. Isn't that amusing?"

"Why? I don't see——"

"Oh, Wistart! It was a little schoolgirl inhibition coming out in my mind unconsciously. It was as if I were saying to myself, I'm going out with a married man, and there won't be many to see us. Do you see? My mother is very Victorian. I was taught when I was young that going out with a married man was something only bad girls did—very wicked girls."

She laughed again to show him she did not think so now.

But he was not satisfied. "Does it really bother you? Do you think we ought not——?"

"Oh no! Not really. Not at all. I don't care. After all, why should I? We're good friends, we meet by accident in a distant city. What's more natural and civilized than that we while away a lonely evening together? It was the way that silly thought of mine brought me up against the traces of my childish upbringing that made me laugh."

She wanted him to laugh too, to be light and amused by it, but he remained serious. "I don't want you to be sorry, Grey, because it's a big favor you're doing me—I can't tell you how big a favor."

His mood sobered and quieted her. It made her somewhat uncomfortable, too, because she did not fully understand what was behind it. She was sure now that he was in some great travail, and she felt drawn to him by sympathy and affection, and she wished to show him that whatever it was that made him unhappy, he had in her a loyal friend.

Quite impulsively her hand stole out and placed itself in his hand, a little pressure of understanding. She felt his hand clasp hers, and she thought he trembled slightly, and was so sorry for him that she did not take her hand away.

For quite a long time they rode in the cab in this rather intimate manner, neither of them speaking much; and when they did speak, referring to casual outside things, such as how white a park which they passed already had become in the snow, and the way the traffic lights at intersections were blurred and softened by the storm, as if they both were at pains to ignore the fact that they were holding hands very like a couple of high school youngsters.

When at last the cab drew up before the tavern, Wistart helped Grey out, paid the cab driver, and together they ran to the tavern door and stamped the snow from their feet on the mat inside the entrance.

3

It was a small tavern, with a bar near the entrance; dimly lighted, cozy and warm with a fireplace blazing cheerfully, tables covered with red-and-white-checkered cloths, and leather-padded booths. Not many people were in it tonight. A few sat at the bar, listening to the music from the Muzak system, drinking highballs, and speaking of the storm. One or two couples were dining. But actually, when Grey and Wistart were in their own circular booth, they felt almost as if they had the place to themselves, a quite pleasant intimate secrecy.

Wistart ordered a scotch highball and Grey a martini.

As she sipped she smiled up at him from under her long lashes in a way he thought adorable.

"What makes you smile?" he asked, leaning toward her.

"Because I'm having fun. Know something? This is the first time in—in absolute ages—that I've been out to a really nice place with a nice man, and dressed up, and had cocktails, and didn't have to hurry or worry about anything. And—and I hadn't realized how much I've missed it until now. And I think it's wonderful that you happened along just the way you did and we could have this evening together!"

"Thank you," he said, his smile responding to her smile. "I can't think of anything I'd rather do than make you happy." Then his face went somber again.

She wished there were some way she could induce him to talk about his trouble, whatever it was. Most sincerely she desired happiness for him, too, but she shrank from asking any question. So they went on talking about unimportant matters and had another cocktail each.

By then it was after nine o'clock, and he asked, "Are you hungry?"

"A little," she said.

"Let's have another drink, and I'll order."

"No, you have your drink. I still have most of my martini left, and—well, two are enough for me, I think."

"All right. Then I think I will." He caught the eye of a waiter, and when his highball was brought, sipped while they ordered dinner.

She was not accustomed to drinking much and the cocktails had sharpened her appetite. The thin soup was excellent, the salad was crisp and tangy, and her rack of lamb delicious. There was a wine, too, a sparkling burgundy, and she enjoyed a glass of it. But Wistart did not seem to be hungry. He took an occasional bite, and chewed slowly, and presently ordered another highball, which he drank rather quickly instead of the wine in his glass.

After a time he said with almost childlike simplicity, "Oh, Grey, I'm such beastly poor company for you!"

"I'm having a good time," she assured him, and added, "I only wish you were, too."

He stopped eating entirely and sat looking down at his plate. His side face was toward her as they sat in the booth, the blunt nose, the rather full lips, the oddly light eyebrows and eyelashes in contrast to his pink skin. In his expression she never before had seen such sadness, almost hopelessness.

"Maybe I'm not really entitled to a good time," he said.

"I think you're blaming yourself for something," she told him earnestly, "and I think you blame yourself too much."

"Do you really think that?" he said, turning to her. "But then you would—you've always been more generous—than anyone—than I deserve. The truth is, Grey, that I'm a terrible failure . . . I've known it a long time, but I've just realized it fully now in its ugliest sense."

She waited. Presently he went on.

"Do you know you're the only person in the whole world I feel I

could talk to—about anything important—and know you were on my
side?"

"You always can," she said simply.

He gave a little nod at that, returned his gaze to the table, and sat
silent.

After a little while she said, "You feel you can talk with me, Wistart.
Why don't you? It might help."

At once she wished she had not said it, for it sounded as if she were
prying into his affairs, as if she were merely curious, and she did not
mean it that way.

But he did not feel so about it, for he said, "I've had a very bad break.
A godawful bad break. I'm here in Chicago because of—because of
that."

"I—don't think I understand."

"Of course not, how could you?" He drew a breath like a long sigh,
and then began speaking in an odd monotone, as if reciting a doom
from which there was no escape. "They're starting a new paper in Jericho. It's to be called the *Morning Sentinel,* and it's backed by big resources. It's got people who know every detail of the newspaper business, big-city style—tricks we've never heard of in Jericho. They're out
to destroy the *Clarion.*"

This was immediately after his fateful talk with John Giddings and
the appearance on the signboards of the announcements of the new
paper. Grey had been in Chicago and it was the first she had heard of
it, and she was so surprised that she did not speak. Nervously he rolled
his napkin into a tight spindle, then unrolled it and spread it in his lap.

"The worst part, the really bad part," he went on, "is that they've
caught us—caught *me*—off base. I don't know why, but we just haven't
been on our toes. I guess we're only country journalists, not ready for
this big-city raid. Anyhow, confronted by this sudden opposition, I find
that they've got practically all the weapons."

"What kind of weapons?"

"The kind of things newspapers live on: features, syndicated columns, comics, all the folderols that you may not think important, but
which are what people buy a newspaper for, as much, or maybe more,
than for the news itself. We've been alone in our field so long that we'd
lost sight of the importance of these things. Now it's too late—because
the other people quietly cornered everything in sight."

"But the *Clarion's* Jericho's old family newspaper," she protested. "People won't desert it——"

"You don't know people," he said bitterly. "Newspaper readers, anyway. They're fickle—now they're with you and now they aren't. They run after anything new, faddish, sensational, exciting, even if it isn't substantial. And that's just what this new paper is going to offer them."

"Then meet that kind of competition. What about all your people who are running the paper? Surely they have some ideas among them——"

"I haven't a good staff, Grey. One good man, maybe. A chap named Dorn——"

"I know him," she said. "He rooms in the house next door to me."

"I intend to give him some responsibility when I get back—maybe put him on the city desk."

"I'm sure Mr. Dorn will do a good job for you." She liked Debs Dorn, although she did not know him well as yet.

"But otherwise I might as well admit it—I have the kind of a staff a man like me would have. I don't crack the whip, and I don't fire people when maybe I should, for inefficiency. Somehow I can't. I've studied all the ins and outs, but they're pretty complicated, and I haven't got all the answers. I'm not a good publisher. What I've learned I've had to learn the hard way, because the people I have around me aren't very competent to teach me."

"Why not get somebody who is?"

"It's not as easy as it sounds. Some of my people—like old John Giddings, my business manager—worked for my father when he first established the paper. Should I throw them out? I just can't do it."

"No. I don't suppose you could. You're too kind—too good."

"Not good, Grey." He thought over that for a moment. "I've done some bad things in my life—some things I'm very ashamed of. Even when I've tried to do something worth while, I seemed to be under an unlucky star. There's something the matter with me; nothing—not anything—ever has gone really right with me."

He seemed now to want to talk, and she encouraged him with her silence.

"As a kid I was too awkward to be good at games, which are so important in a boy's life, and the other kids would jeer at me. In school I was a rather poor student—too lazy, I guess. At the university they took me into my father's fraternity, but I wasn't popular—the other fellows just tolerated me. I graduated without any kind of honors and got no particular pleasure from my years on the campus. Afterward I did nothing that amounted to much—just drifted along. My mother did everything. She ran the *Clarion* so perfectly that there was nothing for me to do there—it would be like tinkering with delicate clockwork. I thought I was in love a few times, like every young fellow, but the girls didn't go for me, not the ones I wanted. When I married Mary Agnes, we weren't in love. Just decided to get married to solve certain problems. It hasn't been much of a success—our marriage."

He paused as if arraying the evidence against himself and ordered another highball. She kept still for fear of breaking his train of thought.

"Mary Agnes is brilliant," he went on, "and she likes brilliant people about her. I'm far from brilliant." He gave her a tired little grin, but the grin faded at once.

This was a subject on which she did not feel free to express herself.

"Until Mother died, all this affected me only," he continued. "But after her death it affected a lot of other people. I wasn't particularly interested in newspapering, Grey—I didn't want the responsibility of the *Clarion,* and I wasn't very well fitted for it. But there it was. A lot of people depended on the paper for their daily bread, some of them practically pensioners, and the Wedge family owed them an obligation. Somebody had to keep the paper going, so I was it."

"I think that kind of a feeling is pretty wonderful," she told him with all sincerity.

"Well, it wasn't very practical. Most people would say I made a big mistake not selling the *Clarion* right after Mother died. It was a very salable property then—before Wistart got his big foot in it. But—Grey, I hope you'll believe this—I knew if I sold, the new owners would have no scruples about getting rid of the old employees—the dead timber— and I couldn't help it, I didn't want that sort of thing to happen. Soft, I guess. Then I had some queer notion, too, of carrying on the family tradition. Funny, isn't it, a 'family tradition' dating back only one generation? So I went on—until now."

The last words were a groan. Grey felt as if she were seeing into some hidden chamber of his soul, reading his humiliation and defeat, and it made her almost ashamed to be looking. At the same time she knew the deep underlying reason for his agony: the *Clarion* was his one great bid for achievement, for justification of his existence. If it failed, he would have nothing worth living for. It would be the final crushing blow to what small remnants of pride and confidence he possessed. More than she had ever wished to help anyone in her life before, she wanted to help him.

"You must stop belittling yourself, Wistart," she said. "It's not true that you have less to offer than—than other people. It's just that something—has been beaten into you—until you believe it yourself——"

Grey would have stopped there, but he was gazing at her very intently and her heart was sore for him. She was very anxious for him, too, so that a sort of recklessness seemed to carry her along.

"Your mother was so competent that she would never allow you to do anything on your own," she said. "And your wife——"

Now she did stop.

"Go on," he urged.

"Doesn't appreciate you, or even *know* you!" she finished.

"Do you . . . ?" he asked in a low voice.

"I think I do!"

"Oh, Grey——" His voice was broken, almost a whisper. "Be my friend always. Don't ever desert me——"

His hand groped for hers under the table with such hungry yearning that again she let him keep it.

"Always," she said. "Always."

She knew now that he loved her, and she knew that he never before had known this kind of love: a pedestal worship which he did not dare offer her, the impossibility of his love one of the things that was destroying him within.

And she knew also that it was in her power to descend from that pedestal and teach him that he did dare offer her his love: that if she were a certain sort of a woman she could do for him what nobody else in the world could do . . . it was as simple as ABC, and she almost wished it were possible for her thus to restore his confidence, complete him, and give him that reason, that justification for his existence, which might replace the great frustration of his failure with the *Clarion*. Love could do that.

But of course it was not possible, and she would not really even think of it, and it was against all her principles and all her training even to allow such a vagrant idea to enter her head. Yet, considering the two of them as if she were considering two other persons remote from her—whose thoughts and emotions she could read without really being personally involved with them—she saw how *that* woman might do all and everything for *that* man: and somehow, viewed from this distant standpoint, it did not seem to her very bad, in fact even somewhat good. Except, of course, for the fact that it was unthinkable . . . between herself and Wistart.

4

"Sir," said an apologetic voice beside them.

Under the tablecloth Wistart's hand released Grey's with guilty quickness. They were surprised, so preoccupied were they were each other, forgetting everything about them. It was one of the waiters.

"I'm sorry, sir," the waiter said, "but the storm's got so bad that the boss wants to close the tavern so the help can get home."

"What time is it?" Wistart asked.

"After midnight," said the waiter.

"Goodness! We've got to be getting back," Wistart said. "Bring the check, please."

Neither of them had realized how time had passed. Now they saw that the tavern was empty, except for a waiter or two in red jackets, the maître d'hôtel, and the bartender near the door. On the window beside their booth a thickness of snow had heaped like white wool on each of the transverse frames of the panes and flakes beat thickly against the glass.

They rose and Wistart helped Grey into her coat.

"It must be snowing harder than ever," she said.

"Call me a cab," Wistart said to the maître d'hôtel as he took his overcoat and hat at the checkstand.

The man hesitated. Black tie, dinner coat, worried look on dark aquiline face.

"Don't know if I can get one, sir," he said. "Traffic's badly tied up by this blizzard. The city snowplows are out, but that's downtown. Out here it's getting worse instead of better."

"Is that so?" said Wistart in surprise. "We've got to get back to the Loop somehow——"

The maître d'hôtel appeared concerned. "This is a bad storm, sir. The buses haven't been running for two hours, and even with our own cars we of the staff have been wondering how we'll get home. There haven't been any guests except yourselves in the place since ten o'clock. I just can't promise you a cab."

"What will we do?" Wistart turned rather helplessly to Grey.

"As a suggestion, sir," said the maître d'hôtel, "there's a little hotel across the street. I might phone over there."

Wistart looked at Grey again, then nodded. The man went to the telephone by the reception desk.

"It may not be first class, but any port in a storm, I guess," said Wistart.

"I don't care." Grey smiled. "Any kind of rooms will do for tonight. It's kind of fun—at least it's a break in the monotony, isn't it?"

She was rather exhilarated by the unusual little dilemma. And she felt that being with Wistart was part of the pleasure of it: he seemed somehow big and pleasant and worth while, in her mood and in the presence of the unimportant little crisis; and she felt that it was nice to have a man to take care of her, an emotional relief to her feminine soul, which had depended entirely on itself for so long.

The maître d'hôtel returned. "Yes, they can take you," he said.

Grey touched Wistart's hand. "Let's go over and see what they have."

Both of them were astonished by the white swirling smother in which they found themselves outside the tavern. It was snowing heavily and the wind, corrosively cold, whirled the thick flakes in clouds almost blinding. A traffic signal gleamed forlornly pinkish, lemonish, greenish in the pallid gloom.

"It's across the street—over there," Wistart said, taking her arm. "Let's run for it."

"O-o-o-h dear!" wailed Grey. "If I'd only worn my galoshes——"

Anticipating nothing of this kind, she had little open-toed velvet slippers on her feet. But she bravely ducked her head, held on her hat with one hand, and clung to him as they fought their way across the deserted, snowdrifted street and through the revolving doors of the little hotel.

Within they stamped their feet and looked around, half laughing and half disconcerted. It was a really second-class place, very small, rather old-fashioned, with almost no lobby.

Behind the desk a little ratty man squinted at them through pince-nez glasses.

"You're the couple from the tavern?" he asked.

"Yes," said Wistart. "We got caught away from our hotel down-town——"

The clerk nodded. "There's others like yourself. Fortunately we have a room left. Twin beds."

"Only one?"

"Yes, sir. We're very crowded tonight—account of the storm."

Grey looked up at Wistart's undecided face and smiled brightly. "Any port in a storm, you said—and this is a storm, isn't it?"

He turned, as if half in a daze, and wrote something on the registration card.

"Mr. Wedge?" said the clerk, reading. "*And* Mrs. Wedge, of course."

He glanced past Wistart at Grey and added a notation on the card. To her his manner seemed conspiratorial, unpleasantly so.

"Our boy's stranded out tonight, and I'm alone," he said. "But since you have no luggage—naturally—if you'd like to go up now, here's your key. Room 334. Hope you have a pleasant night."

He gave them a rodent grin of large yellow front teeth, and Grey disliked the grin. It was as if the man said, "Go ahead. I'm broad-minded. Have fun."

She felt that he had catalogued her in his mind already, no matter what were her motives or the circumstances surrounding her, and she found it hateful. Yet at the same time being judged and found guilty in this manner gave her a strange sensation of having already crossed some intangible bridge.

"Come on," she said to Wistart.

He followed her into the self-service elevator and they found the room on the third floor: cheap and second-class like the hotel, with two narrow beds, a frowsy dresser and mirror, a small closet, a radiator hissing steam gently, and a bathroom containing an ancient porcelain tub, lavatory, and stool.

"At least it's warm in here," Grey said, trying to make the best of it.

"What are we going to do?" Wistart asked helplessly.

"You might close the door. I don't like to have people peering——"

He obeyed and took her coat. She placed her hat on the dresser and stood looking into the mirror, mechanically tucking up her bright hair.

"Your slippers—they're soaked!" he exclaimed.

She glanced down. "I'm afraid they are."

"Sit down, won't you? Let me take them off."

"Oh, I can——"

"Please."

She seated herself on the edge of one of the beds and he threw his hat and overcoat on a chair and knelt to remove her slippers.

"I'm afraid they're ruined," he said.

The small fragile pumps were wet, and he ruefully held them up for her to see.

"Your stocking feet are wet, too," he said.

"I'll take them off. Maybe they'll dry by that radiator."

She reached quickly up under her skirts, unloosed the garters, then stripped the filmy nylon sheaths down over the smooth calves, the slender-boned ankles, the narrow arched feet. Her toes were pink and her feet seemed smaller than ever when they were bare.

Still the man knelt before her, spellbound by the sight of her in the intimate, feminine act of removing her stockings. She appeared to be perfectly natural and serene, but the sensation of being so near her, shut in with her in a sleeping room, made him afraid of his own feelings.

"Here," she said, handing the stockings to him. "O-o-o-h, my feet are cold!"

She drew her legs up and half sat on them, drawing her skirts about them.

"Grey . . ." he said without rising. "Oh, Grey—you mean so much to me—and I'm such an awful dub——"

Suddenly he placed his head on his arm on the bed beside her, and his shoulders heaved with a sob.

"Wistart!" she said. "Stop that. You frighten me!"

She lifted his head, and when she did she saw tears in his eyes.

"Wistart—Wistart, dear!" she said. "Please don't be beaten yet! You haven't even struggled against it yet. Please fight back, Wistart! You may surprise yourself—and everyone else."

"Even you?"

She held his face between her two hands, looking into his eyes. "No, not me. I'd be the one person who'd expect you to win."

She felt very tender toward him, a pitying love, protective and sacrificial . . . not entirely sacrificial, a wish, an actual wish, outside all the realms of thinking and purely instinct, to assuage something . . . his high purgatory, her own . . .

"Grey . . . oh, Grey, darling . . ." he whispered. "I can't help it, I love you——"

His words stopped her speech, but not her heart. She had been reckless, perverse, with a half-formed daring inclination to let events take their course, rather believing they would not go very far. But now all at once the recklessness left her and she felt cowed and abashed. She took her hands from his face and lowered her eyes to keep from looking at him.

It was too late. She felt his arms about her.

The sandpapery roughness of a man's cheek—she had not known it for a long time—or the way a man's strength felt when he held her fiercely close, or the tobacco and shaving lotion scent of a man's kiss, or the manner in which a man's heating excitement set flame to her own excitement.

Fear left her. Some inherent fatalism took possession of her, cupping her in, directing everything.

He whispered hoarsely, her name, endearments. She hardly heard them. Words were nothing, she did not want words.

This time it was she who kissed him, and for the first time in his life Wistart knew what a woman's kiss could really mean in sweetness and fire.

Blood pounded in her temples, something within her clamored fiercely, she found herself lying back on the pillows, her surrender complete and sudden, as if she had dropped in one breathless moment all the watchfulness and guard of a lifetime. She was a feminine nature being, in whom instinct lived not in ruth or scruple, made for love and long denied . . . and she allowed him to come over her, sobbing with her pent emotion until it was eased by him.

Fourteen

I

The room was cold when Wistart awoke in the morning. His eyes opened and he was staring at the ceiling.

His first thought was of Grey: she had not really been out of his mind even in his brief snatches of sleep. He turned and looked at her.

Already she was awake in the other bed, the covers pulled up under her chin, her hair fluffy, her face almost childishly pure from slumber. Her eyes were wide, natural and innocent of any evil, trusting herself and him, but holding an inner wonder.

He felt wonder, too. First there was only the proud possessiveness of the male. She was wonderful, and she had been willing. He had bent her scruples aside, and her unwillingness, if she had any. A triumph for male dominating power, the subjugation and possessing of a woman.

Then his feeling changed. She was not just a woman—any woman. That was *Grey*. Of a sudden he could hardly believe it was she, or the incredible fact that she had been his, was his. He could not understand the great riddle of why she should be attracted to him, why she of all women he knew in the world should have permitted—no, welcomed and shared without reservation—their mighty mutual and intimate sin.

She stirred in her narrow bed and smiled. "Good morning," she said in a small sleepy voice.

"Good morning, darling," he said. Her greeting astonished him, so matter of course, as if nothing had happened; as if nothing *were* happening at that very minute, when you thought of it—the two of them in beds side by side, in arm's reach of each other.

The evidences of intimacy were about him: her suit, hung over the back of a chair; her stockings draped over another chair near the radiator, with the slippers beside them; his own clothing, helter-skelter, where he had thrown it.

"B-r-r-r, it's cold!" she said. "I opened the window a crack—for fresh air——"

Before he could anticipate her, she threw back the covers, rose in her pale sheath of a slip, her nightdress for this night of nights, and ran over to the window. He saw her slim shoulder rise and her elbow bend slightly as she pushed the sash down. For a moment she fiddled with the heat control on the radiator.

She came back. "O-o-o-h, let me in there!" she cried.

He opened his covers to help her come burrowing into his bed, exactly like a child, shivering, squirming, huddling in against him.

She was so small, so delicate as he warmed her with his arms, that he felt an immense tenderness, a protective loyalty toward her. She seemed incredibly perfect and dear; and he held her close until she quit shivering and grew warm and he could ease his embrace.

She gave him a little peck of a kiss. "It's quit snowing," she said. "I looked out of the window. Some traffic's moving, so they've got the streets open."

Still commonplaces. Still ignoring the situation as it existed. Still an attitude that everything about this and them was perfectly natural, as if hedged about by all the proper rituals and conventions. Wistart felt baffled, almost resentful of her calmness, where he was in turmoil.

Grey turned her head and looked into his eyes. She was not calm, she had not assumed in her mind that all of this was natural and that it could be ignored. But hers was the invincible instinct of a woman to smooth over things, to make *him* feel safe and confident, for she felt the disturbance in him.

She snuggled a little closer to him, and she remembered how he had been the night before: how she had been awed into a new respect for him by the change in his face, as if he had grown greater than himself with the importance of his act, his hour of ecstasy . . . and godhood and power . . . and how even in her own blood-leaping passion, she knew pure happiness for him in his happiness suddenly achieved.

She did not want him to forget that hour, ever. Within her, for the moment at least, the feminine instinct of possessiveness, of holding under spell, was in full sway.

With that her mood changed. She began all at once to feel the beginnings of terror in a retrospective look at their wrong. She felt a need to know that she was something more than a thing of pleasure to him, that she had not thrown herself away, that she was important to him now as she had been to him then.

He broke her silence and her thoughts with a kiss on her cheek.

"What's that for—reassurance?" she asked in a little, feminine voice.

"What do you mean?" Her faint hint of doubt, perhaps even resentment, surprised him.

"It was an achievement for you, wasn't it? A seduction always is for the man, so I've been told. A milestone. A conquest. A proof of something or other—isn't it?"

He was aghast. "Don't! Please don't talk that way! It's not right!"

"But you're a success now." She gave him a shadowy, inscrutable smile.

"In what way?"

"By your own standard. Remember the day when you told me that a man wasn't considered a success until he had a mistress and——"

"Grey!" He was horrified. "That was another time—and another man —we were talking about. I'd never think of you as a mistress. One single——"

"One single seduction doth not a mistress make?" she said.

She had grown serious, her eyes turned up to the ceiling, her head cradled on his arm.

"Mistress," she said slowly in a withdrawn, meditative tone. "I've been lying here getting used to the word. I think I don't mind it. Very much. As you said, it's an ancient and not entirely dishonorable estate —depending on whose mistress you are. I've never been a mistress before. I've never been seduced before. It puts things in a—a different light somehow, doesn't it?"

"Stop torturing yourself, darling! I love you—doesn't that mean anything?"

She seemed not to hear him. "Odd, isn't it?" she went on in the same musing voice. "A wife is one thing, and a mistress is another. Both are based on sex, almost no difference at all between them, yet all the social, legal, and moral prohibitions are against the mistress and in favor of the wife."

"Please, Grey——" he begged.

She knew she was making him miserable, causing his conscience to lacerate him with her half-remorseful musings, and she wondered at her own perversity, and at a kind of cruelty in her that made her do it.

"Don't blame yourself," he said wretchedly. "It was my fault—all my fault——"

Another swift change came over her. "No, it wasn't," she said.

"Maybe we were a little high—all those drinks—but here we are——"

"I wasn't a bit high," she said. "The two martinis I had didn't affect me at all. I knew exactly what I was doing."

"I should never have come into this room with you," he said with self-recrimination. "But believe this—you *must* believe it—I love you more than anything in the world."

Every impulse in her urged her now to reach out to him, to reassure him, to tell him that it was all right, that she was not unhappy, that she held him to blame for nothing.

"It wasn't your fault—it was mine," she said. "I was only talking like a typical woman. Seduction—it's the familiar refuge and excuse of my sex, as if we had no volition in what happened, were the victims and not the partners. If there was any seduction, darling, it was I who seduced *you*. I could have sent you away. I could have stood on the conventions and ordered you out of my room. I didn't. I didn't even *want* to. I don't feel like a wronged woman. What happened was what I wanted to happen. I don't know exactly why. Maybe it was the night, the storm, being all at once isolated from the world. But here's something for you, Wistart: I'm not sorry—I'll never be sorry!"

"And I'll never let you be sorry!" he said hoarsely. His spirits lifted with his relief at knowing she was not resentful of him.

"You've given me the moon and the stars, darling—it almost frightens me to receive so much," he told her. "And I don't feel sorry either if you don't. I don't feel guilty. I feel proud. I feel as if having you is the greatest thing that ever happened in my life. I feel honest—somehow this was the most honest thing I ever did."

"I suppose a lot of things we do are dishonest," she said soberly. "Hypocrisies—pretense—going through expected forms insincerely. Of all things in the world it may be that the most truly honest is the love of a man and woman together in bed."

"I love you, darling!" he exclaimed eagerly. "I'm going to prove it to you! Do you love me?"

"Can't you guess?" she smiled.

He kissed her passionately. He did not realize that she had not quite answered his question even when they forgot themselves in the reckless, wayward, tumultuous moments that followed.

He did not realize it later, when they had breakfast together in a little coffee shop, smiling across the table at each other like two half-guilty, half-happy truants; or when they took a cab through the snowy streets for the Loop.

He did not realize it when they stopped in a jewelry store near her hotel before parting.

It was then he bought the magnificent pearl earrings for her. She protested, but he said, "Please. Pearls are the most perfect of all jewels. Only they are worthy of you, darling. Make me happy by taking them, and wearing them once in a while—for remembrance."

So she accepted them, the only gift she ever did accept from him.

2

And all of that happened three years ago. Sitting on this January morning in the dining car, sipping the last of her coffee and watching apartments, houses, and business buildings pass as the train slid smoothly into the heart of Chicago, Grey ran over in her mind the events that had occurred since, and she found that she could not understand herself.

Sometimes she almost felt that she was two persons. There was the practical, law-abiding, responsible, business side of her, in which she lived most of her days, doing her duty conscientiously, devoting her mind and energy to her work, living for her family, above all knowing wrong from right. And then there was her instinctive, feminine, impractical, almost lawless side, willing to surrender every other consideration in the arms of a lover, feeling no sense of wrongdoing, almost blindly risking everything to fulfill itself. These changes in her sometimes were in conflict, and she was indecisive, prone to mistakes and error . . . as now.

She had thought the solitary night of madness in the blizzard-girt hotel was to be a single episode, standing by itself, never to be repeated. It did not happen that way. One night, even one moment, she found, may interweave lives so that there seems no way of unraveling the weft.

She discovered she could never again be a wholly separate being after that night with Wistart. She was bound up with him, he appealed to something in her that was remote, mysterious, unexpressed as the depths of the sea.

She considered the two men, two men only in her lifetime, who had known her in the ultimate intimacy of love.

Jed Rutledge . . . she had been married to Jed, lived with him in the close relationship of husband and wife, borne to him a child. Yet, thinking back, she realized that she never really knew Jed. He was her husband, but not a part of her: self-assured, extrovertic, dominant, not given to thinking except in terms of money and business, or of sports, asking and expecting nothing of her but acquiescent femininity. Even in the last days before his death, when she knew he was greatly concerned over his business, she did not herself worry greatly, because he kept her out of his affairs. She did not know Jed; and he did not need her, except for her sex, and as a symbol of conventional respectability, a mother for his child and a hostess for his home. She wondered if he ever really loved her, or if she was just one of the pigeonholes in his life. She wondered also if she ever had loved him beyond a sense of dutiful loyalty to him.

In contrast there was Wistart Wedge. With Wistart her relationship was not open and unashamed, it was furtive and guilty. Their meetings had been few, usually many months apart, and always by prearrangement at some distant place. She did not want her trysts with him, and yet she went to them again and again, after each time telling herself that *this* time would be the last.

Yet in spite of this, Wistart she knew almost as she knew herself. She could sense his longings and concerns, his depressions and fears, before he even expressed them. Some immense sympathy between them had arisen which was not to be escaped.

Jed was strong; and she had admired his strength, although it did not draw him nearer to her. Wistart was not strong. He needed her: to supply him over and over with new resolution, to give him the feeling of exaltation in successful love.

To be needed is one of the most imperious of all demands to a woman, and perhaps it was Wistart's need that brought him so close to her; closer, truly, than her husband ever had been.

The strong are not the tyrants; it is weakness that requires, demands from strength, tyrannizes over it. After that night in Chicago she saw him fight out his immediate crisis of fear, which was a crisis within himself, on the basis of the new pride in his manhood which she had given him. And in the ensuing months she watched anxiously his struggle, quite courageous, to maintain the *Clarion* against the steadily waxing attack of the *Sentinel*.

He had needed again and again to have his strength renewed, his resolution inspired, and it had become in some manner her duty to give him what he most needed, proof that in at least one respect he was victorious and successful: in his love. More than anything else it was she who by this tenderness had kept him up to what seemed an eternally losing struggle for these three years.

She was sure that though Wistart wanted her bodily her sympathy and loyalty were even more important to him. This was what caused her again and again to renounce her previous determinations and go to him once more.

But there were other reasons why she forgot her self-promises.

The little matter of obligation, for one. Grey was too honest ever to forget the manner in which Wistart had lifted her out of a dreadful, a heartbreaking situation into a new life. On the loan he had made her to start her store she had somehow managed to pay the interest and something on the principal each six months, though often it was a heavy struggle, what with her payroll, the credits she must carry, discounting of her bills, and keeping up her merchandise stock. She was never pressed: Wistart wanted to write the whole thing off. But on this much she insisted for her own pride. At least she could say she had taken no money from him. Yet there it was: however one might look at it, she owed very much to Wistart; more, far more than the money that was involved.

All these formed the basis for her long involvement. Affection based on their mutual understanding and mutual unhappiness, her sense of special obligation to him, her pity for his misery and hopelessness . . . did they add up to love?

Whether they did or not, these things had become a part of her, she knew now what she had sacrificed for them: more than the sacrifice of pride, or of conscience. For them she had somehow forsworn the things a woman desires most greatly: security of place even if it be humble; the right to look everyone clearly in the eye; happiness based on peace.

She could not ever think of marriage. And she was still young, and men found her lovely, and wanted her.

She was everything feminine, and she liked men; and it was not in her nature to be insensible to the admiration of men, or to find it anything but pleasing. Yet she was forced to keep a watch on herself to prevent herself from responding as she might have liked to the men who liked her for fear they might come to like her too much.

One man in particular she was most careful, for this reason, to treat as impersonally as she could and still be friendly to him. Debs Dorn lived next door: had roomed there almost all the time since Grey and her little family moved into the house on the corner of the block. They became acquainted gradually, and all of them liked him: Betty Jean who played games with him in the yard, Mrs. Norcross who considered him "a superior young man," and Grey herself . . . very much.

About him there was something admirable. He worked long hours and intensely at his newspaper job, and sometimes talked about it quizzically, with humorous wry comments of a cynical nature, yet she knew he was deeply serious about it and perhaps deeply dedicated to it . . . and she felt in him, though she never spoke the thought aloud, the imagination and sensitivity Jed Rutledge lacked, and the strength Wistart Wedge lacked, and with these also the ability to dream.

And in this lay a tragedy: she knew how easy, how very easy, it would have been for matters to grow much deeper and stronger than ordinary friendship between Debs and her if things had been different . . . whole worlds different.

But things were as they were, and she had wasted something precious and irreplaceable. So this thought could have for her only the wistful attractiveness of a dream long past and acknowledged as impossible. Even with her entanglement with Wistart ended she could never give herself, being what she was, to a man who trusted her and wished honorably to make her his wife. It would be too deadly a treachery to such trust.

Her life was committed to an unnatural loneliness, and almost at its very beginning. She had made her own bed and she must lie in it; a hard bed, a cold bed, an inexorable fate.

Out of the car window Grey saw that the train already was in the switchyards. She paid her breakfast check and made her way back through the swaying cars to her compartment to see that her bags were taken to the vestibule, tip the porter, and stand in line in the passageway, waiting to leave the train.

"Here we go again," she said half aloud and almost with a sigh.

Slowly the train slid to a smooth stop. In the passageway the line began to shuffle forward and Grey moved with it.

On her ears were Wistart's pearl earrings.

Even yet, three years after, she had never given him the answer to his question.

ANNALS OF THE *DAILY CLARION*
The Raleigh Rabbitry

Mr. Marmaduke Raleigh arrived in Jericho unannounced, a broad, tall, fine-seeming gentleman, with a smooth high forehead, a senatorially aquiline nose, and a long, honest-looking face, such as is commonly associated with the benevolent and upright. His figure was full —pleasantly so—and in his eyes, which were blue, was a faraway look as if he were dreaming of things sublime.

The circumstance that he owned the first air-conditioned Cadillac in Jericho did not detract from the immediate fine impression he created. Nor did the fact that he took the President's suite at the Kansas Hotel: a suite prepared for the reception of a nation's chief executive, who, however, never came; and was reputed to cost fifty dollars a day, although rates could be obtained for steady occupancy.

When, however, it became known that he had a mistress, a "girl friend" in the Jericho vernacular—blondined, curvaceous, given to picture hats and long-stemmed cigarettes, and named Mrs. Toni Gilbert —his career was threatened with wreckage almost before it began.

It was remembered afterward that Mrs. Mary Agnes Wedge saved the day for him, although she did it not as a favor to him, but rather as a means of setting the Junior League back on its collective high heels, a practice she enjoyed.

On that afternoon the Junior League, which contained some ladies hardly junior in years, had resolved itself into an indignation meeting concerning Mrs. Toni Gilbert, who, according to scandalized report, was living openly and flauntingly right in the President's suite with Mr. Raleigh, wore dresses that "showed everything she had," and otherwise violated tenets of Jericho convention.

It was in this gabbling that Mary Agnes intervened. "A mistress?" she said, withering them. "Really, I suppose we're not *all* children."

It was the way she said it, coolly, inquiringly, with an air of amused worldly wisdom that quite squelched them.

The members of the Junior League hastily began to revise their several opinions. *Certainly* they were not children . . . they could be as mature, as sophisticated, as—as—anyone! They began to view matters with a new and somewhat unaccustomed broad-mindedness, and to consider that perhaps the whole question of Mr. Marmaduke Raleigh and Mrs. Toni Gilbert was hardly worth all the pother after all.

Indeed, after Mary Agnes' intervention, and their resulting new viewpoints, the man's daring knavery became something to chuckle over; and if one did not actually receive the woman into one's home, at least one could feel comfortably tolerant, almost a little daring, when one gaily greeted her, as if she were a friend, on the street.

Going from this triumph over prejudice, Mr. Raleigh's steps were well remembered. First he rented a suburban house on a scrub-tufted acreage, established Mrs. Gilbert there instead of in the President's suite, and with her assistance made himself popular as a host and bon vivant. Gentlemen—particularly gentlemen of financial standing—found Mr. Raleigh most personable and friendly. As for Mrs. Gilbert, the same gentlemen found that a plunging neckline is something one can look down upon without disapproving, and that she herself, with her svelte figure, was both alluring and most agreeably flirtatious. After an evening at the Raleigh-Gilbert ménage, such gentlemen left with pleasant remembrances, and sometimes with still more pleasant hopes of the future.

One day a sign went up:

RALEIGH RABBITRY
WORLD FAMOUS
Join this organization for
quick returns

Almost simultaneously, behind the rented suburban house, appeared tier after tier of hutches, quickly and deftly run up, of frame and lath and chicken wire, with tar paper roofs and coats of quick-drying paint. The hutches were populated with rabbits—plump, white, sleek, velvety, long-eared, nose-wabbling rabbits.

Now full-page advertisements appeared in the *Daily Clarion*—this happening was prior to the publication of the *Morning Sentinel*—and on the local radio stations commercials were heard in which Mr. Marmaduke Raleigh announced that he had something new in the world of commerce, something that would coin dollars faster than the mint, because it appealed to a demand hitherto untouched, not even suspected, and girdling the entire globe.

It was an industry, the announcements said, which was based on a new and special breed of rabbits, rabbits without peer and beyond price, developed after years of the most careful scientific study and breeding by Mr. Marmaduke Raleigh himself. His plan was convincingly simple: by newspaper, radio, and in person he promised that if people bought his priceless rabbits from him, in pairs of bucks and does, at a really nominal cost, he would purchase back from them the increase at delectable prices, for the fur, which he could and would market on a world-wide basis.

To prove his words he had samples of what rabbit fur would do in fine felts, and he asserted that Raleigh rabbit pelts were easily worth five dollars apiece, and cheap at that price since, when properly processed, they could hardly be distinguished from seal, mink, or even chinchilla, by the most expert furriers.

Jericho citizens, of high and low degree, made pilgrimages out to the Raleigh Rabbitry to gape. The one breed of the rabbit family with which most of them were familiar was the lean and haggard jack rabbit, a creature indigenous to the Kansas plains, which was said to subsist on sagebrush and barbed wire if it could get no more succulent fare, was capable of working up jet plane speed when inspired, and was utterly unfit for human consumption because of its whang leather stringiness and toughness. For these, to whom the sight of a jack rabbit, all lank bony legs, ridiculously exaggerated ears, and mangy ribs, was familiar, a view of the white, plump, tame, soft Raleigh rabbits was a revelation, carrying conviction.

Still continued the advertisements. One full-page announcement compared the profits of cattle growing and rabbit growing in terms easily understood. The argument was somewhat as follows: A cow cost a hundred dollars, and it could have one calf a year, to be sold at fifty dollars. The feed would cost thirty dollars, leaving a profit of twenty, not counting the investment in land, improvements, and labor. But why buy cows when you could buy a buck rabbit of the peerless Raleigh breed for twenty dollars, a doe for fifteen? Such a pair would produce thirty young rabbits a year, to be resold to Mr. Marmaduke Raleigh himself for five dollars each, or a total of a hundred and fifty dollars. After paying all expenses, the net return on these rabbits—carefully itemized—would be $65.54, on an original investment of thirty-five dollars!

Now if the truth be known, although Jericho prides itself on its metropolitanism, it is too close to the farm and the prairie sod to be anything but strongly bucolic. Raising something, even rabbits, appealed to the instinct.

Mr. Raleigh's prize exhibit, father of the nation, was a big buck rabbit, snow white and fluffy, named Emperor. Mr. Raleigh told everyone emphatically, "Emperor is worth a thousand dollars." Inflection and emphasis made everyone believe.

He launched a half-hour radio show, with musicians impersonating rabbits that could sing, pick guitars, and tell jokes. In Jericho it topped all other programs in the ratings. He hired firecracker young salesmen who raged through the countryside like the ten plagues of Egypt.

On the dizzy stuff handed out by Mr. Raleigh, thousands of persons in Jericho and in the surrounding state, including bankers, lawyers, and merchant princes, as well as the commonality, hurried to the Raleigh Rabbitry, plunked down their money, and got into the game.

In Jericho back yards—even those of the exclusive mansions on Tower Hill—hutches appeared in hundreds, built by the Rabbitry and paid for by the customers along with the rabbits. The city was filled with optimism and enthusiasm, there was universal expectation of quick riches, and a new era of optimism for everyone. There was great talk of a huge packing plant to put up rabbit meat for the foreign trade, of hat factories and fur houses to use pelts; in fact, little was discussed in Jericho but the future of the rabbit industry.

For a long time Jericho had advertised itself and wished to be known as the Wheat Capital, but it came perilously near in those days to having itself permanently tagged instead as the Rabbit Capital.

Delirious speculation lasted for about six months. By the end of that time, having thoroughly covered Jericho and most of the surrounding territory with his hutches and rabbits, to the tune of something in excess of one hundred thousand dollars, Mr. Marmaduke Raleigh, together with Mrs. Toni Gilbert and the air-conditioned Cadillac, all disappeared between an evening and a morning.

Behind them they left hutches open and rabbits milling around, eating alfalfa off the neighbors' patches. They left also a bitterly sorrowing horde of creditors, with at their pinnacle the radio station and the *Daily Clarion,* holding large unpaid bills for promotion. And they left thousands of wailing and caterwauling rabbit growers, who one day before had been happily, if avariciously, counting their prospective wealth, but who suddenly now encountered the cold light of fact. Their "priceless" Raleigh rabbits were no more than ordinary Belgian hares, of use only as pets—but how expensive the pets!—or as dinners—and how costly the dinners!

Let it be remembered that the cardinal rule of the perpetrators of confidence games is that their arts and wiles shall be devoted only to single gullible individuals, or at the most, to two or three persons. The more who know, the less likely is the game to succeed. Secrecy, the quick separation of the victim from his cash, and the prompt getaway are the prime tactics of the bunko steerer.

Even to this day the word "rabbit" is spoken guardedly in Jericho. Those who invested in the Raleigh enterprises—and their name is legion—never again wish to hear the word that brings anguished memories not only of dollars lost, but of an entire city, prideful of its tall buildings, industries, and marts of trade, so innocently verdant that it was not only defrauded, but defrauded over a period of six months, with the full blast of publicity by press and radio and spoken word, openly, blatantly, cynically—and humiliatingly.

In the homes of Jericho for all future time Easter eggs are fetched by storks, angels, even elephants, perhaps. But by bunnies? Never!

Fifteen

I

In Jericho, the same morning that Grey Rutledge arrived in Chicago, the *Morning Sentinel* carried a shrieking headline over a story that gave Debs Dorn a queasy feeling in his stomach:

JERICHO OFFICER SLAIN
IN GRAVEYARD AMBUSH:
LOVE BANDITS SOUGHT

"Hell of a thing," said Jeff Linderman. "Nibs Galloway. Shot in his patrol car."

"Yes," Debs said. "Best man on the force."

He and Nibs Galloway had been friends; but in the curious impersonal manner of the journalistic world he was less concerned at the moment over his own feelings than over the fact that the murder had occurred shortly before midnight, which had given the rival *Sentinel* just about the right time to cover the story fully and completely in its final edition. What was left for the *Clarion* was no more than a follow-up, a sweeping together of crumbs of news to be garnished and rewarmed as well as possible for the readers; at best nothing but leftovers.

Galloway, according to the *Sentinel* account, was shot while he and another officer, Walt Benson, were on a routine tour in their patrol car. The killing occurred on a road leading through one of Jericho's cemeteries; a dark lane, shadowed by trees and fenced by hedges, remote enough and secret enough so that sometimes couples parked their cars there to make love.

This was a practice more dangerous than the lovelorn couples realized, for a certain type of thug, often degenerate, sometimes prowls about such places, finding it easy to steal upon and surprise a young pair when they are so intent on each other that they are deaf to any other thing in the world. Cases of robbery in Cemetery Lane had been reported: and worse, for on one or two occasions a robber had forced the girl's escort out of the car at the point of a gun and driven away with her to rape her.

Although the police did not especially concern themselves about love-making in parked cars, the danger of holdup and assault in this dark stretch was serious enough so that each night one or more patrol cars drove through it. On seeing a parked automobile it was the custom of the patrolling officers to stop behind it, allow the occupants a reasonable time to compose themselves, and then talk to them, pointing out the danger of the place and directing them to move on.

It was on such a routine patrol that Nibs Galloway was killed. Benson, his companion in the patrol car, reported that they encountered a parked automobile which contained, instead of an amorous couple, either two or three men—he was not sure of the exact number. Galloway, who was driving, pulled up behind the other car to inquire what the occupants were doing. Some shots were fired. Benson said he leaped from the squad car and returned the fire with his revolver, but the other automobile sped away. He ran back to the squad car and found Galloway slumped over the steering wheel, shot through the head, unconscious and dying.

Benson's first concern was to get his fellow officer to a hospital. He pulled Galloway over in the seat, took the wheel, and drove to St. Matthew's, but Galloway already was dead when they arrived. Benson telephoned headquarters and later made a full written report.

He said he did not know any of the men who did the killing, had not been able to see them clearly in the darkness. The car they drove was a Buick, he believed, but he did not get the license number in the excitement. Galloway had not spoken from the time the first shots were fired.

Besides all this, the *Sentinel* carried pictures of Galloway and Benson, a summary of Galloway's police career, a personal interview with Benson, and a statement by the police chief, Tex Hardcastle, that every resource of the department would be devoted to tracking down and bringing to justice the killers. There was, Debs confessed, not much left for the *Clarion*.

When Joe Canfield arrived in the office he already had checked at the police station.

"Any new angles?" Debs asked him.

Canfield shook his head.

"What about the love bandit angle?" Debs asked.

"Could be. Three men parked in Cemetery Lane with rods weren't there for their health."

"Your friend Benson doesn't seem to be very much on the ball."

"Why do you say that?"

"According to his story, they pulled up behind the killers' car. With the headlights on it, he ought to have been able to read the license number."

"Maybe if you had two or three guys plugging hot slugs at you you'd forget about license numbers," suggested Canfield nastily.

"Maybe I would," said Debs. He thought a minute. "Did he hit the other car?"

"He doesn't know."

"Doesn't *know?* And he was shooting at it not thirty feet away?"

"Anyhow, it made its getaway."

"A car with bullet holes in it ought to turn up. Even if nobody in it was wounded."

"Maybe so, maybe not. They might junk it in a river or lake somewhere."

"Well," Debs said, "take a photographer, get a picture of the death scene and the patrol car—it may have bullet holes in the windshield. Phone in anything new and we'll have a quick roundup for the noon edition."

The assignment was routine, but there were two or three questions tugging at the back of Debs' mind. For one thing, he did not believe the "love bandit" theory. It had some glaring flaws. Love bandits—the journalistic cliché—usually were furtive, solitary sneak thieves, sometimes with a sex craze. They did not hunt in packs for the reason that the youthful couples they victimized rarely had much money—not the kind of loot to attract three men, all armed. From Benson's description the killers were more of the big-city bank bandit type than the small-time love bandit type.

Debs did not communicate these thoughts to Canfield because he did not fully trust him. If there was some special angle to the story, Debs wanted it for the *Clarion* exclusively, not to be shared with the *Sentinel*. Reporters were inclined to pool information—to protect themselves from being scooped—and he was fairly sure that Canfield and his opposite number on the *Sentinel* had some such arrangement.

2

Sally Sayre read the account of Nibs Galloway's murder with a feeling of personal horror due to the fact that she had met the man who was killed a few days before when she had lunch with Debs Dorn in the cafeteria and was returning to the office. She remembered the detective as a big, bull-necked, polite young man, a trifle uncouth perhaps with all that obvious muscularity, who looked at her, then turned his eyes quickly away as if he should not, in his position, allow himself the luxury of admiring a pretty girl with a nice figure.

She had dismissed Nibs Galloway from her mind; but now he was dead, and that made a difference. Never before had she been even slightly acquainted with someone who had been murdered.

Two or three times Sally glanced down the room toward the city desk. She saw Debs and Jeff in close conference, saw Canfield join them and leave on some errand with a cameraman, saw and heard Samson J. Hudson ask about the story and then go back to his own desk shaking his head.

Sally wondered what was going on up there, but she would not dream of asking. She was, after all, a member of the society-club department, devoted entirely to women's affairs, which she felt was a separate dead-end street of journalism, where one grew old and slaty-voiced, and dyed one's hair, and became accustomed to being patronized, and to growing excited over trifles. As such, Sally felt inferior to the reporters in the mainstream of real news. She hoped Debs Dorn would go to that place across the street for lunch again, and then maybe he would stumble on her and talk to her about what was happening in the Nibs Galloway case.

Then Sally heard her name called. Debs was looking over at her.

She jumped up quickly and went over to the city desk.

"You told me you'd like a chance to handle a news story," Debs said.

"Yes." A smile is a way a girl can sometimes get something she wants, and Sally used her smile freely, instinctively, and almost unconsciously whenever a smile seemed appropriate to the occasion. She used her smile now and nodded. It was a very cute smile indeed.

"You've read the Galloway murder story?" Debs asked.

She nodded again.

"I want an interview about Nibs from someone who knew him well," he said. "He wasn't married. Lived with his widowed mother. Here's her name and address. Take a cab out there. I'll put through an expense account for you. I want you to try to get her to tell you something about Nibs the human being, not the cop. Can you do it?"

"I can try."

"You'll have to hurry. Noon edition deadline's eleven-thirty."

Sally put on her long loose coat and her little hat with the veil that came just under her nose, and touched up her lips and went down the stairs with her heart beating excitedly. She hoped she could do the job and she half feared she could not, but she was determined to do her best —to prove something to Debs Dorn.

As she left, he called after her, "Be sure to get whatever pictures she's got, like snapshots, that might dress up the story."

The cold snap of a few days before had left little skifts of snow in the parkings and it was still frosty, the breath white in the air. The taxi driver found the Galloway house: an old-fashioned frame cottage with gingerbread scrollwork on the porch eaves, and a big leafless elm in the front yard. Along the curb stood three or four cars. They were old cars, with a worn dejected look about them, and Sally surmised that they belonged to friends of Nibs Galloway's mother who had come to share her sorrow.

The sight of those old dejected cars made her feel out of place: like a morbid stranger invading the privacy of suffering grief that ought to be secret and sacred. But she remembered it was her job, and paid the cab driver and went in.

Mrs. Galloway proved to be a surprise. Somehow Sally had built up in her mind a picture of a sweet motherly old lady, perhaps white-haired and with a shawl, sitting in a rocking chair. She found instead a big woman with hair dyed dead black, wearing a cheap wrapper, and surrounded by other elderly women, all poorly dressed, some busying themselves tidying up the house, others in the kitchen, others just sitting.

Mrs. Galloway had been weeping, but when she learned that Sally was from the *Clarion* she sat up and regarded her with eyes black and bright: as if she had expected someone from the newspaper and this was important to her and she was not going to allow her emotions to interfere with it.

"Won't you set down?" she said. And when Sally took a stiff-backed chair, "We're jest fixin' to have coffee. Could we offer you a cup?"

Sally accepted it. She hardly knew how to start, especially in the presence of those other women, who sat staring at her with unblinking curiosity. But the big woman with the dyed black hair opened the interview herself.

"You want to ask me about my boy," she said.

"Yes."

As easy as that. For the first time Sally felt the almost hypnotic effect the press has upon the public. In most instances people will go out of their way to give a reporter all possible information; sometimes even when the information is not entirely creditable to themselves. It is as if they feel a sense of importance and responsibility to the public simply because fate has elected them to the prominence of being in the newspaper.

Nibs Galloway's story, as told by his mother, was not extraordinary. He was born on a farm near Great Bend, Kansas, but his father died when he was fourteen and Mrs. Galloway had to give up the farm and go into town, where she made a living as a cook in a small restaurant. Nibs liked baseball, and had normal boyish fights and escapades, but he was a good son and did odd jobs to help out the family exchequer. When the war came along, he was seventeen and he enlisted in the Navy, being assigned to the shore patrol.

"Stationed at Frisco first, then Guam," said Mrs. Galloway. "He wanted a pigboat because of the extry pay——"

"What's a pigboat?"

"Submarine. Nibs put in for it, but they kept him in the S.P. because he was big an' strong an' good at handling drunk sailors. After the war he come to Jericho, hearin' they was payin' good wages in the plane factories, but disarmament had set in an' they was layin' off instead of hirin'. They needed police officers, so he applied. He could ride a motorcycle an' had this record in the S.P., so they put him in the traffic department. He sent for me to come an' keep house for him. Two years ago they made a plain-clothes man out of him."

All this Mrs. Galloway recited in a methodical dry voice, no sobs, no show of grief, no histrionics.

Sally asked a feminine question. "Did Nibs have any girl friends?"

"A few dates, but no steadies. Him an' Walt Benson—that was his ridin' partner—double-dated a couple of times. Nibs was shy around gals. He'd ruther set home an' listen to the radio, or maybe read. He had whole rafts of paperback books, mostly two-gun Westerns. But I reckon Walt Benson done enough datin' for both of them. I never liked Walt much. Awful gabby part of the time. Sour other times. But gal-crazy."

"Did Nibs ever talk to you about his work?"

"No, he never done much talkin'." The big woman paused, her eyes black and fixed. "But I'll tell you somethin'—I'm jest sure he had somethin' on his mind the last day or two. He was goin' over somethin'—mullin' it over. That was his way, jest mulled a thing over till he got it settled before he ever said or done anything. I could tell. Nibs was worryin' over somethin'."

"Was it connected with his work?"

"Must of been. He didn't have no gal trouble. About all a young man ever worries about is his work or gals, ain't it?"

"I guess it is," Sally said.

The doorbell rang. More of Mrs. Galloway's friends. With their arrival the bereaved mother returned to her role of grief. There were tears, and embraces, and sighs, and broken expressions of sorrow.

Sally excused herself as quietly as possible, got a cab, and returned to the office.

3

"Any pictures?" was Debs Dorn's first question.

"No . . . I forgot to ask," Sally said with a sinking heart.

"You *forgot?*" Debs looked as if he hardly believed his ears. "That's the first thing to ask about—*always!*" He thought a moment. "Well, it's too late to get them now, for today at least. I'll send Canfield over just to keep the opposition from having them—if they haven't been there already."

He spoke without heat. Sally had the humiliating feeling that he really had expected very little of her and was therefore not much disappointed.

"Go write about two pages of copy," he said.

She went to her desk and wrote her story, tearing up two or three leads, and doing her best. At last she gave the copy boy her two sheets of typewritten copy.

A few minutes later, in a voice that made her jump, Debs called, "Sally!"

She rushed over to his desk.

"This is tripe," he said. "Obvious—banal—all that stuff about Nibs Galloway being a good son and a war veteran—the usual, run-of-the-mill. But down in the bottom of your story you've got a real feature. Know what it is?"

She shook her head mutely.

"Galloway was *worried*," he said. "He had something on his mind that he wasn't talking about to anybody—not even his mother. He died without telling it. What was it? Did it have anything to do with his death? Why did he keep it secret? Don't you see? Mystery there—something brand-new in the case. You could have thrown all that bromide stuff into the last paragraph of your story."

He tossed Sally's two pages over to Jeff Linderman.

"Write a new lead, Jeff," he said, "and put that mystery angle in strong. Edit out the rest of the yarn to conform."

Sally went back to her desk feeling crushed and stupid, and hating Debs for being so brutal and superior. At lunch time she stole out of the office and went over to the cafeteria across the street for a salad and coffee and a cigarette to be alone with her insignificance and failure and the hurt of it. When she saw Debs come in a few minutes later, she almost shriveled up inside, and she tried not to look at him and hurried to finish her lunch so she could leave before he came over to her table—if he did come.

But then she reasoned that he knew she had seen him, and it was a little childish to run away before he came. After all, maybe he wasn't planning to come to her at all, and then it would be twice as ridiculous. So she waited, and lit a cigarette so nervously that she got it wrong end to, and set fire to the filter tip, and had to put it out and take a new cigarette. It made her furious with herself and she hated Debs Dorn even more for getting her into a state of absolutely ludicrous agitation like this.

Then she got herself in hand and sat trying to look very unconcerned and poised with her cigarette. And Debs came right over with his tray, and lifted his quizzical eyebrows with a grin, and said, "May I sit down?"

She nodded without smiling and made a little gesture with the cigarette.

He placed his dishes on the table, took the empty tray over to the rack, came back and sat down, unfolded his napkin with the knife, fork, and spoon inside, and placed them beside his plate.

After a while he said, "Sally."

She did not look up. "What?"

"Are you mad at me about that story?"

Now she raised her eyes. He was smiling at her. All at once she felt she was being a trifle juvenile for a girl who ought to have a professional attitude, so she smiled back with a wry little smile, half apologetic and half unhappy.

"I guess I was—a little," she said.

"You said you wanted to be a newspaperwoman." He took a bite of swiss steak, masticated it and swallowed it. "In the newspaper business you've got to learn to take criticism."

"I do—I think I can!" she flared. "But you didn't even let me rewrite my own story!"

"There wasn't time. Had to make an edition. Jeff's a fast rewrite man and knew exactly how to handle it. I didn't take that story away from you to hurt you—I did it because we had a deadline. That's one thing you've got to learn to worship—the Great God Deadline."

She did not reply, so he went on.

"I was going to talk to you after press time, but this is better. You say you don't think much of doing society items—how'd you like to try out on the news side?"

Her eyes opened with a blaze of interest. "You mean—you'd give me a chance—after I flopped like that on my first assignment?"

"You didn't see the feature, but you got the information. I think you'll learn to recognize a feature when you see it."

"But the pictures—you specifically told me to get pictures——"

He nodded. "That was pretty bad. If an ordinary reporter had done that I'd almost have fired him."

"Ordinary? What makes you think I'm not—not ordinary?"

"No girl like you is ordinary. You're attractive, real attractive, but

you try to be something more than just a pretty girl. You're intelligent
and loyal, and aren't afraid of work. And you have nice impulses and
sympathies. You missed on those pictures because you felt so sorry for
poor Mrs. Galloway that you didn't want to ask her for something that
might add to her pain. Isn't that true?"

She gave a little nod, realizing it *was* true.

"It adds up to this: a man will do a lot more, go a lot farther, for a
girl who's young and charming and nice than he would for somebody
else," Debs went on. "Natural instinct, I suppose. So that puts you in
a special bracket. Now don't get me wrong, Sally. This is no more than
the way I'd feel toward any girl like you. No more than the way I'll
probably feel toward a whole succession of girls who'll want to go into
journalism on the *Clarion*."

He paused and drank some coffee. Then he lit a cigarette.

"So I'm going to give you that chance you wanted," he said. "But
remember this, Sally, if you do come over on the news side: being a
pretty girl will be no refuge for you any more. Because there's also
another side to human nature. A man who naturally likes a girl—and
anybody would like you, Sally, everybody does—may go clear to the
other extreme, be twice as mean to her as to an ordinary person just to
prove to people, himself most of all, that her sex hasn't the slightest influence on him in his treatment of her."

She listened, half abashed yet half pleased. Debs Dorn thought of her
as young and charming and nice. Somebody special. Even to the point
of being twice as mean to her . . . if he had to be.

Then she thought of it in a different way. Debs was leveling with
her. She was an attractive young female, and he was nice to her because
of that; but once she became an impersonal member of his immediate
staff—a "she-scribe," as he once had called it—she would have to perform on a different basis, and only results and ability would count,
whereas charm had always counted so strongly before. She almost disliked this different view of her status.

But she said, "Thanks. I'll try to remember—when you get mean
with me."

He grinned.

4

Sally's hint of mystery concerning the brooding Nibs Galloway before his death (rewritten) was the *Clarion's* lead story that day.

People read it and discussed it just as Debs said they would. What, they asked each other, was worrying Galloway? Some kind of a mix-up with a woman? The newspaper use of the "love bandit" angle in connection with the murder gave a feeling that sex might be involved in one way or another, and sex is something the public loves to use its imagination on. Maybe Nibs Galloway was shot by a jealous rival, or even an irate husband or father! The possibilities for speculation were relishingly wide.

But Debs Dorn had different thoughts. Nibs Galloway's mother stated there were no romantic entanglements in her son's life, and besides, Debs knew the dead detective rather well himself. Nibs was serious-minded, no skirt chaser. No more did Debs believe the "love bandit" theory, for the reasons he already had adduced.

He remembered his last conversation with Nibs Galloway, right after the murder of Bonnie Bonner. Words of Galloway's came back to him: *Wasn't sex—I don't think . . . mebbe somebody shut her up . . . hallelujah lassie . . .*

Bonnie Bonner was murdered two nights before Nibs Galloway, and Nibs was working on a theory that she knew something about someone . . . perhaps there was a connection between the two murders. Perhaps somebody wanted to shut up Nibs Galloway also.

After press time Debs left the office without telling anyone where he was going, got into his old convertible with the fabric top that leaked wind and rain, and drove south. The address he looked for had been published in the paper. It was in the Jugtown part of the city, the humble section, out beyond the great sprawling packing plant. He found the house, small, faded yellow, with a chicken pen behind it and a few hens wandering listlessly, their feathers fluffed out in the cold. A little smoke eddied from the chimney.

Debs knocked on the door. It opened. A face peered out: face of an Old Testament prophet, but an inarticulate, illiterate prophet, long hair, straw-colored beard, eyes pale and focusing their attention slowly.

"Are you Dewey Bonner?" asked Debs.

The bearded head nodded.

"I took a chance hoping you'd be here," Debs said. "I'm from the *Clarion*. Can I talk with you?"

Bonner stood aside for Debs to enter, then went over to prod up the fire in the stove. It was apparent that he had only just come home and lit it; the wood in it was beginning to catch, crackling, and the room still was chilly. Behind the stove a box contained more wood, chiefly odds and ends of boards, the trash of carpentering jobs. Poverty advertised itself everywhere in the poor furnishings, the old torn wallpaper, the seedy rag carpet. Curious place, Debs thought, for a glamour girl, such as Bonnie Bonner was supposed to be, to live.

He glanced again at the husband. Bonner was of medium height, thin with an ascetic thinness, and though he wore a suit of black, his feet were encased in work shoes. On the wall hung faded blue denims, his work clothes.

"I see you didn't work today," said Debs.

"Work, yes; for the Lord."

"What kind of work?"

Bonner took two slow steps over to an old mission-style table on which stood a stack of blue-bound books with gilt lettering. Beside the stack lay a very worn and large brief case. He began opening the brief case.

"Here," he said.

Debs took from him three pamphlets and glanced at them. *I Am the Way. The Light of Salvation. Repent Ye.*

Tracts, religious tracts.

"You've been out distributing these today?"

The other nodded.

Debs felt pathos in this inarticulate soul, so uncomforted in his loss, seeking as the only assuagement he knew for his hurt this familiar self-appointed task of spreading his particular kind of religion by distributing from door to door his tracts.

"You sell these?" he asked.

"No. Only the book. I ask two dollars for the book. Just for the cost of printing. I take no profit for God's work. The tracts are free to any who ask."

"Can I see the book?" asked Debs.

"Do you want to buy the book?" Dewey Bonner said. "I'll sell one to you, but they are not for handling for curiosity only."

Debs could read the title from where he was. *Seven Times Seven Keys to the Kingdom*. The books all were alike, the same title. He put his hand in his pocket, then considered that if he bought one of the books it would not help Dewey Bonner, since it would only go to the sect that published the volume. He removed his hand from his pocket.

"You distribute these every day?" he asked.

"Yes. When I don't have a job." Bonner's voice trailed off.

"You're a carpenter, aren't you? Are you on a job now?"

"No. Work has been scarce."

"I want to talk with you about your wife," said Debs after a moment's silence. "Did she help you with—the Lord's work?"

"Yes. Bonnie, my wife, in her lifetime labored also for the Lord."

The face above the straw-colored beard did not change expression, nor did the voice quiver with any evidence of emotion.

"How long have you lived here?" Debs asked.

"In Jericho? Six months."

"Where did you come from?"

"Oklahoma. We came here after we got married."

"You're considerably older than she was, aren't you?"

"Yes. She knew I was a messenger of the Lord. When she believed, we were married and came here to live."

"Why here?"

"Lots of building going on here."

"You two made a good deal of money, didn't you?" Debs glanced around at the poor house.

"It went to God's work. All of it."

"You kept nothing?"

"The work was our life."

Debs did some rapid calculating. Bonnie Bonner had been getting two hundred dollars a week, according to Canfield. Carpentry was well paid. In six months the girl and her husband must have earned together several thousand dollars. And all of this was gone—to some sect, the beneficiary of this religious mania.

He changed his line of inquiry. "Do you have any idea why your wife was murdered?" he asked directly.

A momentary flicker went over the prophet face, a tautness of expression, perhaps an enormous woe. Then it vanished, the stoical look returned, and the pale eyes dropped.

"No," said Bonner dully. "The police asked me that, too. I told them I didn't know. It was the Lord's will. I know she's happy above."

A simple statement, a positive assertion of faith. Debs felt baffled. Never before had he encountered fanaticism so completely able to wipe out any pulse of feeling as this. Was this man deficient mentally, or perhaps emotionally out of balance?

"Did Bonnie have any enemies?" he asked.

"Bonnie didn't have no enemies. She couldn't have."

"Can't you give me *any* kind of a lead that might bring her murderer to justice?"

Again the pale eyes gleamed with the briefest flare of feeling, pain or latent rage, instantly gone.

"Vengeance is mine; I will repay, saith the Lord."

It was intoned like a liturgy. Alone in his house of loneliness Debs left Dewey Bonner.

Sixteen

I

By Debs' watch it was four o'clock as he entered his car again and drove south out of town on the main highway. Three miles beyond the city limits he took a blacktop turnoff toward a grove of trees standing around a brown-stained board-and-batten building with a shake roof. In front a garish neon sign read: CHESTERFIELD CLUB. It was the Draggett roadhouse where Bonnie Bonner had been murdered.

In the rear Debs noticed a car parked as he drove up in front of the club. He tried the customers' entrance, found it locked, and read a notice tacked on it, which set forth in legal phrases that these premises were closed to the public by order of the county attorney as a public nuisance and because of violations of the statutes of Kansas until further notice. Section and paragraph of the code were cited.

Padlocked, as the saying was.

Debs considered a moment, then went around behind. Garbage pails and packing cases. Barrels filled with empty bottles. The seamy side of a public night spot, never intended for the eyes of the public. One of the back doors was unfastened and he entered. It was the kitchen. He went forward through a swinging door into the dining room. As a customer he had been there before, and he knew Earl Draggett.

The interior was bleak and uninviting, chairs stacked upside down on tables, a piano on a slightly raised platform in one corner, all the decorations of the kind that glitter brightly when the lights are on at night but look shoddy and dull by day.

At one of the tables sat a short, swart man with his hat on. He glanced up from the piece of paper on which he was figuring.

"Hello, Earl," said Debs.

"What are you looking for, Debs?" said Draggett without cordiality.

"I'm still interested in the murder of that Bonner girl."

Draggett swore. *"You're* interested? Look what it done to *me*—lost my liquor license—my business is gone—I'm busted!"

"When they find out who killed the girl," said Debs, "they'll take off the padlock order and give you back your license. If you're clean—and I'm taking it for granted you are. Give them thirty days—sixty at the outside. People will come back." He spoke soothingly.

"Think so? Think they'll lift the padlock?"

"Just a matter of time."

"Put in a word with the county attorney, will you, Debs? Appreciate anything you can do. We never was out of line—not very much, anyway."

Debs nodded. "Count on it. But you've got to help me first."

"What on?"

"The Bonner case. What friends did the girl have?"

Draggett became eager to give any information he possessed. "No guys," he said. "Never seen a stripper like her—done her act, and that was it. Plenty of guys wanted to date her, but she never give none of 'em a tumble."

"Gal friends?"

"Wimmin—lemme see. W-e-e-ll, the only one I ever seen her have much to do with was Mamie."

"Who's Mamie?"

"Waitress we had here. They was a whole lot different but knew each other somewheres else, I heard. Bonnie wouldn't step out, but I always thought Mamie done enough of it for two."

"What was Mamie's last name?"

"Slago."

"Was she working here when——"

"Naw. Got another job a couple of weeks before the murder."

"Why did she leave?"

"Dunno. Restless, I reckon. All them hashers is. Work awhile, then go to another place. Move around all the time."

"Did she have any visitors here?"

"Naw. This place was always decent——"

"I don't mean that."

"Well——" Draggett shrugged. "Guys might wait for her an' take her to town when we closed up nights. What people do off hours is their business. Mamie Slago never had none of her boy friends in here."

"Where's she now?"

"I'll give you the last address we had on her. But that's every single thing I know about her. An' speak to the county attorney for me, will you?"

Debs nodded.

2

Back to Jericho, and to an address in the Jugtown district once more: this time on Bede Street, where the packing house workers and Negroes and Mexicans lived. Debs went up a sidewalk that was cracked and full of holes to a rooming house of ancient brick and unpainted weather boarding. In the downstairs hall a gaunt sallow woman with a faded cloth tied around her head was mopping the warped flooring. She stood up, leaned on her mop handle, chewing gum, and stared at him.

"I'm looking for a woman named Mamie Slago," Debs said. "Does she room here?"

"Nope."

"Did she?"

"Used to."

"How long ago?"

"Couple weeks."

"Anybody ever come to see her here?"

The gaunt woman gave him a sour, suspicious look.

"How would I know?" she said. "I don't check up on my tenants as long as they're quiet and don't annoy nobody. Live an' let live is what I say."

"Sure, sure," said Debs.

"It's a free country, ain't it?"

"Sure."

"Well, she may of had friends, an' she may not of."

"Men?"

"Couldn't say."

"You never saw any of them?"

"Never paid them no mind. People come an' go here. I mind my own business as long as tenants pay their rent regular."

"Where's she working?"

The woman returned to her mopping of the worn pine floor. "I don't want no trouble," she said sullenly.

"There won't be any trouble," said Debs. "Could you remember where she works—for five bucks?"

She hesitated. Then she reached out greedy fingers and took the bill he offered her.

"She told me she was workin' at Nick's Cafe on E Street," she said.

"Is that all you know?"

The woman clutched the five-dollar bill. "A bargain's a bargain, mister."

Debs turned and left her.

3

Nick's Cafe was a small hole-in-the-wall restaurant operated by a bulletheaded Greek with a black mustache.

"Do you have a girl working here named Mamie Slago?" Debs asked.

"Mamie? Uh-huh." Nick nodded his head.

"Can I speak with her?"

"She ain't here."

"When will she be here?"

"I do-know. Work morning treek, but she deen't show op thees morning. Wait a minnit."

Nick stepped over to a customer who had just taken a stool at the counter. "Biff stew, appla pie," he said over his shoulder to a white cook's cap seen through an opening in the wall behind the counter. He placed a glass of water, knife, fork and spoon, and a paper napkin before the customer, brought him a cup of coffee, bread and butter, and returned to Debs.

"Trouble alla time," he said. "Gal don' show op, make coff' myself, clean op, wait on counter, cash register—she's fired."

"Maybe you can tell me where Mamie lives," said Debs.

"What you want weeth her?"

"I'm a newspaperman. The *Clarion.*"

"Oh, *Clarion,* hah? I take *Clarion.* What Mamie op to now?"

"Nothing that I know of—a feature story, that's all."

"Feature story, hah? Mebbe som'day you write feature story about restaurant bizness. Nick Popolopolis geeve you planty good story——"

"Maybe, someday. But right now what about Mamie?"

"Sure. I tell you." The Greek, now that he knew he was talking to a newspaperman, became relaxedly friendly. "Wait a minnit."

He took time to place the order before the customer at the counter, consulted a small book beside the cash register, and returned.

"Thees last address she geeve," he said, handing Debs a piece of paper with a number on it.

4

Nobody was in sight up or down the block when Debs parked his car before an ugly brick veneer apartment building on South Market, another cheap rooming house district. He stepped out, compared the number with that on his piece of paper. Apartment 2D, the paper said. That would be on the second floor.

He entered the building, climbed a stair, went down a dark hall, and knocked at a door on which was painted 2D.

No answer.

He rapped again. Someone moved inside. After a considerable time the door opened.

"Well—hello!" said Debs, surprise in his voice.

In the door stood a short, thin-faced man, very dark, with a compressed mouth and heavy brows that met across the bridge of his nose, rather dapper in a brown suit and hand-painted necktie. He was Walt Benson, the city detective who was with Nibs Galloway when the latter was killed.

Benson stared. "What do you want, Dorn?"

212   JERICHO'S DAUGHTERS

Debs grinned. "Guess I'm here on the same errand as you."

"Yeah?"

"I found out Miss Slago knew Bonnie Bonner, too."

"Oh, you did?" Dead-pan inquiry.

"Is she here?"

Benson hesitated. "Yeah."

"I'd like to talk to her."

"I just finished checkin' her, Dorn. She don't know nothin'."

"I'd still like to ask her a question or two."

A woman came to the door and stood behind the detective. She was dark, about thirty, aquiline. Figure not bad though somewhat thin. Debs guessed she wore falsies.

"Are you Mamie Slago?" Debs asked.

"Yes." Hard voice.

"A friend of Bonnie Bonner?"

"I don't know a thing—not a thing!"

"You knew her, didn't you?"

"Just to say hello."

"Know anyone else that knew her?"

"I tell you I don't know nothing about her!"

"But you used to visit with her——"

"Not a goddamn thing! Listen, I ain't got time to talk with you, neither of you. Will you get out an' leave me alone?"

She pushed Benson into the hall and slammed the door.

Debs and the detective looked at one another.

"I think she knows something," said Debs.

"If she does, it's by me."

They walked together down the hall and out of the building. With a perfunctory nod Benson got into a car—not a police car—and drove off.

On his way back toward the *Clarion* office Debs was thinking. He remembered Benson's face when he came to the door. An odd expression, perhaps surprise, perhaps something else. Benson hesitated momentarily when Debs asked if Mamie Slago was in her apartment. Why should he hesitate? Perhaps Benson wanted to say no, but it was obvious the woman was there or his own presence would be impossible to explain. Mamie Slago's voice—tough, resentful. Why should she be resentful? Had Benson been badgering her? And she had pushed Benson out and slammed the door on them both. Why was Benson so noncommittal? It was not the usual manner of a police officer with the press—given a chance to figure in the news, most policemen were only too glad to talk, to be quoted. Was Benson on some kind of a private investigation, conducted perhaps personally and apart from the department's investigation? And if so, had he some definite connection—something more than a mere hunch such as Debs had—between the Bonner and Galloway murders?

All at once Debs had a thought. He knew someone who might have a line on Mamie Slago. A certain kind of line, at least.

5

It was Larry Cameron, the *Clarion's* sports editor, whom Debs wanted to see now—Larry the woman chaser, the self-confessed "expert" on the cheaper types of available sex. He wondered where Larry would be at this time of a late afternoon.

It occurred to him that there was to be a wrestling match that night at the city auditorium. Sometimes Larry took the opportunity afforded by such night events for an assignation with one of his various wantons, but this was a match in which considerable public interest had been stirred up by the usual methods of the wrestling racket—publicity build-ups, phony feuds, nonexistent "championships," villain and hero characterizations of the contestants, and so on. It had been advertised as a "shooting match" between two cauliflower-eared behemoths who allegedly hated each other and desired to commit bloodthirsty mayhem on one another. But Larry, who might be expected to be on the inside and thus know the already arranged ultimate outcome of the match, had found some sucker money and bet a hundred dollars. Under such circumstances he probably would cover the match in person, if only for the joy of witnessing his winning of an easy bet.

Debs parked his car near Jolly Herron's Drugstore and entered. The front end of the store was full, and Herron, a heavy dark man who perspired even in winter, nodded at Debs.

"Meeting of the clans in there," he grinned, jerking his head toward the "Press Club" in the rear.

"See Larry?"

"Yes, he's there. Tod Burdock, too, and Joe Canfield. Some of the *Sentinel* boys. I've been taking in setups. Somebody's got the bottle. What'll you have, coke or plain water and ice?"

"Neither just now, thanks."

When Debs opened the door of the Press Club, it was a scene of curious activity. Stretched on the long table was a man in a rumpled suit and a cashmere slipover sweater, asleep. He was Cody, of the *Sentinel,* and his slumber was undisturbed by the fact that three men were rolling dice on the table at his feet and two more playing gin rummy at his head.

Glasses, sticky and smeared, empty or half empty, stood on chairs, on the floor, on window sills. An empty whiskey bottle lay in one corner, and another bottle, uncorked but not empty, stood on a corner of the table.

Tod Burdock, the *Clarion's* courthouse reporter, a veteran with a face like a disgusted Mr. Punch, was one of the gin rummy players. His opponent was Caddy Rice, his rival on the same beat from the *Sentinel.* Canfield was shooting craps with Brummitt and Yates, of the *Sentinel.* Larry Cameron was not in view.

"Don't you guys get enough of that on your run?" asked Debs, stopping beside Burdock to watch the gin game.

"You know we never play cards at the courthouse, but always attend strictly to our duties as representatives of the metropolitan press," said Rice in injured tones.

"Yes, I know," said Debs. "I had that courthouse run myself once."

"I knock for three," said Burdock, spreading his cards.

Rice looked over his layout, played off one or two cards from his hand, then said "Five." From a little pile of silver he pushed a quarter over.

"Another snort?" said Burdock. He reached for the bottle just in time to save it from being knocked off the table by Cody, who aroused himself and turned over.

"No," Rice said. "I've still got to write my yarns."

"Don't mind if *I* do." Burdock poured a stiff drink on the half-melted ice in his glass. "Here, Cody."

The recent sleeper sat up, his legs hanging over the edge of the table, and reached for the bottle, directly from the mouth of which he took a long gulping drink.

"Debs?" said Burdock when Cody returned the bottle.

"Not now. I was looking for Larry."

"He's in the can." Burdock set the half-empty bottle on the floor under the table, out of danger, and dealt the cards.

"Somebody paging me?" said a voice from the boarded little cubicle in the corner that housed the toilet. Water rushed and Larry Cameron opened the door, zipping up his fly. He gave Debs a glassy grin. Obviously he was preparing alcoholically for the ordeal of watching the wrestlers go through their antics and contortions that night.

"Like to see you just a minute, Larry," Debs said.

"Okay," Larry said genially. "Where's that bottle?"

He spied it, retrieved it from under the table, and offered it to Debs. "Come on, have one," he said.

Debs took it and allowed a couple of swallows to burn down his throat. Larry gulped lengthily when the bottle was handed back to him.

"What can I do for you, pal?" he grinned.

Debs drew him into a corner. "Do you know a woman named Mamie Slago?" he asked, lowering his voice.

"Mamie Slago? Well, I'll say I do! Nice li'l gal. Sure I know Mamie!" Larry was too drunk to keep his voice down.

"What do you know about her?"

"What do I know about Mamie?" Larry leered archly. "Well, I know this much, she won't lay nobody but her friends, but she ain't got an enemy in the world! Say—want me to fix that up for you?"

Debs had his back to the room but he had a feeling the others were listening.

"No, thanks," he said. "How long since you had her out, Larry?" He grinned disarmingly.

"Me? Oh, mebbe six weeks. Just a little casual ride in the hay. We both found other interests."

Again Debs grinned. "You old tomcat, you've got too many interests for me to keep up with."

Larry accepted this as a well-merited compliment. "Oh, a little poontang here and there," he said as one who, being flattered, seeks to be modest.

"But what about Mamie's interest?" Debs continued.

"Her? I think she's been goin' out with some cop. Walt Benson. He picked her up about the time she an' I called it off. Have another slug?"

"No, thanks."

As Larry lifted the bottle to his lips, Debs went out of the Press Club. He noticed that Joe Canfield had departed before him.

6

Tex Hardcastle, the chief of police, was a pompous man in a blue uniform with much gilt braid, whose dark skin contrasted oddly with his white hair. Tex was honest, stupid, and a figurehead, the department really being operated by Vic Hinshaw, the chief of detectives. He gazed at Debs Dorn, who sat before his desk.

"Have you a record on a woman named Mamie Slago?" Debs asked.

Hardcastle was very willing to oblige the press. He pushed a buzzer.

"Get me an R.D. on a woman named Mamie Slago," he said to the uniformed police clerk who appeared.

Within a few minutes the record office reported by telephone that there was no such woman in the files.

"I'll give you something to start on," said Debs. "She was a friend of Bonnie Bonner."

"You talked to her?"

"Just a few words."

"Where's she live?"

"Here's the address."

"I'll have her checked."

"She's already been checked."

"Who by?"

"Walt Benson."

"How do you know that, Debs?"

"When I went to her apartment, he was there. She wouldn't give me anything."

"Benson never said nothing about it to this office," said Hardcastle, frowning. He pressed the buzzer again. "Tell Hinshaw to come up," he told the clerk.

The chief of detectives appeared presently with his hat on the back of his head: a loose-limbed, leisurely man in his fifties, with a long nose and gray eyes, the drooping lids of which gave him a deceptively sleepy appearance. Under his slow drawling manner, Debs considered him not a bad officer. He nodded and took a chair.

"Vic, do you know anything about a dame called Mamie Slago?" asked Hardcastle.

"Slago?" said Hinshaw. "No."

"One of your department's investigating her."

"Who?"

"Benson."

"She's a waitress," said Debs. "I have information she's Benson's girl friend."

"Walt has a taste for hashers," said Hinshaw. "What's the line?"

"She knew the Bonner woman," said Hardcastle.

"Benson was just checking in to Investigation when I came up," said Hinshaw. "Send for him."

Debs made no move to leave. "I'd like to hear what Benson's got to say," he said. "If it's off the record, it's off the record."

Hardcastle appeared reluctant, but policy forbade his ordering the city editor of the *Clarion* out of his office. So he nodded.

When, a few minutes later, Walt Benson entered, his face changed as he saw first Hinshaw, then Debs.

"Benson, who's this woman, Mamie Slago?" Hardcastle asked at once.

"Why—just a hasher, chief."

"You been dating her?"

Benson shot a glance toward Debs, dark with sudden suspicion. Then he nodded. "A few dates. She's good for laughs."

"Did you know she was acquainted with the Bonner woman?"

"Sure, chief." Benson seemed to see his way and relaxed. "She knew Bonnie Bonner just slightly. I happened to remember it. Hadn't seen her in a couple of weeks, an' went over to check her on it."

Hardcastle's face stiffened. "Why didn't you report this matter? Anyone give you authority to make a private investigation?"

Benson shifted his weight, his black eyes glittering angrily.

"It was on my own time," he said. "Mebbe I was wrong, but it's a personal matter with me. My own pardner, Nibs Galloway—killed right before my eyes. I want to get that killer, chief. I remembered Mamie had spoke of the Bonner girl. Them murders happened close together. I thought there might be a connection—just an off chance. So I went over to talk with her. I was off duty, so I thought it would be all right."

"You know damn well that no man in this department is ever off duty!" snapped Vic Hinshaw. "And you know one of the first rules is to report all information to this office. How do you know we weren't investigating her from another angle? How do you know you haven't blown up a whole line of investigation?"

"I—I didn't think of that," said Benson.

"Think of it next time! What did you get out of her?"

"Nothing. Not a thing. Miss Slago ain't seen the Bonner woman for a long time, she told me. It was a water haul, chief."

"It'll be a water haul for you—back to pounding pavements—if I ever hear of anything like this again," growled Hinshaw. "Go back to detective headquarters and make a full written report."

"Okay, chief."

Benson went out, walking slow and closing the door behind him. Debs knew he was mad clear through. Not at Hardcastle or Hinshaw. At Debs.

But Debs was fitting together some things in his mind.

"I'd like to see that Slago woman checked," he said.

"Well—she's been checked——" began Hardcastle.

"I've got a hunch someone else might get something out of her that Benson couldn't. When I was trying to talk to her, she put him out of the room like you would a pup."

Hardcastle tapped the desk with a pencil.

"One thing, chief," said Vic Hinshaw, "she's the only single solitary connection of any kind that's been found with the Bonner case."

"There's something oddball about the whole thing," said Debs.

"How do you mean?" asked Hardcastle.

"I don't know. I'd just like to have someone beside Benson have a talk with her."

Hinshaw rose and stretched. "Reckon it won't do any harm. I'll have her brought in."

Debs was still thinking. "While you're at it," he said, "you might get out a call to the radio patrol cars with her description and have somebody watch the bus depot and the railroad station."

"What for?"

"If there's something wrong with her, she might try to skip town."

Hinshaw gave a nod and departed.

Debs rose. "If there's anything new, let me know, chief," he said to Tex Hardcastle. "I'm going back to the office."

"Sure, Debs."

Thirty minutes later Debs Dorn's telephone on the city desk at the *Clarion* rang.

"This is Chief Hardcastle, Debs," said a voice. "We got that Slago woman."

"Where?"

"At the bus depot, with her suitcase—beating it out of town."

"Has she said anything?"

"No. Won't talk. But we're holding her on a vag charge."

"Thanks, chief."

"Another thing. I've put Benson on temporary suspension."

Debs hung up the receiver with a little whistle.

Seventeen

I

That afternoon the Jericho Art Association was holding its monthly meeting. For the first time in months the hostess was Mrs. Simon Bolivar Butford; and in attendance, also for the first time in months, was Mrs. Wistart Wedge. Though Mary Agnes usually found the meetings somewhat boring, she had personal reasons for wishing to be present at this particular one.

Her first two days at home had been busy ones. After the conversation with her husband, in which she drove her bargain for a controlling interest in the *Clarion,* for which she met the print paper bills, there was some necessary work to be done, with conferences with lawyers and the signing of certain documents. When that was finished, Wistart announced suddenly that he was flying to Tulsa for some sort of a regional publishers' meeting—she did not interest herself enough to make sure just what it was—and so she turned her attention to other affairs. Of these, the Art Association seemed the most immediately important.

The gathering at the Butford house that afternoon was perhaps better attended by the membership than any for at least a year, although it was January and still cold. Plans for the proposed new Gallery of Art were to be discussed and this may have had some bearing on the gratifying show of interest. There is even a possibility that the members were actuated by a sincere devotion to aesthetics. But there is room also for at least a surmise that curiosity was the main factor, for the Jericho Art Association was to be introduced as a body, for the first time, to Mr. Erskine de Lacey, late of Hollywood, who since his arrival in Jericho a few weeks previously had been Mrs. Butford's personal guest at her home.

Mr. de Lacey's importance in the world of art was quite generally accepted in Jericho circles. He had been Mrs. Butford's very assiduous escort to two receptions, a concert, and three dinner parties during the somewhat more than a month he had been in the city, and those ladies who had been fortunate enough to meet him personally had firsthand knowledge of his notable genius and high status as an artist through his own words.

He was, you understood, too much of a prodigy to be falsely coy or modest. He told you frankly and fearlessly what was good and what was bad. And when he said that he himself was a genius of world stature—although his work thus far was known and understood only by the highest and most recondite circles of art experts—he said it so sincerely, and he was backed so strongly by Mrs. Butford in his no doubt completely objective estimate of his own qualities that quite naturally you accepted and believed.

In varying ways, during the short time she had been home, Mary Agnes already had heard this feeling expressed by several of her art-eager feminine acquaintances. She had not ventured to dissent from the prevailing opinion. It was evident to her that Erskine had made a very profound impression on Jericho; and it was general knowledge that Mrs. Butford was enthralled with him, regarded him as her own personal possession, had turned over to him a suite of rooms for his quarters and the late Simon Bolivar Butford's smoking room for a studio, and in every way behaved in the manner of a fatuous old woman who is completely adoring.

Arriving a little late this afternoon, Mary Agnes observed that the driveways of the Butford grounds already were crowded by parked cars of the more expensive makes. It was evident that the ladies of the Art Association were out in force to take in the new marvel from Hollywood, to see him in the flesh, to hear his dictums on painting and other matters, and in general to acquire merit and culture by so doing.

She gave a little sniff, and repeated the sniff when she was ushered into the drawing room. It was filled with women, all formally hatted, all in their best afternoon garb, all silent for once, and listening.

Mrs. Butford, in her almost invariable purple, sat solidly in her usual chair by the glass mosaic fireplace, in which a blaze of oak wood was burning. Her feet were on a stool, she was stroking the wheezing lap dog in her lap, and her broad face with its sagging folds and white bristles of brows wore an expression of complacency.

Beside her stood her secretary, Miss Rose Caruthers: a rather withered rose, a spinster of perhaps fifty winters, thin-bosomed and thin-shanked, with horn-rimmed glasses and that silent self-effacement which seemed to be a hallmark of all Mrs. Butford's secretaries.

All, perhaps, except one. Mary Agnes thought of Mrs. Butford's former secretary, Grey Rutledge, and sniffed for the third time. Grey Rutledge, she remembered, left the old lady most unexpectedly. She was not the type for this office, anyway. Mary Agnes, of course, had nothing in particular against Grey Rutledge except that she disliked any really attractive woman. An idle wonder flicked through her mind, as it had once or twice before, as to how Grey, from obvious poverty, had suddenly found the finances to establish that store of hers. The thought, however, was dismissed at once in favor of something more immediate and interesting.

In the drawing room the women were not looking at Mrs. Butford, or at her secretary, either. They were gazing toward—and listening most raptly to—Erskine de Lacey.

It was the first time Mary Agnes had seen him since that strange night in Hollywood, and his appearance was subtly changed. She decided it was because he was wearing glasses with pinkish rims. She had never seen him wear glasses before; they gave him a slightly scholarly appearance.

He leaned easily against the mantel beside the fireplace and in his fingers he held a cigarette holder with a lighted cigarette—a thing unheard of in Mrs. Butford's drawing room, and proof in itself of the old woman's complete surrender to this object of her new idolatry. Once more Mary Agnes noticed how unusually small were his feet in their perfectly polished pointed shoes, and how he posed with his hands almost as if he tried to mock effeminacy. She noticed also how Mrs. Butford did not take her eyes off him.

She *dotes* on him—the old fool! said Mary Agnes to herself.

Since she was late she made as little disturbance as possible, seating herself near the door at the back of the drawing room.

2

Erskine de Lacey was lecturing on painting. The words flowed smoothly, hardly requiring thought, although he was leading up to a point and a conclusion connected with a definite plan. Talking about art was an accomplishment, a technique one acquired, depending on a natural glibness, plus a study of catchwords, symbolic phrases, a smattering of psychiatry, and always remembering to maintain a mystical vagueness which left the listener, unless he were of the initiates and therefore cynical about the whole matter, feeling there were depths beyond which his own poor intellect could not go.

As he spoke Erskine observed how easily he had engrossed this audience of women, almost breathlessly so, by his facile recital of the old phrases and old postulates, familiar and perhaps a little corny in places like Hollywood and New York, but sophisticatedly new in Jericho. He saw with satisfaction how eagerly these women accepted the most specious casuistries; and that they did not understand at all what he was talking about, but willingly believed him to be a kind of high priest in those realms of mystery which feminine natures seem to crave as an escape from hard realities.

Clearly Jericho was a rich and virgin field for one of his varied talents; and already he was conscious that he had succeeded beyond his imaginings and stood at the threshold of good fortune incredible.

For a long time Erskine had known that to take up painting as a life work was to starve slowly to death. Unless, perhaps, one went into commercial art; and if he had any real ability, it was in this field. He had been offered work by advertising concerns, and could have been a fairly good calendar artist if he had desired. But that meant labor, and he early had acquired the inclination to live by his wits rather than by his sweat. He therefore became successively a futurist, an expressionist, a dadaist, a surrealist, and a primitivist. He spoke with scorn of "philistines" who prowled the land and hooted at any or all of his "phases."

For a time he lived on the small estate his mother left him, but this was quickly used up because he was spendthrift by nature. The problem of simple subsistence became a concern that had overpreoccupied him.

Yet he remained an artist by vocation and maintained a studio. Occasionally he had even fallen so low, when hard pressed for money, as to take commercial work. But this he despised.

The complete freedom, or more exactly, the complete license of action which the public accords an artist, was one of the chief appeals to him. An artist could dress as he wished, talked as he pleased, act in any manner he desired, and the laity was unsurprised, humoring, even perhaps a little intrigued and amused by it.

Erskine could paint, if he chose, rather expertly in the realistic manner, but he considered illustrators beneath the dignity of notice. Furthermore, he had discovered that the public delights in being bedazzled, in being abused and derided for its lack of "feeling," of "comprehension"; and it gave him a sensation of power to slap something off on canvas and then by the very audacity and insolence of his conversational attack force people to blink, and back off, and stare, and doubt their own senses, and finally admit that they must be viewing Art in a great mystical sense, and that he who had created it was a Genius above ordinary human comprehension. To be a successful artist one had, in the argot, "to talk a good line," and Erskine had always been more than successful in this.

He was intelligent and realistic enough to recognize his own weakness, his physical sexual impotence. Sometimes he wondered if he was born with this lack, or this quirk; or if he had acquired it. And often he thought his mother had something to do with it. Madame de Lacey was a masculine woman, with a vestigial mustache, speaking in a voice almost bass in timbre. For years before her death she was a paralytic in a wheel chair, requiring constant attention sometimes of the most unpleasant kind, which he accorded to her because he was financially dependent on her, and also because she was something of a habit to him. Yet though he waited on her and rarely left her alone, his mother was loathsome and repulsive to him, especially in the last months of his servitude before her death: a creature both masculine and feminine, at once a burden and a threat.

To make personal attachments or loyalties was impossible for him, since he felt on the one hand distaste and contempt for women, coupled with deep-rooted fear of them which was shadowy yet instinctive; and on the other hand, a sense of dependence on them. At the same time he lacked all mental or emotional meeting grounds with men.

Not even in the dim borderland between the sexes did he find release. Alone he stood, shunning not only normal sexual attachments which are common everywhere, but also abnormal homosexual attachments such as he sometimes observed in some of the Hollywood circles in which he moved.

Constantly he was experimenting, in his painting, with imitations of this or that artist of one or another of the various modern schools, since secretly he knew himself to have little real originality. Yet sometimes it was as if his nature demanded relentlessly that he go back to realism in the nude, the study of a model, the intense engrossment with the translucent clarity of delicate flesh. From this he derived an aesthetic pleasure similar, he sometimes believed, to that of the ancient Greeks, and there were moods and mutations in this enjoyment.

Sometimes a hired model was all he required. But at other times the model must not be a professional. He found that the selection of a subject, the pursuit of her, the subtle campaign very similar to a seduction conducted perhaps over a considerable period of time, and the triumph at last in overcoming her scruples and bending her to his will was an intense part of the pleasure of the game. When he succeeded in bringing about the surrender of a woman like that and made her accede to his wish, he sometimes felt enormous excitement, especially if his subject showed embarrassment in her nudity, which seemed to give the final fillip to the entire adventure.

On such occasions this excitement found expression in his brush, the placing on the canvas of those smooth soft contours, particularly the attitude of shame. Sometimes he watched with delight the expression on such a model's face when he displayed to her his painting: the shock, the dissent that such a painting as he usually achieved brought. And sometimes he touched his model's body, sometimes even went so far as a kiss. But it always ended there . . . it achieved for him the psychic release he sought.

His women sometimes seemed surprised, even incredulous, when he halted at such a point. Often he surmised their frustration, yet he was through with them. Hardly any of them understood what really had happened. Some of them, he was sure, hated him afterward, and some perhaps despised him. But all of them, without exception, kept the matter to themselves, and no doubt trusted that he would do so also.

This psychic problem was one that never would be solved. But there were others more pressing and practical that required solution; and it now appeared that one of the most important of them was approaching that end.

He could hardly believe it, the quick and enormous influence he had achieved over Mrs. Butford in the relatively short time he had known her. His experience with his mother had been a great resource: he knew the things to say, the little acts, the whole atmosphere of attention and flattery that appealed to an old woman's vanities and her comforts and satisfactions.

To Mrs. Butford's servants, he was "Mr. Erskine"; they hurried to obey his directions as quickly as those of his mistress. He had made himself a combination of courtier, adviser, child, servant, and master to his hostess, by studying her and adapting himself to her wishes, and by fathoming the stupidity of her mind and the unsubtle processes of her thinking, until he ruled the house as he wished and Mrs. Butford looked to him for most decisions with her fatuously fond grin.

He knew now where his future lay. Invariably Mrs. Butford referred to him as "Dear Boy," and he estimated the length of time it would require him to come to an understanding with her about something that was her chief worry: the disposition of her wealth after her death. He was inducing her to see an objective that would relieve that concern. She was beginning to look upon him actually as a son, a child of her old age where she had never had a child in her youth, perhaps something even more. Already she had half expressed the desire to secure Dear Boy's future, to give his genius a chance to flower. How long? Weeks, months? She was old . . . she could not live much longer. It was not impossible to imagine that with proper tact and handling, Erskine de Lacey might, at her death, be the major heir to the magnificent Butford fortune.

Meantime, however, he was the focus of interest of these women in the room, and he now devoted himself to further building up his ascendancy. It was not difficult. As he talked he felt he was being completely successful; they were spellbound by him, every face was eager, accepting.

And then, just when he felt this glow of triumph over what he already had achieved and the greater achievements to follow, he saw someone whom he knew enter the room and seat herself at the rear. Mary Agnes Wedge. In that moment he felt almost frightened. She was one of his women, whom he had courted and seduced into serving him for his odd passion. Fervently now he wished he had left her alone, never sought her or succeeded with her, because intuition told him she was a threat, a peril to him. Mary Agnes, he was sure, hated and despised him. The thought was dreadfully disconcerting.

3

Mary Agnes listened to Erskine's lecture, the smooth flow of which hardly hesitated at her entrance. For a time she scarcely followed what he was saying: it was of a pattern with which she was familiar. Certain pet words, clichés of artistic jargon, appeared again and again.

Suspended architecture . . . rhythm . . . static-dynamic relations . . . architectonic reliefs . . . atonal . . . melodic (in a deprecating sense) . . . violent expressionistic fervor . . . tour de force . . . abstractism . . . essence of approach . . .

About certain great names in art he expressed strong opinions.

Renoir was "utterly boring."

Van Gogh "simply leaves me cold."

But he spoke with enthusiasm of Epstein's sculptured women with huge buttocks and pendulous breasts, and about Picasso, in his most exaggerated moods, he grew almost excited.

Over and over, she noticed, he employed expressions describing pain: "that smothers me . . . gnaws at me . . . batters . . . bruises . . . makes me writhe . . ." He employed such words as if they gave him pleasure at the thoughts they evoked in him. She was reminded that the masochist and the sadist often are combined in the same individual and wondered if this was true in Erskine.

He was nearing the end of his lecture, gesturing with his cigarette holder, from which he now had ejected the cigarette into the fireplace. And she said to herself: His skin looks like an aging woman's skin without that tan he always had, and I believe in my soul he creams his face at nights.

"So we approach the great question," he was saying, "the question of the objective, the central theme of our gallery, which we all hope may be established very soon."

He gave a little bow and smile to Mrs. Butford, who returned to him her gargoyle grin.

"Shall we have a gallery of the trivial, the ordinary, the banal?" he continued. "Grandma Moseses, perhaps?" He waited expectantly for the dutiful titter, and got it.

"Ah, no, I hope not," he continued. "I have nothing against Grandma Moses, I understand she is a very estimable old lady. But anybody can do so-called Grandma Moseses—any sign painter. They are being turned out in carloads by people with no more artistic ability than so many swine—mere crude decoration, perhaps in harmony with antique furniture."

His voice indicated scorn not only of the Grandma Moses school of art, but also of antique furniture. On the faces of some of his listeners might have been detected a faint look of consternation, as the ladies remembered that not only did they have Grandma Moses imitations in their living rooms or dens, but also antique furniture, of which, up to this moment, they had been quite proud.

"Shall we go farther back, to the so-called old masters?" Erskine said. From the floor, leaning against the wall, he lifted a canvas.

"This is an example I found in your collection here. It purports to be a Frans Hals. Precious old boy, wasn't he? One of those dear old boys who painted what they saw and therefore are not to be compared to the moderns." Having sufficiently patronized Frans Hals and the other old masters, he paused. "But this, I'm sorry to have to say to you, is a forgery—an antique oil copy, and I'm afraid not even a very good one."

From the ladies came a little murmur of woe at the thought that the Frans Hals, of which they had been proud since the Charles Sinclairs brought it from Amsterdam and presented it to the Art Association, was not genuine. Mary Agnes observed that nobody thought to ask Erskine how he knew this was a forgery. They accepted his judgment without question.

"It illustrates the dangers a gallery faces," he was saying. "But why need we go in for antiques in the first place? At most a *genuine* Frans Hals would be of interest to us primarily from an historical standpoint. This Art Association, this gallery we hope to establish are too new, too recently in the field to hope to compete as an historical repository. We stand in an era of change, of revolt. Would it not be better, far better, to devote ourselves to modern art?"

He set the despised Frans Hals back on the floor, its face to the wall like a shamed child, and lifted another canvas, which he set on a chair facing the room.

No question that this created a stir, almost a shock, among the ladies. To Mary Agnes it appeared to be a moon with a long tail, like a comet going off into space, on a background of strange liverish patches.

"An experiment of my own," he said. "I bring it before you as an illustration. Here you see emancipation, a painting going beyond any style, a concentration of sensitivity and insight, emphasizing the artist's emotional spirit, conveying the very essence of his approach to life."

He smiled at his obviously stunned audience.

"Continue to look at it. Study it. You will find it has meaning for you—a powerful experience of the soul. The undulating rhythms here, the subtle harmony of tones and textures, is contrasted with the violent maelstrom of slashing strokes and colors there. It jars one out of one's complacency, doesn't it?"

He smiled again with a lift of his brows. It struck Mary Agnes that the ladies might be having their complacency jarred, but there was something very complacent in Erskine's own expression at the moment.

"This canvas, I daresay you will agree," he said, "illustrates the infinitude of opportunity awaiting us. Here is an example of the new focus of painting, having its collaterals in all the other forms of expression—sculpture, drama, literature, music. Need I add that a gallery at Jericho dedicated solely to the newest and most stimulating trends in art would give you national publicity, national reputation? Ladies, it is my suggestion, my earnest recommendation, that in the proposed Jericho Gallery of Art we strike out on new paths, dare to be original, dare to display true *savoir-faire* in artistic appreciation, which cannot fail to make our gallery a shrine in years to come."

Erskine's speech was received with quite enthusiastic applause, led by Mrs. Butford, who clapped her fat old hands and nodded her blue-white head, although it was obvious she hardly comprehended a word of what he had said.

The other women glanced at each other as if to seek reassurance that they were in the presence of something perhaps difficult for their minds really to grasp but no doubt great and new. They were somewhat dazed by all that jargon, but the touch about national publicity could be understood and it appealed to them all. They began to nod at one another and to chatter aloud all at once, as if with relief at being freed from the restraint of having to keep still so long and listen.

Miss Caruthers effaced herself as the women gathered about Erskine with gushing expressions of admiration and enthusiasm. Presently she was back, shepherding in the servants with the tea things. The guests broke into groups, the largest of which always surrounded Erskine and Mrs. Butford, sipping tea and nibbling small thin sandwiches; and all gabbling, making up for lost time by not listening to what anyone else was saying.

4

Alone in all the room Mary Agnes had not applauded. She was smiling a slight, inscrutable smile as she watched Erskine hovering over Mrs. Butford and saw Mrs. Butford's grin of gratification at the flatteries he was offering her along with a sandwich tray.

What is he up to? she asked herself. He's a charlatan and an opportunist, and he's riding the fads wherever they take him, purposely and not because he has any deep-rooted convictions concerning them. Why? His "modern" painting isn't objective. He doesn't have the intellect to conceive of abstract ideas, or the creative ability to express them. He speaks derisively of the "dear old boys who painted what they saw"— yet *he* paints what he sees on occasion, when the dark urge is upon him. I think he *can* paint, if he wants to, but he isn't painting now. He's faking, putting on a performance that is calculated to stun and dazzle these poor women.

Is it purely cynical, this mumbo-jumbo of mystery, the facile, smiling display of something very bad, something meaningless, an insult to the intelligence, presented in a manner so almost contemptuously audacious that these women swallow it, unable to rally their wits and think? And their yearning to be "different," to be "advanced," to be thought "smart" makes it so pathetically easy for him to befuddle them.

Or does he have some scheme, some plan behind all this? Even if he does impress our women, he can't make a living here by that kind of painting. The most gullible of these geese will hardly buy his daubs extensively in this town. Once out of his immediate presence, the sound of his facile tongue, his mountebanking performance, that "art" of his will look the sorry, ridiculous thing it is.

Yet he must make a living somehow, I happen to know. To be curator of a small art gallery which doesn't even have a collection yet and can afford little in salary—certainly that isn't Erskine de Lacey's real purpose.

Suddenly Mary Agnes glanced across the room with a new expression.

Mrs. Simon Bolivar Butford!

Of course! Old, anile Mrs. Butford, *she* is his objective! She dotes on him, he's indispensable to her. He's "Dear Boy" to her . . . over and over, "Dear Boy."

I see it now. Mrs. Butford began by being his sponsor; she's his creature now, a dupe to his flattery, a slave to his charm, his knowledge of her every weakness. Her money—that's what he wants. Perhaps he already has some of it.

And nobody has the brains to see it: nobody knows Erskine de Lacey, nobody understands his kind, so often marvelously acute and cunning, unscrupulous and therefore doubly dangerous.

Nobody but I—who have been exposed to him.

5

Mary Agnes placed her teacup on a table and moved over to the group gathered about Erskine. Instantly he broke off his conversation with Mrs. Dr. Kleaver and gave Mary Agnes his direct attention and his direct smile.

"Darling!" he cried, holding out both hands to her. "I *wondered* when you were going to speak to me!"

"You seemed so occupied," she said. "I thought I'd better wait until the lion had a little more leisure."

He laughed. "There are no lions here. Only people interested in something vital and personal to us all."

He glanced around the circle, and the Jericho women smiled and nodded vigorously to show that, whatever it was, it was vital and personal to *them*.

"We're old, old friends," he said, half placing an arm around Mary Agnes and smiling at the faces about them. "Do you people in Jericho know, really *know,* this charming lady of yours? When she's in Hollywood, I give you my word she's beset with invitations from that whole fantastic town. People fight to have her as a guest, the biggest names in the film colony with the rest of them. I've seen Mary Agnes at the

Ronald Colmans', the Glenn Fords', the Alan Ladds', the John Waynes'
—I can't tell you how many places like that!"

The Jericho women were impressed. Mary Agnes exceeded their
imaginings.

The flattery was quite subtle, being intended not only to win Mary
Agnes' gratitude and friendship, perhaps, but also, incidentally, to enhance Erskine's own prestige. If he had seen Mary Agnes at all those
places, the Jericho women said to themselves, he must have been a
guest at those places too. They ticketed it mentally as a subject of conversation when they had him in the future as a guest.

Mary Agnes smiled. "Yes, Erskine and I have known each other for
a long time. We understand each other quite well, don't we?"

She was smiling directly into his eyes and she saw that he knew she
was completely aware of his scheme.

His next audacity almost surprised her into a change of expression.
"I've even painted Mary Agnes," he told the group. "She's really a
wonderful subject."

"Oh!" "Ah!" came the gasps. To be painted by this genius! "May
we see it?" "Do you have it here?"

"Oh, someday I may let someone have a glimpse of it," he said care-
lessly, his eyes dwelling just a moment on Mary Agnes with a smile that
was not a smile. "Not for the present, though. It's not quite finished
yet. I dislike showing my work in the unfinished state. It does neither
my subject nor myself credit—don't you agree, darling?"

Mary Agnes nodded, her smile becoming rather glassy. She was
furious.

A gauntlet at her feet! He had that damned painting all right, and
he had read her quite correctly, and he was going to hold it as his hidden trump in case she made things the least bit difficult for him.

Blackmail, sheer blackmail . . . but she was helpless and he knew
it. That silly, drunken night in Hollywood . . . posing in the nude had
seemed such an amusing lark at the time, until the curious repellent
aftermath, and the picture, his treachery.

If people here in Jericho ever saw that obscene, shameless thing, so
recognizable in face and attitude, she never could live down the ridicule and embarrassment and outright scandal.

And with that she knew that Erskine would never give that painting
to her, never sell it to her now. Not for ten thousand dollars could she

buy it. Because it was his whip over her, to assure that she let him have smooth sailing with Mrs. Butford and her fortune.

She had never been particularly interested in Mrs. Butford, or her money, or the Jericho Art Association's hope that it would inherit her money. But to have Erskine defy her, and hold over her the threat which alone could control her, aroused every combative instinct in her. She groped in her mind for a way to checkmate him and he read her thoughts.

"Now that you're home, darling," he said, "you must come to the studio and finish our sitting. I've added some touches to the portrait since you saw it."

"I imagine they're very interesting." She smiled with eyes as hard as green stones.

"You may find them so," he said negligently.

"I may have some ideas."

"I suspect you have some now. They'll be most enlightening, I'm sure. But remember, I claim the artist's prerogative—my own ideas must always be the law."

She saw how secure he felt in a position of unassailable strength, and that the mutual understanding they had reached in those few oblique sentences addressed over the not very subtle heads of the women about them made him even more secure.

He had dared her: and she could not take up his challenge.

Eighteen

I

When Mary Agnes left Mrs. Butford's house after the Art Association meeting, she had Suey drive her downtown to the *Clarion*.

It was late, almost six o'clock, when she entered the business office, and the presses had long ceased their rumbling. In the circulation department a few unkempt persons lounged, and a dowdy girl or two stood at the classified advertising counter. Here she did not tarry. Instead, she at once took the private elevator to the second floor.

The door to Wistart's office stood open, although nobody was there.

Already the early winter darkness had set in, and she switched on a light to see around her. It was, she conceded to herself, a rather sumptuous office. She found herself approving Wistart's taste, and approval of anything concerning Wistart was rare with her. Then she remembered that this office originally was designed for Wistart's father, and later improved by Wistart's mother. Very likely all this reflected Algeria rather than her son. Mary Agnes' appreciation of Wistart underwent a decline.

She wished to see what the paper was like. Newspapers had power, and the *Clarion* might, just might, be some sort of resource to her in the delicate matter concerning herself and Erskine de Lacey. After a moment she left the office and went out through the reception room down a hall.

The hall led to the editorial department, and she halted to give it a quick, sweeping little survey. It was deserted except for a rather dark young man sitting alone at a central desk under a green-shaded light, apparently making notations on a piece of paper.

The young man glanced up at her. Debs Dorn had been spending the last hour in intense concentration, trying to put together some pieces in the crazy jigsaw puzzle of two murders. In the mink-swathed figure at the hall entrance he recognized Mrs. Wistart Wedge, although she would have no particular way of knowing him. She had, he thought, a rather aristocratic face, with its hollowed cheeks, slightly aquiline nose, and strongly marked brows. An imperious face, and just now a petulant one, with distaste evident on it.

It was the first time Debs had seen Mrs. Wedge in the *Clarion* office, and he felt apologetic. All city rooms look frowsy and disordered when they are empty at the end of day. He regretted that she could not have observed this one under more favorable circumstances, when it was busy, driving, accomplishing, filled with life and thought and activity and drama.

Somewhat hesitantly he rose and approached her.

"Mrs. Wedge," he said, stopping at a respectful distance, "I'm Debs Dorn. Is there anything I can do for you?"

She turned upon him the green sheen of her eyes. "Are you the only one here?"

"The paper's been out for three hours," he explained. "The staff's gone—I just happen to be here myself."

"What did you say your name was?"

"Dorn—Debs Dorn."

"And what is your—ah—capacity here, Mr. Dorn?"

"I'm the city editor."

Mary Agnes had a hazy conception of city editors derived from popular fiction and an occasional stage play or motion picture purporting to reflect newspaper life.

"City editor?" she repeated. "That's important, isn't it? A sort of manager of the news department?"

"Only the local news, ma'am. The managing editor is Mr. Hudson."

"I have a slight telephone acquaintance with Mr. Hudson," she said dryly. "He's not here, I take it?"

"No, ma'am."

She glanced again at the dreary surroundings, then walked over to the city desk. For a moment she viewed with disfavor its litter—proofs, unedited copy, head paper, spindles, ash trays, pencils, rules, assignment book, rumpled newspapers—and she stood at a little distance from it, as if it might soil her at closer quarters.

"I know very little about newspapers," she said. "But I'm supposed to take some interest in this one."

"Yes, ma'am."

He was thinking that she was now co-publisher of the *Clarion,* with "fullest authority," and he was hoping she was not going to be too much of a headache.

She surprised him with a smile that was not without charm. "Not the way I'm afraid you're thinking," she said. "I detest amateurs who intervene in things they know nothing about."

He gave her a grin of real appreciation for the way she had read his mind. Perhaps he had underestimated Mrs. Wedge.

"You don't look like a city editor," she went on. "I had the impression that all city editors were tyrants, unscrupulous and spectacularly villainous, hard drinkers, and somewhat sadistic toward their reporters."

She capped this light satirical little sally with another smile, but this time he did not respond to her smile.

"No, ma'am," he said seriously. "You can see I'm none of those things. Nothing spectacular about me—just a spear carrier in the ranks, trying to do the best he can."

"When you put it that way, it makes me sure you're far from being a mere spear carrier, Mr. Dorn. May I ask how long you've been with the *Clarion?*"

"About ten years. It's the only newspaper job I've ever had."

"Perhaps you can educate me a little. How do you operate in your job?"

"Well," he said, hardly knowing how to begin, "this is the city desk." And he went on with a swift and sketchy description of a typical day's work on the *Clarion.*

To this she listened keenly.

"That's quite illuminating," she said. "Now, Mr. Dorn, perhaps you'll give me your opinion on something else."

"What is it?"

"Just what's wrong with the *Clarion?*"

"Why—I hardly know what you mean, Mrs. Wedge."

The sudden odd alertness of his glance struck her rather forcibly. She said to herself, He doesn't trust me, and he's on his guard against me. It made her impatient with him that he should suddenly withdraw into his shell and become secretive.

"I think you *do* know what I mean," she said with an edge in her voice. "I presume that in your position you're aware that this newspaper is losing money rather rapidly?"

He answered her levelly but not deferentially.

"I am. We're losing both circulation and advertising. I'd say the competition of the *Sentinel* has something to do with it."

"Don't advertisers prefer to buy space in newspapers with the largest number of readers?" she demanded.

"It works out that way in a general sense."

"And circulation—isn't that based on the interest a newspaper offers to its readers? And doesn't that, in the final analysis, go back to the news and the way it's handled—in other words, right here to this department?"

He believed he saw the trend of her questioning. She was trying to find a scapegoat for the *Clarion's* condition, and she was putting her finger on the newsroom. She was going to be trouble, perhaps big trouble, after all.

"News is only one facet," he said. "There are others."

"Just what?"

"If I explained, do you think you'd understand?"

"And why not?" She sensed his thinly veiled resentment. "Is there some special category of intelligence, Mr. Dorn, that you suppose I lack?"

For a moment their glances met and locked.

"No," he said. "You have plenty of intelligence, Mrs. Wedge. But you're asking something pretty complicated, and I was wondering if without experience and special knowledge behind you, I could make it at all clear to you. But if you want it, I'll try."

She gave a nod, and he felt he had angered her.

"As far as the news itself is concerned," he told her, "I think we handle it as well as the *Sentinel,* maybe better. But there are other things——"

For the next ten minutes he flailed her, unceasingly and almost angrily, with information about the complicated workings of a newspaper. He ran the gamut of features, and showed her how countless readers buy a paper solely for a certain comic strip, or a movie column, or the dress patterns in it—and how the *Clarion* was heavily handicapped because of a conservatism which had not seen the need for them in time. He told her the strategic value of edition times, and railroad and bus schedules; circulation methods and how the *Sentinel's* high pressure was beating down the *Clarion's* old family-style approach; equipment and the necessity for improvement; the shortsightedness of a salary policy that made it virtually impossible to employ a competent staff, not only in the news, but in other departments as well; imagination and the necessity for keeping abreast of new trends; news services, and all the countless matters that must be recorded—markets, and sports, and crime, and obituaries, and radio-television, and theater-amusements, and editorial opinion, and elections, and personals, and business, and society, and weddings, and politics, and world news, and births and deaths, and a myriad other things, it seemed to her, for which the *Clarion's* facilities were inadequate for full coverage.

She felt like wincing, and when he finished all this he said, "But there's something else that's important. Maybe the most important of all."

"What?" she said.

"You think this newspaper's a business—just a business for making your money. Like your store."

"If it isn't that, what is it?" She felt defensive.

"It's a hell of a lot more than a business, Mrs. Wedge! A newspaper's almost like a person—almost *human*. Can you conceive of that? It appeals to the minds of people, and their hearts and their imaginations —not just to their pocketbooks! A newspaper has character, and it should have intelligence and ideals. It ought to have a sense of responsibility, and a sense of good taste, and a sense of honesty."

She gazed at him almost curiously, this was so foreign to her own brittle creed.

"Mrs. Algeria Wedge believed in those things," Debs pursued relentlessly. "Under her the paper had a definite set of policies. Sometimes the policies cost it money and friends, but if they were right the *Clarion* stuck by them just because they *were* right."

Her face drained of all expression, she listened.

"The newsroom was the power and the glory of the *Clarion*," said Debs. "People knew where the *Clarion* stood. They might disagree with it, but they knew it was honest, and they trusted it."

She gave a nod. "That's rather changed—now?"

Again his quick glance, dark and very aware.

"Circumstances have changed, ma'am."

"How?"

"A different kind of journalism in Jericho. The *Sentinel* has succeeded in debasing newspaper character in this town. We've tried to meet it on its chosen grounds, which are sensationalism, sex, trickery, and hippodrome. We should have stood on our own grounds of integrity and truthful presentation of the news. We're scrambling for revenues —and getting licked at it—instead of upholding principles. The newsroom's no longer the power on this paper. The advertising department calls the turn, and the advertising department's like all hucksters—timid to the point of cowardice about doing anything, *even if it's honest,* that might offend someone with a lousy buck to spend. That's the trouble with the *Clarion,* if you want to know it, Mrs. Wedge! Cowardice, superficiality, cheap mountebank stunts! It's become just what you said —a *business* primarily—and it's forgotten to be a *newspaper*. And that's a hell of a sorry situation!"

For a moment there was tense silence.

"And what would you do, Mr. Dorn, if you had the say about it?" she asked icily.

He looked her grimly in the eye.

"At least I'd go down fighting for what I believed, if it was my newspaper, Mrs. Wedge. I'd be honest—with myself as well as my readers. I wouldn't willfully blind myself to facts. I wouldn't lick anybody's boots—not even Cox's, Incorporated! I'd call the shots as I saw them and abide by my convictions. And if that didn't work, I'd say to hell with all newspapers and do something I didn't have to be ashamed of doing!"

He stopped, suddenly aware how far he had overstepped himself. They stared at each other, and he thought Mrs. Wedge was going to speak.

But suddenly she turned, threw a "Good day, Mr. Dorn," over her shoulder, and left the city room without a backward glance.

Debs returned to his desk. Well, he had been undiplomatic, even rude, pouring out his resentments at her, scolding at her, talking to her as if she were some stupid subordinate who had to be told off. And she was the co-publisher of the *Clarion*. She had left him as if she had found him wanting in any value, and cast him aside.

He pictured what Sam Hudson would have done under the same circumstances; how much more wisely he would have handled it, smirking and flattering this haughty woman as she obviously expected.

But with that came a sudden quick stiffening of pride. If he had made an enemy out of Mrs. Mary Agnes Wedge, the hell with it. She had asked him, hadn't she? And he told her. He goddamn well told her the truth.

On consideration, he was fairly certain that she would not forget him. And he also was fairly certain there would be a new city editor, perhaps quite soon, on this newspaper.

2

Mary Agnes, leaving the city room, was hardly as angry with Debs as he imagined. She was impatient with him, true—he was brash and too positive. He had bristled at her, and told her she did not understand things, and lectured her . . . as a matter of fact, a good deal of what he poured out at her she did not understand.

Treatment like this at the hands of any employee was something to which she was unaccustomed, and she did not like it. He seemed really, she reflected, not much concerned whether he kept his job or not.

On the other hand, there was something about that young man, an undertone of sincerity that was somehow refreshing. He spoke of the *Clarion* as if it were a living person, a rather important person, and one in whom he was greatly interested and concerned. He talked of matters that sounded impractical and idealistic as if they were real and solid. She wondered if he knew what he was talking about. Her mood as she left him was one of displeasure, but displeasure tinged by something else: perhaps interest.

What she had seen of the *Clarion* seemed poor and grubby compared to her store, vast, luxurious Cox's, Incorporated. She decided that on the morrow she would instruct her business manager, Edgar Swope, to have his auditors begin at once checking the *Clarion's* books and give her a report on exactly what were the physical assets of the paper.

While she was walking back through the hall from the city room, she noticed she had left on the lights in Wistart's office and went in to switch them off. She wondered just what Wistart did in there; it sounded more complicated than she had thought, from Mr. Dorn's telling. One thing she felt rather sure about: the *Clarion's* organization appeared to have gone to seed. She had no acquaintance with the personnel, or with the nature of the various kinds of work and the abilities required, but there ought to be some way to get better people in charge and get better performance out of them.

She was owner of fifty-one per cent of this newspaper—fifty-one per cent for the sum of one hundred thousand dollars advanced to pay the newsprint debts. She remembered Wistart's reluctance at her proposition and how it made her more determined, more relentless.

Well, she was gambling one hundred thousand dollars, and that is a considerable sum even to a wealthy woman. It would require a bank loan, with Cox's, Incorporated, as the surety.

Nevertheless, perhaps it was worth it. Algeria had been so proud of her success and the power she wielded with this paper. It gave Mary Agnes a little heady feeling of triumph that she was in the same position now. She almost laughed aloud. Algeria would writhe if she knew it, for Algeria never had liked her.

But she sobered. Algeria was not in the position of trying to revive a newspaper that was losing ground in the face of tough opposition. Maybe that hundred thousand dollars wasn't a very good gamble after all.

It would, certainly, require some enthusiasm and inspiration to put the old *Clarion* back on its feet. She had no idea where to begin.

Then she thought about that strange young man, Debs Dorn. She had felt in him resentment, distrust, almost scorn. It annoyed her because she was sure it was based on some sort of masculine antagonism toward women in general, and particularly women in authority. Or perhaps he felt some odd loyalty to Wistart and thought she was crowding Wistart aside, which in a measure might be true, since she certainly intended to see that there was a little more efficiency on this paper.

Well, she had encountered antagonism before, and she could deal with it. Mr. Dorn either would learn to respect her, or she would teach him another lesson not greatly to his liking.

On the other hand, she had to confess that she was rather impressed with him. Whatever else he was, he was loyal to the *Clarion,* and he was no sycophant, certainly. He had told her right in her teeth what he thought, without regard to whether it might be distasteful to her, and in terms so unequivocal that it was evident he was not afraid of the consequences, whatever they might be. Some kind of strength was there, and Mary Agnes was enough of a woman to admire strength. She felt in him also pride, and that was not entirely bad either, if it was the right kind of pride.

It occurred to her that if she could win with his fealty, Mr. Debs Dorn might be valuable to her. He seemed to know about all there was to know about newspapering. She could use that kind of knowledge.

Then the thought of what brought her down here in the first place came to her. The problem of Erskine de Lacey and his threat, the blackmailing of her with that painting. A newspaper ought to have some sort of resources to deal with something like that. She did not know just what, but perhaps through Mr. Dorn, if he was clever, she might devise some plan of campaign that just might work . . .

She was standing before Wistart's desk, her mink coat thrown back, removing her gloves as she thought. The wall behind the desk was entirely lined with bookshelves. At one side of Wistart's high-backed chair, within easy reach, was a radio set in the bookshelves. On the other side, in about the same position relative to the chair, she noticed a gray enameled steel filing case, also set in the bookshelves and probably fixed in the wall.

A slip of typewritten paper in the slot of the steel drawer attracted her attention. She went over and read it.

Personal Papers, Mr. Wedge.

Quite instinctively she tried to pull open the drawer: it was locked. She smiled half guiltily at her own curiosity and instinct to pry, and gave it up.

Very likely the key to the lock was on Wistart's key ring. To keep that kind of a file locked, with so many people around the office, was a perfectly natural precaution, especially when the papers were private.

But . . . *Private.* What kind of private papers did Wistart have?

She shrugged. After all, she told herself, it was no business of hers what he kept locked in his filing case.

She drew on her gloves again, pulled up about her throat the dream-like soft luxury of her minks, switched off the lights, and went down to her car.

And yet, in spite of herself, the question nagged her mind about that private file of her husband's. She felt she must find out what he kept in there: perhaps it had to do with the operations of the newspaper, which she had discovered were far more intricate than she had imagined. Mentally she reinforced her resolve to have another interview with that Mr. Dorn and pick his brains for information about this great new interest of hers, which was somehow becoming more important as she became more acquainted with it.

Private. She had never bothered her head to wonder about what Wistart did in his journeyings away from Jericho on the newspaper's business. But she wondered what he was actually doing in Tulsa now. When he returned, she must inform herself . . .

Nineteen

I

Mrs. Wedge's husband was not in Tulsa as she thought. He was in Chicago on an errand connected in no manner with the Jericho *Daily Clarion.*

The next morning, in Chicago, the sun at last broke through the leaden overhang of clouds which had obscured it for the past several days, giving promise of brighter and more cheerful weather. But to Wistart, gazing out of the breakfast-room window on the eighth floor of the apartment hotel, this was no augury, for he saw neither brightness nor cheer, nor any prospect of either of them in the future for him.

Shaved and dressed, but coatless and with his shirt collar open at the throat, he sat with his elbow on the table, his head leaning on his hand; the attitude of a man at once weary and dejected, not so much physically as at heart. The window of the breakfast room did not present much of a view, facing only the windows and brick wall of the building on the opposite side of the court, but had the vista been magnificent he would not have seen it. He was not looking at anything in particular; his eyes were open, but his vision was inward.

Behind him, in the kitchenette, he heard Grey's quick light step as she moved about making breakfast: a very small breakfast, for on this morning neither of them had any appetite, their emotions being what they were. Wistart was not looking at her now, he could not bear to look at her at this moment, but he knew exactly how she looked, he would never forget how she looked to the end of his life.

To him she seemed especially lovely this morning: diminutive and dear in a pale blue dress-length housecoat with a tiny fitted waist and a whirling circular skirt with two big pockets. About Grey there was nothing slipshod, even in the most minor details. She detested the lazy habit some women have of going around their homes disheveled and unkempt and slovenly: each morning, at home or anywhere, the first thing she did always was to make herself as neat as possible to begin the day, her hair combed and arrayed, her make-up correct, her garb fresh and seemly. It was just another of her traits, and the thought of it gave the man an additional choking, aching feeling of loss; for he was losing her, it was all over between them, ended forever.

Grey had breakfast nearly ready. She always got their breakfasts for them, it had become a rite, a little domestic act which had special meaning. As she worked in the kitchenette she glanced over at Wistart again and again with concern in her face.

Neither of them spoke. Not since what had been said a few minutes before. She knew he was not angry with her, that he did not blame her, but she knew also that he was hurt as deeply as it was possible to hurt him: a hurt perhaps greater than any of the many hurts he had previously suffered in his life.

It seemed very sad to her that it should be she, who hoped so sincerely for his happiness, who inflicted that hurt upon him. She wished he would say something. It seemed terrible to see him sitting there staring unseeing out of the window. Most wistfully she desired to assuage his pain in some manner, if she only knew how. But one thing alone would do that: for her to change her decision. And she could not change that decision because it was not for herself she made it. She had thought everything out to the very farthest conclusions she could reach, and there was no way to solve the complications into which life had led not only her, but others involved with her, except by unalterably putting an end to this relationship with Wistart.

She did not spoil their first night together in Chicago. It was to be her parting gift to him, and she made it as tender and perfect as it could be.

He told her what had happened, why he needed her. He had lost the *Clarion*. He still had, to be sure, the ownership of almost half of it, but Mary Agnes controlled the paper now, would give the orders. In any ordinary husband and wife relationship this might have been supportable, but Mary Agnes was . . . Mary Agnes. He knew her too well to have any illusions about what would happen to him. Already he was no more than a figurehead with no real power any longer; someone to be bypassed and rather contemptuously pitied by his own employees, as if he were shorn of his manhood. It was the final failure: Wistart could only sit in a kind of stupefied despair while he expressed to her, in halting awkward sentences, what this meant to him in terms of pride prostrated and in helpless, hopeless bitterness.

To heap upon this despair the added distress she held in store for him seemed too much, and Grey's heart almost failed her. But she could not do otherwise. At least she had comforted him with sweetness and grace in every way she knew; and for a time, she hoped, she had given him some happiness and even perhaps momentary forgetfulness of his woe.

But the inevitable moment had to come, and it came this morning. Wistart knew it was coming, it had to end, already more than once before she had told him she could not go on. But he shrank from it, he kept hoping, and the pain in his face cut her to the heart when she said this must be the last time for them, ever.

The table was set and now the coffee was ready. She took the juice and toast and marmalade over. Then she lifted the percolator. Still Wistart did not take his gaze from without the window. Standing close beside him, she poured coffee in his cup.

The familiar aroma seemed to arouse him. He turned from the window and all at once his arms went around her hips and he drew her body against his shoulder.

"Oh, darling—darling!" he said brokenly.

She set down the coffeepot and held his head to her, closing her eyes. In some ways this was the hardest thing she had ever done.

After a moment she gently released herself and went over to sit at her place. He raised his eyes miserably to meet hers across the table and she answered the question in them, forcing herself to be firm.

"I'm not thinking of myself entirely," she said. "If anything happened, it would ruin *you*. We've been very lucky so far. It can't continue forever."

At that he protested almost tearfully, and even spoke of divorce . . . longingly, but not with much assurance. He feared too greatly what his wife might do, not only to him but to Grey also, if she ever found they were interested in each other.

The divorce question had come up before in this same indefinite way. Grey had never urged it. She did not expect it, or even want it. If Wistart were free, she did not think she could marry him: she only wanted to feel clean and released from discreditable involvement.

"It's no use to talk about that," she said when he finished. And after a moment, "Wistart, dear, if this means anything to you—I think all the world of you—and—and I'm not sorry—I'll *never* be sorry, for anything I've done, or for what we've been to each other——"

"You say you think all the world of me!" he cried. "That can mean anything—or nothing! I *love* you! Don't you love me—a little?"

Then it was she gave him the answer to the question he had asked three years before, which she had never truly answered up to that moment; and in giving it she forsook feminine ambiguities at last because she wanted him to have something he could keep.

"Yes. Yes, I do love you," she told him. "Of course I love you. Nobody ever was as wonderful to me as you've been."

But when, with hope revived by this he sought to follow it up, she said, "Wait, dear, until I finish. It's not the kind of love a woman ought to have, or want. You say I've made you happy; but I've made myself terribly unhappy. Do you understand how that can be?"

"No; I don't quite," he confessed.

"Maybe a man can't see a thing like love through a woman's eyes," she said. "Maybe it's more important to a woman than to a man— maybe it's everything to her, her whole existence. But when it's wrong, and she has to be ashamed of it, somehow it breaks her heart—or her spirit—or something——"

She stopped, and he sat looking at her.

Presently he said, "Grey—is there—someone else? You can tell me. I have no claim on you, no real claim. And I'll try not to be jealous and I'll be glad if it makes you happy. But if there's someone else won't you tell me?"

She shook her head. "No. There's nobody else. There can't be— can't ever be, Wistart. Don't you see? I'm a sort of lost cause, I guess, because this love affair of ours means I can never think of marriage again. No man would have me if he knew, and I would not go to any man dishonestly without his knowing."

"And I've done that to you!" he exclaimed. "To think that I——"

"No, you didn't do it to me," she said. "I did it to myself, with my eyes wide open. Somehow it didn't seem so very wrong to me then, but it's different now. It's wrong, and I know it's wrong, and I began it and I've got to stop it."

"If it wasn't so very wrong before, why is it now? Oh, Grey, the thought of losing you makes life not worth going on with for me!"

"I have to do something," she said. "I've thought about this from every side, trying to weigh one thing against the other and see where my greatest obligation lay. And it always comes down to the same answer: my little girl. She's old enough to be starting school now, and it won't be long until she'll be able to understand things. Your happiness is terribly important to me, Wistart. I have my mother to consider, too. As for myself—I don't even count——"

Until now she had spoken rather calmly, but at this her voice broke and she halted, bowing her head.

After a moment she went on, "So you see this isn't selfish. You're very important to me, and so is my mother. But Betty Jean is the one who must come first of all. She's my child: I brought her into the world, she didn't ask to come into it, and she has a right to expect her mother to be everything to her a mother should. And her mother—my little girl's mother—has failed her—pretty badly up to now——"

Again she stopped to control herself, and he remained silent.

"I've made up my mind," she said presently. "If I can't do anything else, I'll have to go away. I'll sell the store and—and pay you back everything I owe you—and take my little girl and my mother somewhere else to live——"

"Don't!" he said. "Don't say anything more. I do see now. And I promise you won't have to worry—about me—any longer."

So he accepted it; and he was so gentle and sweet about it that it hurt her almost worse than if he had resisted.

"And you mustn't even think about going away—from Jericho," he went on. "That would be the one last thing I couldn't bear. At least stay in my life a little—as a friend—even if I only say hello to you once in a while on the street."

She went to him then and kissed him with tears in her eyes. Wistart was pathetic and yet somehow wonderful, she thought. He could make a great sacrifice, and do it selflessly, because it was for her.

2

Later they talked over plans.

"I still have some business to do here," she said. "You know—for the store."

He nodded.

"I think that the best and wisest thing, now that we've agreed, is for me to go back to the Sherman right away," she went on.

It was their custom for her to register at a hotel and keep a room there during her stay, looking in each day for possible mail or telegrams or telephone calls, so she could have an address in case her home or the store tried to reach her with a message. Of course she did not occupy the room, they always went somewhere else to stay: the apartment hotel in this instance. And they never went out together, but always separately and whenever possible at different times: another thing that Grey disliked, the guilty hiding, but a necessary precaution for the sake of safety.

"What will *I* do?" he asked.

"Well—I suppose—go home."

"Home!" he exclaimed so bitterly that she knew how cold was the thought of it to him. He looked at her. "Since we're both here now—why do we have to part right away?"

"Just because it's always best to do anything unpleasant as soon as it can be done and get it over."

"But—I'm not due back until tomorrow—and neither are you——"

"No, Wistart. It's no good putting it off. It would just make it worse later on."

"Oh, I can't just part with you now—like this!"

She was thinking and all at once she looked at him with an understanding little smile.

"I know," she said, "and I feel so too. It seems cruel just to walk away from each other, so to speak, without even looking back. And I've just thought of a sort of an idea——"

"What is it?"

"I was thinking—maybe it's illogical—but since we actually *have* agreed not to see each other any more and we're going to be—to be——"

"Friends? Just friends?"

"*Dear* friends. The dearest friends, Wistart, I want you to believe that, because you *are*."

He nodded solemnly. "Thank you."

"So, since we actually *are* friends—no more—it puts us on a kind of a different basis, doesn't it?" she asked.

"How do you mean?"

"Well—look at it this way—we're good friends. We're in Chicago. As—as *friends* would it be so risky if we went out to dinner together, just like friends would do?"

He drew a deep breath. "Maybe not—looking at it that way."

"We've never gone out to dinner together—except once. I just thought it might be nice, and not bad—as I said, maybe it's all illogical——"

"I don't think it's illogical at all!"

"And do you know where I think it would be fun to go?" she said.

"No."

"That little place where you took me that night three years ago."

"In the north end? That little tavern?"

"Yes."

He took up the suggestion eagerly. "I'd like that—I'd like that very much. And I don't think anybody would see us that knew us."

"If they did," she said, reasoning like a woman, "we could have a free conscience—at least a fairly free conscience—because all that—that other is behind us, and we could just feel that we sort of met and went out on the spur of the moment. Or don't you think so?"

"Yes, I think so. I do think so. Only—well, even if there *is* a risk, it's worth it!"

They agreed that he would come for her in the evening at her hotel exactly as he had done that night three years before.

3

So it ended as it had begun.

They even had the very same booth. The waiters were all different, because the staff had changed in three years, but the maître d'hôtel was the same aquiline dark man who had been there before, and he looked at them as if he vaguely remembered them and was trying to place them in his mind.

Grey was sure that if they mentioned the snowstorm he would remember, but they did not enlighten him; and he did not recollect the circumstances, she could see, by the way he spoke to them as he took them to their seats.

At first, over the cocktails, they chatted almost gaily, as if they really had met by accident and were taking a casual dinner out together.

But when the food was brought on a silence somehow fell as they ate. It was hard to keep up that appearance of gaiety when they did not feel gay at all.

When they were having their coffee after the dinner, he looked at the window beside the booth and said, "No snow on the panes this time, is there?"

She knew he was thinking how the snow had piled up there three years before.

"No snow," she said. "All clear this time—the moon's shining."

She meant it to say to him perhaps that not only the night but the path of life was clear now for them also.

But if he caught her meaning, he did not respond to it. "I'll never cease being thankful for snow," he said. "I'll never cease being thankful for *that* snow."

"Why?"

"It gave me three years of happiness. Do you know that even with—with everything else happening—I've been happy, really, these three years? I'm just realizing how happy I've been."

"It's meant so much to you?"

"So much. It's like this. Whatever took place—no matter how rough the going was, or what disappointments or unpleasantness occurred with the paper, or—or with other things in my life—I could always go back to the thought that there was *you*."

"I know."

"It made up for everything else," he went on. "It gave me a sense of being invincible, somehow, as if nothing could harm me very much, because the most important thing of all was there. Three years—they've gone so quickly. I can scarcely believe they're past—and yet so many things have happened. I know I don't express it very well—am I being banal?"

"No. You couldn't say anything more complimentary. Or anything that would make me feel—so miserably unhappy."

"You mustn't be unhappy."

"I can't help it. I feel as if, in a way, I'm running out on you—deserting you just when you need me. And yet I know that I'm really not running out on you, it's the circumstances that have run out on us both. That's not very clear, is it?"

"I think I understand it."

"Anyway, I'm pretty sad."

"Then let's talk about something else."

"All right. What?"

"Where did you go today, for instance?"

She told him the places, and what merchandise she had picked out, and she went on with a whole lot of inconsequential details, keeping up her chattering in hope of taking his thoughts, and hers also, off the central question that shadowed both their minds. She saw now that it was a mistake, their coming here. She only had hoped that it would make the parting easier, a sort of good-by ending on a pleasant note: but it would have been better if the good-by had been said when she left him that morning.

He listened to her, seeing her bright hair under the little black hat and his earrings on her pretty ears, and watching how the expressions changed and played over the sweet symmetry of her face while she talked, and all at once he laughed.

It made her pause and look at him rather in surprise.

"Thank you for doing that for me," he said.

"What did I do?"

"You made me feel better."

"But I didn't know——"

"Just by being the way you are. Just hearing you talk about nothing much, the unimportant little episodes of your day, your way of looking at things and thinking about things. It makes me realize that you aren't going out of my life entirely. I can always think of you like this, and it will make me feel good just to know you're in my world."

It gave her a lump in the throat, because she knew he was lying. And he was such a poor liar. He was lying to comfort her, to make her feel better. She thought he meant more to her at that moment than ever before.

She let him kiss her good night in the cab before they parted at the hotel and she left part of her heart with him when she gave him that kiss. It was their last kiss forever.

Twenty

I

"I went to the wrestling match last night," Jeff Linderman said in the morning as he and Debs were walking over to the *Clarion* from Jolly Herron's after coffee.

"You?" Debs was surprised. "I thought you were fed up with that grunt-and-groan, when-I-say-three-turn-over hippodrome."

Jeff grinned. "I am. But Sally Sayre had never seen a wrestling match. So I got passes from Larry Cameron. I'd rather have gone to a picture, but she seemed kind of thrilled with it."

"Wrestling to women," said Debs cynically, "is what burlesque shows are to men—the opposite sex, doing their stuff, as near naked as possible."

"I don't think that's quite it with Sally. She believed it was a real contest. Got all excited. She's pretty when she's hopped up, know that?"

"Yes. Do you date Sally much, Jeff?"

"Oh, a few times. Nice, real nice. But she hasn't much time for me. Someone else on her mind."

"Yeah? Who?"

"You."

"Me?" Astonishment was genuine in Debs. "I've never gone out with her in my life."

"Just the same," said Jeff moodily, "you're the Big Hero. Shrieking Sam is the Big Stinker."

Debs laughed. "Sally's a little girl with a notion that the newspaper business is more important than it is, and she makes out that the squabbles between Sam and me are bloodletting affairs—just as she goes for the phony wrestling shows."

"Maybe she's halfway right."

"Why do you say that, Jeff?"

"Shrieking Sam's got his knife out for you."

"He's been drinking too much lately. He was half crocked when he came to work yesterday, and he left early. Maybe the pressure's beginning to get him."

"What pressure?"

"I don't know. Something. Maybe the change in the publishing situation. He had some sort of a run-in with Mrs. Wedge the first day she was home. He might be worrying about that."

"Whatever it is, he's a pain in the neck around the office. That yelling's beginning to grow a little old. Don't see how you can stand it."

"May not much longer. Lots of other papers, lots of other jobs."

"Sally's not so far off then."

They went up the stairs to the city room. Debs was thinking that Jeff Linderman was a little serious about Sally, and he didn't blame him much. A real sweet kid, Sally. Sweet and pretty and girly. Maybe not very savvy in a newspaper way, not yet; but smart in other ways—feminine ways. It was nice and a little flattering to have a kid like that looking up to you, thinking you were more than you really were. Cute, real cute, Sally was. He would work with her, maybe make a real newspaper gal out of her. That is, if she didn't go off and marry somebody in the next few months, which she probably would. A girl like that simply couldn't keep from getting married. He remembered once more how she said to him, "I think you're swell," and it still had the power to please him, although God knew he had no notions about Sally . . .

He left off this thinking and plunged into the early work of the desk. When Joe Canfield came up, he called him over.

"What did the cop house drag in overnight?"

"Nothing much. The usual. A prowler. Three or four vags. Drunks. Couple of hopheads. No, three. One's a woman."

"Three dope addicts? Where did they get them?"

"In a rooming house over in the packing house section of Jugtown."

"Any stuff?"

"Couple of needles. Cooking spoons. No dope, but the residue in the spoons could be heroin."

"Is there some dealer working in town?"

"None that anybody knows of." Canfield stood at the desk with his soft hat cocked over one eye, a cigarette in the corner of his mouth, his eyes, as usual, cold and recessive.

"The addicts must be getting it somewhere."

"Some junk peddler could've slipped in and out of town. Happens lots of times. Hard to put the finger on—here today, gone tomorrow. Have a regular route. Make several towns, and have a schedule. Meet the joy poppers at a certain time, at a certain place, and when they unload the junk on their customers, they skip to the next place."

Debs considered that. It might be worth a special story. Then he thought of something else.

"That Slago woman they picked up yesterday, have you ever seen her before, Canfield?"

The other hesitated. "Few times, maybe."

"Where?"

"Here and there. She's hashed all over town."

"Think she knows anything about the Bonner case?"

"No."

"Why not?"

"I've talked to her."

"When?"

"Yesterday. Right after they got her in."

"What did she say?"

"Demanded a medical exam. Says they can't hold her as a vag. The health department can keep a woman locked up if she has a disease, to treat her. But she got the exam and she's clean."

"Is she a prostitute?"

"No. Has round heels, maybe, but she doesn't hustle for a living."

"Ever see her with Benson?"

"Maybe. Don't remember."

Debs' mouth tightened. "You'd better begin doing some remembering."

"What do you mean by that, Debs?"

"Simply this. You and Benson have been palsy-walsy, and I happen to know that Benson dated the Slago woman for some time. Galloway and Benson sometimes double-dated, according to Nibs' mother. So Nibs must have known the Slago woman. There was some kind of a black worry in Nibs' mind just before he was murdered. Worry over what? Was it something he knew, or suspected? Perhaps about someone *he didn't want to suspect*? Do you follow me, Canfield? There are some pretty fishy things about Walt Benson, and about his story of the murder. He said he didn't see any of the killers enough to describe them. He didn't get the license number. He wasn't even sure of the make of the car. The whole story of three thugs waiting in Cemetery Lane with guns sounds silly to me. What would they be doing in a place like that? Waiting to hold up some high school couple for the six bits or a dollar the boy had in his jeans? That's pretty ridiculous. Benson smells bad in this case to me, Canfield. When our dumb cops get around to checking that story of his, I think he's going to have a lot of important things to explain."

"All right. But how does that affect me?"

"You've been pretty thick with Benson, Canfield. And if you want to know the truth, I'll tell you what I think. I don't think you're leveling with me."

Canfield took the cigarette from his mouth and let the smoke curl up around his nostrils.

"If that's the way you think, Mr. Dorn, it's your privilege. I've told you every damned thing I know."

For a moment they stared, eye to eye.

"That's all," Debs said.

Slowly Canfield went down the stairs, hat still cocked over one eye, cigarette hanging in the corner of his mouth. Debs knew he was burning inwardly.

"Did you hear what Canfield said?" he asked Jeff across the desk.

"Yeah."

"Talked with the Slago woman yesterday and made no report of it here."

Jeff nodded.

"Can you tell me why?" Debs pursued.

"I wouldn't know," said Jeff. "But Canfield's an old enough reporter to know better than that."

Debs thought a moment. "Jeff, I'm sorry I said that to him."

"Why should you be? He had it coming."

"Because it brought something out in the open I should have left in the dark. He's going to report what I said to Benson, sure as hell. And that will give Benson a chance to think up a better story. Besides, Canfield knows he's made a butch, and he knows I know it, so he'll be more careful to cover his own tracks, if they need covering."

Again Debs fell silent, thinking of something that happened the previous afternoon. At the Press Club. He had been talking to Larry Cameron about Mamie Slago, and Larry was drunk and persisted in loud comments. When they finished, Debs remembered that Canfield, who had been shooting craps, was gone.

Later on the police picked up Mamie Slago trying to get out of town. Perhaps she'd been warned to leave. By whom? Benson? Not likely. He was at police headquarters and hardly had the opportunity.

Debs disliked carrying this line of speculation to its logical conclusions, and maybe he was entirely wrong. Nevertheless, he knew he could not trust Canfield.

Presently he said, "Jeff, I think I'm going to do some shuffling of the staff."

"How?"

"Put Canfield on the courthouse for a while and take Tod Burdock off that beat and send him to the police station."

Jeff stared. "Canfield won't like that."

Debs was sure he would not.

"He'll try going over your head—to Hudson," said Jeff.

"I might as well find out some things now," said Debs.

When Tod Burdock came in from the courthouse at noon, Debs summoned him over.

Burdock was long, lean, and graying, with a large hooked nose and a jutting chin, one of the veterans of the staff, fairly dependable but a master of all dodges to fool city editors into thinking he was hard at work. He was a sort of town historian, sometimes writing feature stories about Jericho's past, and when some pioneer of prominence died, it was customary to have Tod Burdock write the obituary because, out of his background of local history, he could often insert interesting touches.

About such matters he was cynical, and referred to all Jericho old-timers as "hardy pioneers." Gradually he had grown to employ the word "hardy" as a synonym for "aged." Thus: "How hardy was he when he died?" Or, "You can't get much hardier than Old Man Diver. He fought in the Civil War." Or even, "I played poker and drank too much last night. Feel sort of hardy this morning—could scarcely get out of bed."

Burdock approached the desk. "What's on your mind?" he asked Debs.

"Have you got anything hot?"

"No. Routine meeting of the county commissioners. Damage suit filed against the Westcott Packing Company by a hog killer who cut himself in the slaughter pen. About all."

"Make 'em short and quick. I'm going to send you to the city hall, Tod."

"What for?"

"Anybody on the same old run too long gets in a rut. A new beat wakes a man up, gives him different interests."

Tod Burdock looked quite "hardy" at the thought of this. He liked his courthouse beat. It was comfortable, he was on measurably good terms with all the news sources, had favorite loafing places and an amicable gin rummy game that went on periodically, and the thought of starting on a new assignment, where he would have to be on his toes, wearied him.

But he was too much of a veteran newspaperman to debate the matter.

"All right," he said. "Where's Joe Canfield going?"

"To the courthouse."

Burdock stared, his huge nose a curve of interrogation. Then his eyes went down the room to Samson J. Hudson's desk. The managing editor had come in late that morning, morose and silent. His eyes were pouched and now he sat brooding with the *Morning Sentinel* spread before him, looking for something in the opposition which he could use to hector his own staff. Two years more or less on the wagon had told on Shrieking Sam, and he had fallen off rather devastatingly the past two days. Now he was suffering the black reaction, his nerves jangled, his stomach wretchedly upset, a sour aura of whiskey about him.

"When you finish your stories," said Debs, ignoring the look, "grab a sandwich and then go over and relieve Canfield. Tell him I want to talk with him."

2

Trouble was evident when, right after lunch, Canfield came bounding up the stairs. Pale with wrath, he confronted Debs.

"What's this about switching Tod and me on our beats?" he demanded.

"Just an experiment," Debs said. "To see how——"

"Experiment, hell! Do you mean it?"

"Yes."

Canfield whirled and strode directly over to the managing editor's desk.

"I quit!" he told Hudson loudly. "I don't have to work for this damned bladder! They can't shove me around here!"

Hudson rose, a startled expression on his face.

"What's the matter, Joe?" he asked.

"Debs Dorn just told me I was off the city hall beat!"

Hudson glanced over at the city desk. "He did, did he?" He put his hand on Canfield's shoulder. "Well, don't do anything rash, my boy. Sit down here. Now tell me what's happened."

Everybody in the city room heard it and everybody suspended work to watch. Debs tried to concentrate on a piece of copy he was editing, knowing he was the subject of the low-voiced but heated conversation between Hudson and Canfield over by the window.

After a few minutes Hudson nodded, patted Canfield on the shoulder, rose, and came over to the city desk.

"Who gave you the authority to switch those beats, Debs?" he said.

"I'm the city editor."

Hudson grew ugly. "Just as long as I say so, you're city editor—and no longer!"

"Okay. So what?"

"So I'm countermanding that order. Canfield goes back to the city hall, where he belongs. He's too valuable there. He's got more news sense and more news sources than any reporter in Jericho. Do I make myself clear?"

Thus far Hudson had spoken in a voice almost moderate, although he was scowling, his glasses glittering menacingly. He was getting even with Debs, putting him in his place, showing him where he belonged. They both knew it; the whole staff knew it.

Debs looked him squarely in the eye.

"Is that final?" he asked.

In a single breath Hudson lost his calm, exploded, became Shrieking Sam.

"Final?" he yelled. "You bet it's final! It's goddamn final! And you listen to me, Debs Dorn, I've got my bellyful of insubordination and stupidity on this paper, and I'm getting goddamn tired of it! Jee-zus! Where do you think you get off, not consulting with me? I'm warning you, you've gone too far! A helluva long ways too far! One more crooked move like this, and you'll wish to your goddamn dying day it never happened!"

Not a typewriter in the city room was clicking. The staff sat listening. Canfield was at Hudson's desk, his face expressionless but his eyes containing a gleam of triumph. At the opposite end of the room, over toward the society desks, Sally Sayre was looking at Debs as if she waited for some final answer.

Slowly Debs shoved back his chair and stood on his feet. In the hush which had fallen over the city room his words were clearly heard.

"Mr. Hudson, you can get yourself another city editor."

Still deliberately, he walked around the desk, took his overcoat and hat, and went down the stairs without glancing back.

3

In the home edition of the *Clarion* that afternoon was an obscure item:

Mamie Slago, 30, a waitress, was released today by police after being questioned in connection with the murder of Bonnie Bonner, night club entertainer. Victor Hinshaw, chief of detectives, said Miss Slago had been unable to give information of any material value relating to the mysterious slaying. She was released on her promise to remain in the city in case it is thought necessary to question her again.

Miss Slago, a friend of the murdered burlesque queen, said Bonnie Bonner had no enemies of whom she had knowledge. She said that the entertainer sometimes augmented her income by posing in the nude for an artist, but otherwise lived quietly in her South Jericho home.

That was all there was to it: unimportant and soon forgotten by most of those who read it. But to a few it had some meaning, varying according to the individual.

Debs Dorn read the item in his room and said to himself that the examination of Mamie Slago must have been pretty perfunctory. She ought, he thought, to have been good for something more important than the line about the Bonner girl's being an artist's model. But then he shrugged. He was no longer with the *Clarion*. The matter of news had ceased to be any affair, any interest of his.

Mrs. Mary Agnes Wedge read the story at her home, and the last sentence seemed to leap out of the paper at her. Bonnie Bonner posing —for whom?

She believed she could guess. Nude models . . . the curious erotic necessity of Erskine de Lacey. No doubt he had seen the girl perform at the roadhouse, made the usual artist's approach to her, and she accepted his offer. Where did he paint her? At Mrs. Butford's house? If so it was secretly, and at some risk, with that old dragon's absolutely pathological puritanic prudery.

Mary Agnes knew the kind of painting that came out of that posing. None of Erskine's ugly, affected "abstractions" with which he cynically befuddled the ladies of the Art Association. Something quite different: a naked girl, almost as real as life yet somehow indecent because of the inordinate attention his brush had devoted to every token of her female sex, as if each stroke were a lascivious caress.

The canvas of Bonnie Bonner would join a little stack of other canvases, of similar character, perhaps carefully concealed somewhere and never shown by Erskine. How many there were, and what other women were thus limned, Mary Agnes did not know: but one of them was of intense personal interest to her. Again she said to herself that somehow she *must* get possession of that vile thing and destroy it.

Another thought: the little item in the newspaper did not mention the artist's name, but had not perhaps the Slago woman given the name to the police when they questioned her? And if she did, would there be an investigation?

Mary Agnes' imagination leaped to construct situations where the painting of herself might come to light. Suppose, for example, the police questioned Erskine in his studio: might they demand to see his painting or paintings of Bonnie Bonner? And if so might not other paintings of his strange lust be revealed?

Suppose the filthy *Morning Sentinel* got wind of the picture of herself . . . Mary Agnes, who rarely felt apprehension, was very apprehensive at that moment.

Mrs. Simon Bolivar Butford stopped Miss Rose Caruthers, her secretary, who was reading the story aloud to her.

"Does it say the woman actually posed *naked?*" she exclaimed. "Before a *man?* Dreadful! And right here in Jericho! I thought nobody but Frenchwomen or Italians or some of those other heathenish people ever actually did anything so shameless! She was evil. An evil woman, seeking to lure men to their downfall. The hussy, I can't be sorry now that somebody killed her."

It did not occur to Mrs. Butford's somewhat dim mind that the posing might have been done in her own house, before her own personal protégé, Erskine de Lacey. She was secure in her mind that he painted only those queer things he called "abstractions," which she could not understand even if she could see them well, but which at least did not offend what she considered the decencies.

Erskine de Lacey was not heard to make any comment on the item.

4

It was after dark, but Debs had not turned on the lights. He sat alone in his room, looking out of the window. There was not much to look at: only the shingle roof of the house next door. The shingles were old and weathered, and a few old dead leaves were lodged and rotted in the eaves gutter, but in this dimness he could not even see details like that.

Grey Rutledge lived in that house next door; Grey and her little daughter and her mother, Mrs. Norcross. Debs had been thinking about Grey moodily, as he did sometimes.

But he was not, at this minute, thinking about even her. He was not, in fact, thinking very hard about anything: just becoming accustomed to the idea that he was without a job. He did not need to be sitting alone there in the darkness. He might have been other places, like Jolly Herron's for instance, getting drunk. But he did not feel like getting drunk. He wanted to be alone and not have to talk or even listen to others talk. At first he wondered at the enormous vacuum he felt in his life now that the *Clarion* was no longer the central core of it. Then he thought a little about his future.

There was the *Sentinel,* should he apply for a job there? He had a fairly good idea that they would be glad to hire him on the *Sentinel.* It would be a sort of victory to hire the *Clarion's* city editor and then put him on a beat like any punk reporter, as if he were a captive on exhibition, someone to crow over the *Clarion* about.

On consideration, Debs thought he would much rather go out of town and start over—on one of the Denver papers, maybe, or in Kansas City, or even Wichita. But first he wanted to stay around Jericho a little longer just to satisfy himself about a theory that was growing in his mind in the murder of Nibs Galloway.

He was turning this over in his thoughts, not really arriving at any definite way of proving it, when he heard a knock on his door.

"Mr. Dorn, are you in there?"

It was Mrs. Hillyer, his landlady. Debs got up, switched on a light, and opened the door.

"I didn't see a light, and I didn't know whether you were here or not," said Mrs. Hillyer. She was a widow, sixty years old, and he had been rooming with her for three years, but she still called him Mr. Dorn. She winked rapidly with one eye, a nervous impulse that had flickered all her life, and she put up a finger to rub the eye.

"I was just sitting thinking," Debs said.

Mrs. Hillyer moistened her faded lips with a pointed tongue. "Somebody wants you on the telephone."

Debs felt annoyance. Just at present he wanted to avoid conversation, commiseration, questions. He was lonely, sure, but that could be borne and he was used to it. Some busybody could not be borne nearly as easily.

But after all he could not very well ask the old lady to go back downstairs and hang up on whoever was calling him.

"Thank you, Mrs. Hillyer," he said.

Mrs. Hillyer had only one telephone and it was in the hall. He followed her down the stairs, took up the receiver, and said, "Hello."

"Hello," said the voice. Cute young girl's voice. "Debs? Hey, what are you doing?"

"Sally! Why, nothing—special."

"Sure?"

"Nothing at all."

"You aren't anti-social?"

"Not with you." It seemed to him suddenly that it was very nice to have Sally Sayre, of all people, call him up and talk to him.

"Know something?" said the bright young voice. "My folks have gone off and left me—all alone and without a sitter. Imagine! It's lonesome. There's something to eat in the refrigerator, and Dad has a bottle of bourbon. Strike you?"

Debs thought a second, then grinned. "Strikes me."

"When will you be over?"

"Would about ten minutes suit you?"

"Suits perfect! I'll put the coffee in the electric percolator and some new perfume behind my ears."

Debs laughed and hung up. He suddenly felt real good. When he was back upstairs in his room he saw in his dresser mirror that he was still grinning.

Sally's way of putting it: "My folks left me alone without a sitter." Cute of her, and friendly. He thought a good deal of Sally.

He washed up and combed his hair and changed his shirt and put on a necktie. Then he remembered what she said about perfume. So he dabbed a little shaving cologne on his palm and patted it on his cheeks. If she was going to smell good, he would too.

When he drove up before the Sayre home, a bungalow on Millcreek Lane, the porch light was lit.

He rang the bell. Sally came to the door, smiling brightly and looking pretty and youthful in a jumper dress—different from the suits she wore to the office—and a little frilly apron, and a blue ribbon about her hair.

"Just in time to help with the waffles. Like waffles?" she said.

She showed him where to put his hat and overcoat in the hall closet, and then frisked ahead of him out into the kitchen.

"There's cold fried chicken in the refrigerator," she said, "but I want something hot. Know something? Waffles are the only living thing I know how to make. Coffee and waffles. Maybe bacon. Shall we have bacon? There's some in there."

"Let me fry the bacon," he said. "I'm an old experienced bacon frier. Like yours crisp or limber?"

"Crisp." Her eyes laughed, and she had a trick of wrinkling her nose when she smiled.

He put the thin slices of meat in a frying pan and they began frizzling over one of the gas stove burners while he turned them with a fork.

"How do you like your bourbon?" she asked.

"Plain water."

"I'll get us some drinks. I feel like getting swacked."

"Okay," he said, humoring her. "Let's both get swacked."

He was sure she didn't mean it, but he would go along with the gag. Presently she was back and put a glass in his hand, holding one herself. He took a sip.

"Hey, you loaded this!" he said.

"Sure, wasn't that the idea?"

"I guess it was." He took a long drink. He felt good, real good. He liked Sally, and her little impromptu plan, and the way she looked, and everything about it. It was fun to be getting supper with her, even a supper that was really a breakfast, if you considered its components.

By the time they finished their drinks the waffles and bacon and coffee were ready. They sat side by side at the breakfast table and ate, and he said he didn't want another drink. She said she had enough, too.

After a while he said, "Do you do this often?"

"What?"

"Have gentlemen here when you're alone?"

"Not very. Actually never, really. To eat, that is. I've had boys here, of course. I'm adult, you know. My folks give me credit for being adult."

He felt like saying something very nice to her, but he could think of nothing to say that didn't sound banal. Adult she was, perhaps. But also very young. And very tempting. And he wouldn't risk offending her for anything in the world.

He thought he had better change the subject. "How did things wind up at the office today?" he said.

"Jeff got out the paper. When you walked out, old Shrieking Sam looked as if somebody had hit him over the head with a ball bat."

"I doubt that."

"True. So help me. He didn't expect it. He thought you'd sit there forever and take his brainstorms. It never occurred to him that you'd just get up and leave him standing there with his teeth in his mouth."

"He'd been drinking. I was just fed up."

"Sam's got a problem, and he knows it."

"What?"

"He's got to find a city editor. He knows you're the best city editor this town ever saw. Everyone says you've been carrying the paper. He knows that, and he's scared. He doesn't know where to find anyone to do the job you've been doing."

"Jeff can do it. Jeff's a good man."

"Jeff's all right. Too young, though. Not very mature."

Sally spoke with all the ripe judgment with which any young woman of twenty expresses opinions about young men, particularly when those young men admire her somewhat abjectly. Debs smiled inwardly.

"He's not in your class," she went on positively.

"Flattery, Sally. Sheer flattery."

"It is not! Know something? I'm going to quit too."

"You're not!"

"Yes, I am. It wouldn't be any fun any more on the *Clarion*. I won't work for a man like Shrieking Sam. Just as soon as enough time has passed so they won't say that I—that I—did it because of you—I'm leaving."

He stared at her. She *meant* it.

He had not dreamed of this kind of loyalty in her. It troubled him and all at once it deeply moved him.

"Sally——" He stopped, unable to express what he felt. "You—oh, Sally, you're such a little sweetheart—I don't know what to say——"

Reflex. Sheer reflex action, unconsidered. They were sitting side by side and she came to him unresisting when he drew her.

He held her in his arms, her body bent back across his thighs, and felt the stunning soft abundance of her breasts and hips. She made a little whispering protest.

"Debs——" She breathed it as if the breathing choked back her words. "We mustn't——"

Then the protest died, and there was surprise to him in the fire of her return to his kiss, hot, moist, almost fierce.

He did not let her go for a long time.

When at last he lifted her, taking her on his lap in the circle of his arms, they were both silent except for their panting, and she hid her face on his shoulder so he could not see the trembling of her lips.

All at once he set her on her feet and stood up.

"I've got to go," he said in a low tense voice.

"Why . . . ?"

"You're too much for me. I can't think . . . for both of us. I don't want anything to happen——"

Her cry: "I don't care if it does!"

They were standing now, and she came to him again, lifting her face to his kiss. For long minutes they stood clasped, shaking against each other.

He forced himself to draw his head back and look down at her. Her eyes were closed, her lips half open, as if beseeching. The flushed, excited face of a child, awakened to something it scarcely knew, greater than anything it had ever known. The blue ribbon around her hair, the young little nose, the perfect half-moons of the lashes of her closed eyes against her smooth cheeks all added to the impression she gave him of childishness and innocence.

Firmly he took her arms from around him and held her away from him.

"Sally," he said, "I'm going—right now!"

He kissed her once more, very softly and gently.

She followed him to the front hall as he got his coat and hat.

"Debs——" she said. There were tears in her eyes.

"What, Sally?"

"Is it Grey Rutledge?"

"Why do you say that?"

"It is Grey Rutledge, isn't it? You're in love with Grey . . . I've thought it ever since that day in the cafeteria when I saw you look at her——"

"No! Grey Rutledge wouldn't be remotely interested in me. Particularly when I don't even have a job. And there are other reasons . . ."

"What else?"

"Well, it isn't Grey Rutledge—or anybody. Sally, honey, listen to me. I like you. An awful lot. And I want you to like me—keep on liking me. And I don't want to do something to you that I'd always be ashamed of. Now, good night, Sally. Good night, dear."

When he went out he felt her hands touching his shoulders, a fluttering farewell.

5

Driving the old convertible back through the night toward his rooming house, Debs was still shaken and moved. He had wanted Sally: and he was sure she was in the mood, the reckless mood of forgetfulness and excitement, responding to his sudden urge. He remembered how he said that he didn't want anything to happen. And her wild little cry: *I don't care if it does*. He could have taken Sally, and he did not.

Reaction came, and he laughed aloud, and bitterly, at himself.

Debs Dorn—the knight on a white horse, protecting the chastity of innocent girlhood. Sir Galahad. Noble—very noble indeed. So goddamn idiotically noble that he walked right away from her arms, from her tears, with some inane futile notion that it was sneaking to take advantage of her youth, and her inexperience, and her hero worship. And especially so in her own house, while her parents had gone and left her with her pride in being "adult" when they ought to have been there to look after her.

Debs Dorn, thirty years old, no bargain, who had tomcatted enough in his life so that a scruple like that should have been foreign to him. Debs Dorn acting like a noble goddamn saint; ridiculous, phony, inexplicable.

He remembered once interviewing a very old man who was celebrating his one hundred and fifth birthday. He asked the aged gaffer if there was anything in that long life he regretted.

"Yes, young man," quavered the ancient. "I've got a whole lot of regrets to look back on. And every damned one of them is a temptation that I resisted."

Debs thought of the temptation of Sally, and his own resistance to it. And he swore at himself for a fool. Sally was willing and ready—more than willing, beseeching, if he ever saw a girl who was. A woman was a woman, and he was no virgin. Perhaps Sally was a virgin, but she seemed at that moment most eager to have him rid her of that estate. With bitterness now he said to himself that he had lost a moment in his life forever, and it probably always would be a regret to him.

The thought even came of turning back. Perhaps Sally . . . with that flushed, starry-eyed look on her face . . .

But, no. When a girl has been as near to the edge as that, the re-
vulsion is rapid and violently opposite. Sally probably was well over
her mood of recklessness, perhaps raging at herself, even weeping with
gladness that what she wildly wished to happen had not happened.

Then Debs wondered if he really regretted it after all. Sally . . .
generous, loyal, trusting. So much a winsome child, overwhelmed by
something she hardly understood and was unprepared for, her own
instinct and passion.

He said to himself that her emotion that led up to it was based on the
resentment she felt for him at the injustice she thought had been done
him and her young-girl admiration of him. It would have been pretty
stinking of him to take advantage of that kind of feeling in her: a real,
lousy betrayal, even if she did not so consider it. He would have been
a heel to go through with it. He felt pity for her youth, and the things
she must go through; and he wanted to be a true friend to her, and see,
if he could, that she escaped the kind of danger she had been in with
him, and maybe understand her a little. Because she was such a damned
nice girl; the nicest.

Then, as he turned his car into the street that led to Mrs. Hillyer's
rooming house, he wondered, now that things had turned out the way
they did, if Sally would despise him. Or would she despise herself and
hate him?

He wondered if she possibly could know why he acted as he did.

He was half sure she could not. There was that question of hers about
Grey Rutledge; the natural, instinctive feminine probing for other
feminine interests in a man. Women could never believe, Debs said to
himself, that a man can be interested in no woman at all. Women are
rivals, never ceasing and implacable rivals to one another, but women
unite in one thing, the belief in the invincibility of sex. To believe completely in the one thing about them that is most significant is a fundamental necessity with them. So if one of them does not succeed with
a man it is impossible for her to accept her own failure except in the
terms of the success of someone else of her own sex with him.

Having thus dismissed in his own mind—somewhat didactically and
not very satisfactorily—the question Sally had asked him, Debs found
himself asking himself the same question.

What about Grey Rutledge?

Grey . . . Grey . . . beautiful, unattainable Grey . . .

Well, *that* was something he must not allow himself to think about. It was completely out of the question, utterly foolish, for him to think about it, although he thought to himself that he would do anything in the wide world for her if she would let him.

Yet he could not help thinking about it. And when he thought, he felt he was making himself ridiculous even allowing his mind to dwell on it. But he could not help it.

He thought about Grey. She was two years younger than he, yet somehow she seemed so much more of a woman than he was a man. She was at the perfect age of a woman, when beauty has reached its height and mind and spirit have developed equally to round out the wondrous creature that a woman can be. Already she had achieved success: her store was a proof of it. And he was struggling on a newspaper salary without much prospect of advancing farther in the limited field of journalism. And not even a job right now. A man didn't reach his peak until he was nearing forty, Debs thought, and he felt that Grey was far beyond him.

But even if this hadn't been so, there were other reasons why he couldn't think of her. He had known Grey for three years now, almost ever since she and her little family moved into the house next door to Mrs. Hillyer's; and she had always been friendly, kind, charming—and completely impersonal toward him from the first. It was as if she took care to erect invisible barricades that kept him out of any intimacy in her life.

She was nice to him always. Several times she had him over to dinner, and he had played cards with her in that little neighborhood poker club and invented games for her little girl. Last New Year's Eve, when she had an open house for a few of her friends, the rugs were rolled back and records played, and he danced with her two or three times. He remembered how light she was in his arms, and how precious somehow; and her laughter, and his sensation of almost wondering delight that such a being could exist and be so close to him at the moment; and how she seemed to lift him out of himself to do fairly well on the dance floor just to please her, although he was a marvelously poor dancer and she a marvelously good one.

It was hard not to be terribly interested in Grey . . . in fact, he found himself, in spite of himself, interested in her to the point of danger if he did not keep a strong curb on his imaginings. But he was quite certain that she had not the slightest interest in him. Even allowing for her manifold attractions to him, he could not let himself be in love with Grey Rutledge . . . for a number of reasons.

Like a pendulum his mind swung back to Sally. Was he, perhaps, a little in love with *her*?

So fresh, so young, so obviously adoring: there was nothing, not one thing about Sally, that wasn't sweet and tempting. The way she looked with that schoolgirl ribbon in her hair, the way she thrilled when he held her in his arms, the fragrance of the "perfume behind the ears" and of her own clean healthy young self, the taste like sweet-spice heady wine when his lips mingled with hers: they came back to him like a spell woven about his heart and mind.

Women wove such spells, consciously or unconsciously. It might not be entirely unconscious in Sally; but at least it was instinctive. About one thing he was sure: there was nothing designing about Sally. She was a child, really, though so proud of being "adult," a danger to herself more than anyone else unless someone protected her.

Debs had protected her: against himself. It still surprised and in its way puzzled him.

When he thought into it farther, the reason for it surprised him even more. As much as anything, it was her hero-worshiping of him. It touched his vanity, there was not much question of that: he wanted still to be a hero to her, and it is hard to be a hero to a woman when once a man has shown his weakness to her. Having found a chink in his personal dignity and reserve, having touched him where his defenses do not serve him, her hero is revealed to her as vulnerable, and ceases to be heroic. Debs did not want that to happen with himself and Sally.

Twenty-one

I

Debs suddenly felt low: very low. He had quit the *Clarion,* and under present conditions he would not work there again for any money; but in leaving the paper he had disrupted his life more deeply than he had thought. Ten years, almost all his adult working years, had gone into the *Clarion*. It was a part of him, and now that its problems and its work no longer were the focus of his thoughts and actions, he felt empty.

This was a bitterness, but not the only one. The other had to do with something else, a resentment brought to the surface, when it previously had lain below the surface of his consciousness, by the episode at Sally Sayre's. Involved in it was not only Sally, but Grey Rutledge also, as Sally had divined. Yet, further, it involved not only the two of them, Sally and Grey, but all women, women in general.

Grey and Sally merely became the immediate nexus of the whole problem of women, because they were the two most appealing and desirable women in his personal orbit of existence.

He remembered that day when the two of them sat across the table from him in the cafeteria, dressed and adorned with all possible feminine art; enticing, an enhanced suggestion of sex traveling with them as the atmosphere travels with the earth, an instinctual snare so difficult for a man to avoid because it is so attractive.

They were consciously gay and chattered inconsequentialities in a manner apparently empty-minded: but they were not empty-minded, and because he was the only man present, they both turned upon him the charm that is a practiced lifelong preoccupation of women. Yet though they devoted themselves to him for the moment, he had said to himself with cynicism, they might in another moment be devoting the same arts just as unflaggingly to another man; it really made little difference to them what man or men were handy so long as they could practice their little wiles and indulge their vanities.

Thinking back upon that day, he said to himself savagely that women not only were erratic, changeable, fickle, not to be relied upon, but he felt in them rapacity and an irrational, yet crafty and even cruel scheming. They lived to uproot and twist the lives of men, seeking to catch them in a web of desire and subdue them by stealing into their souls; and not for love, but rather for a craving to gain power, to convert men into instruments for furthering their interests, the things important to their parasite sex.

In the mood of misogyny induced by his frustration, he wanted to rid himself of the influence of women, of the hold they and sex had on his thoughts even now when he did not wish to think of them.

With that, all at once, he stepped on the accelerator of his car. He was near Mrs. Hillyer's, but instead of stopping before the house he gained speed, swung around the corner, and headed south down the lamplit street toward Jugtown with a sudden, solid purpose.

It was still early: he had been at Sally's no more than an hour and a half. He believed he knew a way to snap all the invisible threads that seemed to web him, the unpermitted longings, the unconscious imaginings concerning women, all women, but particularly those two women, Grey Rutledge and Sally Sayre.

At a liquor store on the way he stopped and picked up a bottle of whiskey. Then he drove on, down South Market Street, to the rooming house section. The ugly brick veneer apartment building was familiar; he had been there before. He parked his car, mounted the stairs to the second floor, and knocked at a door on which was painted 2D.

Mamie Slago's room. His mind turned to her because he had read of her release by the police that afternoon; and because he had sensed in her a peculiar depravity and debasement which his nature at this moment sought.

The door opened: Mamie, in a gaudy quilted housecoat, stood staring at him.

"Hello. You got company?" he said.

Her eyes grew recessive. "What do you want?"

"Want to talk with you."

"I've said all I'm going to say."

Debs put out his hand and held the door from being shut.

"Listen," he said, "I don't want to talk about that murder. I'm not even interested. Why should I be? I'm not with the newspaper any longer—quit this afternoon. Leaving town tomorrow. But before I left I thought—well, I thought I'd like to see you—you know, friendly like. Just to visit. On the level."

She still stood in the doorway, holding the housecoat together at her breast with one hand. He thought: You've been celebrating already, haven't you, baby? He could smell the odor of liquor even where he stood.

"I've had enough trouble." She seemed undecided. "No job——"

"Nick fired you? He was pretty sore when you didn't show up yesterday morning. If you want that job back, I can fix it for you. Nick will do me a favor."

"Yeah?" A half sneer.

"Nick knows me. He'd be tickled to death to do me a favor. I promise you'll get your job back tomorrow. Okay? Now what do you say? At least you'll take a drink with me, won't you?"

He took the bottle out of his pocket.

"Well——" Her voice changed slightly. "I guess—all right, come in."

"Got any ice?" he asked as he entered and closed the door behind him.

"I'll get some. Glad you brought that hooch—I just had barely 'nough for a couple little snorts myself, *all* by myself. Gimme the bottle. You hang your overcoat and hat there in the closet."

With his bottle she went to the kitchenette a little unsteadily. He followed and stood in the door watching while she loosened the cubes in an ice tray under the tap in the sink, put ice in two glasses, poured a big slug of whiskey over the ice, and added water. She glanced up at him, a question still in her eyes.

"You make a good bartender," he said.

"I wanna get hookered."

"Don't blame you."

"That woman's jail! Crummy, and it stinks. Took two baths today since the cops let me go."

"Too bad."

"Them cops couldn't hold me. Knew they couldn't all the time. I work and I've got a place to live. No vag. I hate cops."

She handed him a glass and stood by the sink, not sipping her drink but draining it to the bottom. Knowing she already was at least two and probably more drinks ahead of him, he also drank.

"You don't hate Walt Benson, do you?" he asked.

"Him too! He never come near or acted like he even knew me when they had me in poky. He might of been the one that got me picked up, for all I know. I wouldn't spit on him!"

"I heard you were going with him."

"Naw. Him and me broke up two weeks ago. He's too jittery. All fired up one time, chasin' a kite; bellyachin' and singin' the blues next time. Gets mad, too. I've been scairt of him once or twice when he went on the prod and begun havin' a hemorrhage. Any little thing, seemed like, could set him off. It quit bein' fun. I ain't seen him for days except the time you was up here. And he wasn't here for no good then."

"What was he after?"

"Oh, hintin' around, tryin' to find out if I'd heard anyone say anything about them two murders."

"Did you?"

"Naw. I didn't know nothin' special. I was acquainted with Bonnie Bonner, but I only met Nibs Galloway once or twice. Seemed like a nice guy. Who bumped 'em off, I couldn't guess. Here, lemme have your glass."

Debs gave her the empty glass. He decided she was still suspicious of him.

"Well, let's forget that," he said. "Like to dance?"

"Yeah. Do you?"

"Sometimes. I'm not very good, but I like it."

"A man doesn't have to be good. Just a strong leader."

"We might try it sometime."

"Okay. That'd be okay." She gave him a speculative glance, and the change of topic seemed to alter her attitude toward him.

She had refilled the two glasses. "Let's go and set down," she said. With a glass in each hand she started out through the door past him.

Debs wondered just how real was her change of heart toward Benson and what she thought about Debs himself. She was no angel, and it was natural for a woman of her type to deny any connection with another man, because she knew that men detest rivals, even absent rivals, and male jealousy sometimes takes the form of sudden departure, leaving a woman without any man at all.

He did not greatly care. As she passed him in the door, he put his arms around her and stopped her. Holding up the liquor glasses, one in each hand, to keep them from spilling, she halted. His hand stroked up from her waist, cupping a breast. It was small and rubbery, but she was not wearing falsies under this housecoat.

On her painted lips came a little knowing smile and her manner subtly changed when she felt his embrace, as if she were now on safe and familiar ground.

"You feeling that way . . . ?"

She stood still, the glasses filled with liquid and ice in her hands providing her with an excuse for not making any resistance, and he lowered his head to kiss her at the place where her neck joined the shoulder. But when he began taking greater liberties with her, she pulled away and faced him, still with the knowing smile.

"Here," she said, offering him his glass.

Debs took the glass and sipped. To his surprise she drained her own drink again in a few hurried gulps.

"You *were* thirsty, weren't you?" he said.

"I sure was."

He had come here deliberately for a purpose: to have her, because a beastly rutting with a woman so abased would give him distaste and scorn not only for herself but for everything she represented, the whole race of women, all sex; a release and a purgative at least for the time being from his turmoil of doubts and confusions. Rather grimly he set out to carry out this purpose.

He set his glass, half emptied, on the table and moved toward her, but she retreated, holding him off as if she were fencing with him, yet still with the little smile on her lips.

"I thought you wanted to talk," she said.

"I do. But I want something else, too."

"What?"

"You." He reached out, took the empty glass from her hand, and set it down.

"What do you think I am?" she asked with weakly counterfeited indignation.

"I know what you are. A girl. I need a girl. Need a girl almighty bad right now——"

"Wait." She half giggled. "Wait——"

He pulled her to him. She made a faint struggle, turning her face this way and that from his kiss, but he held her close against his body. She was thin and sinewy, with compact small buttocks in keeping with her small rubbery breasts, giving him a sensation almost snakelike with her writhing. He turned her face with one hand, feeling her hard cheek under his palm and kissed her. Her breath smelled of tobacco and liquor and her lips were sticky with rouge. Suddenly she ceased any pretense of struggle and opened her mouth, thrusting her tongue into his mouth.

All at once he felt revolted, an intense disgust with himself and her. He released her hurriedly and stepped back.

An hour ago he had held Sally in his arms, and the recollection of her delicacy and softness compared to this woman's hard vulgar boldness made him almost shudder at what he had just done. He could have Mamie without any question, right now or whenever he wanted her. But suddenly he did not want her. He knew how she would be without experiencing her: familiar with all forms of sex, all the techniques; probably even counterfeiting a shadow of excitement and response to him in the manner of her kind; but as cold inwardly as an iceberg and as calculating as a stockbroker. A night with her would be shameful, a depravity that would soil him instead of releasing him.

He had come here to obtain a catharsis: and he had obtained it with a vengeance. He glanced at her with loathing because she looked so cheap and unhealthy, with an uncleanly streak of mascara on one lean cheek where he had smeared it when he turned her face to kiss her, her lips appearing sharp and hard, the lipstick on them smeared.

That lipstick . . . he wanted to wipe his own lips clean, because he knew he was stained and soiled also.

"Let's have another drink," he said.

She nodded, and he took the two glasses and went into the kitchenette. There was a paper towel hanging on its roller and he tore off a strip; wiped his mouth and saw the red smear upon the paper; wiped his lips again; took a fresh strip, wet it under the tap, and washed his mouth so vigorously that it hurt.

Then he threw the two strips into a wastebasket under the sink. He wanted now nothing except to get away from her, but he tried to make his departure seem not too precipitate.

"Why were you trying to leave town?" he asked over his shoulder through the door as he melted out more ice cubes.

"Somebody told me to," she said.

"Why?" He was pouring the whiskey: considerable for her, not so much for himself.

"Said the cops were going to pick me up for hustling. It's a lie. I'm no hustling gal. But I didn't want no trouble. Thought I'd visit a gal friend I know in Emporia for a week or two until it blowed over. A gal gets a stinkin' raw deal when the cops gets after her—if she ain't got connections."

"You're going to stay in town now?"

"Yeah. All they wanted was information about Bonnie Bonner. When they turned me loose they made me promise to stick around in case they wanted to talk to me again."

He took the two glasses and went back into the living room. She was sitting on the cheap davenport, one bare shaved leg tucked under her, the other stretched out toward him. When he held out her glass to her she took it and drank quickly again. He wondered how long it would take her to pass out at this rate, and thought that maybe after that happened it would be the best time to go.

"Who told you to leave?" he asked, sipping. Even he was beginning to feel the liquor slightly, and she had a lot more than he had.

"Somebody," she said.

"Benson?"

"No."

She would not tell him, but Debs thought he knew. Joe Canfield. But what was Canfield's interest in the matter?

"You said you knew the Bonner girl," he said to her.

"Yeah, I knew her before she married Dewey." Her speech was becoming a little thick, and with the whiskey she had drunk she seemed to grow talkative and less guarded. "She's a lot younger than me—only nineteen. Just a kid, a dumb little country punk, who didn't know what it was all about. Dumber than dumb, really. Bonnie wasn't much more'n simple-minded, if you ask me. Simple but sweet. Anybody could put anything over on her. Her folks was farmers, an' she got a job car-hoppin' at a drive-in where I was workin'."

She was beginning to slur her words, saying ashk for ask, shimple for simple, and so on. He was in no haste now to go, hoping she would not pass out before he learned more from her.

He made conversation. "Was that before she was married—when you got acquainted with her?"

"Yesh. Dewey used to come t' the place for hamburgers. He'd just hit town. Workin' as a nailer on a housing project. I remember thinkin' how goofy he looked with that billy goat beard. But he was bugs on religion, an' he got to talkin' to Bonnie, an' firsht thing I knew, she was bugs on religion too, an' they was married. Her folks was dead againsht it—didn't like no part of Dewey. But she thought he was the Second Coming, or shomething like that. Jesh' a dumb kid, mebbe a li'l *dumber* than dumb. You know what I mean?"

Her articulation was becoming thicker and she spoke in a jerky, stumbling manner. But the incredible things she was saying seemed to clear the liquor from Debs' brain.

"I think I know what you mean," he said to her.

"Anyway, her folksh raised so much hell that Dewey took her away."

"To Jericho?"

"I didn't know they come here—until—until I run onto Bonnie by acshi—accident—when I shtarted as a waitress at the Chesh—Chesterfield Club. She was doin' that strip act then. Knew her routines an' how to do a li'l belly dance with a few bumps an' grinds—but she wasn't no smarter than ever. Somebody taught her the movements, mebbe 'twas Dewey, though where he learned 'em I dunno." Mamie paused, took another pull at her glass, and then giggled drunkenly. "You know, I never thought Bonnie half wanted to strip. She done it, but she didn't like doin' it."

"Why did she do it if she didn't want to?" Debs asked.

"Dewey made her, I reckon. Bonnie minded him like a shlave—slave. He had some kind of hold on her, almost hypnotized her, seemed to me. Like when she—when she posed for that artist feller. She never wanted that, neither, 'shpeshially after the first time she posed for him. But Dewey, the ole goat, he made her go jesh' the same. Sunday nights, too, her only night off."

"Funny," he said, "a religious fanatic insisting on his wife's posing in the nude."

"Mush—musht of been their religion. Ever hear of them Dook—what d'you call 'em?—Dukhobors? Goin' naked is one of the things they do, I don't know why—gimme 'nother drink, my glash's empty."

He went into the kitchenette and mixed her a drink, a light one this time.

"I remember," he said when he returned and gave her the glass. "Some of the Dukhobors left Canada, didn't they, because people objected to their naked processions? Were the Bonners Dukhobors?"

"I dunno for sure," she said. "Mebbe jesh' an offshoot, or took part of their ideas from 'em—Dewey, anyway. Bonnie b'lieved anythin' he said, an' did what he told her." She lifted the glass and sipped. "About her posin' bare-naked that way, an' doin' that strip tease—he said it was her only way of makin' big money for the Lord's work. Said the end jush-tified the means—or somethin' like that. She minded him, but she didn't like it."

"Who was the artist?"

"Mr. de Lacey. Has a shtudio in that big house on Forest Boulevard. I posed for him once myself. He wants a gal to take off everything. Ten bucks."

Debs knew of Erskine de Lacey. The *Clarion* had carried news stories about him when he first arrived in Jericho, and Kay Roberts had interviewed him once about the proposed gallery of art.

"Does he make passes at the girls posing for him?" he asked.

"Oh, not too much." She giggled tipsily again. "When he had me in there he jesh' wanted to love it up a little. An' me naked as a jaybird. I thought mebbe he—he felt the urge. But he only done a little kissin' an' feelin', an' that was all." She looked at Debs owlishly. "If you ashk me, I think he's a *queer*."

"How many times did you go?"

"Jesh' once. I must not of been his type. But he had Bonnie back."

"Do you suppose he——?"

"Naw." She made a jerky gesture with her glass, spilling some of the whiskey on her housecoat. "Not her. He might of got his hands on her—but that'd be all. Jesh' the same he was crazy 'bout paintin' her. An' he made a deal with Dewey, so Dewey made her go back."

"You got acquainted with Bonnie and her husband in Oklahoma?"

"No, Joplin. Joplin, Missouri."

Joplin? It sent a question twisting through his mind. He was sure Dewey Bonner had told him they came from Oklahoma.

She finished her drink and gagged. "I'm tired of talkin', sugar. Less go to bed——"

He shook his head. "I'm not sleepy."

She gave him a bleary grin. "Not shleep—wouldn' go to shleep on you, sugar——" She chuckled and stretched an arm out toward him.

He disliked now to have her use any endearment toward him. "Not now."

"Well, if you don' wanna go, I do," she said.

She finished her glass, tried to rise from the davenport, and collapsed back upon it. The empty glass rolled across the carpet.

"Reckon—jesh' stay here——" she said.

Again the little chuckle, then all at once her eyes were closed and her mouth open. She began breathing noisily and deeply. Mamie Slago had passed out cold all in an instant.

For a moment Debs stood looking at her. One of her lean legs hung over the edge of the davenport, her clothing so disarrayed that it was exposed almost to the hip. Her hair was disheveled and her lips drawn in what seemed to him almost a ghastly grin.

He leaned over and raised her leg, placing it on the couch, and drew down over it the housecoat. She was limp and motionless, too deeply sunk in stupor to know that anyone was handling her.

Drunk, dead-drunk. Debs went over to the sink in the kitchenette and from the remnants of the bottle of whiskey poured a good stiff drink for himself. Then he set it down without touching it.

After that he turned off the lights in Mamie's room and went out, setting the night latch and closing the door carefully behind him.

He had a sensation akin to nausea, a violent rejection by the fastidious side of his being at any contact with the woman. He was very glad he had not carried out his original purpose with her, because he could think of her only with disgust now. At least he had no entanglements or obligations to settle for.

Nevertheless, there was one thread left: her connection with Bonnie Bonner. He would have to keep in touch with her because of that.

2

On the sheet of paper the pencil made diagrams and arabesques next morning in the fingers of Vic Hinshaw, chief of detectives.

He looked up, hooded gray eyes, long sly nose, hat as usual on the back of his head.

"We've already questioned Dewey Bonner once, Debs," he said.

"All right, just what did you find out about him?"

"Nut on religion. Half crazy. Sells books and tracts. Harmless."

Debs said, "Have you thought about it this way: what if Dewey Bonner isn't as religious, or as crazy, or as harmless as you think?"

"What are you getting at?"

"I talked to Bonner, too. He told me several things. He came here with his wife from Oklahoma. He wasn't working just now, because work is slack. He gave all the money he made, and she made, to their church. Some of those statements don't check with the facts."

"Which ones?"

"He didn't come here from Oklahoma; he came from Joplin, Missouri. Work isn't slack here in his line—carpentering—the builders are

using everybody that can hammer a nail or use a saw. That's two. Do
you know what I've been doing this morning?"

"No; what?"

"I got a list of all the religious denominations in town from the Coun-
cil of Churches office. I've telephoned every little off-brand religion on
that list to find which one the Bonners belonged to. Not one of them
knows Dewey Bonner."

"Maybe it's a sect that ain't listed," said Hinshaw.

"What would you say if there *wasn't* any church?"

"But—the tracts and religious books——"

"I've been doing some thinking, Vic. Bonnie Bonner was pretty, but
she wasn't very bright. She was getting good money strip teasing, and
she did some modeling for an artist, but she didn't want to do either
of them."

"How do you know?"

"From somebody that knew her. She did it because her husband made
her. I believe she thought he was some kind of a prophet, handing down
the commandments from Mount Sinai. What if *he* was the church
himself? A one-man religion with one disciple—her?"

Hinshaw continued penciling his diagrams.

"She was always reading the Bible," Debs said. "Why, do you
reckon?"

"Part of her religion, I'd say."

"I'm wondering a little farther. Even with the whammy he had on
her, could Bonnie Bonner have been wondering about Dewey's holi-
ness? Could that Bible reading have been to check up on what he told
her—among other things that it wasn't sinful, but God's work, to strip
off the clothes from her gorgeous body before a crowd of goggle-eyed
drunks at the Chesterfield Club every night?"

"You're trying to tell me that Bonner didn't believe it himself?"

"I'm not sure. But there are some mighty funny things about it. And
since we're speculating, what if Dewey wasn't giving the money his
wife made to *any* church? She was getting two hundred a week from
Draggett, and believe me, they spent none of it on their living or their
house. What if that pious prophet beard of Dewey Bonner's was a
cover-up? Did you ever consider how a set of whiskers can change a
man's appearance? He might even have a record."

"You've got a point there, certainly."

"Then let's go a little farther," Debs said. "The murder report stressed that Bonnie Bonner didn't make any outcry when she was murdered by a blow on the head. It was surmised that the assailant was hidden in her dressing room somehow and she didn't see him. What if she *did* see him—and *knew* him? What if he was Dewey, her own husband? That could account for her not screaming, couldn't it?"

"Yes, I reckon it could."

"He could have been there on some excuse, and as soon as she turned her back, hit her one hard lick on the head with something. Nobody checked on her. He might have stayed right in her dressing room until everyone was gone and then let himself out and returned home. Walking, likely, because the car was left there at the roadhouse."

Hinshaw pursed his lips. Then he lit a cigarette and puffed on it, studying.

"All this *could* be," he said at last. "But there isn't a shred of evidence that it *was* that way. There ain't enough motive, for one thing, to base suspicion on."

"Couldn't you pick him up and fingerprint him to check if he's got a record somewhere?"

"I've got to have some evidence for an arrest. Something at least to base a suspicion of murder on."

"You could get a search warrant for the house, couldn't you?"

"Yes, I reckon."

"There's one thing you might look for," Debs said. "He might have it on him, or it might be somewhere around the house."

"A gun?"

"No, a bankbook."

A gleam came into Hinshaw's eyes. "Stashing that money away?"

"If he was, it's a motive, isn't it? The girl might have been turning against him, getting ready to expose his racket."

"W-e-e-ll, a *kind* of a motive," said the chief of detectives slowly. "Not a very good one." He straightened up in his chair. "Just the same, I think I'll go down and have another talk with Mr. Dewey Bonner."

Twenty-two

I

It was eleven o'clock in the morning when the police car pulled up in front of Dewey Bonner's faded yellow shack. In the wire pen at the rear chickens were pecking and scratching the ground, but no smoke came from the chimney and there was no sign of life in the house.

"He must be gone," said Hinshaw.

"Let's find out," Debs said.

They got out of the car, the four of them: Hinshaw, Debs, and two detectives named Biggers and Childreth.

"Jim," said Hinshaw to Biggers, "you go to the back door. Stay here in front, Jerry," he added to Childreth. "Keep anyone back."

He and Debs went to the front door, and Hinshaw knocked.

He knocked again.

"Skipped," he said.

Debs reached out and tried the knob. It turned. The door swung open.

Hinshaw started to enter but halted, a look of surprise on his face.

Standing in the middle of the room, wearing only his long baggy underwear, and staring wildly as if startled out of his senses, was Dewey Bonner. His large feet were bare, and his hair was tousled. His whole appearance, in fact, was of one suddenly roused from deep sleep. In the shadowy room his face appeared even more gaunt than when Debs had seen it before, as if he had undergone a long penance of fasting. His beard bristled and his eyes were hazy, heavy-lidded, with pupils that seemed to have contracted to mere pinpoints. Like one who is ill he stood in the middle of the floor, almost swaying as if with weakness, peering dully at the intruders.

"Hello, Mr. Bonner," said Hinshaw.

For a moment Bonner stared as if uncomprehending, then he seemed to get command of himself by an effort of will and spoke.

"What—what d'you want?" he said, his voice hoarse and a little thick. "Who told you that you could come in here?"

"We want to talk to you," said the chief of detectives.

Bonner's eyes drifted vaguely about the room, then came to a focus. He drew himself up.

"Who give you permission to walk into a man's house without his leave?" he demanded. Though his voice was still thick, it contained a note of anger. "A citizen's got some rights left, ain't he? You men get out of here now, an' leave me alone!"

"Be reasonable, Mr. Bonner," said Hinshaw. "No call to get excited. Just some routine questions."

"I've already told you everything I know," Bonner said querulously. "You cops never know when to leave a man be. I'm wore out. Now listen, I ain't foolin'. I'll go to court over this. You got a search warrant? You can't come into private premises without permission even if you are a cop, an' you know it."

His gaze shifted to Debs. "An' what's *he* doin' here? He ain't even a cop!" For some reason his voice changed.

"We knocked and you didn't answer," said Hinshaw soothingly.

"I was comin'. Can't you see? I was asleep. Never even took time to get dressed."

"You're sleeping a little late, ain't you?"

"I was up late," said Bonner. "Readin'. Say, lemme get some clothes on, won't you? This floor's cold."

"Sure, Mr. Bonner." Hinshaw made as if to follow the bearded man into the lean-to sleeping room.

"You don't need to come in here," Bonner said. "This here's a private room—nothin' here that can be of any interest to you. I'll be out in a minute."

Hinshaw acquiesced. Bonner disappeared and the chief of detectives went over to the stove, got a newspaper and some kindling from the box, and lit a fire to take the chill off the air.

Debs looked about the room. Old chairs; gaudy flowered wallpaper; Dewey Bonner's battered brief case on the floor by the wall; the table with its stack of blue-bound books entitled *Seven Times Seven Keys to the Kingdom*.

Curiosity caused him to walk over to the table. He remembered that Bonner was unwilling to let him touch the books on his previous visit and he wondered what their import was. From the top of the stack he took a copy and opened it, glancing at chapter heads and stray sentences.

Nothing remarkable about the book. It was a religious treatise of the familiar type, written by some not overliterate tent evangelist, full of platitudes and pious banalities, reinforced by Biblical quotations.

He was about to replace the book in the stack when he heard Bonner behind him exclaim, "What you doin'? Get your hands off them books!"

Surprised by the harsh quality in the voice, Debs turned. In his pants and shirt, his feet shod now but his suspenders still hanging about his hips, the fanatic stood in the bedroom door, bent-legged as if he suddenly had crouched.

"Look out!" cried Hinshaw.

Across the room Bonner made a leaping rush and snatched the book from Debs' hands.

So sudden and unexpectedly violent was the act that Debs lurched backward, blundering heavily into the table. There was a crash behind him. The jolt had toppled the stack of books over on the table.

"Now see what you've done——" Bonner began furiously.

Then he stopped. For a moment the three of them stood in a silence so complete that it seemed almost religious.

One of the middle books from the stack had fallen open, face down, its cover thrown back. From under the cover rolled what looked like three or four white medicine capsules.

The book had been converted into a sort of box by pasting its pages together, and then cutting out the printed center, leaving only the glued margins of the leaves.

"What's that?" asked Hinshaw.

Bonner spoke quickly. "Quinine! Just quinine. I'm subject to ague."

"Let me see one of them."

"No you don't."

Again Bonner suddenly galvanized into action. He leaped to the table, clawing the scattered capsules with his hand. Before they could prevent him, he bounded across the room to the stove and stuffed the little cylinders and the false book into the blazing fire which Hinshaw had kindled.

Then, panting and glaring, he turned on them.

"Heroin!" exclaimed Hinshaw. "That was heroin!"

He drew his revolver and held it low, muzzle pointing at the bearded man.

"What proof you got?" Bonner was grim and defiant.

"I've got enough proof to arrest you for the murder of your wife," said Hinshaw coldly. "Now I know why we've had a raft of hopheads in jail lately. You've been shoving the stuff in them books, lettin' on you was goin' your rounds spreadin' the gospel. You're a junkhead yourself—I saw you was glass-eyed as soon as I come in. Your wife tumbled to it—you were afraid she'd squeal on you, so you bumped her off."

Bonner made a half twist of his body, gazing about wildly as if for an avenue of escape.

"Don't move," said Hinshaw. "It would be a pleasure to drill you." He jerked his head toward the back door. "Debs, go tell Jim Biggers to come in here."

A half sob from Bonner. "I ain't no chronic. I'm off it—been off it. Had to have a fix—had to have it—God, ah God——"

2

Debs stepped out of the little yellow house. He had experienced none of the man-hunter's exultation which Hinshaw and the other officers seemed to feel; which they showed especially when an examination of Dewey Bonner's arm revealed the needle scars along the vein; when they discovered a hypodermic hidden under the mattress of the bed; when after a long search among the scattered books on the table one capsule was discovered on the floor, where it had fallen, a piece of certain evidence against the prisoner.

Debs felt an inner sag, an emptiness, but he had a story.

For the first time in his life he had a big story that he did not know what to do with.

Habit is very strong. He glanced at his watch. Eleven-thirty.

He owed nothing to the *Clarion*, still less to the *Sentinel*. But he remembered that Sally told him Jeff Linderman was on the desk now, and Jeff was a good friend. Perhaps getting the news break would do him some good.

Before the Bonner house, kept back by Detective Childreth, had gathered a small crowd of people, shabby women, dirty-faced kids, one or two men in overalls.

He walked over toward them. "Anybody here got a phone I can use?"

"You kin use ourn, mister," said a big, slatternly woman with a man's jacket over her shoulders. "What's goin' on in there?"

"Arrested Dewey Bonner," said Debs. "Suspicion of murder. Which is your house?"

"The white one across the street. Go right in." The woman did not want to leave for fear she would miss some of the excitement.

Debs crossed the street, entered the shabby little bungalow. The telephone, an old-fashioned upright instrument, stood on an old table in the front room. He dialed the *Clarion.*

"This is Debs," he said when he got Jeff at the other end of the wire.

"Debs—*Debs?* Good God, am I glad to find you! Listen, Debs, come up to the office right away, will you?"

"I got a story for you."

"We can talk about it when you come up——"

"This is an extra-edition story."

"What's that? It is? Extra? Hell, give it to me——"

"They've just arrested Dewey Bonner for the murder of his wife, and got a cache of dope in his house. Heroin."

Rapidly Debs gave Jeff sufficient information for a flash street banner. Then Jeff said, "Debs, come on up, won't you?"

"If you want to see me, come down to Jolly Herron's. We'll eat lunch together."

"No, Debs, listen. It's not me. It's Mrs. Wedge wants to see you. I'll give it to you straight. She found out you were gone and she's down here at the office in person. She's got Hudson in the publisher's office now. I don't know what it's all about, but hell's sure popping. Debs, I wish you'd come up—I've been phoning all over town trying to reach you."

"Mrs. Wedge made you personally responsible for corralling me?"

"No, but Shrieking Sam sure did. Please, Debs, come up. I've got to get busy and write that lead—please, Debs——"

Debs ran his hand along his jowl. He had not shaved that morning. He felt hollow-eyed and grimy.

"I've got to clean up," he told Jeff.

"No, don't waste any time! Please, Debs—I'm telling you this is *important!*"

The urgency in Jeff's voice was unmistakable.

"All right," Debs said. "I'll come in with the police. You can tell that skirt-wearing boss of your damned broken-down sheet that I'll be there in fifteen minutes."

3

The obscure mention in the previous afternoon's paper that Bonnie Bonner had posed for an artist, unnamed, brought about Mrs. Mary Agnes Wedge's intervention in the affairs of the *Clarion* that morning.

She had thought about Erskine and that painting he had made of her, and she found that her feelings toward it had considerably changed. At first—and entirely surprising to her when she fully realized it—she had been simply, old-fashionedly, femininely, horribly ashamed: in the final analysis as shocked at herself as Jericho would be if it found out.

But as she considered it further, she said to herself that it was something else. If it had been a really first-rate artist who painted her in the nude, she might have brazened it out, carrying it off by sheer boldness, by being amused at provincial attitudes, by pointing to some lofty precedents: Goya's celebrated painting of the Duchess of Alba, for instance. There might be a little eyebrow lifting over it, and some spiteful behind-the-back remarks, but in the end wouldn't people rather shrug their shoulders and dismiss it as perhaps a little daring and even risqué, but not really so terrible?

The trouble was that Erskine was not a first-rate artist. He was a phony, and a dilettante; and his paintings were not art, they were pornography. An obscure night club entertainer might display her body for him, and nobody would think anything of it perhaps. But for Mrs. Mary Agnes Wedge, mistress of a fortune, head of an important business and co-publisher of the *Clarion,* the envied, hated, and admired leader of Jericho's society, to do so was far different. Her very prominence would turn what in another woman was no more than perhaps an indiscretion into something far worse in her case.

It would make her appear shoddy, common, cheap. Worse, it would make her a fool and a laughing stock: a silly, inane simpleton who allowed herself to be deluded into being displayed on canvas indecently for the gaze of the vulgar. She writhed inwardly at the thought of the laughter, the ridicule of all Jericho. It was the one thing Mary Agnes did not think she could survive. Her whole life's fabric of pride was terribly involved and threatened: somehow she must prevent anybody from ever seeing or even knowing about that painting.

She needed time to deal with Erskine, and to have a police investigation of him might be fatal to her plans. She was aware that newspapers sometimes have considerable influence with public officials, and she decided to make her first official act as co-publisher of the *Clarion* a rather personal one. She was in the position of having to request that the *Clarion* in turn request the police to keep their hands off Mr. de Lacey. That brought her up against the fact that she hardly knew anybody on the *Clarion*. Only one person, really—that brash young man, Mr. Debs Dorn.

At eight o'clock that morning—an hour so early that to anyone who knew her it would have indicated her state of mind—she telephoned the *Clarion* and asked for the city editor.

She got hold of someone who said his name was Linderman and who informed her that Mr. Dorn was not there.

"Can you tell me when he'll be back?" she asked.

"May I ask who's calling?" Linderman replied.

"This is Mrs. Wistart Wedge."

"Mrs. Wedge? Wait a minute, Mrs. Wedge——" She detected consternation in the voice, and it was obvious that a hand was held over the mouthpiece of a telephone while some kind of colloquy was held at the other end.

Then a different voice came on the phone, a voice consciously bluff and hearty. "Hello. Hudson speaking."

"Mr. Hudson, this is Mrs. Wedge."

"Oh yes, Mrs. Wedge! Yes indeed! What can I do for you this morning?"

Her prejudices always strongly influenced Mary Agnes, and her prejudices were sometimes quickly, even superficially, formed. She had not liked Hudson before, and now his oiliness increased her distaste.

"I asked for Mr. Dorn," she said.

A moment's hesitation. Then, "To tell you the truth, Dorn isn't with the paper any more, Mrs. Wedge."

"When did——?"

"He resigned yesterday."

"Why wasn't I notified of this?"

"Oh, a minor administrative problem, Mrs. Wedge. Why should we trouble you with an unimportant detail like that?"

For a moment she was silent. Now that she was told she could not see him, her reasons for wishing to see Mr. Dorn seemed more important to her than before. Furthermore, she felt that she was being ignored, pushed aside in this matter, whereas she was sure that if Wistart had been in town he would have been consulted, and it made her resentful.

She spoke decisively. "I don't think, Mr. Hudson, that the resignation of a city editor from a newspaper is a minor matter, and I want to know more about it. Besides, I have some business with Mr. Dorn. I want you to find him and have him up to the office before noon."

To Hudson this had an ominous sound. "I can't promise to locate him, Mrs. Wedge. He may have left town for all I know—newspapermen are birds of passage, you know——" Ingratiating cackle.

She cut the cackle short. "Find him, Mr. Hudson! I'm coming down."

4

Samson J. Hudson sat back with a decided sensation of alarm. He was confronted by a contingency on which he had not counted. The showdown with Debs Dorn had come at a very bad time. Had Wistart Wedge been in town, he would have been inclined to listen to explanations, accept recommendations. But Hudson was dealing instead with Mrs. Wedge, and she had given him an order that was sharp and characteristically imperious, and took into account no difficulties in compliance or excuses.

Why was the woman interested in Debs Dorn, and what business could she possibly have with him? If he had known this . . . but Hudson had not known it, and now all he could do was curse his luck.

An order, however, was an order, so he set Jeff Linderman frantically at work trying to locate Debs.

After that he felt need of something to brace his quivering nerves. He fumbled in the drawer of his desk, slipped into his pocket a half-pint bottle, went back to the washroom, and after making sure no one was in it, took a long pull at the whiskey.

Later in the morning, still feeling the need of it, he returned to the washroom and finished the half pint. After that he took a small vial of breath deodorant and poured a few drops of aromatic liquid in his mouth, gargling with it and expectorating in a urinal. He had a belief, not entirely justified, that it would kill the whiskey on his breath.

By this time the alcohol had warmed his blood and increased his confidence so that when, a little before eleven-thirty, Miss Finch came in with word that Mrs. Wedge was in the publisher's office and wanted to see him, he went in somewhat jauntily, even planning tactics which he hoped would mollify the lady.

She was sitting in her husband's high-backed swivel chair behind her husband's desk, and some of his confidence oozed away as he thought to himself that her face was hard enough to cut glass.

"Have you located Mr. Dorn?" she asked at once.

"No, ma'am." He attempted to be cheery. "But we should have word of him any minute. I told Linderman to call in here if they get in touch with him."

"I want to know why he left the paper."

"Well," said Hudson uneasily, "there's not much to be said about it. He simply resigned suddenly yesterday and left. Without giving even a minute's notice."

"But *why?*" she insisted.

"To tell you the truth, Mrs. Wedge——" Hudson paused and scraped his throat nervously. "I hate to say anything unfavorable about any man, but I've had trouble with Dorn. He's a fair newspaperman, but he can't take discipline. Yesterday, in a clear case of insubordination, when I had to take matters into my own hands because of my responsibility to the paper, he quit in a huff."

The telephone on the desk rang. Mary Agnes lifted the receiver.

"Yes?" she said. "Yes. Oh, he is? Now? Very good. Thank you."

She hung up and turned her jade green gaze on Hudson. "That was Mr. Linderman. He says Mr. Dorn just phoned in. He has some kind of a story. Didn't you say he'd quit the paper?"

"He has."

"Then why is he bringing the story to us? Mr. Linderman says it's important. They're getting out an extra. Mr. Dorn's on his way in now."

"An extra?" Hudson jumped to his feet. "Jeez—I beg pardon, ma'am —I'd better get out there——"

Mary Agnes was not a newspaperwoman and did not know the overwhelming eagerness to be in on a big story; but she did have some ideas about executive management and delegated responsibility.

"Sit down," she said coldly. "I'm sure Mr. Linderman can carry on for the present. You were saying Mr. Dorn quit—in a huff, I believe your words were?"

Hudson twisted about in his chair in an agony of desire to be gone out of the presence of this unyielding woman. But he could not leave against her direct command. He realized that his position was very weak. His actions in the Dorn matter were subject to criticism since he had acted on an impulse not entirely praiseworthy. Furthermore, his story to Mary Agnes was not exactly the truth.

But he knew the strategic value of the first presentation of evidence, and he made an attempt to convince her that he had acted for the best interests of the paper by setting forth things in the most favorable light to himself.

"Dorn walked out," he said, "walked out before the paper even went to press. A very unethical thing to do from a professional standpoint. Almost unheard of. I had to get the paper out myself on the spur of the moment with what help I could find——"

"You mentioned insubordination. What was it?"

"He went contrary to my orders. He made a very bad blunder, and I overruled him——"

"What was the blunder?"

Hudson felt he was being driven into a corner. "Well—he took a very valuable man off a beat which that man knows better than anyone in town and put someone else on who wasn't at all familiar with it; and at a time when important news was breaking——"

"Who was he replacing?"

"Joe Canfield is the man. He's on police—the best reporter in Jericho, does an outstanding job——"

"Then why did Mr. Dorn wish to transfer him?"

"I can't imagine why, Mrs. Wedge. Canfield so obviously belongs where he is." Hudson stopped a moment, and then, speaking as if he were unwilling to say it, went on. "I'm very much afraid it was a personal grudge on Dorn's part. I simply intervened, and without explaining himself, Dorn walked out."

Mary Agnes knew the man had been drinking. Even across the desk she could detect the sour odor of liquor, overlaid by something else. Her opinion of Hudson underwent a further decline, because she disapproved of a man's drinking when he was at work. But, more importantly, she sensed his uneasiness. She felt that something more underlay this whole question. Hudson was too plausible. The more she estimated him, the surer she was that he was lying about something, and she resented having someone lie to her.

"You're trying to tell me he lost his temper over nothing?" she asked.

"Lost his temper. Lost his head. That's bad enough in a man who's supposed to be holding down an important desk. But what I can't forgive is his lack of loyalty to the paper. I believe the *Clarion* can get along without that kind of a man. Loyalty's the first requisite with me."

The last sentence had a false ring to Mary Agnes' ears.

"And yet he goes to all the trouble of getting this story for the *Clarion*," she said. "If he's so disloyal, why would he do that?"

She watched him squirm as he tried to frame an answer to that. Before he could do so, Miss Finch opened the door.

"Mr. Dorn's here," she said to Mary Agnes. "He's in the reception room."

"Ask him to come in at once."

When Debs entered, Mary Agnes was surprised at his appearance. He needed a shave and he had not bothered to dress well to go to the police station that morning: he wore an old pair of slacks and a jacket that looked as if he had slept in it. Without speaking, he nodded and sat down. Obviously, she thought, he was carrying a chip on his shoulder; and she felt a little weary and impatient over the problem of dealing with a man who was evasive and probably lying on the one hand and with one who was antagonistic on the other. But she began coolly.

"We're interested," she said to Debs, "in this story of yours."

His eyes lit with a momentary gleam. "They've got the murderer of Bonnie Bonner. Her husband."

"Husband? Jeez——" Hudson half rose, but subsided when Mary Agnes raised her hand.

Briefly Debs outlined the main points of the story. She listened with intense interest: with a feeling of relief, too. She said to herself that the murder of the Bonner woman had been solved, which meant that no police investigation of Erskine de Lacey was now necessary. On that score at least she could set her mind at rest.

Meantime she returned to her inquiry.

"Who did you say our police reporter is?" she asked Hudson.

"Canfield."

"The man you told me was so outstanding?"

The managing editor hesitated uncomfortably. "Well—yes."

"If he's so good, why didn't he get this big story instead of Mr. Dorn?"

It was a question Hudson had been asking himself, and he had thus far found no answer to it.

Mary Agnes saw Debs glance quickly from one to the other of them, and she was sure he had divined the direction of their conversation before he came in.

"Mr. Hudson says you're no longer a member of our staff," she said. "May I ask why you gave this story to the *Clarion?*"

"I hate to see a good story go to waste," Debs said gruffly.

"Wouldn't Mr. Canfield have got it later?"

Again that gleam in his eye. "We were right up against the noon deadline." Debs did not notice that he used the personal pronoun. "There wasn't time. If I hadn't phoned in, the opposition might have got the jump on the extra——"

The gleam faded and he sat back.

With interest she studied him. For the first time something of the hidden coiled-spring tension latent in newspaper work was being revealed to her, and it fascinated her, excited her. Almost she could imagine the *Clarion* as a living creature, alert, fierce, watching to counter the competitive moves of an antagonist equally aggressive in a continuing duel. What Debs told her a day or so before about the difference between a newspaper and an ordinary business was beginning to be understandable. At the same time she sensed in Debs himself an inborn instinct, something as much a matter of the blood as it is of the mind, the difference between an exceptional performer in any field and all those who remain ordinary no matter what their training and experience.

"Mr. Dorn," she said, "I'm interested in your reasons for leaving this paper."

Again his eyes traveled swiftly to Hudson and back to her. "I imagine you've had a pretty full report on that," he said.

"I'm here to listen to all sides."

"Let's just say I was fed up." He was curt.

Mary Agnes was not a patient woman, and this young man was trying her patience sorely. Nevertheless, she sought to be winning.

"I don't think you see what I'm trying to do," she said. "There's evidently been a misunderstanding. With everybody's co-operation we may be able to work things out."

He shook his head. "There's no misunderstanding."

Still she kept her patience, and it was a growing effort for her.

"I understand that your abrupt action came as a result of some question over Mr. Canfield," she said. "Also that you have a personal grudge against this man."

"I have no grudge against Canfield."

"Then why did you change him against orders——?"

Debs' head jerked up. "Against *orders?*" She saw that now he was angry. "What orders? Nobody gave me orders not to change staff assignments. It's a city editor's job. Nobody gave orders until *after!* If you want to know it, *that's* why I quit—I was told that I didn't have that kind of authority. When a city editor loses his authority, he ought to step out for someone else!"

"Let me have a word——" began Hudson.

Mary Agnes checked him. "I'd prefer Mr. Dorn to continue for the moment. What's wrong with this man Canfield?" She looked at Debs. "I don't consider him trustworthy," he said.

"Now wait a minute!" exploded Hudson. "I don't suppose Mrs. Wedge wants to pass judgment on who is and who isn't to be trusted on the *Clarion*——"

"I think we must at least consider Mr. Dorn's opinion in this matter," said Mary Agnes.

Hudson rose, his face reddening. "Let me remind you, Mrs. Wedge, that this man isn't even on the staff. *I'm* the managing editor of this paper, and the responsibility's *mine!*"

"In this instance, I'll assume the responsibility," she said coldly.

Had he not been drinking it is improbable that Hudson would have done what he next did. His face flushed still more deeply.

"If that's the case—I can see no further necessity for my presence in this conference!" he exclaimed angrily.

He was playing his last trump, but he played it against the wrong opponent. Mary Agnes' patience suddenly snapped.

"Do you feel that way, Mr. Hudson?" she said. "Then I quite agree with you!"

His jaw fell as he stared at her. He was not sure how far the implications of this went. He was not sure that he even had a job on this paper any longer.

He went back to his desk in the city room. There he sat for a while, not looking at anyone or speaking to anyone. After a time he took his hat and coat and left the office. Nobody would see him any more that day.

Shortly afterward the staff saw Debs Dorn come from the publisher's office and go over to the city desk. He exchanged a few words with Jeff Linderman, then took his usual seat and went to work exactly as if nothing had happened.

Twenty-three

I

The conference with Hudson and Dorn had not taken long and Mary Agnes flattered herself that she cut rather shrewdly to the core of things. She had reversed Hudson and reinstated Dorn. The fact that her decisions were based on personal prejudices rather than careful consideration did not concern her if it even occurred to her.

She simply did not like Hudson. Because she did not like him it was clear to her that he was wrong; he would have been wrong, to her view, if he had been right.

She had made a choice between the two men, and it might have a highly important bearing on the future of the *Clarion*. But the fact was —although she did not think along these lines—that a much wiser and far more temperate judge than she might have done no better. Credit to feminine intuition or luck, when the moment came for making her choice, Mary Agnes unerringly chose the better man.

But first she had to convince her man. After Hudson walked out, she had a few more words with Debs.

"I want you to reconsider your resignation," she said.

"On what basis?"

"On this basis: you have a definite future on this paper, Mr. Dorn— if you want it. I have some plans, which I'm going to carry out. And I've made my mind up definitely on one thing. Mr. Hudson doesn't belong where he is. Does that hold any meaning for you?"

"Perhaps," he said.

"Why perhaps?"

"If I knew what reason you had for coming to such a decision."

"You think I have some capricious *woman's* reason?" She emphasized the word with irony almost bitter.

"I don't know what is your reason." He was uncompromising.

"Then let me tell you this, Mr. Dorn. I don't admire a man who drinks on duty, and Mr. Hudson has been drinking heavily. I don't admire a man who is a toady, and Mr. Hudson makes a career of toadyism. I don't admire a man who lies, and Mr. Hudson sat here and lied in his teeth to me!"

For a moment he regarded her almost expressionlessly. Then he said, "If those are your reasons, and you know they're true, I wouldn't call them capricious."

"*You* know they're true!"

"You're the boss. What I know or don't know isn't of much importance."

He was refusing to commit himself on Hudson's shortcomings, she saw, and she respected him for it even though it annoyed her somewhat.

So she said, "I believe we understand each other, Mr. Dorn. What we've just discussed I'd like you to keep in confidence. And I hope I can count on your loyalty and willingness."

He gave a curt nod, but remained silent.

"For the present," she said, "until I have a chance to go over matters with Mr. Wedge, I can at least promise you that you will have full authority within the limits of your position on the city desk."

He considered a minute. There was in this an assurance as well as an implied promise, and he had watched the rather impressive decisiveness of her dealings with Hudson. Though she did not know it Mary Agnes already had gone far toward winning Debs Dorn's full respect.

"Very well, I'll try it," he said, and on that understanding returned to the city room and his job.

Mary Agnes left the *Clarion* and went home, feeling rather well satisfied with herself. Not until four o'clock that afternoon, when the paper arrived at her home, did the satisfaction fade with the sudden realization that she had overlooked something very important. By that time it already was too late.

The headline stared blackly:

MURDERED DANCER'S HUSBAND ARRESTED AS WIFE'S SLAYER

Debs Dorn had written the story himself, and she read the opening paragraphs:

Dewey Bonner, 39, self-styled prophet and religious cultist, was arrested shortly before noon today by Victor Hinshaw, chief of detectives, for the murder of his wife, Bonnie Bonner, 19, night club entertainer, who was found dead in her dressing room at the Chesterfield Club last Monday. He has confessed the crime.

Disclosure that Bonner, picturesque in appearance, is not the fanatical religious worker he was supposed to be, but an ex-convict and parolee, who had been living a Jekyll and Hyde existence as a dealer in illicit narcotics, lends a bizarre touch to the murder which has mystified police for several days. Hinshaw says the prisoner has been using his humble dwelling in South Jericho as headquarters for a widespread dope traffic, his Biblical beard and pious bearing a perfect disguise for such activities.

The story went on to say that in Bonner's house a cache of heroin was discovered, and that, although the accused succeeded in destroying most of it, enough was saved for evidence. Police pointed to a great increase recently in the number of narcotics addicts taken into custody, as caused by the captured man's dealings.

A telegraphic check on fingerprint identifications with the FBI established the prisoner as an ex-convict, Calvin Finley, alias Casey Clark, who had served a prison term in the federal penitentiary at Atlanta, and was at present under parole. Rogue's gallery photographs subsequently verified the identification, although Finley, alias Bonner, had grown a beard to alter his appearance.

Keys to a safety deposit box found in his possession led officers to a vault of the First National Bank, where more than ten thousand dollars in large bills was found, accounting for his profits from his heroin sales, and also for the money earned by his murdered wife, which he previously had asserted was given to religious work. A former drug addict himself, he had been given the cure during his prison term, Bonner said, but returned to the habit since slaying his wife, because his nerves needed to be quieted. He was under the influence of narcotics at the time the police entered his house and arrested him.

Down in the body of the story was a paragraph of speculative interest:

On the theory that there is a link between the murders of Bonnie Bonner and Detective Nibs Galloway, slain the next day after the entertainer was killed, police questioned the prisoner, but he denied all knowledge of the identity of the slayer of Galloway. In spite of his denial, however, it is believed that Bonner has an accomplice or accomplices, or if not, was paying off someone to protect him in his drug selling.

It is recalled that prior to his death Galloway was depressed and uncommunicative. He was at the time working on the Bonner murder. Police speculate that he may have found evidence pointing to someone he knew, perhaps someone he did not wish to suspect, and discovery by the guilty person that the officer had this evidence led to his slaying.

Reading it, Mary Agnes wondered what the police had in mind and whom they suspected. It was the first big newspaper story in which she had been close to the drama of the handling for publication, and she was excited by it and quite proud of it; and of Debs Dorn, who wrote it.

She went on with the story. Confronted by positive identification, it said, Bonner signed a confession that he had murdered his wife in her dressing room, by hitting her on the head with a gas pipe, because she became suspicious of his activities and he feared she would give law officers information that might lead to discovery of his narcotics selling.

Then came three paragraphs that riveted the reader's most rapt attention:

Bonner's confession, as dictated by him, further revealed that he had for many months forced the murdered girl to perform acts she detested, by a Svengali-like ascendancy over her, due to her belief that he was an incarnate prophet, an assertion which her childlike mind accepted when he made to her what he called a "revelation" shortly before their marriage in Joplin, Mo.

Among these were her performances as a strip-tease dancer, for which she, naturally modest by upbringing and traits, had an aversion, but for which he trained her and acted as her agent, obtaining an engagement for her at the Chesterfield Club.

Questioned farther, Bonner placed in his confession, which he later signed under oath, a statement that his wife also disliked another occupation he obtained for her, as an artist's model for Erskine de Lacey, 1341

Forest Blvd. Asked why his wife objected, the prisoner said she did not like to appear completely nude but that the artist demanded that she pose without even the very scanty garments she wore during her performances at the night club.

Pressed to explain why he forced her to do these things, Bonner only answered that her beautiful body was her sole asset, since she was not educated or trained for any other kind of money-making occupation, adding that "she was too dumb." The dead girl, it has been learned, seemed to be of somewhat subnormal intelligence. Neighbors told police that though she was of a pleasant disposition they regarded her as "simple-minded."

The story continued along these lines. Debs Dorn was a top-notch reporter and he devoted more than a column to exhausting every pertinent detail. The only important point he withheld was that one Debs Dorn had provided the deductions, the impetus, and the actual discovery of the narcotics cache which led to the arrest of Dewey Bonner.

It was an exclusive story and a well-handled story, and Mary Agnes as co-publisher of the *Clarion* should have been elated by it, as indeed she was when she first began reading it. But her elation faded and her attention was fixed only on the paragraphs concerning Erskine de Lacey.

Why had it not occurred to her that clearing up the murder of Bonnie Bonner might release the very information she had dreaded to have appear—in her own paper, particularly? And Erskine certainly would hold her responsible. There was no telling what might be his spiteful or vicious retaliation.

She was furious with herself for failing to caution Debs Dorn about Erskine. And she was even more furious with Debs for publishing the item, even though he had not been warned against it.

2

"*Clarion!* Big murder myst'ry solved! Extry speshul!"

The boy stood at the corner beside a mailbox and a city trash bin, crying his wares. On the sidewalk was a heap of papers fresh off the press, an old paving brick on top of them preventing them from blowing away in the prevailing Kansas "scurrying winds." Under his arm he held a dozen more copies of the paper while he brandished one with his free hand so that passers could see the black headline as a stimulant to reading appetites.

The boy's years were no more than twelve, but he had spent enough of them in this special trade of selling newspapers on the street so that his sense of what appealed to the public was sharpened to a precocious degree. Now his vivacity as a salesman proclaimed his own belief in the quality of his merchandise. With assurance and fire, he vociferated. Sometimes he cried the headline itself, sometimes he reached down into the story, which he had read, and dragged up details, which he yelled with the frenzy of a courier just arriving with astonishing details, whenever anything like a purchasing face came in sight.

"Murder myst'ry! Big local artist involved!" shouted the boy.

A bareheaded man with a crew haircut and pink-rimmed glasses turned toward him.

"Paper, mister?" said the boy hopefully. Then, as if reluctant to keep the general public waiting, he lifted his voice to its top again, "Big murder myst'ry! Soci'ty artist involved. Read all about it!"

The man with the pink-rimmed glasses held out a dime and took the paper held out by a grimy hand. Then he fell back to read it as the youthful merchant of news continued to remind the whole street that he was free again to supply its needs. He seemed to have made his most recent sale on that line about the artist, so he changed it slightly, bringing in the feature which to his own mind had the appeal.

"Big local soci'ty artist named in myst'ry slayin' of woman!"

Erskine de Lacey, who had bought the paper, glanced at the column of type under the headline. With curious psychological magnetism his eyes were drawn to the paragraph near the bottom from which his own name seemed to glare out at him, as if in fiery type.

"*. . . his wife also disliked another occupation he obtained for her, as an artist's model for Erskine de Lacey, 1341 Forest Blvd.*"

Savagely he crumpled the paper in his hand, then uncrumpled it to go back to his car, sit in it, and finish reading the story. When he did so he felt a chill and then a flush as his blood receded from his face with acute alarm, then rushed back with a surge of anger.

Though neither the headline nor the story itself laid special stress on his own entirely indirect association with the murder, the boy selling the papers had done so, and it seemed to Erskine that was almost certain proof that the public would do so also. It was a treacherous blow, he said to himself, a blow beneath the belt, which might very well be disastrous to something which was very near to fruition, indeed already under way toward completion, and of desperate importance to him.

As yet that day Erskine had not seen Mrs. Butford. His quarters, a small suite including bedroom, dressing room, and bath, were on the third floor but at the opposite end of the hall from Mrs. Butford's own suite, which gave him complete privacy and enabled him to come and go as he pleased.

So much in awe of him was Mrs. Butford, and so eager for the attentions he bestowed on her, and his flatteries—the broader the better, for the old lady's mentality was not one to catch or appreciate subtleties—that she never questioned him in what he did. She had even placed five hundred dollars in a checking account in his name at the bank on his somewhat transparent urging that he needed it for "research" in connection with the Gallery of Art.

As compensation he dined with her two or three evenings a week, and for this she was almost flutteringly grateful. On occasion, also, he escorted her to a concert or reception where invariably he was the center of attention.

Among his accomplishments was the trick of preparing a small repertoire of French dishes of the fancier sorts, and he had so rallied his hostess on the lack of imagination her dinner menus presented that she had been induced to try some of his specialties. These were highly successful. He oversaw their preparation in the kitchen; and then he would serve the particular dish of the evening to Mrs. Butford with all the mannerisms of a magician producing a miracle, keeping up meantime such a flow of entertaining conversation that the old lady was enthralled and clapped her hands like a child when, for instance, he dramatically set ablaze the brandied crepes suzette.

Yet however much he was beholden to her, Mrs. Butford's company was too tiresome for him to spend much time in it. He therefore went forth frequently and gave the old woman exactly as much time as was necessary to make her feel he was doing her a great favor.

Life at the Butford house had one consolation. Almost invariably her age induced his hostess to retire early, so that Miss Caruthers, who always dined with them, could read her to sleep.

This was the time when Erskine painted: late at night.

The whole household had been told that no one, under any circumstances, was to disturb Mr. Erskine or intrude on him in his studio, which he had fitted up in what formerly was the smoking room on the lower floor. This was a rather large chamber, and save for its lighting, ideal for his purposes. He installed some special lamps—at Mrs. Butford's expense—and substituted for the Japanese and Hindu arms and the Tibetan devil masks on the walls some of his own cynical "abstractions." Then, with easel and smock and palette, he was ready.

An artist must paint. Even more importantly, an artist must talk about his paintings.

Sometimes he painted still lifes, smeared and plastered and awkward, making them distorted and beautiless with a purpose, because such canvases gave him the opportunity—which he enjoyed—of discussing them with a viewer in such increasing complications as to mystify her —it usually was a woman, or women, for few men came to see his paintings.

Sometimes he painted clowns. He had a great predilection for clowns, in this respect trying to imitate Picasso. He had read that Picasso "sought the company of clowns, a thing he always longed to be himself." Picasso made the clown a rage among his genre of painters, and although this rage by now was passé on Montmartre, Erskine took it up. No actual clowns were at hand here in Jericho, but Erskine did not really need them as models. A clown face could be painted from imagination, the grotesquery of the daubed features lending themselves to the illogical and irrational color splashes he preferred. Furthermore, a clown face was safe to paint since he could exhibit it, like a still life, to Mrs. Butford.

When he brought up one of his paintings to her, he displayed it invariably with flourishes and volubility that left the poor old dull mind confused and at the same time conquered. Mrs. Butford, unable to comprehend anything he said, could only believe in him as a sort of god, and be content to hear, and nod her head, and blink her myopic eyes—she hated glasses and she was so nearsighted that even when the paintings were brought up close to her she did not see them well, though she made a great pretense of doing so, and a rather wistful effort to appreciate them.

So far had Erskine progressed, with the spell his loquacity and audacity held over her, that she was giving him increasingly and almost pathetically the childish trust of the aged. Only a day or so before this had enabled him to make it clear to her that she should have a business manager to take the irksome details of business off her hands, leaving them free for more pleasant tasks. She agreed at first somewhat half-heartedly, and then under his persuasion, quite enthusiastically. Her lawyer was at present drawing up a power of attorney for him, and once she signed the paper and it was in his possession, he felt that the first important step would be taken toward where eventually he might almost count the Butford fortune his own: at least the lion's share of it, with perhaps a small bequest for the Gallery of Art and such other charities as she might wish to favor in the new will which he would induce her to draw up.

All this was well enough, but there were times when he could not bear Mrs. Butford, or her house. She had, for example, a phobia in anything which she thought might deal with sexual morals that was disconcerting.

Nudes in art she uncompromisingly regarded as immoral. Never could he think of displaying to her a nude; even an abstract nude. The only thing he had been utterly unable to overcome in her was this psychic aversion, which in her case, as in most instances of excessive prudery, was a combination of an unconscious prurience of mind; the frustration caused by the subconscious knowledge that her own body was so repulsive that she could not bear to have a more attractive female body even portrayed in her presence; and feminine jealousy, in spite of her age, over the interest of a man in another woman—which she perhaps did not even realize.

Almost at once, when he first knew her, he discovered this intense prudery, but he then expected to be able to win her away from an attitude so ignorant and puritanical. Her prejudices along this line, however, were so strong as to be almost violent, and it was dangerous even to bring up the suggestion by indirection, so he desisted and felt shackled and correspondingly resentful.

With increasing frequency he found that he needed a holiday from Mrs. Butford, and it was on such a search for relief from her, and all she represented in strait-laced and crabbed confinement of thoughts and actions, that he first saw Bonnie Bonner.

Alone one night he went to the Chesterfield Club, south of the city, which had been described to him as one of Jericho's few bright night spots. Mincing over a filet mignon, he watched couples dance, and after a time saw the "floor show." Most of it was excessively boring: a pair of bucolic comedians with ancient gags, and then a falsetto soprano. But the last act made him sit up. The girl who did the strip tease had an incredibly beautiful body.

Up to this time he had moved carefully in the matter of models in Jericho, because there was some risk involved. Hard as it was to believe, there appeared to be a rather universal and remarkable false modesty among the females of this city about their bodies: a holdover, perhaps, from the mauve generation that was passing, and from which this inland place was recovering more slowly than the rest of the world. Even to suggest to one of the ladies he met socially that she disrobe for him might be an irreparable mistake, entirely apart from Mrs. Butford: and he wished to make no mistakes just at this time.

Nevertheless, he took the risk partly because of the necessity he felt, partly in a spirit of audacity and daring, bred from his feeling of command over Mrs. Butford. The first model was a waitress: Mamie Slago. But she was too plainly for hire, too brazen and lacking in scruples or embarrassment to give him the subtle stimulation he desired when he painted her. He did not have her back.

Bonnie Bonner, however, was different, and from the first she intrigued him. He arranged an interview through the proprietor, but when he explained to her that he was an artist and wished her to pose for him, she surprised him by her reluctance.

He was struck by a lack of mental response in her. The girl was quite pretty and her body was exceptional; but he thought to himself that mentally she perhaps was no more than capable of a task as simple and instinctive as twisting herself about to the music of the small orchestra while she took off her scanty spangled garments to the whistles and cheers of the audience.

Nobody cared about her mind anyway when she was doing her act. The curves of her body, the smoothly contoured legs, the perfect breasts hardly concealed by her filmy brassière, the marvelous hips and buttocks, almost undisguised by the G-string with which she finished her act, were what the eyes of the spectators were occupied with solely.

Erskine asked Draggett, the proprietor, if the girl had an agent. He was informed that her only agent was her husband, and he was astonished later when he met the husband at his home in the poor south part of the city.

The man, Dewey Bonner, seemed to be a religious fanatic, but when Erskine broached the subject of his wish, he displayed a far from saintly keenness in haggling over her services, which he seemed perfectly willing to sell.

While they chaffered, the girl herself came in from some errand and went about her household tasks. In spite of the fact that she must have been earning a rather good salary, she evidently did her own work. With a face as expressionless as if she were not being bargained for like a piece of furniture, she listened silently while they discussed her, including her most intimate physical good points.

At last Erskine agreed to pay fifteen dollars for not more than two hours of sitting: it was above his usual fee, but he was obsessed with the desire to have her, and her very reluctance seemed to inflame him. She had nothing to say about it—absolutely nothing—and she shrank from the nudity he emphasized, but she was submissive to her husband's commands.

They agreed on hours: ten o'clock of Sunday nights—which were Bonnie's nights off—when the Butford house was asleep, the servants in their quarters in the back. Erskine went for her in his car and took her home after the sitting. He was careful that nobody saw him smuggle her through the back door leading to the furnace room, to which he had a key, and through that to his studio.

3

When he first heard that Bonnie was murdered, the thought fascinated him in a horrible way that twisted and jangled his nerves.

She was so pretty, so defenseless, so helplessly compelled to do things she did not wish to do. It was cruel, really, to take advantage of her almost pathetic childishness; and this, in spite of himself, was one of the things about it that appealed to him secretly.

When she obeyed his orders and came before him in her superb nudity she almost cowered, and in that attitude she reminded him of the celebrated Venus de Medici. Painting her was to him an intense pleasure, because she shrank from his gaze with such charming embarrassment.

Although she showed no curiosity about the picture he painted, the ritualistic image of her body he placed so furiously on his canvas, he insisted that she look at it, and her shame and repugnance delighted him. He made no attempt to touch her, finding he had a sufficient psychic thrill from her without it.

Once more he painted her, purposely this time in the coarsest and most indecent manner. This time, when he forced her to look at it, she appeared startled, and displayed such evidences of disgust and shock that he was afraid she might create a commotion. But she only hurried into her garments, almost weeping, and on the way back to her house he had to quiet her and convince her that nothing very bad had happened to her, because he was somewhat fearful of what her husband might do if she returned home in a semi-hysterical condition.

Before he could see her again, Bonnie Bonner was dead, murdered by a blow that broke her skull, the paper said.

He found himself imagining over and over, morbidly, that shapely head, its darkly rich hair and childishly pretty features, deformed perhaps by the assassin's bludgeon. The thought repelled him, but his mind kept reverting to it with a strange, almost ghoulish fascination from which he could not free himself.

Yet it had not actually occurred to him that he might be involved personally until he read the story in the *Clarion* in which he was mentioned by name in a most distressing manner. The story even gave the address: 1341 Forest Boulevard, the home, as everyone knew, of Mrs. Simon Bolivar Butford.

He wondered if Mrs. Butford had seen the article yet, and he was almost sure that Miss Caruthers would by this time have read it to her. He dreaded encountering her, so he threw the paper out of his car, pulled away from the curb, and for a time rather aimlessly drove out in the country, covering many miles of Kansas roads in speeding transit, because only the sensation of acceleration seemed to soothe his spirit. Darkness fell, and he ate dinner at eight o'clock in a small café, hardly knowing what he ate, except that the food was not very good.

When he left the café, the streets were dark except for the corner lamps and the illuminated houses. By this time he was beginning to argue himself into a more optimistic frame of mind. Perhaps Mrs. Butford was not offended, after all, by the article, if indeed she had read it. Artists are supposed to paint, even Mrs. Butford knew that, and the nude is as old as art. It was even possible, he told himself, that his own sophisticated aestheticism might insensibly have penetrated and overcome the old woman's bigotry. She may have dismissed the article with a shrug, as any sensible person would.

Almost at once, however, this relieving thought was replaced by a return of his fears, not nearly so pleasant, but more realistic. Mrs. Butford was never one to be sensible, or liberal. She was outrageously set and stubborn, and he was fairly sure she might be furious as well as shocked over the use of her house in what she almost certainly would construe as a bawdy and indecent consorting with a naked woman.

By policy Erskine was audacious, cynical, and insincere, making a career of disregarding the opinions of others. Sometimes he carried this off with triumphant success, even with persons of superior taste, by deliberately complicating the issues until he had his adversary mystified and silenced.

But now he found himself in the outlandish situation where the opinion of someone whose intellectual capacities were hardly worth even his contempt was all-important to him. It was almost maddening to think that Mrs. Butford, so archaic, so stupid, so lacking in all imagination and taste, held such power over him.

Yet it was something he must face. And all at once a thought came to him, and with that he turned his car and drove up the avenue which led to the top of Tower Hill.

4

Shortly before nine o'clock the telephone rang and Suey brought the extension to Mary Agnes where she sat in the library catching up on some correspondence. Wistart was still out of town, at that Tulsa meeting, and she was alone except for the servants. Ordinarily she would have had someone in, for cocktails and bridge or canasta, but this night she rather welcomed a chance for quiet and relaxation.

She took the receiver and a voice said, "Hello, Mary Agnes? This is Bess Attwater."

Mary Agnes made a grimace. Bess Attwater was a pest, who made the most of the not extremely lofty position her husband held as cashier of the First National Bank and continually pushed in where she was not wanted and where, really, she did not belong. She was one of those gadfly creatures whom people tolerate, partly because they are so innocuous that they can be ignored, partly because they do not know, actually, when they are being snubbed.

"Yes, Bess," said Mary Agnes. "When did you get back from New York?"

"Just Tuesday," Bess said. "We saw every show that was worth while

—Sidney had to pay *outrageous* prices for tickets—and I went on a regular shopping splurge—I have a *yummy* cocktail gown from Saks and some——"

"That's nice," interrupted Mary Agnes. At the moment she did not feel like a personally conducted conversational tour of Manhattan Island's shopping districts. "Did you have a good flight home?"

"Real smooth. We stopped in Chicago to see Sidney's aunt who lives there. Poor old soul, you'd think a puff of wind would blow her away— and Sidney's *all* she's got except all that stock in General Motors. But that wasn't why I called you. My *dear*—I've just finished reading the paper! That awful murder—and what do you think of our *artist?*"

"What should I think of him?" asked Mary Agnes.

Bess gave a little laugh. "Of course, as you must know, *I've* no prejudices along that line. You have to be broad-minded these days, I think. And I suppose if an artist wants to paint nudes he has a right to do it, although why they have to paint them when they have scenery and vases and flowers to paint, I never understood. But it wasn't Mr. de Lacey I was thinking about as much as Mrs. Butford!"

"I think I know what you mean," said Mary Agnes dryly.

"Poor old Mrs. Butford!" chattered on Bess Attwater. "She must nearly have blown an artery when she read that story. With her notions! I'm sure she'd consider a woman standing around naked to be painted as immoral as if she—as if she were there for—well, for any *other* purpose. *You* know Mrs. Butford!"

"Yes, I know. Anthony Comstock wasn't even in it with Mrs. Butford as a self-appointed guardian of public morals."

"Anthony Comstock? . . . No, I suppose not," said Bess vaguely. It was obvious she had no idea who Anthony Comstock was, but she rushed on eagerly. "And for all this to happen in Mrs. Butford's own house, too—the studio's in the smoking room made sacred by the late Simon Bolivar Butford, isn't it?"

"Yes," said Mary Agnes. She was sure that Mrs. Butford, with her peculiarities, would be convinced that her home had been turned into a seraglio, complete with every form of orgy her mind could conjure up; and minds like that usually were able to conjure up plenty of filth.

So involved was she with her thoughts along this line that she hardly paid any attention to the seemingly endless stream of words coming over the wire until something brought her mind suddenly to a focus.

". . . and saw Wistart for a moment," Bess was saying.

Mary Agnes had failed to catch the first of the sentence. "You saw Wistart?" she echoed. "Where?"

"Why, in Chicago, as I was telling you, when we were taking the plane Tuesday morning——"

"Oh, you must be mistaken," said Mary Agnes. "Wistart's in Tulsa."

"Tulsa, my eye! I tell you I saw him right in Chicago!"

"But I happen to *know* he went to Tulsa."

"Listen, dear, I saw him as plainly as I see this table right in front of me this minute! We were waiting at one of the gates in the Midway Airport to go to our plane, and he was coming down the corridor from a plane that had just landed. Sidney was busy with the tickets and didn't see him, but I yoo-hooed at him and waved. He didn't stop or look around, so of course he didn't hear me. I'd have run after him to say hello, but just then our gate opened and we had to go through and get our seats. I spoke to Sidney about it right after our plane was in the air. Don't tell *me,* darling, that I didn't see your husband there in Chicago! If it wasn't Wistart Wedge, it was his twin brother!"

Mary Agnes recovered herself. "All right, Bess," she said with a little laugh. "I believe you—and it's not at all unlikely. I was just surprised, that's all. He probably changed his plans and had to make a quick trip up from Tulsa. The publishing business takes you all over the country, you know. Naturally, I can't expect to keep abreast of every single move he makes. And, after all, it isn't so very important, is it? Anyway, so nice to talk with you."

They said their good-bys. Mary Agnes felt she had satisfied Bess Attwater's curiosity, but she had by no means satisfied her own. Wistart in Chicago Tuesday morning—he must no more than have changed planes in Tulsa. Why? Was the Tulsa trip a blind, his real destination Chicago all the time, and if it was, why did he go to such pains to keep it secret?

Her mind leaped at once to the suspicion that almost universally occurs under circumstances of this kind: was it some woman?

But the very nature of the question, when she considered Wistart as she knew him, brought a feeling of contemptuous amusement. Wistart —poor, slow-witted Wistart—the mere thought of him in the role of a Don Juan was ludicrous. Even if he had inclinations along that line he was too inexpert, too unattractive, too stumbling to have any success as a lover.

Inclinations? It brought a curl to Mary Agnes' lip. Wistart not only had no inclinations, he had no desires. No sex. She dismissed *that* possibility; and while she was in the act of dismissal, she heard the doorbell.

A moment later Suey came into the library.

"Gentleman to see you, Mrs. Wedge," he said.

"Who is it?"

"A Mr. de Lacey, ma'am."

A look of annoyance passed across her face. She had no wish for a scene with Erskine, and she was sure it would be a scene; but there was nothing much she could do about it now. As well have it out with him.

"Show him in here," she said after a moment. "And, Suey—bring the Courvoisier."

"Yes, ma'am." The butler departed.

She mentally braced herself, yet when Erskine entered the room his appearance almost startled her. His face appeared drawn, and at the same time the lines about his mouth and his compressed lips seemed to express an almost venomous fury.

"Erskine!" she exclaimed.

With what seemed to her a pace sinister in its deliberation he advanced toward her.

"You did it, didn't you?" he said bitterly. "You did it good!"

"What do you mean?"

He halted a pace from her. "You know what I mean! Was that smear in your paper necessary? Why did you go out of your way to do a thing like that to me?"

"I didn't know——"

"Don't lie! I ought to break your neck——"

"Don't touch me!"

He had not moved, but she almost believed that in his madness he would lay violent hands on her. Then she heard a step, and to her relief Suey came in with a tray bearing a bottle and small snifter glasses.

Erskine fell back a pace or two, but he kept his eyes fixed on her as Suey placed the tray on a coffee table.

"Have some brandy?" Mary Agnes said, striving to speak casually.

"No, I thank you," replied Erskine rigidly.

She gave a little shrug and forced a smile. "You may pour me a very little, Suey." And when the butler brought her glass, "Remain in the hall, please, where I can summon you if I need something else."

With his usual grave dignity Suey inclined his head and departed.

"That precaution wasn't necessary," said Erskine when he was gone.

"Why do you think it was a precaution?"

"It's pretty obvious. But I'm not insane—what good would it do me to harm you physically?"

"I'm not at all afraid of you."

"No? You'd better be!"

"I don't intend to listen to threats in my own house——"

"This isn't a threat, it's a promise," he said grimly. "If you've ruined me, Mary Agnes Wedge, it will be the saddest day you ever saw."

"Just how?"

"A great lady—a sanctified sprig of society hyssop," he said with a sneer. "Her reputation's pretty precious to her, isn't it? What I can do to that reputation if I just want to!"

She regarded him silently, her face cold and devoid of expression.

"Do you know what the *Morning Sentinel* would pay for that picture?" he went on. "And a statement I'd make, which you could deny until you're blue in the face but you could never make people disbelieve?"

"The *Sentinel* won't risk that kind of libel!"

"It wouldn't be libel—not if I take an oath on it—and I will! Your word against mine, and people will always believe the worst—won't they, darling?"

Mary Agnes was raging inwardly with the shame of being bullied and threatened in her own home, but she was certain he would do as he promised.

"If it's money you want," she said, "I'll pay you five thousand dollars for that picture, delivered to me——"

"I don't want money! I want a retraction! I want a story in your paper tomorrow saying that everything it printed about me today was a lie—a barefaced, malicious lie! And I want it printed just as prominently as the story in this evening's paper!"

"Do you think that will convince Mrs. Butford?" she asked.

"It had better! And perhaps you'd better call her up and give her your personal assurance——"

"I said five thousand. I'll make it ten."

"You can't bargain with me. This is an ultimatum!"

She felt she was cornered. "All right, Erskine," she said. "I'll go down to the paper and see that it's done to your satisfaction tomorrow."

"It had better be right."

"It will be."

"I'll be in touch with you."

He turned and left the room.

A moment later she heard a tactful cough. Suey was at the door. "I saw the gentleman out," he said. "Is there anything else?"

"No, Suey. Nothing. Good night."

When the butler was gone, she sat for a long time motionless. She felt defeated, humiliated. All her life this had never happened before and she found it very bitter to the taste.

5

It was after nine o'clock when Erskine drove into the grounds of the Butford house, and the huge old edifice seemed utterly dark.

He congratulated himself on the thought that by this time Mrs. Butford would have retired; but he resolved he would thrash matters out with her in the morning.

He would tell her that the whole story had been grossly exaggerated, and to wait for the *Clarion,* so that she could read its retraction herself. In any case, he would convince her that his painting was no more than an abstract, like everything else he showed her. He remembered now that he had that fuchsia-pink distorted nude which formerly hung in his studio in Hollywood. In a pinch he might use it to convince Mrs. Butford.

Once she saw that, he did not think even she could take very seriously as a violation of morals his painting of figures, nude or otherwise; and he would assure her that his models, when he had any, were sufficiently clothed to meet even her exaggerated ideas of decency, and that all his posings were for pure esoteric experiment in planes and colors, no more connected with sex than the dissection of a cadaver on the table of a scientific medical investigator.

He was feeling much happier as he parked his car in the dark driveway, and assured himself that the household was abed. It would be best at the present time to steal up quietly to his rooms and retire without arousing anybody; and for this reason, instead of going through the front door, which was below the windows of Mrs. Butford's suite, where he might perhaps awaken her, he chose the back door, through the furnace room, to make his entry.

With his key he unlocked the door. As he stepped into the furnace room, he thought he noticed an odd odor from the big hot-air furnace with its twisting conduits rising upward. But something else occupied his attention immediately. Light was shining through the crack beneath the door leading from the furnace room to his studio. Somebody had a lamp on in the place.

He rushed across the dark furnace room and threw open the door. For a moment he stood blinking his eyes, trying to adjust them to the light, and his heart sank as he did so.

Seated in the middle of the room was Mrs. Butford.

How long she had been there he did not know. But he had an impression of immobility like an ancient stone, as if she had been sitting there through the ages, without motion, waiting.

"Mrs. Butford!" he exclaimed.

"Mr. de Lacey," she said in a voice that seemed to come from a tomb, "I found those paintings—those secret, vile, obscene paintings you have been doing in this house. I have burned them. Every one. And you will leave this house at once."

ANNALS OF THE *DAILY CLARION*

"Jousts and Tourneys Gay"

The amours of a town frequently are the private information of the newspaper fraternity, which knows how to enjoy a story and at the same time keep it confidential, if for any reason it is important or necessary to keep it in confidence. It is a noteworthy fact that any good journeyman reporter who has been in a city for as much as a year could generally quite disrupt the community if he but published a tithe of what he knows of the secrets of its most prominent citizens.

Nevertheless, the most expert adultery in Jericho's history escaped both the newspaper fraternity and the gossips because of its nature.

The staid offices of the Jericho Chamber of Commerce were humming with industry like a hive of faithful bees one apple-blossom May morning when a young woman walked in and asked to see the secretary, Mr. J. Leniton Jones.

At her appearance the hive-like humming ceased, because the bees turned their undivided attention upon the newcomer. This attention was not undeserved. She was youthfully mature, full-blooded, full-figured, slim of waist, round of arm and calf, neat of ankle, with bosom at full tide. Her skin was creamy white, her hair gleamy dark, and her eyes dreamy blue.

When J. Leniton Jones, the august secretary of the Chamber of Commerce, came from his holy of holies to hold converse with her, he looked upon her with a benignant and at the same time a fervent eye, and acknowledged to himself that she was a dish, a treat to gaze at. The young woman gave her name as Kay Wallis, and J. Leniton, though portly, bald, and a model of propriety, felt the stirrings of an inner appreciation, an allurement the sensations of which he had all but forgotten. He, consequently, virtually turned over to Miss Wallis the keys of the Chamber.

The lady, it appeared, was running some sort of a "survey"—a sociological study of a typical midwestern city, backed by a foundation of some kind in the East—and she would reside in Jericho for some months to accomplish the statistical studies and the personal interviews necessary. Thereafter, she took an apartment, and besides busying herself with her case histories—which included the rich and notable as well as the poor and obscure—she identified herself with the community by taking a willing, helpful, and merry part in the activities of the Community Chest.

Persons hitherto lukewarm to the doings of that charitable body discovered an interest in its activities now that Miss Wallis was so charmingly identified with it. The younger bucks swarmed around. Rather graciously she shadowboxed them off. She was interested, she said, "in men who do things"—mature men, she indicated, men who had experience and character, suitable for her studies.

Some of the mature men with experience and character were highly flattered by this preference of the winsome visitor. Quite eagerly they received her for conferences in their private offices, gave generously of their time, and outlined to her their histories and backgrounds; being charmed by her smiling and understanding sophistication, and the knowledge that—in the interests of scientific study and in pure anonymity, of course—they might relate to her, even perhaps a little boastfully, episodes of the kind one would not ordinarily disclose, particularly to one's wife.

Miss Wallis said frankly that she liked a man who *was* a man, and her admiration encouraged confidences. Furthermore, it was perfectly safe, and the precedent had been well established by the researches of Dr. Kinsey, and she showed them that they were listed only as Case A, or Case B, or whatever initial was the designation; with nothing whatever to identify them as individuals, or even as Jericho citizens since, as she explained, the town itself would be anonymous in the report.

It was not noticed that the gentlemen for whom she showed a particular predilection were those with families and reputations, and bank accounts.

Among those she had no trouble in interesting were Charles Sinclair, of the real estate family; Sidney Attwater, cashier of the First National;

Dr. Edwin Kleaver, a popular and successful dentist; Avery Galt, head of Jericho's largest grocery chain; and similar purse-heavy but hypocritical gentlemen of mature years and spotless public reputations.

One whom she interested, but in whom she displayed no return interest, was J. Leniton Jones, of the Chamber of Commerce. He did not realize that his stipend as secretary did not qualify him for her close attention, especially after she ascertained that he carried a heavy insurance program and a heavy mortgage on his home, which prevented his keeping much of a balance in his bank account.

As time passed, Miss Wallis developed warm friendships with Messrs. Sinclair, Attwater, Kleaver, Galt, et al. And these friendships, naturally, could hardly be expected to remain purely platonic when on the one side was Sex so alluring and on the other side Vulnerability so tempted.

Friendship developed into something more intriguing and delightful: coquetry. The luscious-bosomed Kay seemed to become more than friendly, even accessible. A proposition, eventually, could hardly fail to follow. She heard it, considered, hesitated, and then, as if in surrender to a wild rush of emotions, allowed herself to be kissed and fondled in the private office. In the heat of eagerness inspired by such delicious intimacies, the somewhat mature gentleman felt that he had recaptured his lost youth; and as a final climax to all this, she would reply to his whispered importunities by suggesting, as if unwilling and frightened but unable to still her own wayward heart, that they meet at her apartment.

There are women who lure men on with no intention of rewarding them. Not so Kay Wallis. Once in her apartment the elderly admirer found her both winsome and willing. Clothes were dispensed with, and all was as free and thrilling as in the days when satyrs pursued and made love to nymphs in the sylvan glades of classic Arcady. Miss Wallis said she thought it evil for a woman to pretend she was going to satisfy a man and then not go through with it. No gentleman could charge her with that particular evil who enjoyed an assignation with her in her apartment.

After a number of weeks Miss Wallis suddenly left town, but whispered to her several admirers—each one of whom believed he alone had won her favors—that she would communicate with him in a circumspect manner.

Anon to each his secretary bore a message from a man in the waiting room who said he had word from Miss Wallis. Gladly admitted to private conversation by the quondam elderly lothario, the visitor turned out to be young, personable, soft-spoken.

He was, he said, a disabled war veteran, and Miss Wallis had become interested in his case and suggested that he see Mr. Sinclair, or Mr. Attwater, or Dr. Kleaver, or Mr. Galt—or which of the late admirers it happened to be—because she said he was *such* a good friend of hers and might help a struggling young war veteran. He was selling pictures . . .

A sigh from the lorn suitor. "Well, let's see the pictures."

A private decision that he might give the poor fellow a five-dollar bill and try to get word from him about where the fascinating Kay was at the moment.

The pictures appeared from a brief case: a series of vivid and recognizable photographs of Self and Miss Wallis on that holy night of nights when Self was up there in her apartment naked and deliriously happy!

The visitor said, "I thought you'd be interested, sir. Now this set of views, with the negatives, will cost you . . ." The figure he named was reasonable. Perhaps fifteen hundred dollars, or two thousand, or perhaps four thousand dollars. It was nicely figured at all the traffic would bear, based on Miss Wallis' own previous very careful research into just how much the sucker could raise without too heavy embarrassment and too many questions.

"And," added the visitor quickly, "I might say that let's have no violence. I'm not in good health. If anything happens to me, either with you or with the law, there are a few sets of copies of these ready to be mailed to your wife, your minister, the newspapers, and the heads of all the women's clubs."

The last clinched it. Your wife you might bully, your minister you might silence, your newspaper you might buy off. But nothing under God's holy sky could keep the heads of all the women's clubs from scattering like a gaggle of geese and spilling everything they knew to every acquaintance they had.

What could you do? You could pay off. You did. The guy vanished.

Presumably he had a rabbit's-eye camera and had been stationed in hiding in that apartment to take those snapshots so intimate and indiscreet. He and Miss Wallis must have worked town after town in this manner—Omaha, Kansas City, Wichita, Dubuque, Denver, Oklahoma, Tulsa, as well as Jericho—and for upwards of fifteen thousand dollars each.

Nobody was ever arrested or even sought by the police, because no complaints ever were made. And in Jericho, where each paunchy suitor so betrayed naturally supposed he was the only dupe and victim, not a word was ever breathed by anyone, to anyone, of the story.

Twenty-four

I

It had not occurred to Mary Agnes that she would encounter dissent, much less outright refusal.

Shortly before eleven next morning she was in the publisher's office at the *Clarion,* and she asked Miss Finch to summon Mr. Dorn to her presence. Very soon he appeared, in shirt sleeves as usual, his hair rumpled and a now-what-in-the-hell-do-you-want look on his face.

"Morning," he said. "You sent for me?"

"Yes," said Mary Agnes. "Sit down, please."

"Mrs. Wedge, I've got a deadline coming up. I know you're not up on our schedule yet, but——"

"This won't take long."

With what seemed ill grace he took a chair.

"I'd like you to put a story in the paper this afternoon," she said.

"Of course, if you want it."

"Something that says we made a mistake yesterday," she went on, "in what we published about Mr. de Lacey having that woman posing for him at Mrs. Butford's. Mr. de Lacey objects to it very strongly, and so, I'm sure, does Mrs. Butford. Just say it was an error, no such thing happened, and put a headline on it to make it prominent on the first page——"

"A retraction?" he interrupted, rising suddenly to his feet. "You ask us to deny that story? But it was the truth!"

"Perhaps it was." She was reasonable. "But of what discernible importance can it be to anybody if we gloss over a small detail in the interests of——?"

"It's important to the *Clarion,* Mrs. Wedge!"

He was so uncompromisingly positive that she felt baffled, and for the moment not even annoyed.

"Why?" she asked.

"It's a question of this paper's integrity. To deny the truth is as bad as it is to publish the untruth. Worse—after you've once printed the truth!"

"Hardly anybody will know it, I think."

"Well, *I'll* know it. And the staff will know it. Do you realize what you're asking of me? That I declare in public print that I lied, that I wrote and published a deliberate falsehood. I've spent a lot of years trying to build a reputation as a good newspaperman, Mrs. Wedge. This is a mighty personal thing to me."

She sat back in her chair. Decidedly newspaper people were different from people in other lines of business; different and more difficult to handle. This talk about integrity and personal reputation for veracity sounded unrealistic, especially when coupled with what amounted to a refusal to obey orders. And these people weren't even paid very much —she had checked on this young man's salary, for instance: she was paying assistant department managers at Cox's, Incorporated, more than he got.

"Sometimes it's necessary to do things that are—are unpleasant," she said, trying to be patient. "It happens I have a very important personal reason for wishing this."

That sudden, searching dark glance of his. "De Lacey is a close friend of yours?"

The question nettled her, surprisingly, and she felt impelled to set right the implications in it whether they were intended or not.

"No. Not a friend—far from a friend!" she said. "I despise the man. He's a phony, an adventurer, a fortune seeker, and worse——"

She stopped; he was looking her fairly and fully in the eye.

"If you'd explain what's behind this, Mrs. Wedge, perhaps I can be of considerable help."

"What do you mean, Mr. Dorn?"

"I'll speak plainly. You detest De Lacey. Yet you're willing to compromise your newspaper's reputation, because he demands it. Obviously, since it's not a matter of friendship, the guy is using some sort of a threat. That comes under the head of blackmail——"

"You're assuming an awful lot!"

"Not assuming. Not even guessing. It's quite likely something that doesn't involve you personally—maybe somebody else you wish to pro-

tect. That's none of my business. But *blackmail* is—when it involves
this newspaper! And you never get away from blackmail, it will never
stop, until you face it and kill it——"

"Mr. Dorn!" she broke in. "This whole matter's different from what
you think, and I must insist——"

"Not me," he said grimly. "This is your newspaper. You can order
that story in. But I'll not be on the staff when you do it. You can't pay
a man enough money to disgrace himself, Mrs. Wedge!"

They faced each other across the desk tensely.

"Now I'm going to have to ask you to excuse me," he said. "It's
edition time."

She did not try to stop him as he turned and left her.

For a moment she sat still thinking. Blackmail it was, and what he
said was true—you cannot get away from blackmail. But also it was an
emergency. If Mr. Dorn thought he had a reputation, *she* had a reputation, too, and it was worth a whole lot to her, and she intended to
save it. She could fight Erskine later, but just now time was precious.

She swung around in the big swivel chair behind Wistart's desk and
as she did so her knee came in contact with the shallow center drawer.
She glanced down: the drawer was unlocked.

Idly she drew it out and glanced into it. Nothing of special moment
was there: paper clips, pencils, two ball-point pens, a small sheaf of
stationery, stamps, two or three old keys—nearly every desk in the
world seems to contain two or three rusty keys the very use of which
long has been forgotten—other trivia. She closed the drawer and rose.

After all, she was boss of this newspaper, and she might as well establish the fact here and now. She wanted something done, and it was
important that it be done, and if some feelings were wounded, that was
unfortunate but could not be helped. She walked out of the office to
follow Debs to the city room, and this time it would be an *order* she
gave him, not a suggestion or a request.

When she came to the end of the hall which opened into the city
room, she stopped suddenly stock-still with a gasp. Before her was a
scene of frightening drama.

At one end of the long room, in the society department, a couple of
women sat, one of them no more than a girl. The telephone girl was at
the PBX box near the head of the stairs. Others were gone, to lunch or
assignments, or in the case of Jeff Linderman, to the composing room.

Not a person in the city room stirred: all were silent, rigid, as if stricken by some sudden palsy of horror, the telephone girl for once not even chewing gum.

In the center of all this, at the city desk, stood Debs Dorn. Across from him was a man with a revolver in his hand and a look of murder in his eyes.

2

The story he wrote the day before, which already had so many repercussions, was what brought the crisis to its sudden head, Debs knew later. It was the paragraph in it that concerned Nibs Galloway and suggested that his murderer may have been someone the dead detective knew, someone he suspected but did not wish to suspect.

The object of the story was simple: Debs had a well-founded suspicion that Detective Walt Benson knew more than he had told about the murder, perhaps was involved in Bonner's narcotics traffic by way of paid protection, and he wanted to raise such a question that the police department would be forced to take action and directly examine the man as a suspect.

What Debs did not know when he wrote the story was that he was dealing with a madman.

When Debs returned from his conference with Mrs. Wedge, Jeff Linderman had gone out to make up the noon edition and the city room was nearly empty. He decided to let Jeff finish the make-up job alone while he considered some problems.

He was shorthanded, for one thing. When he came back on the city desk the day before, Joe Canfield, as he expected, quit. He had not heard what Canfield was doing, but expected to learn soon that he was on the *Sentinel* staff. Meantime Tod Burdock was trying to get the hang of the police beat, and his opponent from the other paper was giving him a bad time of it. Someone must be found, also, to take Burdock's place at the courthouse, and a capable man like Burdock would be hard to replace.

Hudson had not been back in the office since his clash with Mrs. Wedge. He was reported to be home consoling himself with whiskey and blasphemy. There was a rumor, also—nobody knew where it started—that he had received his walking papers and severance pay and was leaving town. Debs did not know how true this was, but the

report had come up from the business office, and after what happened
in the publisher's office it could be so. He really had no time to think
about it, because he had too much to do. His own great spate of work
as city editor was complicated by the fact that he had to handle, on an
emergency basis, some of the more pressing details of the managing
editor's job until the situation in that respect was clarified.

He was looking at a piece of Burdock's copy when he heard someone
come up the stairs, and he paid no attention until the person stopped
directly across the desk from him.

Then he glanced up. It was Walt Benson.

"Why, hello, Benson——" he began.

Then all at once he fell silent. He had expected that Benson would
resent the story, but what he saw was something beyond ordinary resentment. The man's eyes were unnaturally black and staring. His
mouth was drawn into an almost beastly snarl, and his brows, which
met across the bridge of his nose, were locked in a scowl.

Beyond this Benson's appearance was changed in other ways. Usually
a careful, even dapper dresser, his attire today seemed wild and disarrayed. The hand-painted necktie was askew, the collar open as if he
had torn at it to ease his breathing, his coat unpressed and slovenly. It
was obvious that he was laboring under some great suppressed excitement.

"What's the matter?" Debs asked in surprise.

When Benson replied, it was in a low, almost guttural voice, which
gradually rose as his excitement grew.

"*You* know what's the matter!" he said. "You're on my back, ain't
you, Dorn? You're out to get me, ain't you? I know about it. I know
all about it!"

Staring at him, Debs suddenly realized that the man's attitude was
more than hostile; it was deadly.

"You wrote that piece about me!" Benson continued almost wildly.
"Don't you try to lie out of it!"

"What piece?" Debs knew, but he was playing for time, eying the
other closely.

"There!"

On the desk Benson tossed a corner torn out of the *Clarion*. It was
the previous day's story about the Bonner arrest, and the paragraph
concerning Detective Nibs Galloway was underlined heavily in ink.

Especially so, as if it had been done over and over, were the words, he may have found evidence pointing to someone he knew, perhaps someone he did not wish to suspect . . .

"That's *me* you was shootin' at!" said Benson in a furious, shaking voice. "It's me you've *always* got it in for! You said I was a bum for not gettin' that car license, didn't you? You said I ought to be sweated on Galloway's murder, didn't you? Well, you're a liar! You're a goddamn yellow liar! What you got to say to that? You been called a *liar* —what you got to say?"

His voice had risen in pitch and volume and his black eyes danced and gleamed crazily.

"Now look, Benson——" Debs began, rising.

"No you don't!"

In one whipping motion the man drew a police revolver from a holster under his armpit.

"Don't you move, Dorn! Don't nobody else in this room move, neither!"

Debs did not move. In that moment he knew he was facing one demented. In that moment also he knew he faced death: irresponsible, maniacal death.

Anything, a sudden movement by someone else in the room even, might cause the trigger to be pulled, the bullet to crash into his body. He felt the perspiration on his forehead and hoped most fervently that Jeff Linderman would be kept busy at the make-up and would not come through that door from the composing room.

"I got you now—I got you just where I want you!" Benson went on with a frenetic rising excitement. "You know what I'm goin' to do? You been askin' for it! I'll tell you what I'm goin' to do—I'm goin' to *kill* you, Dorn! *Mister* Debs Dorn, the wise guy! I'm goin' to kill you, hear that? I'm goin' to sock a lead slug in your guts, a whole *lot* of lead slugs! I'm goin' to watch you kick your heels a-layin' on that floor and laugh while you die! How d'you like that? Don't like it, do you? But you're too scared to move. I *said* you was yellow—*always* said you was yellow——"

"Benson, you're talking foolish. I don't know where you got this—if it was Canfield, he's the biggest liar in Jericho, and you know it as well as I do——"

"Don't say nothin' against Joe Canfield! Don't you do it, hear? Joe

Canfield's a gentleman, and nobody can't call him names around me!"

The revolver flourished menacingly.

"You're wrong," said Debs. "I've got nothing against you personally."

His voice was low, reasonable, quite calm, but he did not for one instant take his eyes from the other's.

"I know better than that!" Benson was yelling now. "I know you're a snitch, and a goddamn yellow, sneakin', belly-crawlin'——" He went off into an impossibly lurid and indecent series of insulting expletives.

Debs saw him cock the revolver, and heard the click even through the shouting, ranting stream of abuse. He saw also that Benson was trembling with still more violent agitation. He felt sick at the pit of his stomach, and he experienced a small sensation of surprise at himself that he could stand there and at least make a pretense of coolness.

"All right," he said when the other paused for sheer breath, and he was glad his voice did not shake. "What's it going to get you if you do kill me? You've got people looking on. They've heard every word you said. It would be first-degree murder, Benson. Not a chance for you. Not a chance."

"I don't give a goddamn—I'll have mine first——" Another stream of wild, almost incoherent profanity.

And now Benson began to beat the revolver muzzle down on the desk in a hammering rhythm, emphasizing the words. Forever afterward that desk bore the half-moon dents where the lower end of the gun barrel battered it.

In the back of his mind Debs wondered if this beating with the cocked weapon might cause it to discharge. But that was unimportant compared to the immediate thing, the immediate problem. He was dealing with an insane man armed with a deadly weapon, completely irrational and irresponsible, and with a murderous purpose directed against himself. He must keep his wits about him and hope.

"Did you ever see a man hanged?" he said, still calmly, his voice not raised above an ordinary conversational level. "It ain't good, Benson. Makes you a little sick at the stomach. He pitches down through the trap and gives a little bounce at the end of the rope, and then his feet kick, but they can't kick much because they're ironed together. And then he spins around and around, his breath cut off, looking as if he's been stretched out about ten feet long, just so much dead meat. It isn't the best way to end up, Benson."

At the hall entrance, frozen with horror and fear, stood Mary Agnes. The girl at the PBX box did not stir although her buzzers were working insistently. The society-page editor held her breath, and Sally Sayre felt as if she were suffocating with her heart in her throat as she watched the ugly drama.

None of them moved. None of them dared to move because a sudden action of any kind might cause lead to be sprayed by the madman not only into Debs' body, but all over the office. It was up to Debs alone, and nobody could help him. And Debs was fully aware of it, and aware of his helplessness and of the fact that at any moment, on any pretext or excuse, if he made the slightest mistake, or even showed a trace of fear, he would die where he stood.

Breathlessly the others in the room watched as Debs, never raising his voice, always talking calmly and reasonably, debated with Walt Benson the question of his own life.

"You're not feeling well, Walt," he said. "I know you're not. This isn't like you. You haven't been feeling well for days, and you're just a little confused. You'll feel different after a while. You'll feel a lot better. Take it easy—just take it easy——"

It was almost miraculous. They saw Benson, listening to the calm voice, gradually lose his extreme excitement. An almost piteous look came into his eyes. He lowered the revolver.

"That's right," he said, his voice still shaking but no longer loud. "Debs—I ain't been feelin' right. God, I feel terrible—I wish—I wish——"

"Sit down, Walt. Take that chair. You need a doctor—I'll call a doctor." He held out his hand. "You don't want that gun. Let me have it. I'll keep it for you."

But Benson shoved the revolver into his holster. "No, I'm goin' back. I'm goin'——"

Hardly believing, they watched him turn and uncertainly descend the stairs, to disappear below.

Debs sat down as if he suddenly had lost the strength in his legs.

The society editor was on her feet, and Sally, weeping with excitement, was running to the desk. The switchboard girl became suddenly busy answering her signals. Mary Agnes caught her breath again and went over to Debs.

"What was it—what was the matter with him?" she heard Sally ask.

Debs did not answer her directly. "Sally, run down the stairs, please," he said. "Run down and watch what direction he's going."

Sally went at once and obediently, and he picked up his telephone and dialed.

"Chief Hardcastle, this is Debs Dorn," he said. "You've got a crazy man on the street. Walt Benson. He was up here, gone berserk. We talked him out of shooting, but you better get him. He's got a gun and might go dangerous again any minute. One of our girls is at our street door. She'll tell you which way he's gone."

"He was going to kill you!" Mary Agnes said.

Debs looked at her. "Manic-depressive. The depression comes sometimes as quick as the frenzy. He must have been at the top of his disturbance when he got up here. The only chance was to talk to him until the spell passed. I saw a case like this once before—when I was on police. Only the crazy man killed that time."

"You—you didn't act as if you were at all afraid."

Debs gave a little mirthless laugh. "I was, though. Scared all over. But I knew the violent period sometimes fades. He had the compulsion to kill, but I let him relieve his emotions by telling me off. Then I talked him out of his spell and the mood passed. For a time. I don't mind telling you, Mrs. Wedge, right now I feel as weak as a cat."

A police siren went past outside.

"They'll get him," said Debs.

"Will he shoot?"

"Not now. Not in his present stage. He's in the depressive stage. If they get his gun from him and take care of him in a hospital, he won't do anything."

She looked at him as if she could not comprehend him. She felt proud of him, proud of the *Clarion,* which had people like him on its staff. What she had seen was raw courage, and she wanted her paper to have that kind of raw courage. All at once she saw her own situation in a strangely different light. Compared to what almost happened to Debs Dorn, whatever might happen to her as regarded Erskine de Lacey was very unimportant. It was as if everything came into a new perspective. She would not ask Debs to do violence to his own integrity or that of the paper, which he seemed to value as highly as his own. She would face the question of that painting when it arose, how it arose.

Now Jeff returned from the composing room, received a quick ex-

cited recital from the society editor of the events just passed, and
hurried over to the city desk.

Sally came back up the stairs.

"I showed them—he went up toward the First National," she said.

"Thanks, Sally," said Debs.

"Oh, Debs! I was so frightened!"

Looking at Sally, Mary Agnes said to herself that the child seemed
near to crying.

Debs grinned. "You weren't the only one. And I'll tell you something
else. I was awful wrong about Benson."

"How were you wrong?" Jeff asked.

"I thought he was in this dope racket. Getting a pay-off. I thought
Nibs Galloway got wind of it and Benson killed him to shut him up."

"And you were mistaken?" asked Mary Agnes.

"About the dope racket. Walt Benson never took a dime of pay-off.
And if there was a connection between the murders of Bonnie Bonner
and Nibs Galloway, it wasn't like I thought. Shows how badly you can
miss."

"Then who killed Galloway?"

"Oh, Benson, of course. But not because he felt guilty of anything.
He thought Galloway had it in for him, was doing him wrong some
way. And somebody put that idea in his head, kept feeding it to him.
Galloway wasn't worrying about Benson's connection with the Bonner
case. People who know Benson told me he had spells of talk and spells
of silence, and he was sometimes ugly and bad-tempered. I should have
figured it—what was the matter with him. Nibs *did* figure it. But he
wasn't sure, and he didn't know what to do about it. That was what
was worrying him. Before he made up his mind, Benson, in one of his
maniacal fits, killed him."

"Who put that in Benson's mind?" asked Sally.

Debs looked at her. "The same person who convinced him that I
needed killing. Joe Canfield."

"Why?"

"Canfield doesn't like me. And he may have known something
about Bonner's dope selling. Canfield has connections in the underworld——"

"You mean *he* was getting a pay-off?" asked Mary Agnes.

"I don't know. But we're sure going to find out."

3

Decidedly, Mary Agnes thought, a newspaper office was no place for a nervous person.

But this crisis was over, and she had come to one settled decision. Debs Dorn was the man to take the managing editor's job. She had felt so before, and this convinced her beyond any question. Hudson had received his notice and a check for six months' pay. The office rumor which Debs had heard was based on that check, issued by the business office the afternoon before. As soon as Wistart returned, Mary Agnes would go through the form of consulting with him, and then make the promotion for Debs official.

Then the thought of Wistart suddenly brought something else into her mind that almost caused her to forget for a moment what she had just witnessed. She turned hurriedly and left the newsroom, going directly to the publisher's office as if she had a fixed and immediate purpose.

Entering the office, she closed the door behind her. Then she went over to Wistart's desk and opened the central drawer again.

Those keys! It was as if she had suddenly received an inspiration: those keys might have an importance she had not even suspected.

She looked down at them in the open drawer. They were rusty, and she stirred them around with her forefinger. Two were looped together with a bit of wire: obviously mates, and equally obviously keys to this very drawer. Since the drawer was not kept locked, they had been permitted to lie in it unused, probably since the desk was first moved into the office.

But the third key had no mate, and that was what had aroused Mary Agnes' sharp interest. What had happened to its duplicate? The thought had come to her that perhaps Wistart carried it on his key ring. People frequently did that—one key on the ring, the other in a drawer somewhere, and the one in the drawer after a time forgotten. She had done the same thing herself.

But if Wistart carried a key on his ring, it must have some importance . . . that filing case in the bookshelf marked *Personal Papers, Mr. Wedge*—perhaps it was that!

Mary Agnes glanced around. The office door was closed. Save for the faint rumble of the presses down below turning out the noon edition she heard no sound. With the rusty little key in her fingers she went to the filing case. The key fitted. So far her deductions were correct: it turned, the lock opened.

Hurriedly she drew out the sliding metal drawer as if she feared someone might catch her in this not very dignified act of prying into someone else's affairs and began glancing through the papers in the file. Disappointment quickly took the place of interest. Even Wistart's private correspondence was dull. Letters from people she did not know, or hardly knew, on subjects unimportant or uninteresting to her. Notations of a business nature. Insurance papers. Idly she flipped them over, preparing to close the drawer and lock the filing case again.

Then suddenly, with a cat's feral instinct, she pounced.

In the very last compartment of the file was an envelope, plain and without any written notation on it, not sealed but with the flap tucked inside. It was like any other envelope, but some queer instinct within her seemed to say its contents differed importantly from any of the others.

A moment later she was seated at the desk with the envelope's contents spread before her.

Item, a letter which began:

Dear Wistart: I'm here at the airport, and it's 9 o'clock at night, and I'm waiting for my plane, which is due in half an hour . . .

Oh, Wistart, how can I ever tell you what you've done for me? I feel like a new person, altogether, entirely different . . .

The letter was signed, "Devotedly, Grey."

Item, a Christmas card from Grey Rutledge, Sportswear, thanking the store's customers for patronage and encouragement. It carried a little personal handwritten note: *All this and a thousand times more to you, dear friend. G.R.*

Item, a personal note for five thousand dollars made out to Wistart Wedge and signed by Grey Rutledge. On the back were some dates and notations of payment of semi-annual interest and small payments on principle.

Item, a lease agreement. The store, of course! *Grey Rutledge, Sportswear!*

Mary Agnes sat back in the big padded chair and her eyes first widened, then narrowed. *So he set her up in business.*

That call of Bess Attwater's the previous evening—Bess had seen Wistart in Chicago, when he was supposed to be in Tulsa!

Mary Agnes lifted the receiver of the telephone on the desk.

"Outside, please," she said to the operator, then dialed a number.

"Grey Rutledge, Sportswear," said a voice.

"May I speak to Mrs. Rutledge?" Mary Agnes asked.

"I'm sorry, Mrs. Rutledge is out. This is Mrs. Hedcomb speaking. May I help you?"

"Oh, Mrs. Hedcomb? This is Mrs. Wistart Wedge. No—it was a personal matter. Will she be back shortly?"

"No, Mrs. Wedge, we don't expect her back in the store until tomorrow morning. She's out of the city, supposed to get in tonight."

"I didn't know she was gone."

"Yes, one of her buying trips."

"Does she go frequently?"

"Oh, New York usually in April and September. Los Angeles in June. Chicago in January. She's in Chicago now—or rather, on her way home."

Chicago!

Mary Agnes said quite calmly, "Thank you, Mrs. Hedcomb."

"Shall I tell Mrs. Rutledge you called?"

"No, it's not necessary, she'll be hearing from me later."

Mary Agnes replaced the receiver on its hook.

So Grey Rutledge was in Chicago . . . and Wistart had gone there, so secretly that he took the trouble to fly out of his way by the roundabout route through Tulsa. And this, with the papers she had found in the locked filing case . . .

If anyone had suggested to Mary Agnes that she could ever be a jealous wife, she would have laughed. She considered jealous females and their behavior ridiculous; and besides, she always supposed that to be jealous one must think the man worth it, which she did not.

Nevertheless, she trembled now with sudden fury.

All these years Wistart had been uninterested in her. And she in him, for that matter. Nevertheless, it was jolting to discover that in *his* case it was because he was interested in someone else, in Grey Rutledge.

With that Mary Agnes made a discovery: jealousy can be based on another emotion, vanity. She was wounded, wounded in an unsuspected spot of tenderness: her dearest, most secret, most surprising pride. Her pride in her sex. That was outraged. She had been outplayed, defeated, perhaps laughed at by another woman. Mary Agnes' brittle, gleaming surface of sophistication was badly cracked and seamed.

Her face stiffened as she regained self-possession.

She began placing the papers on the desk back in the envelope. The envelope she placed in her handbag; and it chanced to be the very handbag Wistart had bought for her at Grey Rutledge, Sportswear, a few days ago.

When she left the Clarion Building, her mood had changed and she was walking almost magnificently, an invariable sign in her of elation. Seating herself in her car, to be driven home by Suey, she laughed a little light laugh.

Wistart's secret: what a surprise it would be to him to find she knew it! She pictured his stupid face, its slow comprehension, its aghast alarm, and the picture gave her a bitter zest.

She began to consider the best way of breaking this news to him. Should she simply make a blunt announcement, a cold accusation which he could never deny successfully? Or would it be better to do it gradually, with a series of hinting references, leading him through the beginnings of apprehension to final dread conviction, perhaps climaxed by something dramatic, like laying before him with a gesture the damning documents she carried at that moment in her handbag?

She would make him squirm, she promised herself that. Even more importantly, she would make Grey Rutledge squirm and cringe.

Mary Agnes remembered that Grey Rutledge had gone out of her way to be nice to Wistart in the days when they were seeing something of the Rutledges, before Jed's death. Rather far out of her way, in fact. Perhaps there had been a motive all the time in what looked then merely like a bit of misplaced sympathy.

Well, things were going to be different, just a whole lot different, for Grey Rutledge from now on. She had used feminine trickery to take in foolish, stupid Wistart—she must have—but she was going to find herself dealing now with someone who knew and understood every female trick and wile, and just how to meet them. And someone who would never soften or be merciful: a woman dealing with another woman, whom she hated.

Twenty-five

I

When the paper had gone to press at three o'clock, long after Mary Agnes was driven home in her car with her evidence of a husband's unfaithfulness in her handbag, Debs came back from the composing room and saw Sally still at her desk.

She was pecking on her typewriter, trying to write a story, with her nerves still squirming from that awful moment of deadly peril that had happened in the city room when Debs stood at his desk while the madman beat on it with a pistol and shouted lurid threats.

The police had taken the man to the hospital, and doctors had him under observation. They had told a *Clarion* reporter that, yes, the man was suffering from severe nervous emotional excitement, and that, yes, judging from the symptoms, it was probable that it was a case of manic paranoia with depressive periods. The patient alternately raved and sat dully quiet, and in one of his babbling periods he had told quite childishly that it was he who killed Galloway. He was dangerous and should be restrained, and a sanity hearing would be held on him as soon as possible, so that he could be sent to a veterans' hospital for mental diseases.

Benson's statement concerning Galloway's death cleared up one important mystery, and was the subject of an important headline in the *Clarion*.

There was another important headline. Police were seeking Joe Canfield because, confronted with his name, Dewey Bonner the wife murderer, badly shaken by his craving for narcotics which were denied him, confessed that Canfield had been a "missionary" for him. This term, it was explained, meant, in underworld slang, that he was a contact man who informed addicts where and when they could go for their drugs— to Bonner. Since Canfield had long been a semi-member of the underworld, none of this was too surprising. But it did explain some things, including the reason why Canfield played on the mind of the crazed Benson to induce him to kill Galloway, who was getting too close to the facts, and later almost to do the same thing to Debs for a similar reason.

Canfield apparently had left the city, but other points had been notified to look for him and provided with full descriptions. Police felt they would have him before very long, and when they did arrest him, the entire mystery revolving around the deaths of Bonnie Bonner and Galloway, and the narcotics dealings of Bonner aided by Canfield, would be cleared up.

All of this going on around her added to Sally's excitement, but even had she been fully calm the story she was working on would not have been very inspiring to her. It was a routine story, a promotion story.

The *Clarion* was holding its annual essay contest for high school students, and she could not imagine anything duller. Small cash prizes would be given for the best essays on *The Two Greatest Americans*. That meant George Washington and Abraham Lincoln in this contest, and the awards were always made at a program in the city auditorium on Washington's birthday, February 22. People said it was a worthy thing for the *Clarion* to do, because it inspired the young folks with a reverence for great men, and there was always quite a little crowd at the awards, mostly members of the PTA, which co-sponsored the program, and parents and friends of the winning essayists. But it didn't add up to much in Sally's young life.

For one thing, the story had to be written every day until the contest was over and the prizes given, and she had to think up some new angle each day to lend freshness to something pretty moldy to begin with. Sally reflected that it was almost as bad as writing about weddings and canasta parties for society: the grubby routine work of the news side was something she had rather overlooked in her wish to become a real reporter. She had, it must be confessed, thought mostly in terms of big, front-page stories, where she would be in the very thick of the excitement.

But she had this assignment and it was her baby and she had to stay with it until the contest was over, the entries judged, and then write the final story about the award program. There were other assignments, of course, but most of them were minor, and she had come to realize that experience and enthusiasm were two very different things; and while she had started with a sufficiency of the latter, she must acquire more of the former before she was trusted with anything important. Acquiring experience required time, and any young woman feels she has so little time.

Sally thought about what Debs said about career girls always being second string, and the girls who got married and had homes being first team, and she wondered if maybe it wasn't true. She thought to herself that if a certain person asked her, she'd marry him so quick it would make his head swim, and start keeping house and maybe having babies, and forget all about being a newspaper gal and wanting a career just to make him happy.

But it didn't look as if he had any intention of asking her.

She was a little resentful and hurt because Debs hardly had spoken to her since he came into the office yesterday, so unshaved and disheveled-looking, after he talked to Mrs. Wedge. And that was the very next day, too, after he had been at Sally's house for supper and there had been those few moments when things were so different: when there was no boss-and-subordinate relationship between them, but a breathlessly thrilling equal status of man-and-woman. At least it was breathlessly thrilling to her, and something she would never forget, and wonderful. She wondered if it was anything like that to him. He seemed so different now: it was as if he were too busy for anything as trivial as Sally, and when he spoke to her at all in giving her small assignments, he spoke to her as if he were barely acquainted with her instead of having held her tight in his arms and kissed her furiously and almost frighteningly, and then dragged himself away from her as if he were doing something as difficult as . . . well, as it *was* . . .

As a newspaperwoman she felt that he had put her in her place, but as a girl she had a deeper instinctive feeling that maybe he was only trying to put himself in *his* place.

So she wasn't a bit surprised when Debs came over to her desk, but she looked up at him all innocent-eyed, as if she had no idea at all about what he was going to say.

He said, "Are you about through, Sally?"

"Yes," she said, "I've only got one more paragraph."

"When you finish it, how'd you like a lift home?"

She tried to keep from showing how glad she was, but she hurried through the last of her story, and took it over and put it in the wire basket where the copy went, and verified her complexion in her compact mirror, and put on her hat with the cute little veil under the nose, and got her coat, and was ready in about ten minutes, no longer.

When they were in his battered old convertible, he drove for a while without saying anything, and she didn't say anything either.

Finally he said, "Mad at me?"

"What for?" she said.

"Because of what happened—the other night——"

"Not exactly."

"What do you mean, not exactly?"

"I'm madder at you because you've treated me like a stepchild since."

He laughed. "Little Sally! You're not a stepchild. Not to me. But I've been awfully busy."

"Yes, I know. What did you do after you left my house?"

He took a little time replying. "I went out and got good and drunk."

"You looked it next morning."

"I know. You wouldn't understand it."

"That men want to get loaded once in a while?"

"No, the reason why they do."

"Well, what was the reason?"

"Men are different from women, Sally. When women get full up to the chin with frustration or bewilderment or disappointment or anger, they can break out weeping, or have hysterics, and blow off steam——"

"I know that's what hysterics means—wild emotionalism—related to the womb—I learned that in Psychology B in college——"

"But a man can't do those things. His substitute is getting pie-eyed and making a fool of himself."

"That's why you did it? Frustration and bewilderment——"

"All those things. I didn't have a job. That wasn't so much, but you made me realize something that I'd never let myself really think about before. And that was pretty bad."

They were in her block, nearing her house.

"Something you couldn't have?" she said.

"Something I can't have."

"Was that—was that why—you did that way—with me——?"

The convertible slowed to a stop by the walk that led up to Sally's front door.

"Sally," Debs said, "no, that wasn't why I did that way with you. I did that way with you because it was *you*. You know how I think of you? I think you're just about the bestest and mostest in girls. I—pretty near lost my head—and if I hadn't, there would have been something wrong with me. A girl like you is born to make men lose their heads. It'll happen to you a lot of times, and someday——"

"Someday what?"

"You'll find somebody you like well enough to give newspapering up for and marry."

"I—already have——" she said in a little muffled voice.

He gave her a quick glance and saw her eyes filled with tears.

"No, you haven't," he said. "Believe me, Sally, you haven't. You're just a baby, dear, you may think you have, but you'll find——"

"You say *you've* got something you can't have," she said with a half sob. "What about *me?*"

His arm went around her shoulders.

"Sally, don't cry. You know how I feel about you——"

"Do I?" she said rather violently, wiggling away from his arm. "Yes, I do! A baby. A kid, just a fresh-faced kid, to have a little fun with, and get all wrought up, and feel sorry for!"

She put her hand on the door handle and started to get out, dabbing her eyes with her handkerchief.

"Wait a minute, Sally."

She hesitated.

"Would it have made you feel any better—if we'd gone through with —what we started the other night?"

She thought a second. Then she shook her head.

"No, it wouldn't. I'd have felt terrible—especially since you—don't feel that way about me at all——"

Now a real sob.

"Just think then, Sally. I was a friend, a real friend to you when that happened. It was the biggest act of friendship I could do for you. I thought too much of you to do anything you'd regret later—as you would have. Even if you wanted it at the moment—as you did. I made a pretty big sacrifice myself, if you only knew it."

She controlled herself, and sat a moment in silence, to think. Then she wiped her eyes. "I'll have to put on my sunglasses," she said.

She made a dive or two into her handbag and found the sunglasses and put them on. With that kind of a disguise for her tear-dampened eyes she felt more confident and poised.

"I guess maybe that's true, what you said," she told him. "And maybe I ought to be thanking you."

"You don't need to thank anybody but yourself for being the kind of a girl you are."

Another silence.

"Debs," she said after a moment, "if things had been different— would you——?"

"Different?"

"If you weren't—in love already."

He ceased looking at her. He could not see her eyes anyway behind the expressionless shields of the sunglasses.

"Sally, all I can say is this. There isn't one single thing about you that isn't lovely and beautiful and sweet."

She seemed to consider that. Then she said, "Why don't you try?"

"Try what?"

"Try and find out if what you think is impossible really *is* impossible."

"I know already."

"Have you tried?"

"No."

"Then how do you know?"

"Because I know the reason, that's how."

She mused a moment. "Funny, isn't it," she said. "I'm carrying a torch for you. And you're carrying a torch for Grey. And Grey's, what? Carrying a torch—for somebody else?"

"I don't want to talk about it."

"All right."

He gave her hand a quick hard little squeeze. "You're a pal, Sally."

"Pal it is."

She smiled bravely under the sunglasses.

Then she got out of the car and watched him drive away.

Pal. She hated the word.

But that's what she was. A pal. Nothing more.

If she'd been just a little older, maybe—that was it, she was too young. He thought of her as a child.

She hated her own youth at that moment. And then she bit her lip, and she didn't hate anything any more. There was a big pain in her heart, but it was a growing pain. Part of her growing up.

2

Grey Rutledge came in on the train at nine o'clock that evening with no premonition or apprehension of disaster.

She had closed a chapter of her life firmly, finally, and she hoped mercifully. It was not easy, and Wistart was hurt, and she did not want to hurt him, but at least she had done it.

So now she was home, and she felt somewhat drawn and weary, but not very sinful. Riding into Jericho in the Pullman car that night, she believed she was stepping out into a cleaner air of existence, leaving behind forever discreditably furtive murks and shadows. And guilt.

Yet her thoughts were painful.

She wondered why she had confessed to Wistart that she loved him after evading confession these three years. She did love him, she told herself, but it was a love she had difficulty in defining.

She was honest with herself: perhaps it was a justification, because love is the only excuse that can be accepted for a woman's being what she was—even by the man himself. The world may condemn a mistress as immoral and loose, but it may also sympathize with her and pity her if it thinks she has given her heart to her lover. Perhaps that was it.

But turning it over in her mind she saw that it had greater complexities than that, which had to do with the complexities of her nature as a woman.

She knew Wistart's love: an unthinking passion, dependent, desirous, seeking, masculinely selfish although he did not realize it was selfish.

But her love was compounded of many factors: fondness, gratitude, and anxiety for him, among them. But unthinking passion such as he knew? She met him, responded to him, gave him kiss for kiss, embrace for embrace. Yet all the time she was thinking . . . and thinking is no hallmark of true passion.

Then was it some weakness that impelled her to go on with this so long? Her basic physical instincts? Yes, of course, that had something to do with it. She was young, and a woman, and not frigid.

But beyond and beneath this there was something else: a woman is supposed to use her head in love. She should plan and think for the future instead of feeling only for the moment, because men plunge so heedlessly and recklessly into the whirlpool of their emotions. Most women have at least something of this thinking, calculating part of love, the practical planning for security, which men often seem to lack. Love at first sight, she thought wryly, probably is possible for men, but it does not frequently occur with women, because female passion catches fire from male passion.

Yes, that was what she was trying to grasp. Women fall in love often with men because the men have first fallen in love with them. Having inspired a great passion, a woman has an inborn urge to reward it, a duty inbound in her by the instincts of the race.

That supplied her final answer, the other facet of her love for Wistart, a somewhat typical case, she supposed, of behavior by her sex. Because she was so certain he loved her overwhelmingly, she had been impelled against her better judgment to reward that kind of love.

Fondness, gratitude, anxiety, and a desire to reward. A strange love; not a happy love.

Because with it always was a gnawing sensation of guilt.

She was mature enough and intelligent enough to realize that this guilt, which ate at her like an acid, was partly a reflex of her early training, the conviction in which she was brought up: that sex was wrong, perhaps even legal sex was slightly wrong. The Bible: *In sin did my mother conceive me* . . . and this referred to the married state!

But particularly sex was unthinkably wicked and shameful outside of legal bounds, and there was no forgiveness for it under the old standards.

Of course she was modern, and she long ago had reasoned those old conventional moral scruples away. She told herself that no marriage is broken up from the outside, and if Wistart's wife had made herself attractive and necessary to him, nothing Grey could have done or said would have made any difference. She had read Dr. Kinsey, too, and from that reading told herself that sex morals are artificial anyway: marriage was evolved to protect the children and not from any intrinsic value in itself.

Almost always she managed to reason matters out thus: and yet, after all her reasoning, the guilt remained and with it the emotional conflict which was unceasingly hard to live with.

Then why the heavy guilt? Fear: she knew that her guilt was fundamentally fear. A woman's guilt cannot, absolutely cannot, be separated from her fear, and the worst fear is the fear of discovery. Relationships

are incomparably important in a woman's life. Her guilt is most intimately associated with "What would people think?"

But the guilt was not all fear: part of it was conscience, old-fashioned,
instinctive conscience, which prodded her in the midst of her most
logical reasonings.

Grey thought of her pearl earrings, the gift of remorse and gratitude
from Wistart after their first time together.

Sometimes she wore them rather defiantly in her store, because they
touched something quite primitive and almost unrealized in her: a little
secret wish to flaunt a woman's victory. Once or twice when Mary
Agnes came into the store, her eyes appraised the earrings. Mary Agnes
had shrewd greenish eyes and she was a good judge of values in anything that cost money. Sometimes Grey felt a moment's chill, wondering if Mary Agnes guessed the true worth of the earrings; and if she
guessed, what she suspected concerning the source from which they
came. But always Mary Agnes' eyes wandered on to some other object,
and Grey was sure she never really surmised anything.

Grey did not like Mary Agnes: nobody liked Mary Agnes, really.
But she was afraid of her, and she resented her, not because of her
arrogance and wealth, but because of her cruelty, especially to Wistart.

She knew what a hell Wistart's life was, and this knowledge, thoroughly laced with indignation at Mary Agnes, was another factor in
her long affair with him. Through Wistart she revenged herself, and
also him, on smug, sneering, supercilious Mary Agnes. It was not admirable, perhaps, but it was human to be proud that she was in this
respect superior to that woman who possessed every other thinkable
advantage.

And yet, in spite of being modern, in spite of telling herself that she
had done something perhaps even a little worthy in giving Wistart
happiness where otherwise he knew only misery, in spite of her detes-
tation of Mary Agnes and moral indignation against her, Grey really
was no siren with a compulsion to break up another woman's home.
She could not quiet the stabbing of her conscience and the weight of
her guilt remained upon her.

It affected her in various subtle ways, but it was not all selfish. Far
from entirely selfish. The fear that was so much a part of her guilt was
not so much for herself as for her child.

Sometimes Grey felt a clutch at her heart when she thought of the fatefulness of being born a little girl. Girls grow up to be women. Some are born to be wanted: others know from the beginning, almost, that they are to be the lonely ones. No one, themselves least of all, can change the forces directing their lives.

Grey hoped that Betty Jean, with her great trusting eyes and her cute winsome little ways, would be one of the wanted ones: yet even in that there were also great risks and dangers, as Grey's own life experience proved. If Betty Jean were a boy, she would become a man someday, and men were so much more self-determining than women. But Betty Jean wasn't a boy; and because her little daughter was so greatly a hostage of fate, Grey's love for her sometimes seemed so poignant as to be almost despairing.

There, in the final analysis, was where her fear focused. Disgrace for herself, Grey could endure. Perhaps it might shatter her, but that did not greatly matter. What it might do to her child was the nightmare . . . the thought that Betty Jean, who was in no way to blame, would be forced to live under the black shadow of her mother's wayward transgression was the terror.

Grey sighed. At least she had finished the episode about which hung all that pall of fear and guilt. She could almost believe she was younger, a different person, happy at beginning life afresh, as the train pulled under the snow sheds of the Jericho Union Station.

3

When she went down the ramp, she saw a man coming to meet her, and she greeted him with glad surprise in her voice.

"Debs! What are you doing here?"

He said, "Came to meet you."

"Meet *me?*" She thought for a moment that he was joking. "Why? You never did before. And how did you know I was coming on this train?"

"The last part of that I can answer easier than the first. I called up your mother, and she told me when you were getting in."

She was still bewildered. "It's really sweet and thoughtful of you, Debs, but I don't understand——"

"There comes the redcap with the luggage truck. Give me your checks. My car's in the parking lot."

She surrendered the checks and stood under the high-vaulted ceiling

of the big station lobby watching him as he claimed her bags, tipped
the boy, and came carrying them, one in each hand. His being there
mystified her, but she decided it was very nice being met, and Debs
was one of the nicest people in the world.

They talked about how it had warmed up since she left as they went
to the parking lot; and he put the bags in the trunk of the convertible,
and helped her in, then went around and took his seat at the wheel.

"Had dinner?" he asked as he started the car.

"Oh yes. On the train."

"Would you care to stop somewhere for a cup of coffee?"

"Oh—Debs," she said, "Mother and Betty Jean will be waiting for
me, and it's Betty Jean's bedtime. I don't think I ought, though I'd love
to—I'll tell you what! You come in and we'll have a cup of coffee when
we get home. How's that?"

"Fine," he said, but something in his voice said it wasn't so fine.

She almost acted on impulse and told him to stop somewhere, she'd
have a cup of coffee. But some imperative instinct in her told her not
to do it.

He seemed abstracted or moody, and after a while he said, "I wanted
to have a talk with you, Grey."

She knew all at once what it was about, and she was terrified that he
might go on and speak about it. She didn't want him to speak about it
. . . and yet she knew she would love to hear him speak about it if
things were different. But things *weren't* different, they were like they
were: and that was so final and beyond appeal that she must prevent
him from saying what was in his heart, and what also was wistfully
hopeless in hers, if she could possibly do so.

She tried to pass it off. "We can talk any time, can't we?"

"Not about this," he said.

He kept on driving, looking straight ahead, and she gazed sidewise
at him, studying his profile, the good jaw, the sensitive mouth, the way
his dark hair came down thickly on his temples, cut off straight there
by the razor, and his eyes that sometimes seemed so alert but now were
dark and brooding. Above almost anything else she did not want anything to hurt Debs Dorn.

They were driving up a residential street, with wide spreading elms
extending their leafless arms in a long arch over the pavement and the
houses all lit up pleasantly. People were in those homes, watching

television, or talking, or reading, or playing cards, or maybe just doing the dinner dishes or putting the children to bed: happy, unworried people, living normally and pleasantly, not carrying around a weight of depression. Riding with Debs along the street seemed to emphasize all this to her, and made her feel even more poignantly what she had lost, and the tragedy of it.

"Grey, I want you to know this," he said rather awkwardly after a time. "If you ever need a friend, I'm there for you."

"Thank you, Debs," she said, and was uncomfortable because of the tone of his voice. "I know you're my friend—I—I'm very grateful for it."

"Sometimes people need friends," he said.

"People always need friends."

"Mind if I say something that sounds pretty ridiculous?"

"Why—no—I suppose not——"

"Then it's this: I think you're wonderful—just simply wonderful— the most wonderful girl—the most wonderful *person*—I've ever known."

She felt a catch in her throat at the way he said it, continuing to look straight ahead, as if he thought she would reject it. And he thought *that* sounded ridiculous! She wanted to tell him it wasn't, and what a grateful balm it was to her sore spirit just to have a man like him think that way. But she did not dare, because she knew if she did it might bring something else, even deeper in emotion, to the surface and she must be wary and take care.

So she thanked him, almost primly, almost formally.

He was silent and she glanced at him sidewise again. She had known him long, but in some manner it seemed to her she did not know him at all tonight. Her woman's instinct told her there was some secret mystery in him, some suppressed thought or feeling. He repressed it not from timidity or awkwardness. His mouth was the key to his character, that sensitive mouth. It was tact, a really delicate intuitive tact, that was keeping him from saying what another man might have poured out, and she knew it and felt almost humbly grateful for it.

"I didn't have a job—yesterday," he said.

"Debs! Really? But it's all right now?" She spoke almost vivaciously, immensely relieved by his abrupt turn of the conversation away from something that had been so intensely personal.

"Yes. I quit, but they hired me back."

"What happened?"

"I had a row with Hudson. Walked out. The matter was straightened up."

"How?"

"Mrs. Wedge."

"Oh——?" In spite of herself, Grey knew her voice sounded flat. Mrs. Wedge. Mary Agnes Wedge. So now she held a determining power over Debs also . . . Was there anyone touching Grey's life over whom Mary Agnes did not hold some kind of power, some kind of threat?

"It may mean promotion for me," Debs went on.

"If you please *her?*"

For an instant his glance shot toward her with a sudden, searching awareness. Then he gazed straight ahead again and brought the car around an intersection corner.

"That's right," he said. "If I please her. Of course you know she's boss of the *Clarion* now."

It was her turn to glance sharply at him. "How should I know?"

"Why, it's on the masthead of the paper. Co-publisher. 'With fullest authority,' to quote the memo sent around to all departments."

She relaxed and breathed more freely. For a moment she had almost been afraid he guessed . . . something she did not want him to guess, ever.

"Well, here we are. There's your house and your folks are waiting up for you, I can see," he said.

When he drew up in front, she put her hand on his arm.

"Debs, please I just want you to know this much. What you said—back there—isn't ridiculous. Not to me. *Anything* but ridiculous. And of everyone I know in the world I—I believe I'd rather have you than anyone else think I'm 'wonderful'—though I'm not. And I want you—very much—for a friend——"

"Just a friend, Grey?"

"What else could there be?"

She got out quickly.

"Come in," she said, still holding open the car door. "That coffee will be ready in just a few minutes——"

"No, Grey, thanks. I'll help you in with your bags. Then I think I'll go on up to my room, and maybe hit the hay. Hard day today."

In silence he unlocked the trunk and carried the bags up the porch steps for her. At the door he set them down.

"Good night, Grey." He gave her his hand.

Twenty-six

I

Her welcome, when she entered her home, made Grey's heart leap as it always did. A piping voice cried, "Mommy! Mommy!" And a little wild sprite, all eyes and tossing curls and clinging arms, came sailing through the hall to her.

Grey lifted her and hugged her and was kissed and hugged in return, and she laughed as Mrs. Norcross came in the hall laughing.

"You'd think I'd been away a year!" she said. "Now, honey, let me put you down. You're getting so big you're nearly as big as your mother! And I've got something for you—and for Grandma too."

Only then could she kiss her mother and exchange a few words with her about the trip, and what had happened at home, while she gave them the gifts she had brought: a new robe for Mrs. Norcross, a set of tiny dishes like miniature spodeware for Betty Jean.

After that she sat happily on the rug by the stairs in the hall, adoring her little girl, who with a child's instant acquisitiveness had forgotten her ecstasy at her mother's return in a new ecstasy over her possessions. She was arranging the doll dishes on the bottom step of the hall stairs, a vision of delight with her curly head on one side, her little pink-tipped fingers caressing each new addition from the box before she placed it delicately in what she considered its proper spot.

It was then that the telephone rang.

"Grey, it's for you," said her mother.

For some reason she could never have explained, Grey felt the muscles of her stomach grow tense with a nameless dread as she took the receiver.

"Yes?" she said.

And over the telephone came these words: "Grey, this is Wistart. I've got to see you. Right away. It's something—terribly important."

"I just barely . . . got home," she half faltered.

"I know it. That's why I waited until now to call. Please—please—meet me somewhere as soon as possible, won't you? This can't wait."

"Where are you now?"

"At the Kansas Hotel. I have a room here."

It was like a spray of icy water in her face. The Kansas Hotel. He had a *room* there . . .

"It's pretty bad," he said, his voice showing agitation. "No time to lose——"

She made up her mind. "Come by my house. I'll be on the front porch," she told him.

When she lifted the receiver she had been in terror, but when she replaced it she was almost stonily calm. It was as if suddenly she were moving by some weird mechanism, without any sensation, without any thought.

"I've got to go out, Mother," she said, and wondered at the steadiness of her own voice. "I don't think I'll be long, but it seems to be important."

"Something about the store?"

"Yes," Grey said, desperately grasping at the idea. "About the store."

It was not so much of a lie: it *was* about the store—about everything else in her life, too.

2

She switched the porch light off and stepped out, closing the door behind her. For a moment she stood in the darkness, buttoning her coat and tying a scarf about her head. A figure came up the walk and turned in next door. Grey did not think she was seen, but a voice said, "Good evening, Mrs. Rutledge. You back?"

"Oh, hello, Mrs. Hillyer," said Grey. "Yes, I just got back a little while ago."

"Going out already?"

"Oh—just a little errand. I'll be back soon. Did you want to see me?"

Mrs. Hillyer stood on her own porch and chuckled. "Well, it can wait," she said. "Things have been happening since you left. You know old Mrs. Butford? There's some kind of a scandal about that artist she has living at her place—I'll tell you about it sometime."

"Yes—I'd love to hear. Later on." Grey was in terror that Wistart would come while Mrs. Hillyer stood there talking to her. But after a moment the woman went on into her own house.

Almost immediately automobile headlights turned the corner and came down the street. Grey ran out to the curb and was in the car almost before the wheels stopped turning.

At first neither of them said anything. Wistart turned the next corner and drove toward the city's outskirts.

"She . . . knows?" Grey asked at last.

"Yes." It was as if he expelled his heart with the word.

Another silence while she groped for strength.

"How did she find out?" she asked after a time.

"I don't know. But she did. Somebody saw me in Chicago—when I was supposed to be in Tulsa. This afternoon when my plane landed at the airport, I was surprised to find Suey waiting for me with the car. Thought it was unusually thoughtful of her to send him. But she wasn't doing me a favor. She just wanted to make sure I came in on that *Tulsa* plane, instead of one from Chicago, because it would prove I was deceiving her."

"But—how could *that* be so important?"

"Because it was the final piece in a little deduction she worked out. Somehow she got into my private file down at the office. There were some papers there—I'd kept that letter you wrote me, and some other things——"

Wistart groaned. Etched in his mind as by some corrosive was the picture: himself, sitting in the library, looking dully at his wife as she swished back and forth, her face terrible and strangely white with fury under its Honolulu tan.

"Admit it!" she was saying. "You may as well admit it! I've got the evidence—all the evidence I want, Wistart Wedge! This correspondence—you set that scheming, conniving woman up in business!"

He was sure she knew everything. There was nothing he could say. How could he tell her how far, far from scheming and conniving had been Grey's story and his?

"You've been in Chicago with her!" Mary Agnes cried, and that made him catch his breath. "Oh yes, you were with her there, and you came back by way of Tulsa thinking nobody would guess, didn't you? But somebody saw you, Wistart! Somebody saw you there, and the crows are coming home to roost now, aren't they, Wistart?"

She laughed shrilly, hatefully.

It did not occur to him that Mary Agnes might not really know as much as she indicated she knew, or that she spoke and acted with such vicious assurance because she wanted to break him down. Sitting there while she badgered him, he was as badly routed as she expected him to be. He had no way of knowing that it was Bess Attwater who saw him; or that it was only at the airport by himself; or that the especial evil luck had befallen that she had tried but failed to speak to him, which if she had succeeded would have given him warning so that he might have flown straight home from Chicago with a reasonable story instead of sneaking back roundabout by way of Tulsa. Instead, he believed fully that someone actually had seen him with Grey, perhaps when they were out at dinner, or even at their hotel, and his only emotion was sodden despair.

"Well, speak up," Mary Agnes said bitterly. "Are you tongue-tied? What have you got to say about that filthy little slut?"

Filthy slut . . . she meant *Grey!*

All at once anger brought him out of his dull reverie. Surprisingly, he found that he was not afraid of Mary Agnes any more. He felt that she had lost her power to intimidate him.

He stood up, suddenly stronger than he had ever been in his life.

He said, "All right. I'll speak up. And here's what I've got to say. Go ahead! Just crack your whip! Do any goddamn thing you want! Get your divorce—you she-devil! Take everything—I don't want a thing. I'm so fed up with you that the very sight of that hag face of yours makes me sick. But keep your dirty tongue away from Grey Rutledge. You wouldn't even know what she is—that spider's nest of selfishness and inhumanity and vanity which you call your mind couldn't conceive of a person like Grey. She's everything wonderful and beautiful and good, where you're everything stinking and ugly and evil. She's so much above you that you can't even touch her. Get that divorce, or if you don't, I will!"

He turned and took two steps toward the door.

"Wait just a minute!" she cried.

He halted and she stared at him, feeling her stomach grow unaccountably tense under the taut white skin. She had not expected this defiance, and it almost frightened her. At the same time it increased her fury.

"You think I'm going to let you go that easily to the arms of your new sweetheart?" She sneered; and then she seemed to gloat over a sudden thought. *"New?* What am I saying?" She gave him a satirical glance. "How long has it been going on, anyway, Wistart? A long time —years! I can get the exact dates you and that—that woman—have been out of town at the same time. There's a child, isn't there? How old? Six? *Your* child, Wistart? Ha!"

He gasped. "That's the evilest thing I ever heard said by a human being in my life!"

"Is it?" She was elated at the way she had found a new spot of anguish in him. "Well, you're going to hear it said—that I promise you! I'll get the divorce. Count on that. And I'll get it right here in Jericho! And I'll get the best damned lawyer in the state to handle it! And I'll drag out every bit of filthy information on you and that dirty little tramp of yours that the law will let me put in the complaint! You're going to have to come to court, Mr. Wistart Wedge, whether you like it or not, because you'll have to *swear* before the judge that child isn't your bastard. And nobody—but *nobody*—is going to believe you under oath! Oh, the newspapers are going to have a field day with the vulgar details of a swine and a bitch and their fornications! I'll drag you and that blonde through the courts and the newspapers until there's not a shred left of either of you! *Now* you can go! Get out of here, get out of this house, and I don't want to see that rotten face of yours again until I see it in court!"

For a moment he stared, hardly believing the complete extent of her malice. And he knew he had been mistaken when he thought he was not afraid of Mary Agnes any more, or that she had lost her power to intimidate him. He was stricken with desperate fear.

Very stiff and pale she stood, her eyes like slits burned by acid into her face, until he turned and stumbled out of the house.

All this, or the substance of it, as much as he knew of it, Wistart conveyed to Grey as he drove her through the night across the town. Looking straight ahead and sitting very tensely upright, she listened without a word.

"Oh, darling," he said as he finished, "I spoke my mind to her. I stood on my feet and told her what she was to her face. I told her she wasn't fit to even speak of you. I know I've done a terrible thing—but I love you. I love you more than anything in the world. And I'm going to make it up to you. Somehow I'm going to make it up to you. When this whole thing is over, Grey—oh, Grey, darling—will you marry me?"

She said, "Wistart, please take me home." ·

"Promise me—won't you promise——?"

"I can't promise. I can't think. I haven't anything to say. I just want . . . to go home . . ."

She did not weep. She showed no anger or resentment. She was like a wooden woman, a lifeless figure, hardly seeming to breathe, saying nothing as he drove her home and let her out at her front door.

Neither she nor Wistart knew that at a window in a darkened upper room of the Hillyer house next door someone stood looking down at them as she left the car and ran into her home.

3

Above everything she must keep control of herself. Until she knew exactly what was going to take place, there must on no account be a breakdown, she must save her little family from fear as long as possible, each day of peace was a boon for them which they might not know, but which she, with doom over her, did know.

When she entered the house Grey was so pale that her mother looked at her strangely, though she did not question her.

"I'm tired, Mother," she said. "Will you put Betty Jean to bed? I'm going up to my room—I—I'm very weary."

Mrs. Norcross assented, and it was in itself most unusual that Grey would surrender the last rite of seeing her small daughter bathed and read to and kissed and tucked in for the night. So unusual that Mrs. Norcross was deeply concerned, fearing that Grey was ill.

And Grey was ill, but not in the way her mother thought. She went to her room and closed the door, and sat down for a minute before she began slowly to undress for bed.

Her mind felt numb, as the body is sometimes numbed temporarily by a stab that is mortal. But the numbness wears off, and the pain eventually comes with anguish terribly increased. She felt the agony twofold, and the despair.

The little rituals of life are mechanical. One watching this girl could hardly have known what suffering was hers. Her face was devoid of expression as she did, without realizing them, the things she did each night, hanging her clothes up carefully, placing her jewelry in their case, cleansing her face, slipping over her head the exquisite filmy nightgown which was one of the extravagances of her happier days, and the other little acts of the routine of retiring, before at last she was in bed.

Yet all the time that she went about this with face outwardly calm, she was writhing inwardly with torment. And as she lay in her bed she thought to herself that every fear, every apprehension she had ever felt, was fulfilled. Only it was infinitely more terrible than her imagination had pictured it.

Be sure your sin will find you out . . . the old Biblical injunction. It had found her, nailed her down.

It was what was happening to Betty Jean that was the horror of it, that tore at her heart and vitals.

She had barely spoken to them downstairs and come up at once to her room, because at that moment she could not look her child in the face.

Almost as if they had been kind and beneficent, she now remembered her previous terrors. Her concern over her little daughter had only been the fear of an indirect stain of disgrace that might smirch her. But what really faced her child now was something infinitely uglier.

You'll have to swear . . . that child isn't your bastard. And nobody—but nobody—is going to believe you under oath!

Those were the fiendish words of Mary Agnes, as repeated by Wistart when he told Grey of his interview with his wife.

What could she do . . . what *could* she do?

If somehow she could see Mary Agnes, perhaps she might appeal to her. Grey thought how gladly, how eagerly she would do anything, undergo any abasement, to have her baby left out of this. She would grovel, get down on her knees, go through any humiliation Mary Agnes might require of her if only, only she would spare Betty Jean.

But it was a futile thought, and she knew it at once. Mary Agnes would grant nothing. Mary Agnes Wedge, the implacable, would only laugh at her, would only enjoy her rival's agonies.

So great was Grey's despair that she considered the thought of death. Desperately, yet as sanely as possible, she computed the effect her suicide might have. It would be easily done: sleeping pills, or the little pistol she kept in her dresser, almost forgotten, in case of burglars.

Death had no terror, it would be a relief compared with what faced her now. Joyfully would she take her own life, even knowing the dreadful shock of it to the ones she loved, if that would erase the terrible doom hanging over her child.

But again the thought of Mary Agnes came. Would Grey's suicide appease her? No. She still would have Wistart to wreak her malevolence upon. Even dead, Grey still would be dragged through the newspapers as Wistart's wench, his slut. And even with Grey dead, her daughter still would be branded as illegitimate in countless minds, too ready to believe what they wished to believe, too ready to discount any denial by the man accused of fathering her on the cynical grounds that he was swearing only to protect her.

No, death would not help. Were only she herself concerned, Grey might have been greatly tempted: but if Betty Jean ever needed her before, she needed her infinitely more now. Death was no solution. Grey must live on and try to think what to do.

They could only flee: she and her mother and Betty Jean, seeking someplace so remote, so hidden, that perhaps the malice of the woman who hated them could not seek them out there. But where was such a place? And if they found it, how could they live once they reached it?

Mary Agnes held every weapon, all the keys. Only Mary Agnes could decide. Only one remote and impossible solution existed: if something happened to Mary Agnes, she became sick or some other thing occurred to her, they might be saved.

But nothing would happen to Mary Agnes. She was too hard, too secure, too strong to be deflected.

Only one expedient did not suggest itself to Grey as she lay on her bed that long night, sleepless, half driven out of her sanity by anguish and terror.

Murder. Mary Agnes' death might solve many things.

But the idea of murder, which might have suggested itself to another in her desperate straits, never suggested itself to Grey. Of even the thought of taking any life, save only her own, she was incapable.

Twenty-seven

When the bus halted at the First National Bank corner at eight o'clock that morning, an elderly man wearing a long overcoat and rubbers descended, assisted a woman down the steps, and lifted his hat to her as they separated.

The raising of the hat revealed a fine head, an impressive head in its way, as a matter of fact, a rather well-known head. It belonged to Judge Thomas Jefferson Pollock, who had for years ornamented the bench of the federal district court before retiring to private law practice mingled with congenial dabbling in politics. Among his eccentricities was the fact that he had his white curly mane of hair cut seldom, and his profuse gray mustache almost never, so that it bristled wildly, somewhat in the manner made familiar by the celebrated Dr. Albert Schweitzer.

The judge preferred riding the bus to his office, since he did not like to drive a car, especially in winter; and also because it sometimes gave him an opportunity for interesting conversation with a seat companion. On this morning he had more than a usual opportunity for conversation, at least the listening part of it, for his seat companion was Mrs. Hettie Hedcomb, the saleslady at Grey Rutledge, Sportswear. She kept up an uninterrupted flow of words, and the judge listened encouragingly. He believed in talk.

"It's a theory of mine that men and women are sometimes destroyed by untalked talk," he said once. "They've got to have a listener—a creative listener who stimulates them—or they gradually fill up with unexpressed emotion until they explode."

Judge Pollock was a very creative listener and Mrs. Hedcomb was in no danger of exploding from untalked talk, at least this morning. She was a widow, and she had known the judge since his wife died ten years ago; and she took a personal interest in his affairs, as she took an interest in the affairs of everyone else she knew; and she considered it a shame that he had never remarried. He had his maiden sister, of course, Miss Janet, sixty-five years old, to keep house for him; and Mrs.

Hedcomb expressed herself as being devoted to dear Miss Janet. But a man should have a wife, she always said, and even at seventy it was not too late. There were plenty of women, not exactly old but mature enough to be sensible, who would make wonderful wives for the judge.

Mrs. Hedcomb did not mention herself as a candidate; but after all— she bridled inwardly—she was rather well preserved, she thought, and if it came to that, she believed the judge could look much farther than his present seat companion and do worse.

This she kept to herself; but she harped on the subject of marriage, and by the time they reached the downtown district she was on the subject of her employer, Grey Rutledge.

"Why doesn't *she* remarry, dear lamb?" Mrs. Hedcomb said. "She's young, and *such* a lovely person. And there's plenty who'd like to get her, if she'd just give them any encouragement."

Judge Pollock knew Grey Rutledge, had known her for a considerable number of years, in fact; they were friends of long standing, going back to his acquaintance with her father, the late Barnaby Norcross, and he agreed in his own mind quite heartily that she was all Mrs. Hedcomb said of her. The question Mrs. Hedcomb asked sometimes had puzzled him also.

"She has her business, and her mother, and her little girl," he ventured.

"What's that got to do with it? She could have them and still be married. A woman ought to have a husband, I always say—at least a young woman should."

"Maybe she's still in love with the memory of her dead husband," the judge suggested mildly.

"Stuff! A woman can get over any man. Grey's no more than a girl. Her life's before her. Besides, what did Jed Rutledge ever do for her, except leave her with a baby to provide for and all those debts? Everything she's ever accomplished she did on her own."

The judge considered there was a good deal of truth in these statements, but he did not commit himself.

"No, there's some other reason," Mrs. Hedcomb said. "I wonder sometimes if she's in love with somebody, and for some cause they can't get married. Understand me, nothing improper. That could never happen with Grey. But she just isn't herself these days. Why, just before she went to Chicago—she got back last night—she seemed as if her mind was in the faraway. It wouldn't surprise me if she's heading for a nervous breakdown. Some man ought to come along and just carry her away in spite of herself——"

"I believe this is our corner," said the judge with some relief.

As he bade her good morning, before turning toward the bank building in which he had his offices, he noticed a car passing. At the wheel he recognized Wistart Wedge, of the *Clarion.* Wistart glanced toward him but did not seem to see him. Judge Pollock, for his part, did not nod or speak. There was a long-standing feud between Wedge's paper and himself, and the judge believed in living up to public opinion on how he should behave under such circumstances.

In Jericho it was generally agreed that Judge Tom Pollock was the cleverest lawyer in town: some said the crookedest—it depended entirely on which side you were on. The *Clarion* avowedly was his foe, partly because he was the leading Democrat in the city while the *Clarion* was Republican; partly because of a long history of disagreements going back to the days of prohibition, which the *Clarion* upheld, but with which the judge was not in sympathy; partly because of a ruling the judge had made when he was on the bench in a libel suit against the *Clarion*—newspapers forget political foes slowly, but their memories are even longer for those who cause them to lose money. But these offenses were compounded by the greatest of all: Judge Pollock, on occasion, had acted as attorney for the hated *Morning Sentinel;* it was he, indeed, who presented to Wistart Wedge the proposal from the people he represented, to buy the *Clarion.*

Like most newspapers, the *Clarion* was prodigal of descriptive adjectives for its enemies, but it had been especially generous over the years in this respect toward the judge. "Crook," "boodler," "jackleg" and "ward heeler" were a few of the mildest epithets. One inspired editorial writer had described him as "debauched and whiskey-poisoned," which was considered good by Jericho connoisseurs of newspaper phraseology. But those with a taste for such wares always held that the phrase "gasconading reptile," as applied to Judge Pollock during a campaign, was the peak of all these delicacies of verbiage: a conviction in which, it must be said, the judge himself, who had no mean taste for words, rather agreed.

People in general were sure that the slurs and epithets of the *Clarion* had made him a deadly enemy not only of the newspaper, but of the entire Wedge family. Yet it is an interesting commentary on the judge that he inwardly felt no very bitter resentments against either the newspaper or its owners, being of a philosophic turn of mind and holding the opinion that a man engaged in politics should cultivate a very thick hide or else withdraw from the game.

He took an elevator to the fourth floor and entered his office, greeting with his usual old-fashioned courtliness Miss Cardwell, a rather formidable female of indeterminate age, who had been his secretary for many years. Miss Cardwell was faithful and efficient, though she disapproved of some things about her employer: the manner in which he now tossed his hat on a hook in the coat cabinet, hung his coat loosely by the collar, and threw his rubbers in a slovenly heap, for example. As soon as the judge went into his office, she would arrange these things more neatly, and she thought rather grimly that she could never change him: it was too late to teach an old dog new tricks, she supposed.

For the present she said, "There's somebody waiting to see you, Judge."

"Who is it?" he asked.

"Mrs. Rutledge. Since she's a friend of yours, I told her to have a seat in your office."

"Well, well," he said, smiling, for he enjoyed the prospect of talking with Grey, whom he considered one of the bright spots in a somewhat imperfect world. "Strangely enough, I was just talking about Mrs. Rutledge with a mutual friend on the way down. Thank you, Miss Cardwell."

The smile was still on his face when he entered his inner office. Grey was sitting by a window, gazing out with a singularly bleak expression. She rose quickly to her feet.

"Judge——" she said. "Oh, Judge——"

His smile faded. In her he recognized distress.

"Sit down, my dear," he said, closing the door. He went to his desk, seated himself, and for a moment his shrewd old eyes studied her face.

"What can I do for you?" he said presently.

"I don't know," she said rather wildly. "I don't know—if you—if anyone can do anything——" She broke off, almost with a sob.

"Is it as bad as that?" he asked. "Suppose you tell me."

His kindly voice seemed to reassure her. For a moment she hesitated as if trying to think how best to describe her situation to him.

"Well—to begin with—Mrs. Wistart Wedge is going to file a divorce suit against her husband," she said at last.

"Ah?" The judge was surprised. Then he remarked to himself how distraught Wistart's face had looked just a few minutes ago when he drove past on the street.

"But—the dreadful part of it—is this: she's going to name *me* as co-respondent!" she cried.

Now he was thoroughly astonished. *"You?"*

Grey nodded.

"But this is impossible!" he exclaimed.

Wearily she shook her head. "No, it isn't."

He stared at her unbelieving. "You—and Wistart?"

Almost tonelessly she said, "His wife has just learned the truth."

For a time he sat quite still, digesting this news. Then he said gently, "Tell me how this thing happened, Grey."

"It was loneliness, I guess," she said. "Loneliness, and the need for someone to turn to for—understanding and sympathy—and—and—love —both of us."

He nodded.

"It began in friendship," she went on. "It developed—into something else. I won't go into details. She knows about it, that's all."

"How much does she know?"

"Everything, I suppose. He—Wistart—confessed it to her when she showed him the proof she had."

"What proof?"

"Some—documents."

The judge looked grave. To the legal mind documents are more deadly than artillery.

"What's Wistart going to do?"

"What can he do? He asked me to marry him when—when this thing —is over."

"Will you?"

"No! Oh, I don't know! How can I know? I don't think I can ever do anything that's normal and happy again. I want to crawl in a hole where nobody will ever see me——"

"You can't do that, my dear."

"It's not myself I'm thinking about, Judge! It's—it's my little girl— she's going to be dragged in this—what it will do to her!"

"She? How?"

"Mary Agnes has threatened to charge in her complaint that Betty Jean is—is Wistart's illegitimate child—and it's a lie, you know it's a lie, Judge!"

"Of course I do. When will Mrs. Wedge file?"

"I don't know. That's the worst part of it—the suspense. It may happen any minute—it may delay for some time—trying to keep myself ready to face it is almost—more—than I—can stand——"

The judge was moved with profound concern and pity for Grey, who seemed so near the breaking point.

"I know I—did the wrong thing," she half sobbed. "But isn't there *something* I can do—you can do for me——?"

The appeal touched him, but he slowly shook his head.

"Under the law—nothing," he said. "If what you have told me is true, Mrs. Wedge has all the weapons in her hands. She has also every advantage of the initiative. She can file any allegations she wants to make in her petition, and the courts are notoriously inclined to believe the story of the 'wronged' wife, however much she is herself actually to blame. Everything depends on her whim—and I fear, from what I know of her, that I can't extend to you much hope of forbearance. Mrs. Wedge is a determined and unyielding sort of woman. We can only wait and see what kind of action she will take."

"Then—there's no hope for me——?"

Her voice was faint and piteous, as if she prayed; and praying, knew the prayer was useless.

"I'll do everything—everything possible, my dear," he said.

2

"It's Mrs. Simon Bolivar Butford, ma'am," said Suey as he brought Mary Agnes the telephone extension.

"What can she want?" Mary Agnes said aloud but to herself. She was so bitterly preoccupied with affairs this morning that she had no wish for a long conversation with the garrulous old woman.

"I wouldn't venture to surmise, ma'am," said Suey, who did not realize that the question was not really addressed to him.

"Very well, Suey. Thank you." She took the telephone receiver and spoke into it. "Mrs. Butford? This is Mary Agnes Wedge."

"Well! Mrs. Wedge!" said the voice over the wire, speaking in the old lady's usual pompous manner. "I've got a little piece of news that I thought might interest you and the rest of the Art Association. I'm taking the trouble to call all the members of the board of directresses."

"Really?" Mary Agnes was completely uninterested in view of her own much greater concerns. But Mrs. Butford's next words riveted her full attention.

"Mr. de Lacey is gone."

"Gone? Gone where?"

"I regret to say this, but we have been nurturing a snake in our bosom, Mrs. Wedge. The man is a moral leper."

"In what way?" Mary Agnes felt the first beginnings of apprehension.

"He has made a practice, while my guest, of having indecent women in my house, carrying on with them—*naked,* if you will believe me!"

The word "naked" was uttered with horror which would have been almost laughable had not the situation been so serious.

"How do you know this?" Mary Agnes asked.

"You remember the story in the paper about the arrest of that man who killed his wife? It said that the murdered woman had been *here,* to be painted in the nude by Mr. de Lacey—and I don't know what else——"

"He left because of that?"

"He left because I ordered him out of my house!"

"And—and did he—take those—those paintings—the ones he made of the naked women you mentioned?"

"No. I anticipated him. I went to the studio he had fixed up for that shocking and disgusting purpose, and I found the paintings, secreted, mind you, in the Korean money chest that belonged to my dear dead husband, Mr. Butford himself! There were at least twenty of them— and, oh, Mrs. Wedge—they were the most shameless, indecent, obscene things I ever rested my eyes on! Why, it almost took my breath away!"

"And then?" Mary Agnes felt that her own breath was almost taken away.

"I burned them. I put them in the furnace with my own hands. And when *he* returned, I was waiting for him. He did not spend another night under my roof, I can assure you of that! He's gone—back to Hollywood—that Sodom and Gomorrah!—where he belongs. Driving, so the servants tell me. What a relief it is to me! There's no telling what a man like that might do——"

"But those pictures—did you see them?"

"Every one of them, Mrs. Wedge."

"And did they—was there one——?"

"I have no wish to discuss them further, Mrs. Wedge."

"I mean did anything—did something strike you——?"

"They are too revolting to dwell upon farther."

Mary Agnes hung up the receiver with a distant look in her eyes. Erskine de Lacey—gone. And because of that story . . .

She remembered Mr. Dorn's words, *You can never get away from blackmail, it will never stop, until you face it and kill it . . .*

And she had faced it, or rather Mr. Dorn and the *Clarion* had: because he refused to deny the truth, because of that integrity he seemed to consider so important. Mr. Dorn was right, he had strength and thinking power, and she felt confident in him. She knew what she was going to do with him. Managing editor at once, later maybe general manager. He would be the instrument through which she would operate the *Clarion*.

She felt relieved and grateful to him, with the threat lifted from her which Erskine had held over her. Now she was free to do as she wished. That picture was gone—up in flames in Mrs. Butford's furnace. And nobody had seen it——

Unless Mrs. Butford had seen it! *Mrs. Butford!*

Indecent, shameless, obscene—Mrs. Butford's words. And Mrs. Butford said she had seen every painting with her own eyes. Had she recognized that one of Mary Agnes, her white nude body, her face even to the greenish hue of her eyes? Or in her myopia did she only see it as another nude and consign it to the flames without really marking who it was?

Mrs. Butford grimly had said, "I have no wish to discuss them farther."

But if she had recognized Mary Agnes, how long would she wish not to discuss it?

How long before she would begin to tell everyone that she had seen Mary Agnes Wedge naked, shameless, indecent, painted on a canvas by a man who was a "moral leper"?

It was a question that was destined to cause Mary Agnes anxiety

many times thereafter. A question that raised itself like a cloud whenever she saw Mrs. Butford in the future. Behind that dead-white, aged
face, what ideas lay? What was the old woman thinking, when would
she speak? Perhaps not until Mrs. Butford's death would that question
be answered, perhaps before . . . It was one thing with which Mary
Agnes Wedge would have to live, like the sword hanging by a hair
continually over the head of the fabled Damocles.

3

That afternoon Judge Pollock glanced up from the brief he was studying as his office door opened. It was Miss Cardwell.

"Judge Pollock—Mrs. Wedge is here to see you," she said.

The judge rose in haste occasioned by surprise. If anyone had suggested that this particular visitor would come to him today, he would
have been unbelieving.

"Please tell her to come in," he said.

A moment later Mary Agnes entered and closed the door behind her.

"Mrs. Wedge!" he exclaimed. "I'm highly flattered by a visit from
you to this small, dusty old den of mine. May I be of some service to
you?"

She took a chair and began to peel the gloves from her hands, throwing her mink coat back off her shoulders.

"Yes, Judge Pollock," she said, giving him a measuring glance as if
estimating him. "I want to retain you in a case I am going to bring into
court."

"And this case?" But already he knew.

"A divorce suit against my husband."

A singular expression crossed the old man's features. "May I ask why
you seek *my* services in this matter?"

"Because I've been told you are the best lawyer in Jericho. And because I'm going to make this divorce one that will be talked about all
over the United States. I have some very interesting bits of information,
Judge. Knowing your personal feelings toward Mr. Wedge, I think it
will be a case you may take considerable pleasure in."

"Why so, Mrs. Wedge?"

"You have reason to hate him, haven't you? Well, so do I. Please take
my word for it, Judge Pollock, I'm prepared to give you enough am-
munition so that you can pay back all those long arrears of debt you owe

Wistart Wedge and the *Clarion* for the abuse they've dealt out to you."

His deeply lined face was intent with thought. Strict legal ethics demanded that he should here and now tell her that he was on the other side in her case, that he already had been informed of the nature of it and promised to do all he could for the informant. Judge Pollock believed strongly in the ethics of his profession, and observed them. But there were very strong human considerations here also, and now, for perhaps the first time in his life, he did something a little unethical, hoping by doing so that he might achieve some good, in what manner he did not exactly know.

So he said, "Perhaps you'll tell me a little more about it."

"Very willingly," she replied. "To make it brief, I've caught my husband in adultery. Not one episode, let me add, but an affair that's gone a long way back. He confessed the whole thing to me. The woman's name is Grey Rutledge, and she has been my husband's kept mistress for years. Wistart Wedge can never live in Jericho again when I get through with him. Nor can that woman, either. My fee to you will be liberal, just name it. I want you to draw up my petition, putting into it all the accusations I intend to make—every single one of them." She glanced at him with a sparkle of added malice. "There's a possibility that her child may be his—that they were lovers even before her late husband's death. I may not be able to prove that, but at least I can put it in the complaint, and I will!"

"I see," the judge said. He had in his legal life considerable experience with the sometimes rather appalling spleen which women display in matters affecting their personal domestic lives, an exaggerated, sometimes almost irrational venom, because it touches their deepest instincts, which they hardly understand themselves. But this was an especially virulent case, and he wondered how he could possibly temper such fury.

"You came to me because you feel I am your husband's greatest enemy?" he said.

"Exactly."

Mary Agnes studied him. For some reason the judge did not at once take fire as she had expected. He sat for a time pondering, his fingers pyramided in front of his face, pursing his lips under the wildly bristling mustache as if he were silently whistling some faraway tune. His heavy black brows, which contrasted so strongly with his white hair, drew down in concentration and his eyes seemed remote, viewing nothing, almost as if they saw backward into his mind.

"Have you considered all the effects such procedure as you propose might have?"

"I think so."

"I'm not quite so sure." He shot a piercing glance at her. "This would affect many more people than your husband and yourself, or even Mrs. Rutledge."

"I see no reason why any of that should concern me."

He made no reply for a time and she felt impatient at his apparent reluctance. After a time he cleared his throat.

"Forgive me if I seem to proceed slowly in this matter," he said, "but the implications are of such gravity that I must stop and think. First, my dear lady, let me say that if what you say is true, you have every right to a divorce. Yet let me beg you to consider for a moment the matter from a long view. There is no question that you can punish your husband very bitterly, and also his—the woman who is involved. But has it occurred to you that you also might suffer?"

"In what way?" she demanded.

"No action is ever possible," he said, "without its compensating reaction. If I have learned anything in my seventy years of existence on this interesting but somewhat contradictory sphere, it is this: nobody can absolutely separate himself from the consequences of disaster which he institutes. It is as if an arsonist set fire to a house and was himself seared by the falling embers. You can bring disgrace and ruin on the two people against whom your present indignation is directed, but you will not yourself get off scot-free. You will find that in spite of any art put into this petition and the trial to follow, sympathy will not be entirely undivided. You will become the subject of much and severe criticism. There may be accusations made against you by people whom you least suspect. One cannot use the tarbrush without getting tarred. If this case should be long drawn out in the courts, you may well become a sort of byword: the dignity and reputation which you now enjoy, and which I am sure you deserve, will in very large measure be smirched. You will not come out of it the same woman you went in, Mrs. Wedge."

"Are you trying to tell me," she asked, "that you don't want to take this case?"

"No, not exactly. I'm merely suggesting some possibilities that might be involved, and perhaps a slightly different course of action."

Her head reared back angrily. "Just what are you preparing to suggest?"

"That you get your divorce, if you must, but get it quietly. Even better, I offer the thought that a reconciliation would be preferable to either alternative we have discussed. I urge you to consider it. You and your husband represent great interests, and a city like Jericho would be profoundly shaken by something so violently disruptive as this which you plan. Let me ask you: if Wistart will agree to give up any further contact with Mrs. Rutledge, would you take him back?"

She gave an icy little laugh. "I'd see him in hell first!"

She rose, pulled her mink about her, and began drawing on her gloves once more. "I'd hoped to find in you an ally, Judge Pollock," she said. "Your attitude astonishes me, but let me assure you of this: if you don't want to take the case, I'll find a lawyer who will—and I'm not going to make it easy either on my husband or that woman!"

The judge raised a hand. "Please, don't be hasty. It's a lawyer's duty to look at all sides of a situation."

His mind was filled with wonder at the strangeness of the circumstances. He remembered Grey's stricken face, her pleading and tears, not so much for herself as for her child. For a long time he had known her, had been a guest at her home not infrequently, had admired her beauty and the freshness of her mind. Never had it occurred to him that she could possibly conduct a lawless love affair such as the woman standing before him had outlined. Yet Grey herself had confessed it to him this very morning and begged his help.

Mary Agnes lifted her chin. "Will you take it or won't you?"

A remote possibility suggested itself to him. "On one provision," he said.

"And what's that?"

"That we have Wistart Wedge here in my office so that I can talk to the both of you together."

For a moment she stared at him. Then she nodded. "I'll agree to that. I've got a few more things to say to him, anyway. He's probably at his office now. Telephone him."

4

In his life Wistart had known no torment that approached this. When he told Grey of the catastrophe he had brought upon her, he had seen her seem to curl up like a feather seared by flame, and he could not forget it.

He still was not entirely clear as to how his wife had obtained the information on which she based her accusation: but she had seemed so sure, so invincibly armed with every fact, that he felt there was no recourse but to make a clean breast of it.

The real extent of her rancor had not been grasped by him until she stated it: and then it was stunning. He was no psychologist and therefore he could not reason that Mary Agnes' bitterness was occasioned by the wound to her pride. She did not want him, but she would not let any other woman have him. And she had the deadly female instinct, enhanced, to hurt as deeply as she could, and if possible destroy, a rival of her own sex.

He did not eat lunch that day, having no appetite and feeling as if his emotions had tied his stomach in a knot, giving him the sensation of indigestion. Neither did he do any work. Late in the afternoon he was sitting where he had been almost all day, dazed, unable to think, almost unable to move. He wished he could talk with Grey, but he knew she would not want to see him under these circumstances, and that it would be unwise to be in her company just now even if she did agree to it.

As for his own fate, he found that he did not care much what happened. He was ruined: Mary Agnes had majority control of his newspaper already, and she would take the rest and drive him out of town as well. But he seemed to have acquired something of the mental anesthesia which comes to some men condemned to death when they know the hour of their execution is approaching, and which enables them to mount the gallows steps almost as if they welcomed the conclusion of their fears and worries.

While he sat in this mood of almost unthinking unhappiness, his telephone rang.

He was surprised when he answered, for it was Judge Pollock, and he had not spoken to the judge in years except on the most necessary business.

"I'd like to see you," said the judge. "Could you come to my office? It's very important."

All at once Wistart knew why. "Is it my wife?" he asked.

"Yes, it is."

"She's asked you to handle the divorce?"

"She has. But she has just agreed to a conference with you and myself before she takes any steps."

A conference? What kind of a conference, and for what purpose?

Wistart wondered if it could possibly be that Mary Agnes was relenting somewhat. But he could not believe that.

With a sensation of being impelled, almost without any will of his own, he replied that he would be over at once.

5

As a man braces himself for a plunge in icy water, Wistart braced himself when he entered Judge Pollock's inner office.

They sat there, the two of them: Mary Agnes' hard uncompromising face; the judge's expressionless wrinkled mask. In them he felt he was confronting his two most deadly enemies, and desperate hopelessness swept over him like a dizziness.

"Sit down, Wistart," he heard the old man say.

He almost groped for a seat across the room from his wife and sank into it.

Silence held sway in the room until it seemed to Wistart to become almost a substance, pressing against him until he felt as if he were suffocating, while the two of them studied him.

Unable any longer to bear it, he spoke first.

"You sent for me, Judge?"

"Yes. I wanted to talk to you. As you know, Mrs. Wedge is contemplating a suit for divorce."

Wistart nodded.

"Let me ask this question," the judge went on. "Are you willing to give up any contact with—with the woman in question—should this divorce be postponed, halted, or the terms of the action changed to allegations less drastic?"

Wistart raised his head, trying to comprehend. But before he could even begin to frame a reply, Mary Agnes was on her feet, her eyes blazing.

"What are you trying to do?" She turned furiously to Judge Pollock. "You said you wanted to talk to us! Did I give you any authority to propose terms to him?"

The old man was unruffled. "I beg of you, Mrs. Wedge—a lawyer always seeks to explore conceivable possibilities in preparing any case."

"Well, *that's* no conceivable possibility!" she cried. "If he gave her up, or gave a hundred of them up, he's going to sweat!"

She turned on her husband. "Do you hear that, Wistart? You're going to sweat—sweat blood, my friend—sweat till you're down on all fours, howling for mercy! You and that—that *thing!*"

Watching the angry scene, unable to intervene and seeing his hopes of softening Mary Agnes' fury lost, Judge Pollock noticed that a sickly pallor had come over Wistart's face, as if her scorn and spite had driven the blood from it.

All at once she gave a laugh, strident and mirthless.

"Do you know what's funny?" she said. "Well, I'll tell you what it is! The joke's on you, Wistart Wedge—the ever living joke! I've got you—got you where you can't wiggle. I've got all the evidence I need, and more. *Everything* I want, to do *anything* I want. And do you know where I got it? From *you!*"

He stared at her, stupefied, still with that pallor on his face.

"From you—*you!*" She laughed again. "Here's the little secret, Wistart. I didn't have a thing on you, *not one damned thing!* A suspicion, maybe, but that's all. Nothing I could prove. But when I accused you, I *knew* you'd blunder it all out! And that's just what you did!"

He half rose from his chair, his eyes starting.

"You mean you *didn't* know—that I——?"

He sank back in his chair, his head hanging on his chest.

"That's exactly what I mean!" She laughed cruelly once more. "You convicted yourself—and *her*—out of your own big fat mouth——"

All at once she stopped. Her expression changed from triumph to question.

"What's the matter with him?" she asked.

"Why—I believe he's ill," she heard the judge say.

She stood rooted. Judge Pollock half rose at his desk.

As he did so, Wistart collapsed off his chair to the floor.

Mary Agnes uttered a little scream.

"He's—look—look at him!" she cried. "Oh, do something—*do* something——"

Wistart, lying on his back, gasped horribly, and for a moment that seemed dreadful his heels hammered the floor.

Then all movement ceased.

Judge Pollock was kneeling by the prostrate figure, lifting Wistart's head, feeling his pulse.

Then he lowered the head again and looked up at Mary Agnes.

"Mrs. Wedge," he said, "I'm afraid—this poor man is dead."

Twenty-eight

I

Death, which invests with dignity those whom it claims, provided Wistart Wedge at last with that public respect which he never had received during his lifetime. The news of it was of state-wide, even national interest, since he was the publisher of a rather well-known newspaper and a member of a family also well known.

The papers reported that the widow, Mrs. Mary Agnes Wedge, was at her home under the care of a family friend and physician, Dr. Murray Clifton, who prescribed complete rest for her and absolutely forbade any newspaper interviews. She was, he said, under sedation and suffering from shock.

Denied access to Mrs. Wedge, the reporters sought Judge Pollock, who gave a guarded statement. The Wedges were, at the time of Mr. Wedge's sudden and tragic death, discussing with him details of a private nature, he said, concerning a contemplated reorganization of their business and financial interests, on which he had been asked to give his legal services.

In general, people considered that while Wistart's death was sad, it was hardly surprising. The death certificate, signed by Dr. Clifton, gave the cause as a coronary occlusion, and it was remembered that both parents of the dead publisher had died of heart ailments, which indicated a probable hereditary weakness in him.

Wistart Wedge's funeral at St. Albans Church was largely attended and there were many floral offerings. Most imposing of these was a standpiece, perhaps a little showy and overdone as well as quite expensive, in which a cross of white gardenias was superimposed on a heart of pink carnations, with the word *Rest*. It came from the brothers Eddie and Tony Ender, of the *Morning Sentinel*, who had learned how to pay proper tribute to a dead rival in the days of the gangster funerals in Chicago.

A smaller but far more graceful remembrance was a simple spray of rosebuds, the color of the heart's blood. They were sent without a name: but of the tears shed for Wistart, the most sincere were shed by Grey Rutledge. Sitting far back in the nave of the church that afternoon, and listening to the solemn intonation of the Order for the Burial of the Dead, she saw that someone, perhaps inadvertently, had draped those flowers on the casket itself, where they would go down with it into the grave. And she wondered wistfully if this would please Wistart, if he knew.

So they laid poor Wistart Wedge to rest, in security and honor at last, in the burial plot where his father and mother had gone before him. And thereafter, as is the way of the world, he was forgotten quite rapidly by almost everyone who knew him; for the world must look forward, not back, and life rather than death is its continuous concern.

And yet, though he may have been forgotten by all but a few, Wistart perhaps in all his life never achieved anything as important as in his death.

2

There was Mary Agnes. The morning following Wistart's death she sat alone in her bedroom. She was dressed but she had not yet gone downstairs and her breakfast tray had been taken away with the food almost untouched.

Some of her friends had been over: Gilda Clifton with sympathy, and Bess Attwater with curiosity. She found the sympathy almost as trying as the curiosity, and sent them away.

She could not get the events of the preceding afternoon out of her mind. As if they were being re-enacted before her eyes over and over, she saw again Wistart's startling collapse; Dr. Clifton's arrival in Judge Pollock's office, his quick concern and sorrow as he turned to her after the examination; the ambulance attendants coming in with the stretcher, pushing their way through the crowd of curious already gathered in the hall outside the half-open door.

With fascination almost hypnotic, mingled with horror, she watched them place the still form of her husband on the stretcher. As they drew the sheet over the body, she caught a last glimpse of Wistart's face, and that was what shattered her glassy poise. It was not the face she knew, the pink, good-humored face she often had derided but to which she was accustomed: it was a different face, and it seemed to be molded out of some cold gray putty.

In that moment Mary Agnes felt suddenly like a murderess; she was sure her cruel taunts had killed him. And shaken by the dread and terror of it, and by her own stabbing guilt, she wept so hysterically that Dr. Clifton took her home in his own car and remained with her until the sedative he gave her put her into a drugged, almost deathly sleep.

This morning she was still weary and drawn; and the feeling of guilt was still with her. Belatedly though it came, she did have a conscience, and she would have given anything to recall the past and make some restitution. But that was impossible now, it was too late, what was done was done and from that was no appeal.

While she sat in this mood of depression, Clara, her maid, came up with word that a gentleman was downstairs wishing to speak with her.

"I'm not to see anyone!" Mary Agnes exclaimed. And then, "Who is it?"

"Jedge Pollock, ma'am."

Mary Agnes hesitated, then rose. "Tell him I'll be right down."

When she descended she found the judge waiting somewhat apologetically in the living room.

"I didn't wish to intrude on you at this time," he said, "but—there are certain threads left untied. I thought we should talk as soon as possible."

"Very well, come in here." She led him into the library and seated herself by the oriel window.

He took a chair and for a moment regarded her as if measuring her; and he thought that he would need all his wisdom and tact, perhaps, in what he sought to accomplish now.

"May I ask," he said presently, "if you have told anybody about the—ah—circumstances leading up to the tragic occurrence in my office yesterday?"

"No. Not yet."

"Not even your doctor?"

"Dr. Clifton didn't question me. He was only interested in quieting me."

Judge Pollock nodded his white head. "Had you discussed your divorce plan with anybody prior to coming to me?" he asked.

"Only—Wistart."

He seemed relieved. "That is most fortunate. Then only two persons —you and I—know what happened in my office. And only three, the two of us and Mrs. Rutledge, know the occasion for the conference. As a lawyer I strongly advise you to tell nobody about it. For you it may be of the utmost importance that no breath of the quarrel between you and Wistart, and the imminence of the divorce, ever gets out."

"What about——?" She hesitated. *That woman?*

"Of the whole world, she would be the very last to reveal this secret."

For a moment the old Mary Agnes was back, and she raised her head, her nostrils flaring angrily. "I haven't forgiven her!"

He smiled slightly. "Is it, after all, so very important?"

"What do you mean?"

"Pride was hurt. Wasn't that all? Pride cannot be touched now— unless you wish to have it so."

Her head bent down and the anger faded. She was realizing how helpless she was in respect to the vengeance she once had craved so fiercely. It was as if Wistart had died purposely to cheat her of it. And yet there was something in what the judge was saying . . . only her vanity had been touched, and nobody knew. Pride that is not publicly affronted can be swallowed; perhaps even in the end forgotten.

"You have suddenly inherited a great responsibility and a great prospect: they make these petty feelings trivial. Be a great woman, Mrs. Wedge."

"In what way?"

"You combine in your own person the destiny not only of a vast commercial enterprise, your store, but also of a mighty molder of public opinion, your newspaper. What are you going to do with them?"

"I really haven't—had time to think."

"I know somewhat of your affairs," he went on, "perhaps more than you realize. Because of the negotiations for the purchase of the paper I was called upon to conduct, I know, for example, the financial condition of the *Clarion*. I know that Wistart obtained one hundred thousand dollars to pay his most pressing obligations, the newsprint bills, and it is no secret that the money came from you. This can only mean that you placed an obligation on Cox's, Incorporated. The *Clarion* is still heavily involved and it will require wisdom and hard work to bring it back to a solvent position. And you must do it, or else seriously impair your store property."

He paused and regarded her shrewdly. "There is one alternative. What if the offer to purchase the *Clarion* is still open?"

She flared. "The *Clarion* is not for sale!"

The judge smiled in sincere admiration. "I applaud you! I thought you would say that. And I predict freely you will succeed if you act wisely. That is why I counseled you to keep this purely personal matter of the estrangement and its outcome to yourself. You can depend on it that I will say nothing of it to anyone. Mrs. Wedge, I know you to be a woman of more than ordinary intelligence, and I know therefore that when you have given the matter some thought you will reach conclusions that will make you very glad that all this is between ourselves."

Mary Agnes was not looking at him. Her eyes were remote, gazing out of the window, seeing nothing. For the first time she envisaged what was before her. A life of work where she had been idle; wide horizons where hers had been narrow; interest, responsibility, dangers, and achievement where she had been occupied with petty matters and boredom. Her ambition rose, she accepted the challenge, welcomed it, was ready for it.

The judge watched her face and it was as if he could read the thoughts flashing through her mind.

"The *Clarion* will need every asset it can muster, and the opinion of its community is one of the most important," he said. "Such opinion is a delicate thing, easily lost and won with difficulty. Sympathy is a mighty factor, and the public has a heart, if sometimes it appears to have no head. A brave woman carrying on the work her dead husband left in her hands has already gone far toward winning the support of the people who admire courage and devotion."

She faced him and gazed directly into his eyes with almost a flame-lit intensity; and he felt within himself that this woman had been wasted, she had imagination, great force of projection, resolution which had been choked until it became ingrown, explaining the bitterness of her sometimes violent emotions and acts. Perhaps now these qualities—which might have made her fine, but instead had only made her hateful—would have opportunity to develop in the right direction and achieve notable things.

"I see now," she said, "how the purely personal matter, while perhaps it may not be forgotten entirely, need never be spoken of again."

"In that case you will have the most indispensable of all assets—the goodwill of the people."

He rose to take his departure.

"Dear lady," he said with his peculiar stately charm, "command me if I can ever assist you. And let me say this to you: I have never been the enemy of the *Clarion* that you and some others suppose. I do not deny that the *Clarion* takes out hard after those it condemns—as I have reason to know with many a reminiscent twinge." He smiled half ruefully. "But I respect and hold no grudge against a newspaper that fights hard against a man who has been its opponent politically. In fact, I'm rather fond of the old *Clarion* and proud of it. And I see the beginning of a new existence for it, because I am assured you have plans for it; and also that you have what it has needed, the basic judgment and the basic courage to restore its greatness."

He was gone, and she sat for a while alone, thinking. Perhaps what the judge had said was flattery, and in her present mood of humility Mary Agnes could think of it in that manner. But on one thing she was determined: she was going to fight for the *Clarion* with everything in her and every resource she had. And if she did not perhaps herself have exactly all the knowledge and courage the judge ascribed to her, she believed she knew someone who did have them.

3

And there was Grey Rutledge. She learned of Wistart's death at her home, where she had hidden herself on a plea of slight illness, dreading the ordeal even of showing herself, not knowing when the blow would fall.

Betty Jean was not yet home from school and Mrs. Norcross, who felt her daughter was suffering some emotional distress but wisely did not seek to probe into it, was downstairs sewing and listening to the radio. It was she who called suddenly to Grey, who was upstairs in her room.

When Grey came to the head of the staircase, her mother was standing in the hall below, her sewing in her hands.

"Grey—Mr. Wedge is dead!" she cried. "It just came over the radio!"

So the news was broken to Grey, who listened numbly while Mrs. Norcross gave such details as the broadcast had contained. A heart attack. In some lawyer's office. His wife present when it happened.

Mrs. Norcross added, with ready sympathy, that it must have been very hard on Mrs. Wedge, poor thing, to be a witness to the tragedy.

"Oh—Mother——" Grey said, and her mother was surprised at the emotion in her voice.

"You knew him, didn't you?" Mrs. Norcross said.

"Oh yes, I knew him!" Grey's eyes filled suddenly with tears. "I knew him, Mother—he was a—a good man—a fine, gentle, kind man——"

She fled to her room and shut the door.

Wistart was dead. It seemed incredible, and she found it difficult to believe. When she did believe, sorrow and pity flooded over her still more intensely. Poor Wistart. Poor, dear man. So unhappy, so alone. And he had been good to her . . . loved her.

She wept for him, lying face down on her bed.

But after a time she bethought herself that she could not afford this grief: one of the inexorable conditions of her relationship with Wistart was that she could never permit herself the luxury of expressing openly the affection and sorrow she felt for him. So she composed herself, bathed her face, and at last went downstairs, feeling emptied of emotion and with a void in her life: left by the man who had gone out of it, and who had meant so much to her in concern, in conflict of emotions and thinking, and also happiness too at times . . . she must remember that.

Next day she remained home, only telephoning Mrs. Hedcomb at the store to see how things were going, and to explain that she still was suffering from her slight indisposition.

The third day was the day of Wistart's funeral. It was in the evening after it, and Grey was at home feeling sad and solemn and somehow alone, when the doorbell rang.

She answered it and it was Debs Dorn who stood under the porch light.

"Why, Debs!" she cried, surprised and also glad to see him.

"Do you have company?" he asked.

"No. Please come in."

He hesitated. Then he said, "Grey—could I talk with you—a little while—alone?"

She gave him a close little look, as if trying to understand why he desired a private conversation with her at this time.

"Why, yes, I suppose so," she said. "Where would you like——?"

"Well," he suggested, "there's my car——"

She took only a moment to make up her mind.

"Let me tell my mother and get my coat," she said.

They were in the old car, and under way, and he spoke at first about matters of general interest only. A man named Canfield, it appeared, had been arrested that day by police in Kansas City, and was being brought back to Jericho to face charges of several kinds: among others that he was an agent for Dewey Bonner in selling narcotics, and that he was directly responsible for the murder of Nibs Galloway by stirring up a madman to kill him.

"I don't think they can do anything to him on that last charge," said Debs. "It's an interesting theory the county attorney's working on: that since Benson was mentally irresponsible he was actually a lethal weapon used by Canfield for the murder. But I'm afraid it's a little too indefinite and original for the average jury, and though the case will be unusual, I don't think they'll convict him on that charge. But on the other charge —being an agent for a dope seller—he'll certainly go to the pen for a long rap. He had it coming, he's a grade-A rat, and I'm considerably relieved that they've got him."

She was glad to have him talk to her thus calmly and almost casually, because it soothed her and quieted her. Then he said something that interested her even more, because it was personal.

"I've got a new job," he told her.

"New—what is it?" she asked quickly.

"Starting tomorrow I'm managing editor of the *Clarion*. It was made official this morning."

"Oh, Debs—I'm so very, *very* glad for you!" She gave his arm a little squeeze of pure happiness.

He went on to tell her a few of the things he intended to do. Jeff Linderman would go on the city desk, he said. Jeff deserved the promotion and would make a fine city editor with just a little experience. Already Debs was looking for two or three more good people for his staff; the budget for them had been allotted by Mrs. Wedge when he explained the necessity. Things would be run much more efficiently in all departments, he was sure. The morale of his own staff was good, and he felt the *Clarion* could and would make a great comeback and win its fight in Jericho.

While he talked easily to her on these lines, they drove out past Tower Hill, out of the city limits to the Country Club, and on beyond that.

At last Grey said, "This wasn't what you wanted to talk to me about alone—was it?"

When she said that, he brought the car to a stop at the side of the road near a small creek which lay frozen in the gully below. For a time he sat with both hands on the steering wheel, gazing ahead where the headlights illumined the blacktop pavement.

"No," he said, "it wasn't. I wanted to talk to you—about Wistart Wedge."

She was struck silent with wonder and fear.

"What was it—about Mr. Wedge?" she asked him finally.

"This: you don't need to be afraid any more."

But he was wrong. At his words a new kind of terror surged over her.

"What do you mean, Debs?" she cried. And then, almost despairingly, "Oh, *what* do you know—about *me?*"

Still not looking at her, he said, "I've known it almost from the beginning, Grey. He was a pretty fine man. I never really blamed you."

Far over on her side of the car she drew herself, staring at him with eyes widening with horror.

"Oh, Debs——" she began brokenly, and then stopped.

He went on. "For you the most important effect of his death is this: whatever you were to him, or he to you, no longer has any meaning in court. His wife was going to do her worst against you by her divorce action. It was to be the vehicle through which she would put on public record her accusations and insinuations."

For the first time, now, he looked at her seriously.

"Well, it's impossible for her to bring a divorce suit against a dead man," he finished. "And therefore she can never make those charges."

For the first time, actually, this aspect of Wistart's death appeared to Grey. And she was struck with wonder at the realization that the sudden and unexpected death of the man who had loved her had provided a solution equally sudden and unexpected for the tangle of fears, confusion, and despair which had enmeshed her. And now thinking of it she saw how, undreamed and unplanned and tragic though it was, it was the only possible solution, for he was the key to the entire tangle. It was almost as if he had done it for her, and she felt like weeping for him anew.

Then another thought submerged all this.

"Debs—how do you—how can you *possibly* know all these things?" she said.

"I'm a fairly good reporter."

"But—even——"

"Well, here's how I figured it. I saw you—I'm sorry, I wasn't intending to spy—when he came for you night before last, and when he brought you back a very short time later—and something told me you were very much agitated. With that to go on, it wasn't hard to guess what must have happened in Judge Pollock's office next day. The judge is a friend of mine. I paid him a visit this afternoon and laid my cards on the table. He's a friend of yours, too, and he knew he could trust me. So he explained exactly how, with Mr. Wedge gone, his wife's action collapses."

"Laid your cards on the table . . . then he knows that *you* know—about me——?"

"Yes. He knows."

"And—how many others?"

"He and I only. Except of course you——"

She could not help it. The enormity of this, which she had never dreamed . . . that Debs should know about her . . . what she was . . . when she wished so longingly for his regard . . . she bent her head, put her two slim hands before her face, and her shoulders shook with sobs as the tears came wildly and without restraint.

He looked down at her bowed head; then he reached forward and switched off the headlights, letting the night darkness suddenly possess them, so that nobody should see her tears.

"Grey—poor, poor little girl——" he said, and he drew her over, his arm around her, letting her sob on his shoulder while he softly stroked her hair.

For a long time she wept, as if she could not stop; and when at last the storm of emotion passed, she did not at once leave his arms but clung to him like a child seeking comfort and refuge.

But at length she knew this could not continue, and so she freed herself. He did not try to constrain her but let her go.

For a time she sat very straight in the darkness, regaining her self-control. About them lay the night, the sky above a deep sapphire blue with myriads of stars burning in it, quiet and secret and serene.

At last she said, "Debs, I didn't want you to know it, ever . . . you of all the people in the world . . . I didn't want you to think of me—as you must be thinking——"

He interrupted, "I think of you now just as I thought yesterday, and the day before, and a month ago, and for the last three years."

"What . . . do you mean?"

"That I love you."

Perfectly still she sat, hardly breathing, hardly believing.

Then she said, "But—how can you——?"

"Maybe I can make you understand," he said. "I've been in love with you for three years, Grey, almost since the first day I met you, I suppose—but all the time I knew I could never have you. In those three years I think I'm the only person in the world to whom everything you did was of the utmost importance—just when you went away from town and when you returned meant something to me, for instance. And then, when I discovered that someone else came and went at those same times . . . I put two and two together."

"And never told anybody?"

"And never told anybody—even you."

"But *knowing*—you could still——"

"Knowing you and what you really are is what makes me want you." He hesitated. "Oh, I don't want you to think it wasn't a little tough on me. When first I was sure, I just about hated you for a while. But then I saw it really was no business of mine—I had no claim on you, you were 'way out of my reach." Again he paused. "This may sound corny—but there's not much logic to love, is there? I tried my best to forget you, but I could never do it. This—this thing that happened—I didn't know the reason for it—but knowing it was you, I was sure of one thing—it wasn't sordid or cheap. And I knew that someday it would be over. Although I never dreamed it would end . . . this way."

"And you could forgive it?"

"There's nothing for me to forgive. I'm not a saint, Grey. Very, very far from a saint. I couldn't sit in judgment on you even if I wanted to, which I don't."

For a little time she sat in perfect silence. Then she said, "Debs, if I tell you something—will you believe it?"

"I know you'd never lie to me," he said simply.

"Then I want you to know one thing. It *was* ended between us. And before this happened—before he died."

He waited.

"That was the reason—for this last trip," she went on. "We had to discuss things. He was so generous—and—and understanding. That's the tragedy of the whole thing—I came home feeling that—that I was through with everything in my life that was wrong—and then—and then the skies themselves seemed to fall on me."

After a moment he said, "Did you love him very much, Grey?"

The question almost startled her, and it brought her to a sudden close contemplation of herself. She had believed that she could never dream of love again, because no man would have her if he knew, and she could not, in honor, go to any man without his knowing. Yet here was Debs not only loving her, but having loved her patiently and silently all this time, knowing her secret and not condemning her.

She wanted Debs to love her, and keep on loving her. And she wondered if his question were some sort of a test of her, on which everything might hang.

But whatever happened, she could not deny Wistart . . . not now. Slowly, very slowly, she answered him.

"I loved him . . . yes, Debs. He was so terribly unhappy and alone . . . he needed someone so dreadfully. Oh, I sometimes think he was the saddest, most pathetic human creature I ever imagined in my life. That was what it was, really. He needed me. I couldn't deny that need for the only spot of brightness in his life."

He took her hand. "That explains everything. It's what I wanted to hear you say. I knew there was some great generosity about it. And I don't care anything about your past, darling . . . I want your future."

She was overwhelmed by it, and all at once the tears came again, but tears of a different kind.

"Would there ever be a chance for me," he went on, "not now, of course—but maybe sometime? I haven't much to offer. I know you've got a successful business, and I know that a newspaper salary isn't much——"

"Oh, Debs—you darling—you *darling!*" she cried. "My business isn't *that* successful—and a newspaper salary isn't *that* much to be despised —and, oh, Debs—please keep on being good to me—and understanding me—and please be patient with me——"

For just an instant he felt the softness of her cheek against his, and the wetness of her tears, and the quickness of her kiss. And then she was back on the other side of the car.

He did not even offer to take her in his arms. He did understand. And he would be patient. This was not the time. It was hardly fair to ask her to give him an answer just now.

And yet, though she had not spoken it, he did have an answer. As much of an answer as she could give at a time like this.

He switched on the headlights and swung the car around in the road, starting back toward the city. They rode in silence, but she sat close to him. When they reached her home they said almost nothing at parting.

There really was no need to say anything. Everything had been said that needed to be said about the past. The future lay all before them.